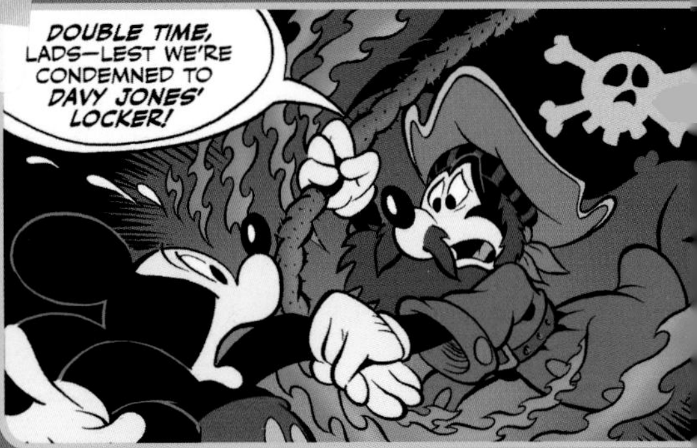
DOUBLE TIME, LADS—LEST WE'RE CONDEMNED TO DAVY JONES' LOCKER!

The Mouse Collector
From French *Le Journal de Mickey* #2998, 2009
Writer and Artist: Noel Van Horn
Colorist: Digikore Studios
Letterers: Nicole and Travis Seitler

Mynah Mistake
From *Mickey Mouse* Sunday comic strip, 1952
Writer: Bill Walsh
Artist: Manuel Gonzales
Colorist: Digikore Studios

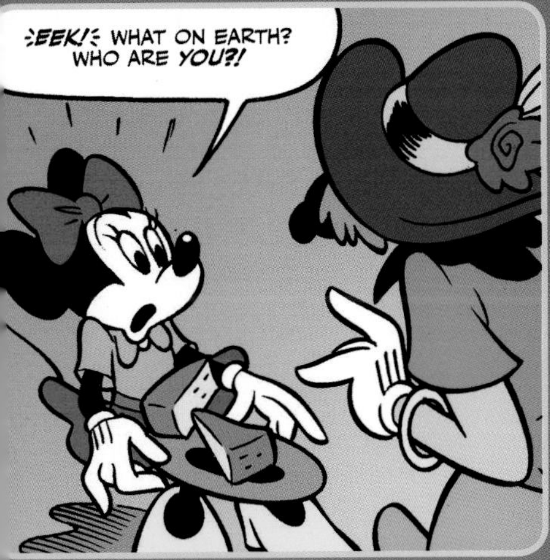
EEK! WHAT ON EARTH? WHO ARE YOU?!

The Clones of Channel 3000
From Italian *Topolino* #3000, 2013
Writer and Artist: Andrea "Casty" Castellan
Colorists: Disney Italia with Nicole and Travis Seitler
Letterers: Nicole and Travis Seitler
Translation and Dialogue: Jonathan H. Gray

Fancy!
From British *Mickey Mouse Annual* #12, 1941
Writer, Artist, and Letterer: Wilfred Haughton
Colorist: Digikore Studios

Adieu
From British *Mickey Mouse Annual* #10, 1939
Writer, Artist, and Letterer: Wilfred Haughton
Colorist: Digikore Studios

Series Editor: Chris Cerasi
Archival Editor: David Gerstein

Cover Artist: Jonathan H. Gray
Cover Colorist: Marco Colletti
Collection Editors: Justin Eisinger & Alonzo Simon
Collection Designer: Clyde Grapa
Publisher: Ted Adams

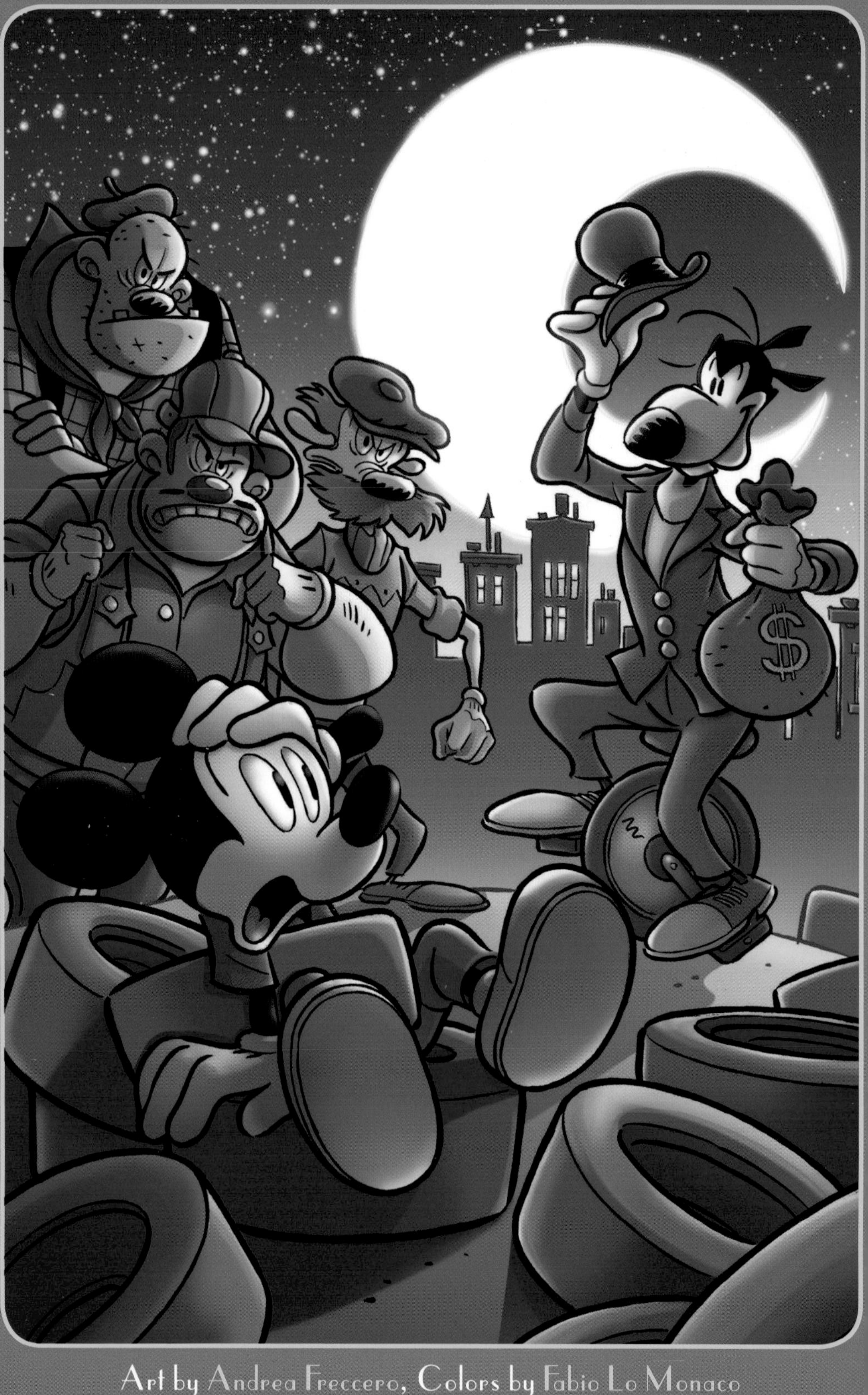
$

Art by Andrea Freccero, Colors by Fabio Lo Monaco

Walt Disney's

MICKEY MOUSE

The Magnificent Doublejoke

From Italian *Topolino* #2535, 2004
Writer: Andrea “Casty” Castellan
Artist: Massimo De Vita
Colorists: Disney Italia with Nicole and Travis Seitler
Letterers: Nicole and Travis Seitler
Translation and Dialogue: Thad Komorowski

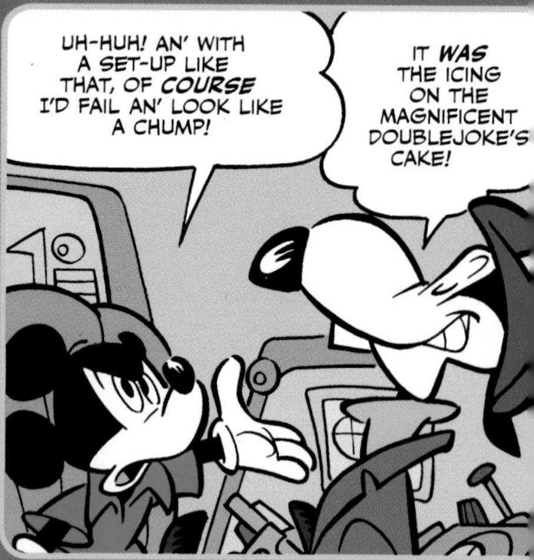
UH-HUH! AN' WITH A SET-UP LIKE THAT, OF *COURSE* I'D FAIL AN' LOOK LIKE A CHUMP!
IT *WAS* THE ICING ON THE MAGNIFICENT DOUBLEJOKE'S CAKE!

Stormy Weather

From *Mickey Mouse* Sunday comic strip, 1951
Writer: Bill Walsh
Artist: Manuel Gonzales
Colorist: Digikore Studios

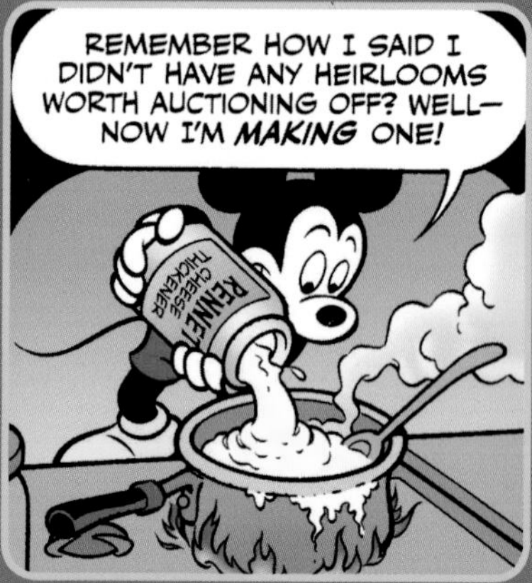
REMEMBER HOW I SAID I DIDN'T HAVE ANY HEIRLOOMS WORTH AUCTIONING OFF? WELL— NOW I'M *MAKING* ONE!
RENNET CHEESE THICKENER

Early To Bid

From Swedish *Kalle Anka & C:o* #37/1997
Writer: David Gerstein
Artist: Jorge David Redo and César Ferioli
Colorist: Digikore Studios
Letterers: Nicole and Travis Seitler

A Goofy Look At Cooking

From Dutch *Donald Duck* #10/2003
Writer: Pascal Oost
Artist: Michel Nadorp
Colorist: Digikore Studios
Letterers: Nicole and Travis Seitler
Translation and Dialogue: Jonathan H. Gray

For international rights, contact **licensing@idwpublishing.com**

Special thanks to Eugene Paraszczuk, Julie Dorris, Carlotta Quattrocolo, Manny Mederos, Chris Troise, Roberto Santillo, Camilla Vedove, and Stefano Ambrosio.

ISBN: 978-1-68405-094-9

20 19 18 17 1 2 3 4

IDW® www.IDWPUBLISHING.com

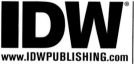

Ted Adams, CEO & Publisher • **Greg Goldstein**, President & COO • **Robbie Robbins**, EVP/Sr. Graphic Artist • **Chris Ryall**, Chief Creative Officer • **David Hedgecock**, Editor-in-Chief • **Laurie Windrow**, Senior Vice President of Sales & Marketing • **Matthew Ruzicka**, CPA, Chief Financial Officer • **Lorelei Bunjes**, VP of Digital Services • **Jerry Bennington**, VP of New Product Development

Facebook: facebook.com/idwpublishing • Twitter: @idwpublishing • YouTube: youtube.com/idwpublishing
Tumblr: tumblr.idwpublishing.com • Instagram: instagram.com/idwpublishing

Originally published as MICKEY MOUSE issues #19–21 (Legacy #328–330).

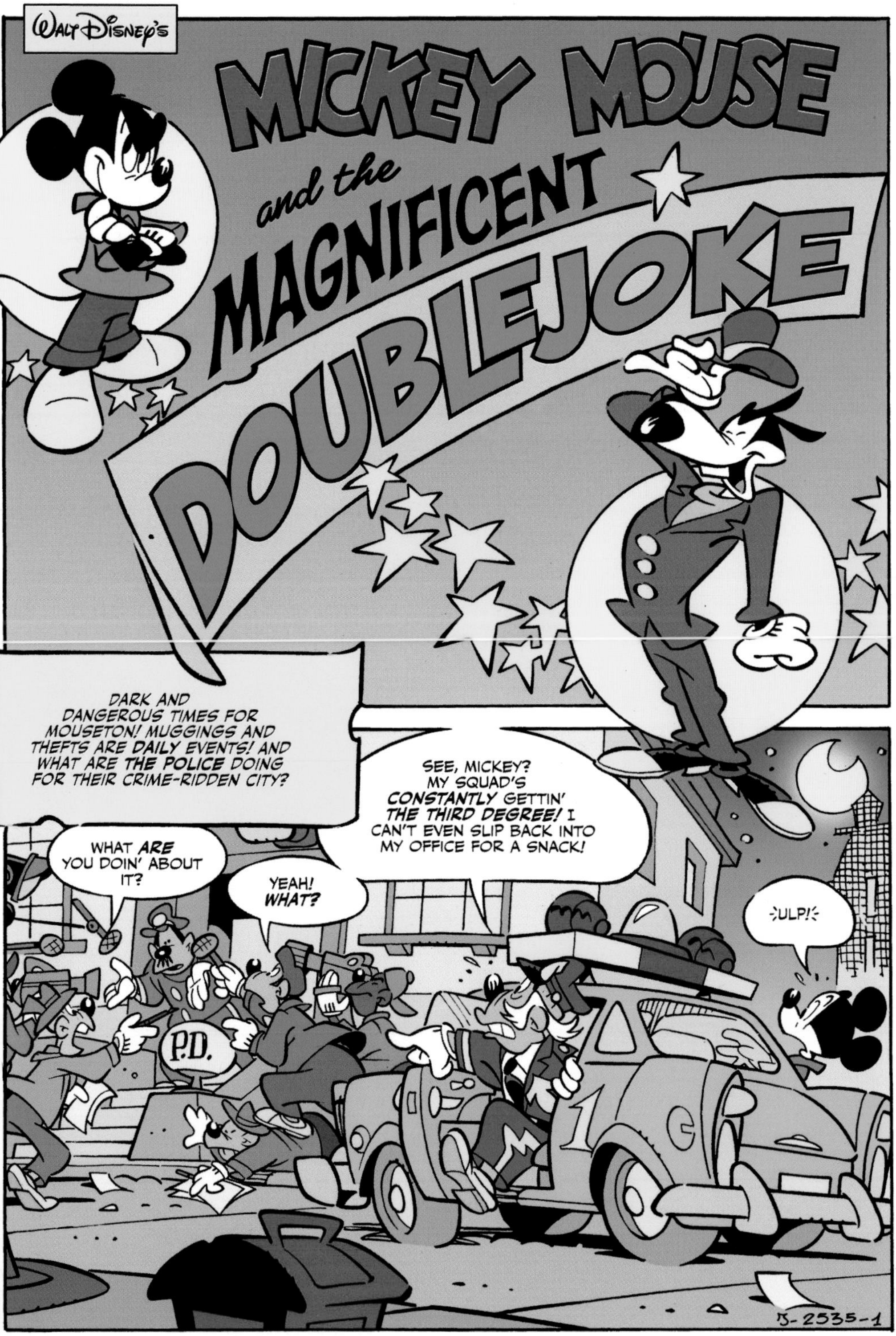
Walt Disney's
MICKEY MOUSE
and the
MAGNIFICENT
DOUBLEJOKE
DARK AND DANGEROUS TIMES FOR MOUSETON! MUGGINGS AND THEFTS ARE DAILY EVENTS! AND WHAT ARE THE POLICE DOING FOR THEIR CRIME-RIDDEN CITY?
WHAT ARE YOU DOIN' ABOUT IT?
YEAH! WHAT?
SEE, MICKEY? MY SQUAD'S CONSTANTLY GETTIN' THE THIRD DEGREE! I CAN'T EVEN SLIP BACK INTO MY OFFICE FOR A SNACK!
ULP!
P.D.
I-2535-1

Originally published in *Topolino* #2535 (Italy, 2004)

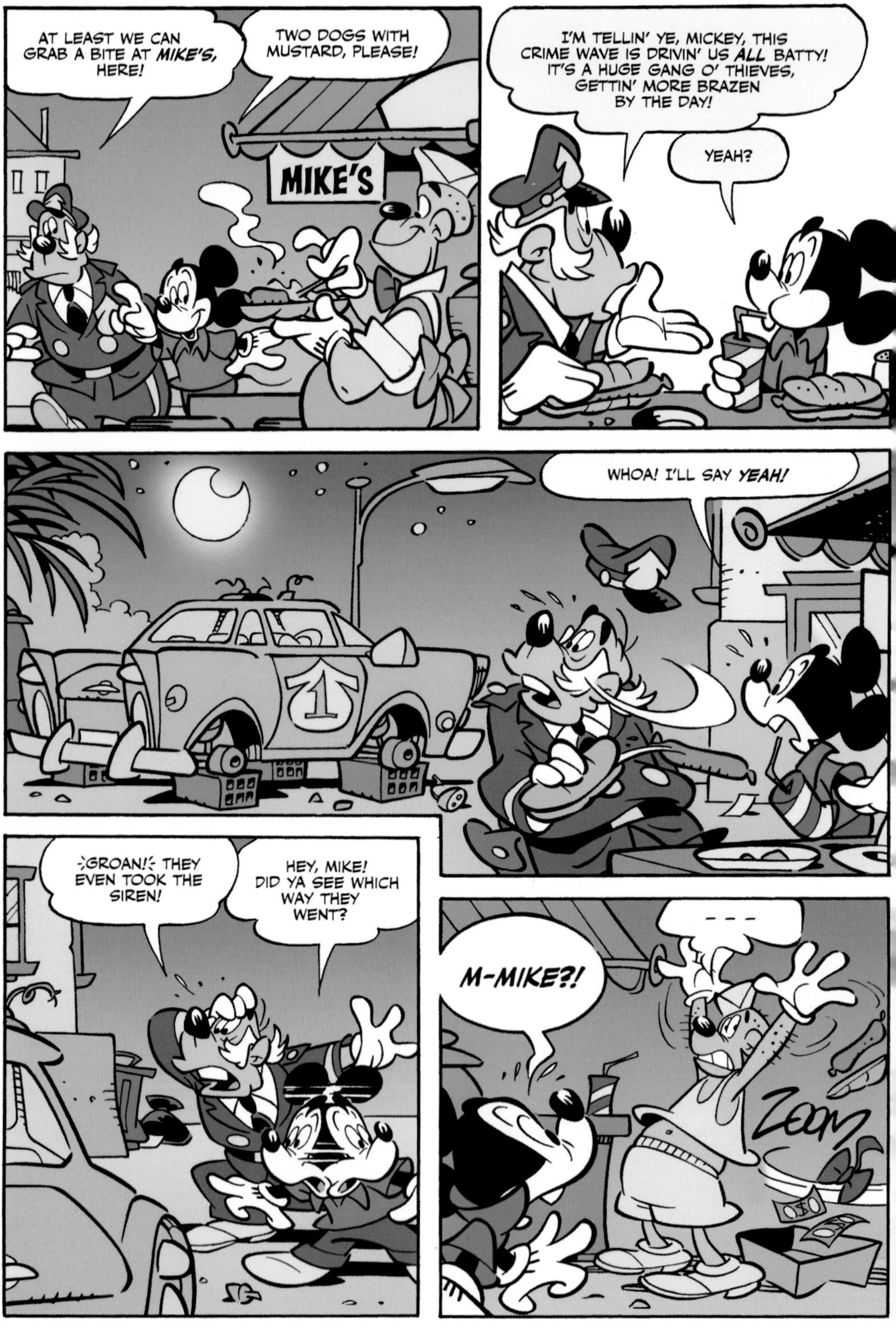
AT LEAST WE CAN GRAB A BITE AT MIKE'S, HERE!
TWO DOGS WITH MUSTARD, PLEASE!
MIKE'S
I'M TELLIN' YE, MICKEY, THIS CRIME WAVE IS DRIVIN' US ALL BATTY! IT'S A HUGE GANG O' THIEVES, GETTIN' MORE BRAZEN BY THE DAY!
YEAH?
WHOA! I'LL SAY YEAH!
GROAN! THEY EVEN TOOK THE SIREN!
HEY, MIKE! DID YA SEE WHICH WAY THEY WENT?
M-MIKE?!
- - -
ZOOM

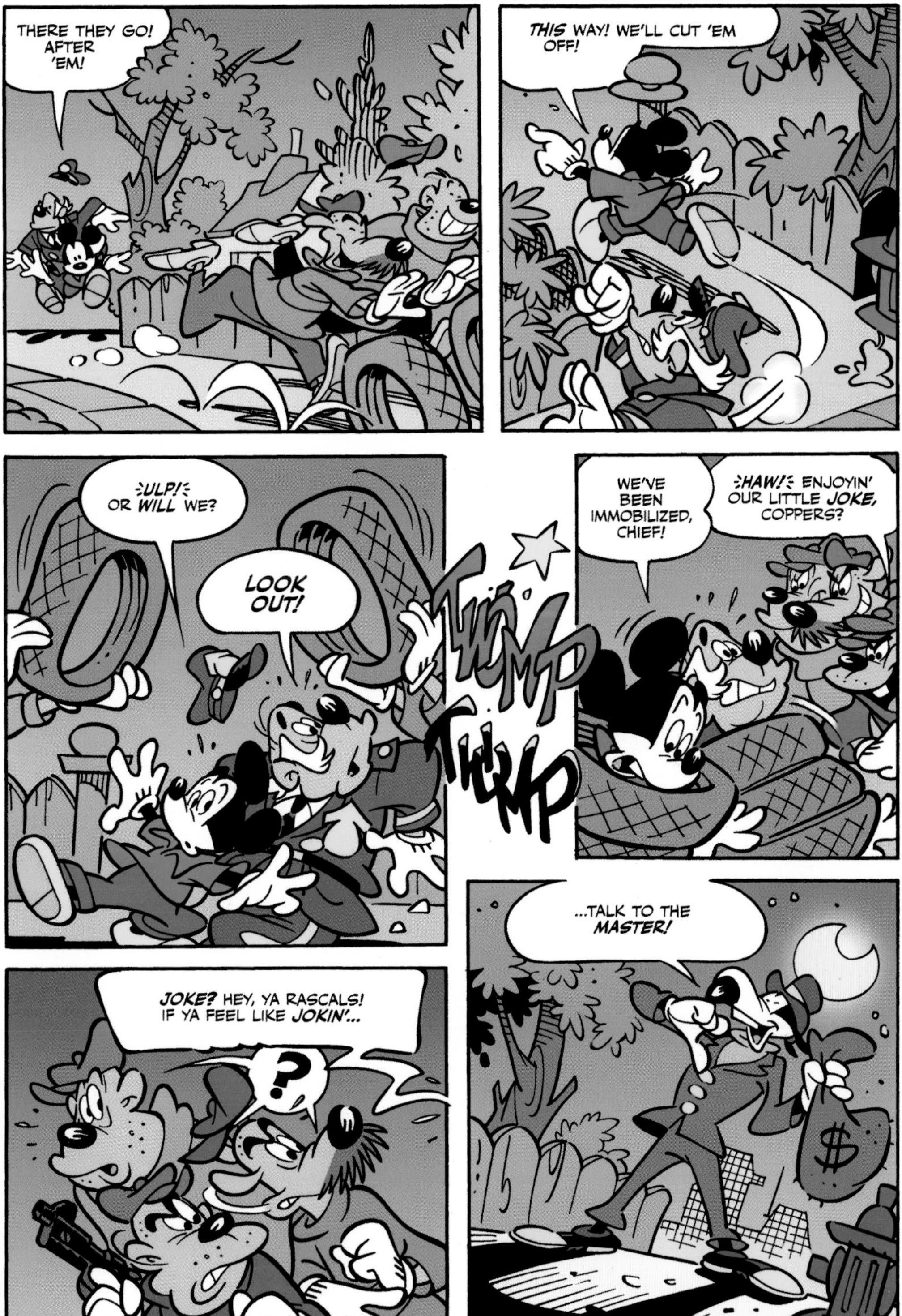
THERE THEY GO! AFTER 'EM!
THIS WAY! WE'LL CUT 'EM OFF!
ULP! OR WILL WE?
LOOK OUT!
THUMP
THUMP
WE'VE BEEN IMMOBILIZED, CHIEF!
HAW! ENJOYIN' OUR LITTLE JOKE, COPPERS?
JOKE? HEY, YA RASCALS! IF YA FEEL LIKE JOKIN'...
?
...TALK TO THE MASTER!

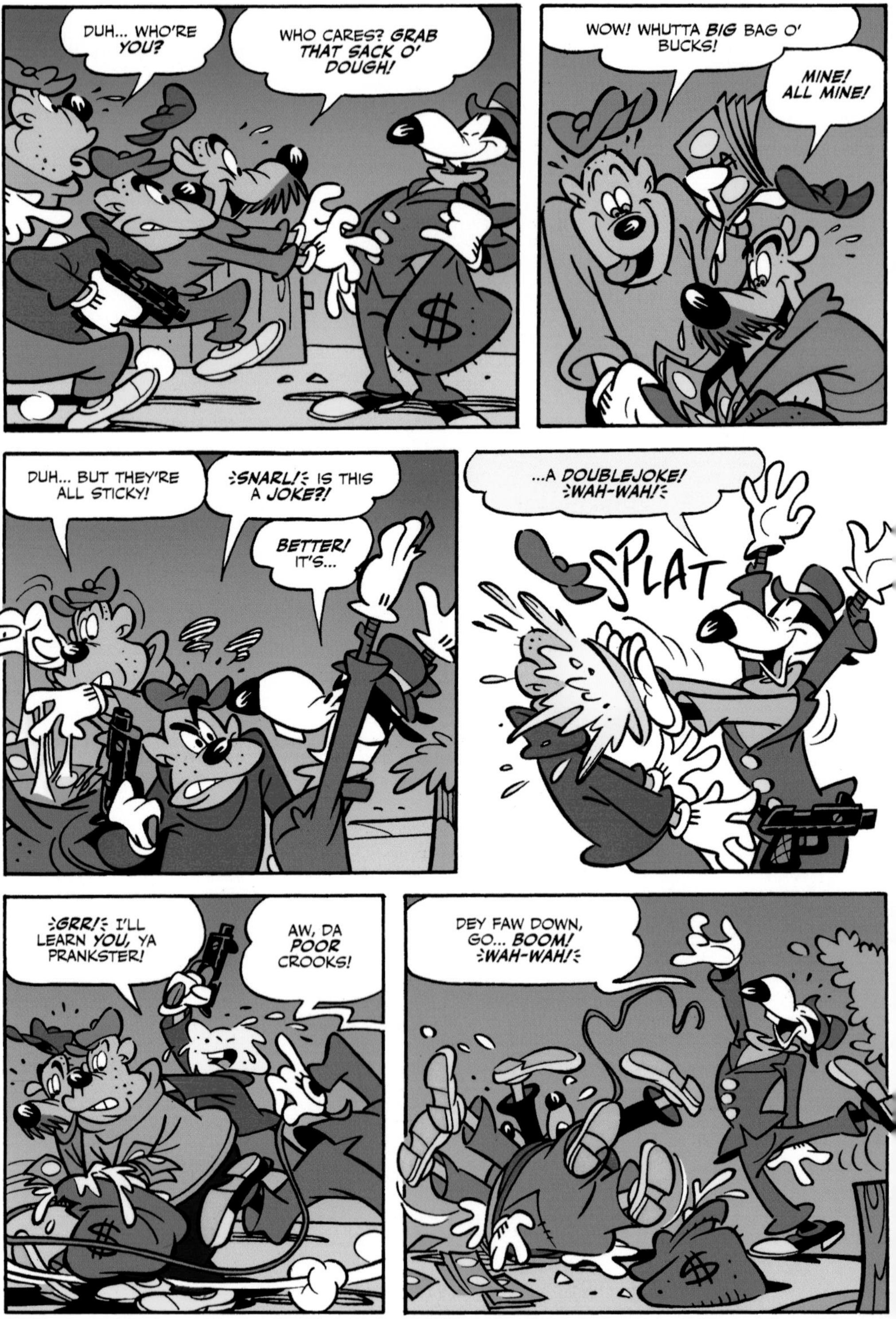
DUH... WHO'RE YOU?
WHO CARES? GRAB THAT SACK O' DOUGH!
WOW! WHUTTA BIG BAG O' BUCKS!
MINE! ALL MINE!
DUH... BUT THEY'RE ALL STICKY!
SNARL! IS THIS A JOKE?!
BETTER! IT'S...
...A DOUBLEJOKE! WAH-WAH!
SPLAT
GRR! I'LL LEARN YOU, YA PRANKSTER!
AW, DA POOR CROOKS!
DEY FAW DOWN, GO... BOOM! WAH-WAH!

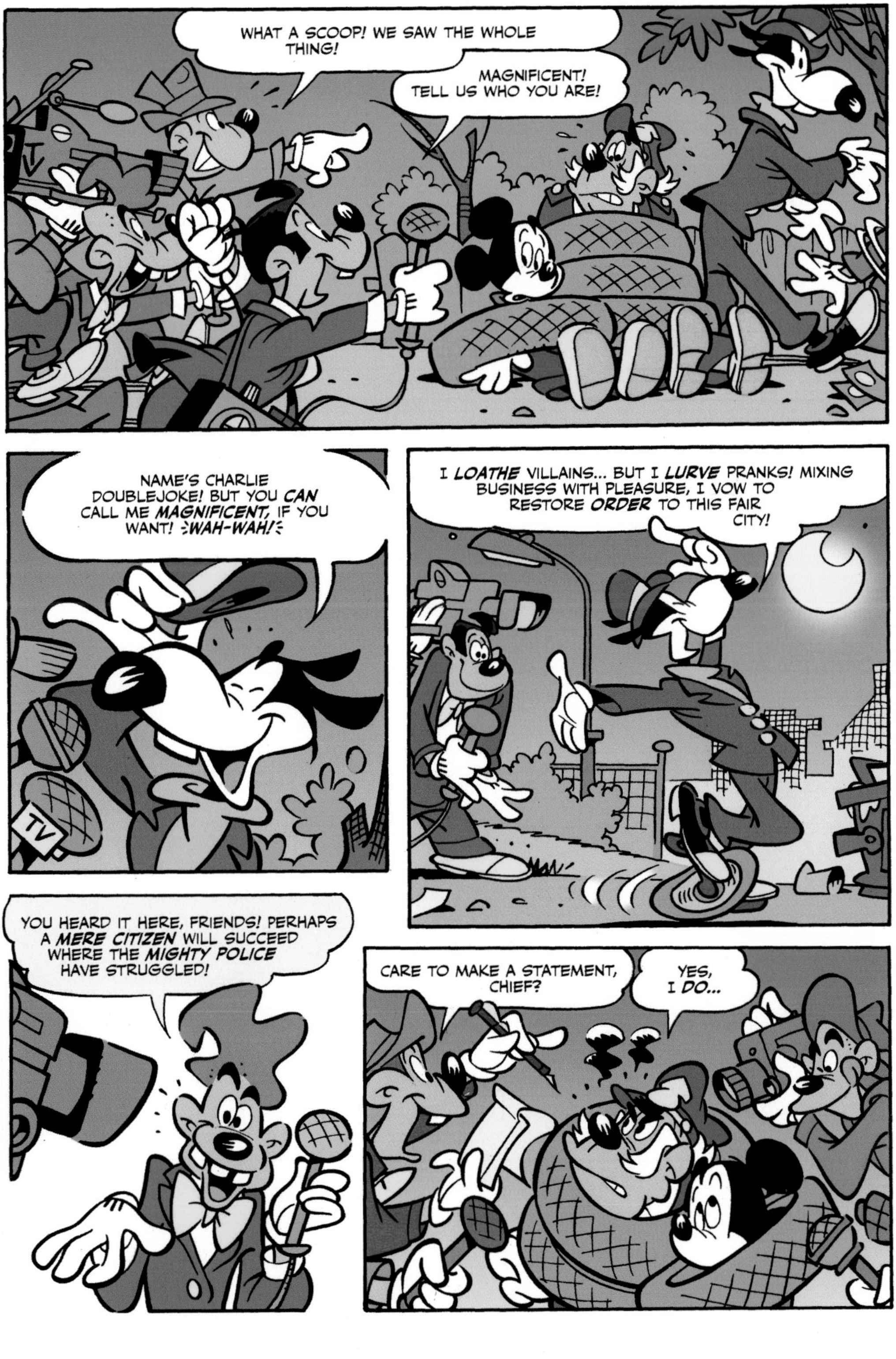
WHAT A SCOOP! WE SAW THE WHOLE THING!
MAGNIFICENT! TELL US WHO YOU ARE!
NAME'S CHARLIE DOUBLEJOKE! BUT YOU CAN CALL ME MAGNIFICENT, IF YOU WANT! WAH-WAH!
I LOATHE VILLAINS... BUT I LURVE PRANKS! MIXING BUSINESS WITH PLEASURE, I VOW TO RESTORE ORDER TO THIS FAIR CITY!
YOU HEARD IT HERE, FRIENDS! PERHAPS A MERE CITIZEN WILL SUCCEED WHERE THE MIGHTY POLICE HAVE STRUGGLED!
CARE TO MAKE A STATEMENT, CHIEF?
YES, I DO...
TV

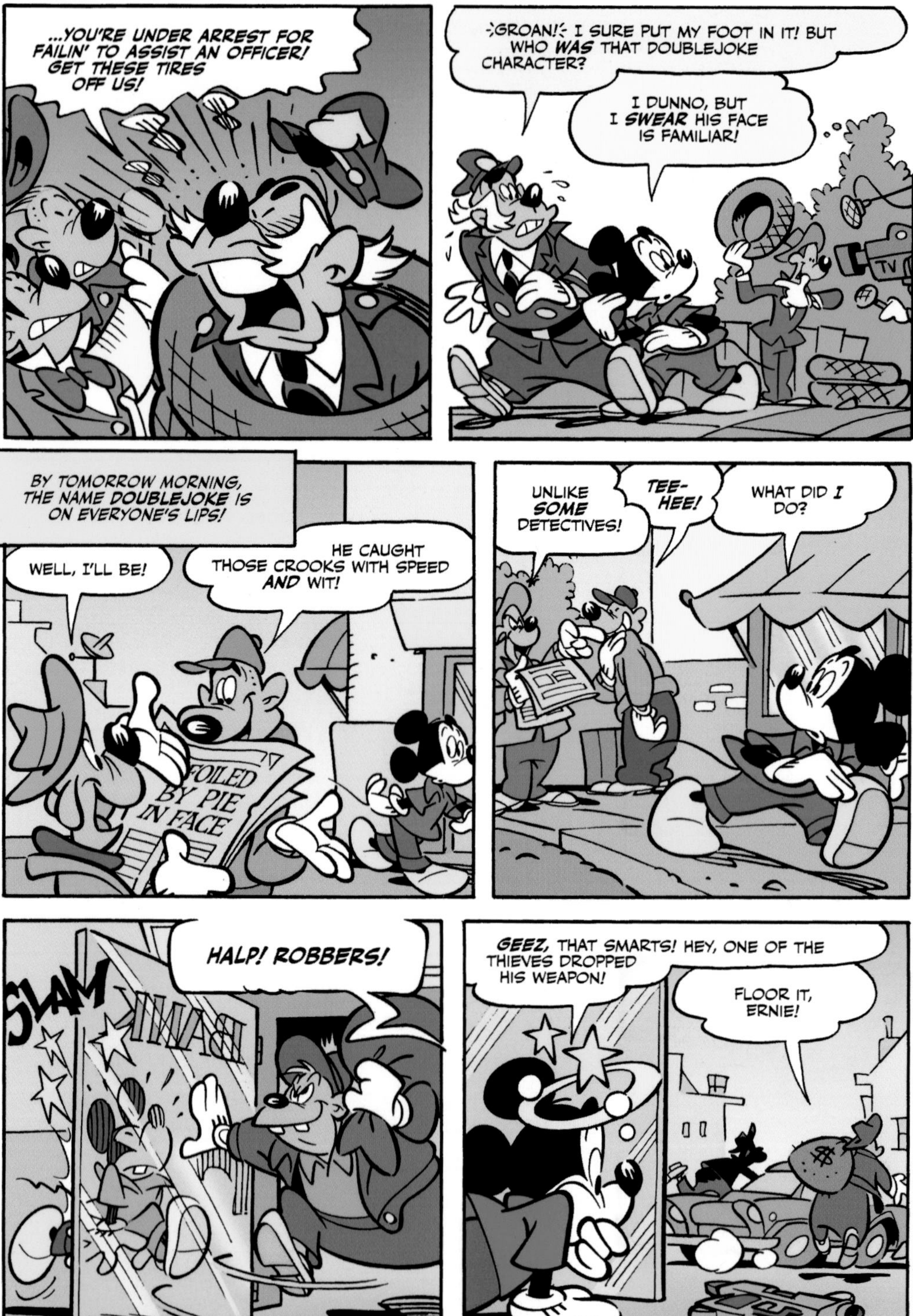
...YOU'RE UNDER ARREST FOR FAILIN' TO ASSIST AN OFFICER! GET THESE TIRES OFF US!
-GROAN!- I SURE PUT MY FOOT IN IT! BUT WHO WAS THAT DOUBLEJOKE CHARACTER?
I DUNNO, BUT I SWEAR HIS FACE IS FAMILIAR!
TV
BY TOMORROW MORNING, THE NAME DOUBLEJOKE IS ON EVERYONE'S LIPS!
WELL, I'LL BE!
HE CAUGHT THOSE CROOKS WITH SPEED AND WIT!
FOILED BY PIE IN FACE
UNLIKE SOME DETECTIVES!
TEE-HEE!
WHAT DID I DO?
SLAM
HALP! ROBBERS!
GEEZ, THAT SMARTS! HEY, ONE OF THE THIEVES DROPPED HIS WEAPON!
FLOOR IT, ERNIE!

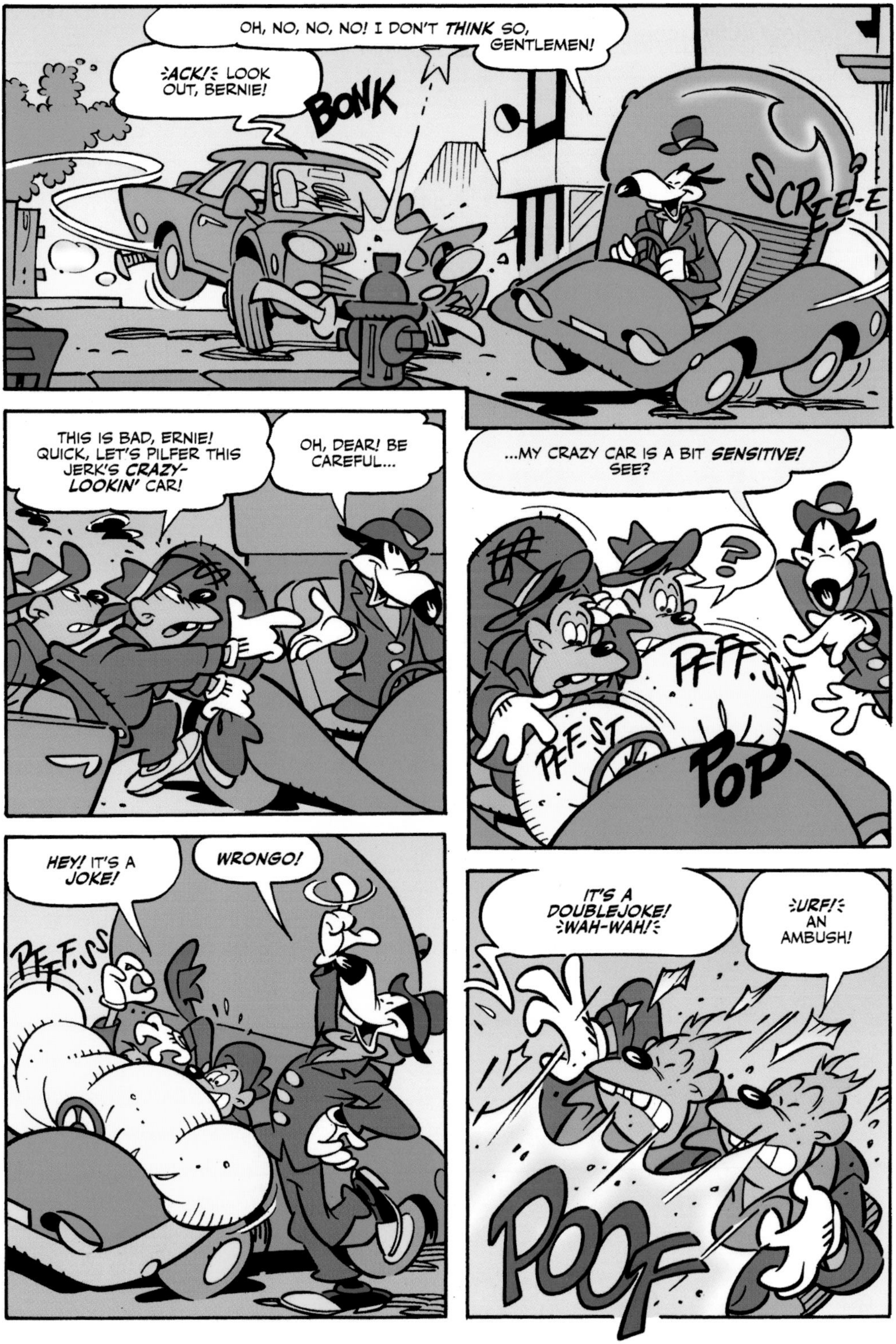
OH, NO, NO, NO! I DON'T THINK SO, GENTLEMEN!
ACK! LOOK OUT, BERNIE!
BONK
SCREE-E
THIS IS BAD, ERNIE! QUICK, LET'S PILFER THIS JERK'S CRAZY-LOOKIN' CAR!
OH, DEAR! BE CAREFUL...
...MY CRAZY CAR IS A BIT SENSITIVE! SEE?
?
PFFFST
PFFST
POP
HEY! IT'S A JOKE!
WRONGO!
PFFFSS
IT'S A DOUBLEJOKE! WAH-WAH!
URF! AN AMBUSH!
POOF

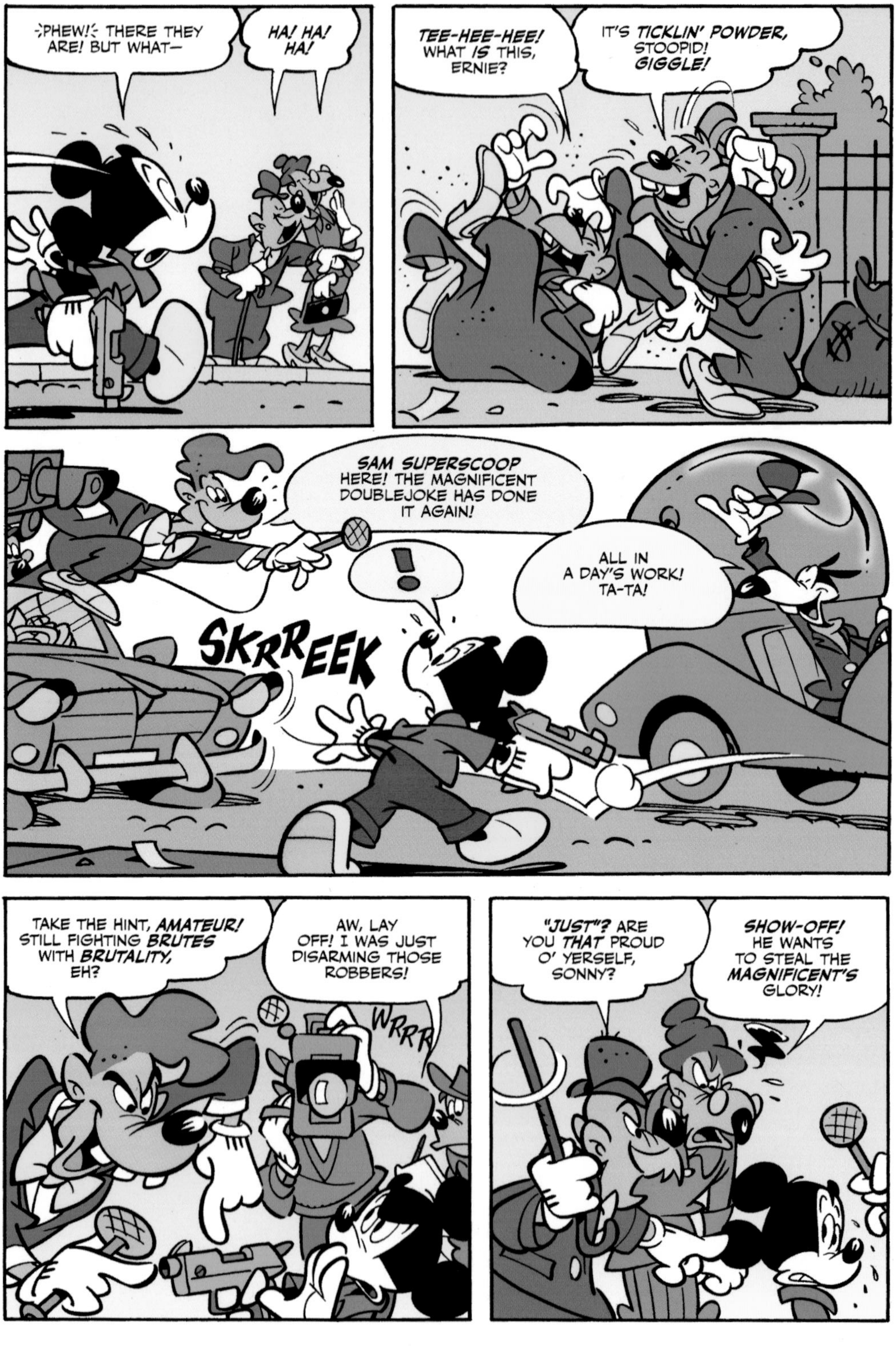

PHEW! THERE THEY ARE! BUT WHAT—
HA! HA! HA!
TEE-HEE-HEE! WHAT IS THIS, ERNIE?
IT'S TICKLIN' POWDER, STOOPID! GIGGLE!
SAM SUPERSCOOP HERE! THE MAGNIFICENT DOUBLEJOKE HAS DONE IT AGAIN!
ALL IN A DAY'S WORK! TA-TA!
!
SKRREEK
TAKE THE HINT, AMATEUR! STILL FIGHTING BRUTES WITH BRUTALITY, EH?
AW, LAY OFF! I WAS JUST DISARMING THOSE ROBBERS!
WRRR
"JUST"? ARE YOU THAT PROUD O' YERSELF, SONNY?
SHOW-OFF! HE WANTS TO STEAL THE MAGNIFICENT'S GLORY!

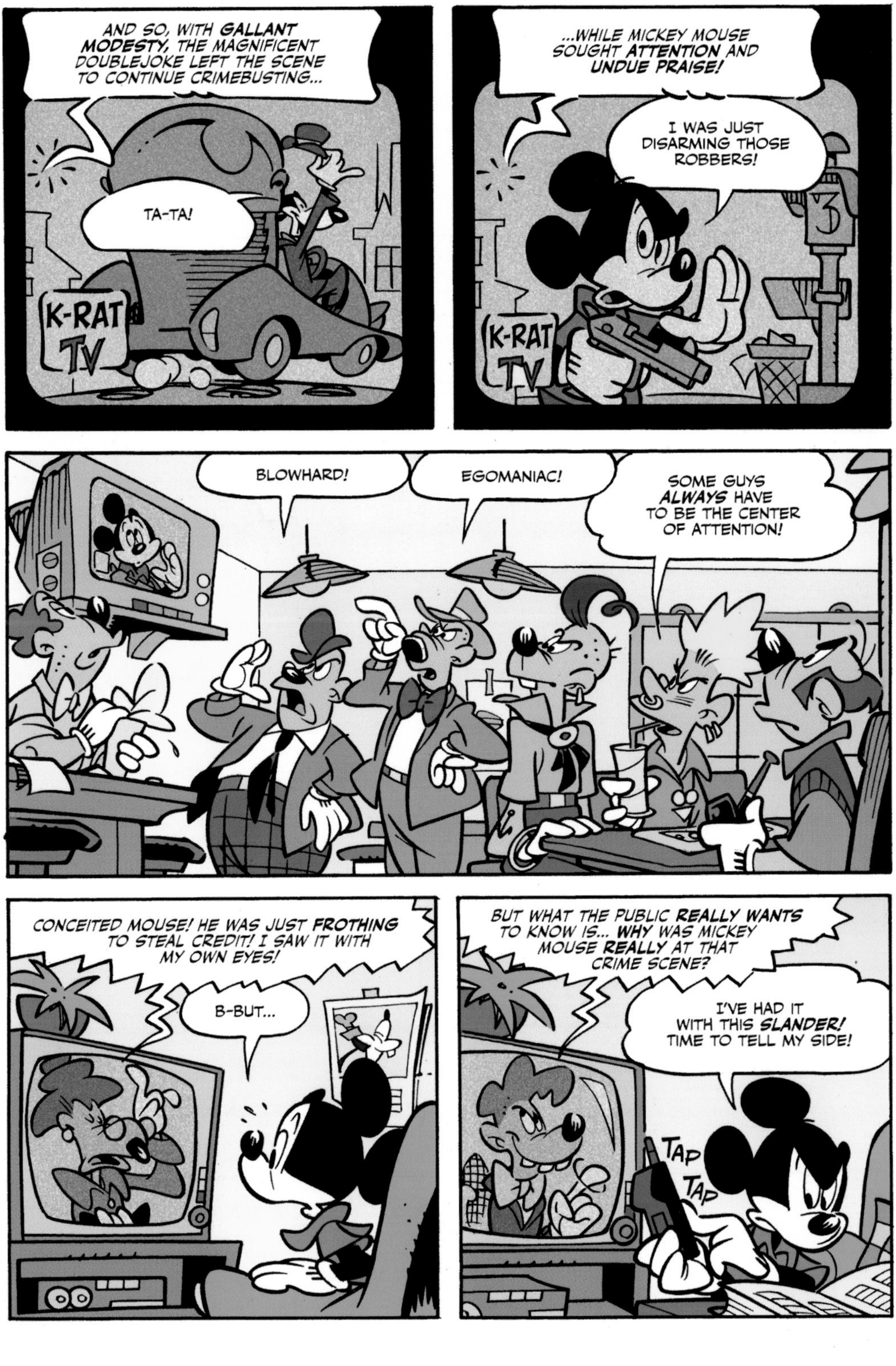

AND SO, WITH GALLANT MODESTY, THE MAGNIFICENT DOUBLEJOKE LEFT THE SCENE TO CONTINUE CRIMEBUSTING...
TA-TA!
K-RAT TV
...WHILE MICKEY MOUSE SOUGHT ATTENTION AND UNDUE PRAISE!
I WAS JUST DISARMING THOSE ROBBERS!
K-RAT TV
BLOWHARD!
EGOMANIAC!
SOME GUYS ALWAYS HAVE TO BE THE CENTER OF ATTENTION!
CONCEITED MOUSE! HE WAS JUST FROTHING TO STEAL CREDIT! I SAW IT WITH MY OWN EYES!
B-BUT...
BUT WHAT THE PUBLIC REALLY WANTS TO KNOW IS... WHY WAS MICKEY MOUSE REALLY AT THAT CRIME SCENE?
I'VE HAD IT WITH THIS SLANDER! TIME TO TELL MY SIDE!
TAP TAP

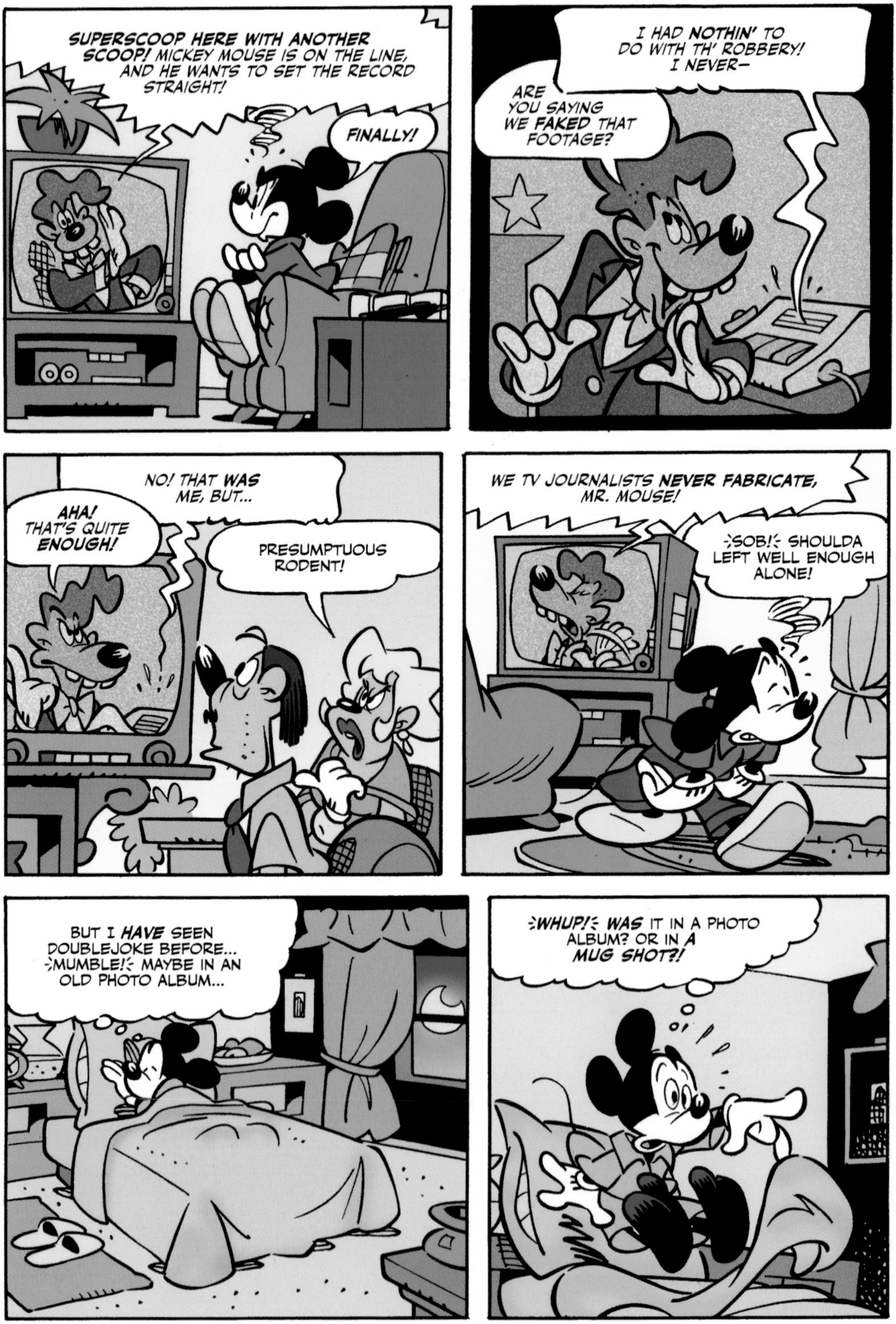
SUPERSCOOP HERE WITH ANOTHER SCOOP! MICKEY MOUSE IS ON THE LINE, AND HE WANTS TO SET THE RECORD STRAIGHT!
FINALLY!
I HAD NOTHIN' TO DO WITH TH' ROBBERY! I NEVER—
ARE YOU SAYING WE FAKED THAT FOOTAGE?
NO! THAT WAS ME, BUT...
AHA! THAT'S QUITE ENOUGH!
PRESUMPTUOUS RODENT!
WE TV JOURNALISTS NEVER FABRICATE, MR. MOUSE!
SOB! SHOULDA LEFT WELL ENOUGH ALONE!
BUT I HAVE SEEN DOUBLEJOKE BEFORE... MUMBLE! MAYBE IN AN OLD PHOTO ALBUM...
WHUP! WAS IT IN A PHOTO ALBUM? OR IN A MUG SHOT?!

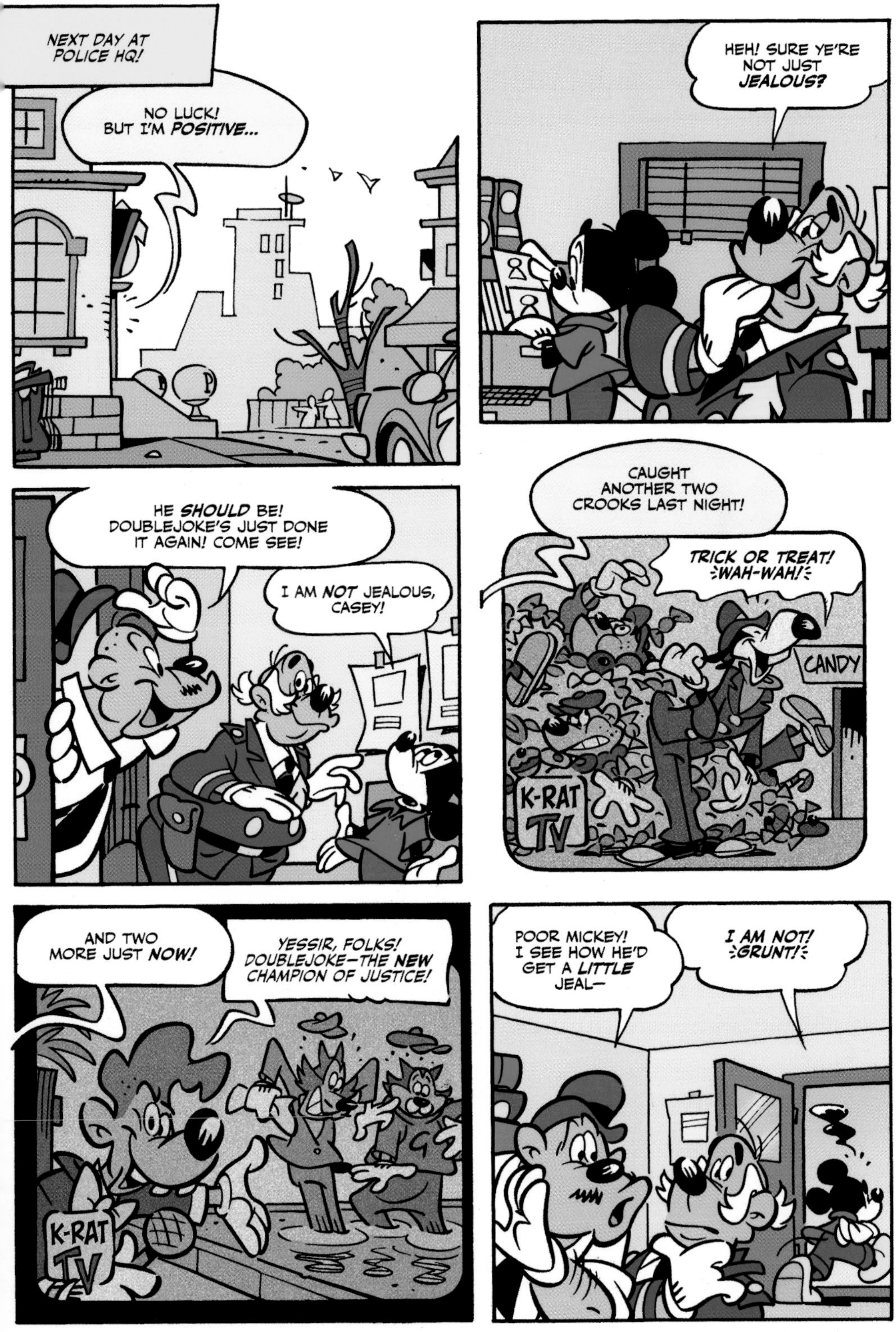
NEXT DAY AT POLICE HQ!
NO LUCK! BUT I'M POSITIVE...
HEH! SURE YE'RE NOT JUST JEALOUS?
HE SHOULD BE! DOUBLEJOKE'S JUST DONE IT AGAIN! COME SEE!
I AM NOT JEALOUS, CASEY!
CAUGHT ANOTHER TWO CROOKS LAST NIGHT!
TRICK OR TREAT! WAH-WAH!
CANDY
K-RAT TV
AND TWO MORE JUST NOW!
YESSIR, FOLKS! DOUBLEJOKE—THE NEW CHAMPION OF JUSTICE!
K-RAT TV
POOR MICKEY! I SEE HOW HE'D GET A LITTLE JEAL—
I AM NOT! GRUNT!

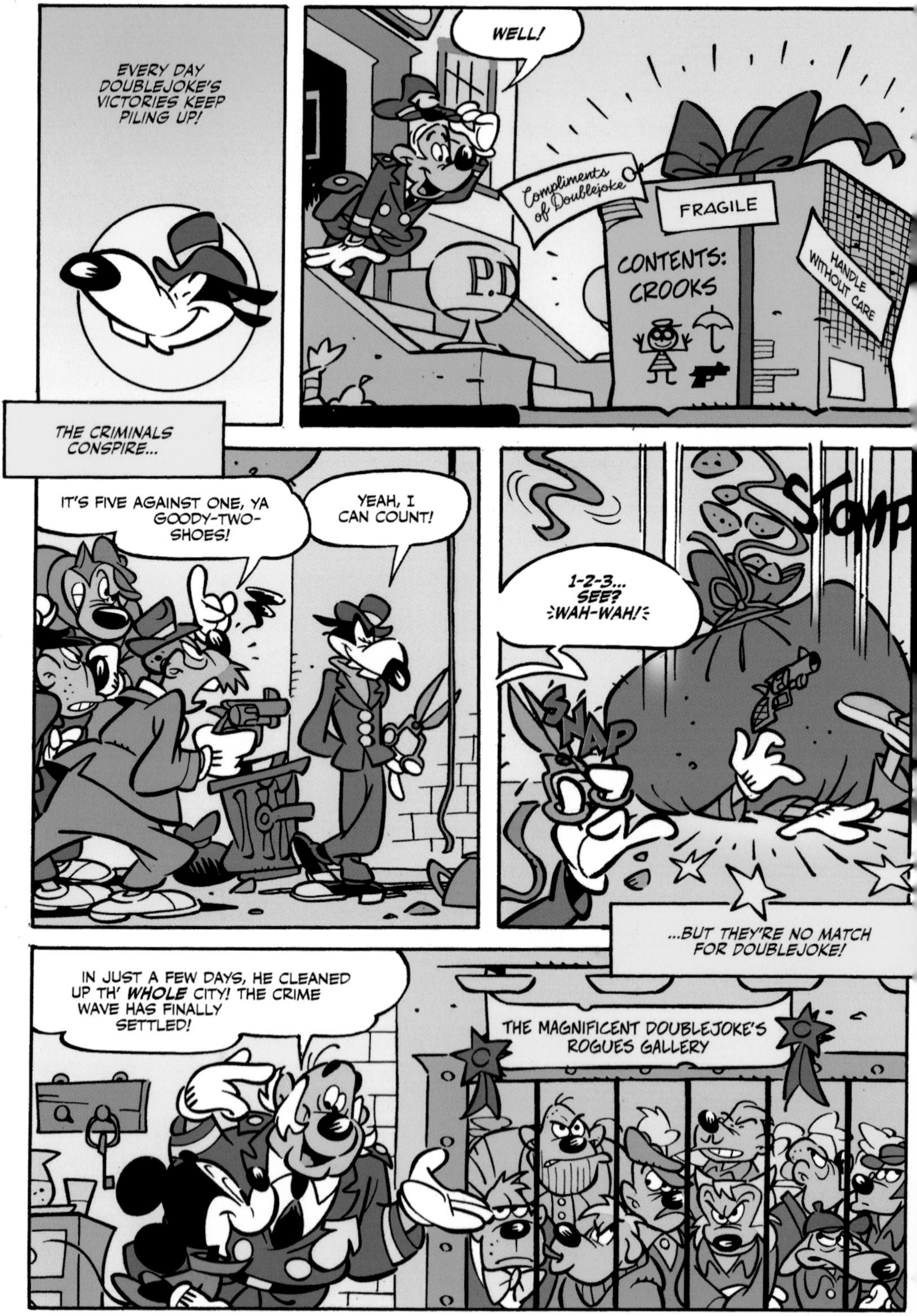
EVERY DAY DOUBLEJOKE'S VICTORIES KEEP PILING UP!
WELL!
Compliments of Doublejoke
FRAGILE
CONTENTS: CROOKS
HANDLE WITHOUT CARE
P.D.
THE CRIMINALS CONSPIRE...
IT'S FIVE AGAINST ONE, YA GOODY-TWO-SHOES!
YEAH, I CAN COUNT!
STOMP
1-2-3... SEE? WAH-WAH!
SNAP
...BUT THEY'RE NO MATCH FOR DOUBLEJOKE!
IN JUST A FEW DAYS, HE CLEANED UP TH' WHOLE CITY! THE CRIME WAVE HAS FINALLY SETTLED!
THE MAGNIFICENT DOUBLEJOKE'S ROGUES GALLERY

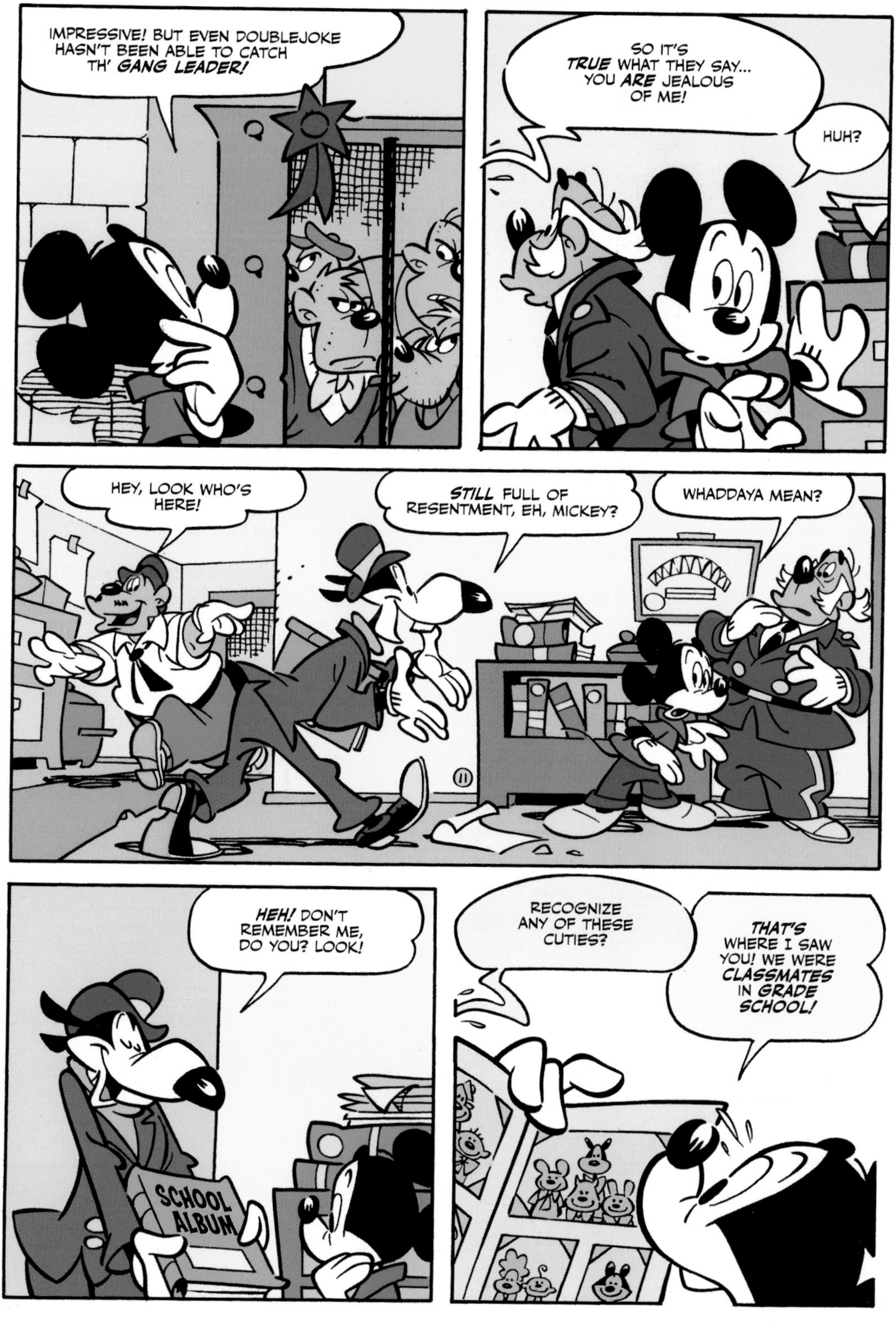
IMPRESSIVE! BUT EVEN DOUBLEJOKE HASN'T BEEN ABLE TO CATCH TH' GANG LEADER!
SO IT'S TRUE WHAT THEY SAY... YOU ARE JEALOUS OF ME!
HUH?
HEY, LOOK WHO'S HERE!
STILL FULL OF RESENTMENT, EH, MICKEY?
WHADDAYA MEAN?
HEH! DON'T REMEMBER ME, DO YOU? LOOK!
SCHOOL ALBUM
RECOGNIZE ANY OF THESE CUTIES?
THAT'S WHERE I SAW YOU! WE WERE CLASSMATES IN GRADE SCHOOL!

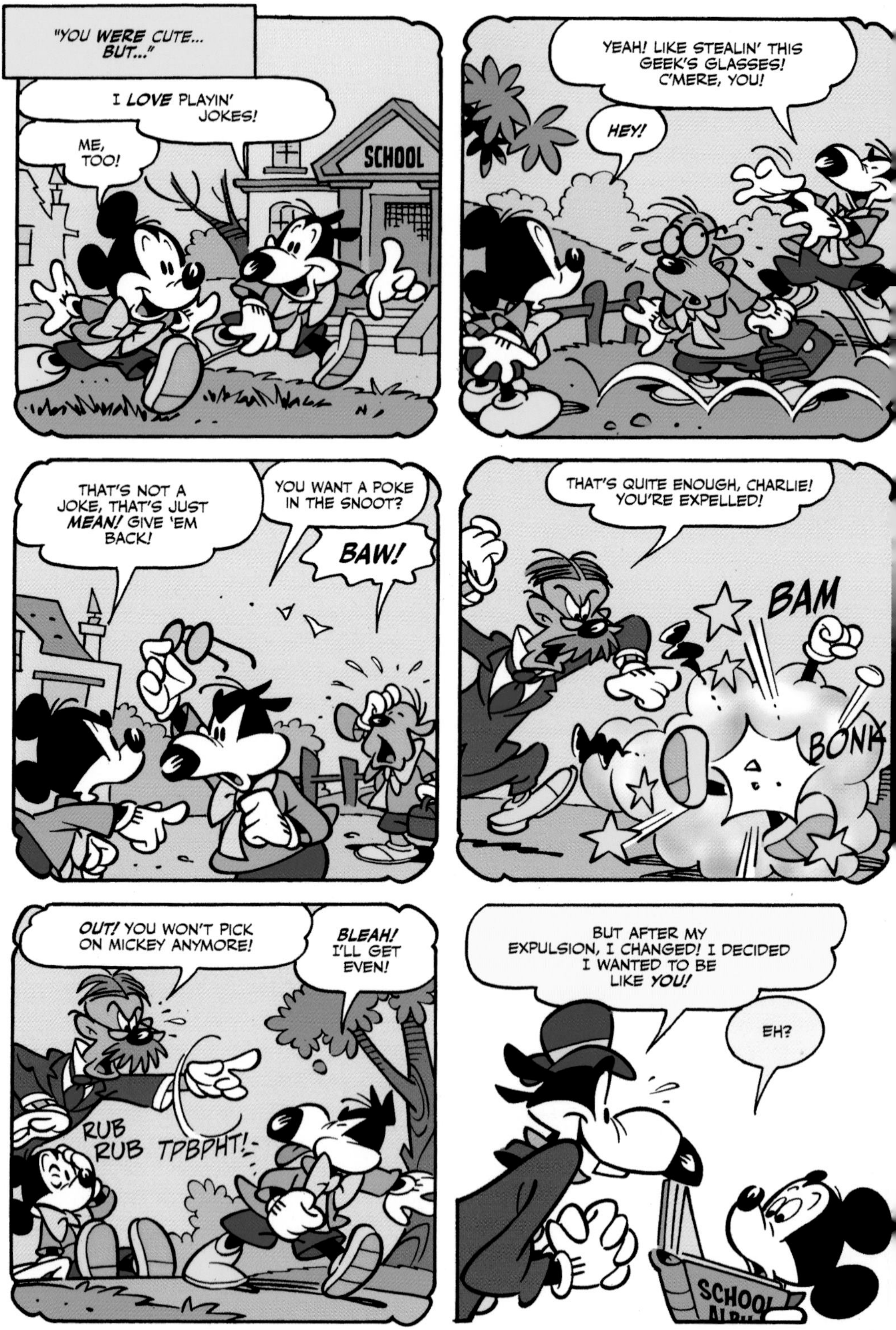

"YOU WERE CUTE... BUT..."
I LOVE PLAYIN' JOKES!
ME, TOO!
SCHOOL
YEAH! LIKE STEALIN' THIS GEEK'S GLASSES! C'MERE, YOU!
HEY!
THAT'S NOT A JOKE, THAT'S JUST MEAN! GIVE 'EM BACK!
YOU WANT A POKE IN THE SNOOT?
BAW!
THAT'S QUITE ENOUGH, CHARLIE! YOU'RE EXPELLED!
BAM
BONK
OUT! YOU WON'T PICK ON MICKEY ANYMORE!
BLEAH! I'LL GET EVEN!
RUB RUB
TPBPHT!
BUT AFTER MY EXPULSION, I CHANGED! I DECIDED I WANTED TO BE LIKE YOU!
EH?
SCHOOL

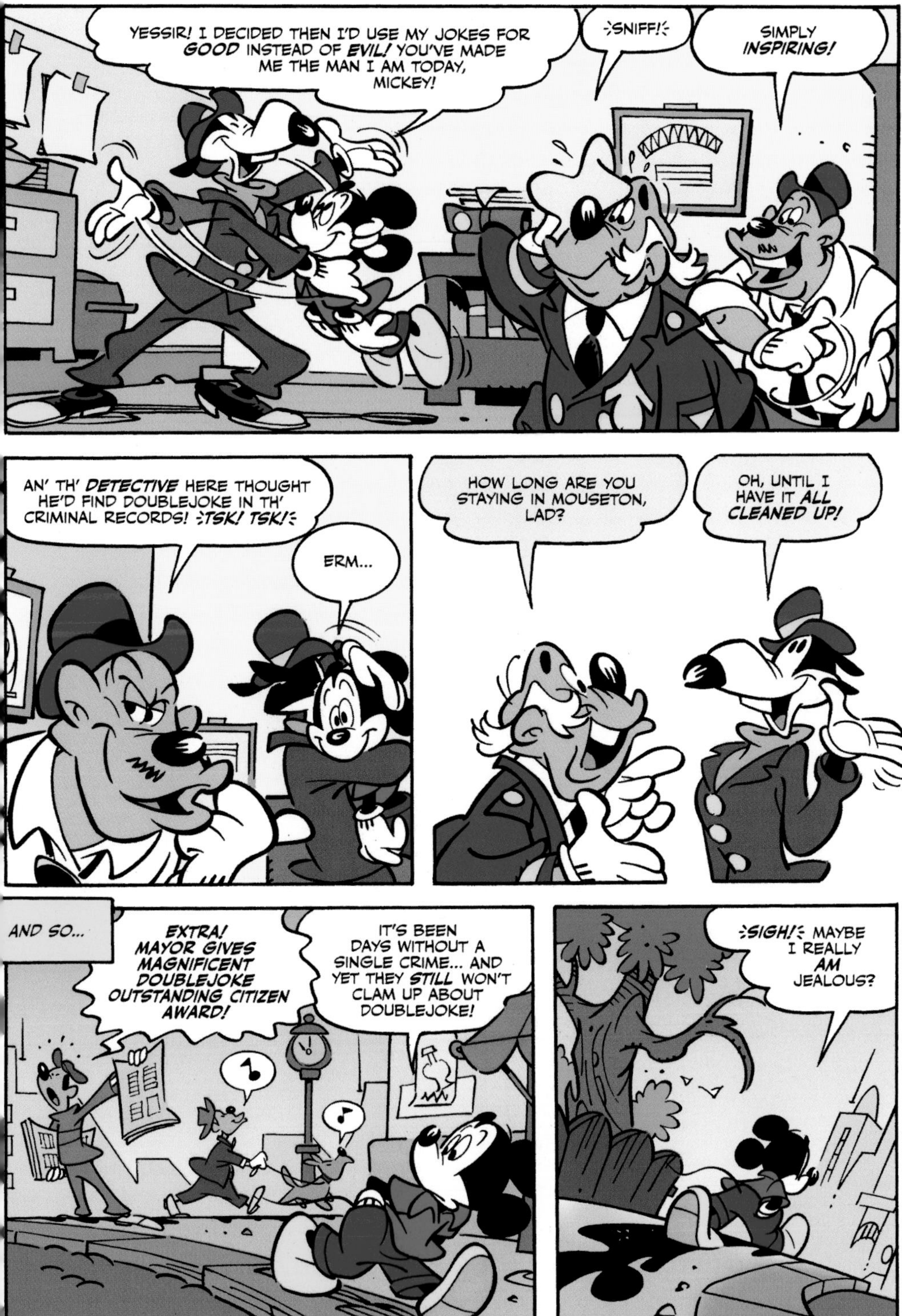

YESSIR! I DECIDED THEN I'D USE MY JOKES FOR GOOD INSTEAD OF EVIL! YOU'VE MADE ME THE MAN I AM TODAY, MICKEY!
:SNIFF!:
SIMPLY INSPIRING!
AN' TH' DETECTIVE HERE THOUGHT HE'D FIND DOUBLEJOKE IN TH' CRIMINAL RECORDS! :TSK! TSK!:
ERM...
HOW LONG ARE YOU STAYING IN MOUSETON, LAD?
OH, UNTIL I HAVE IT ALL CLEANED UP!
AND SO...
EXTRA! MAYOR GIVES MAGNIFICENT DOUBLEJOKE OUTSTANDING CITIZEN AWARD!
IT'S BEEN DAYS WITHOUT A SINGLE CRIME... AND YET THEY STILL WON'T CLAM UP ABOUT DOUBLEJOKE!
:SIGH!: MAYBE I REALLY AM JEALOUS?

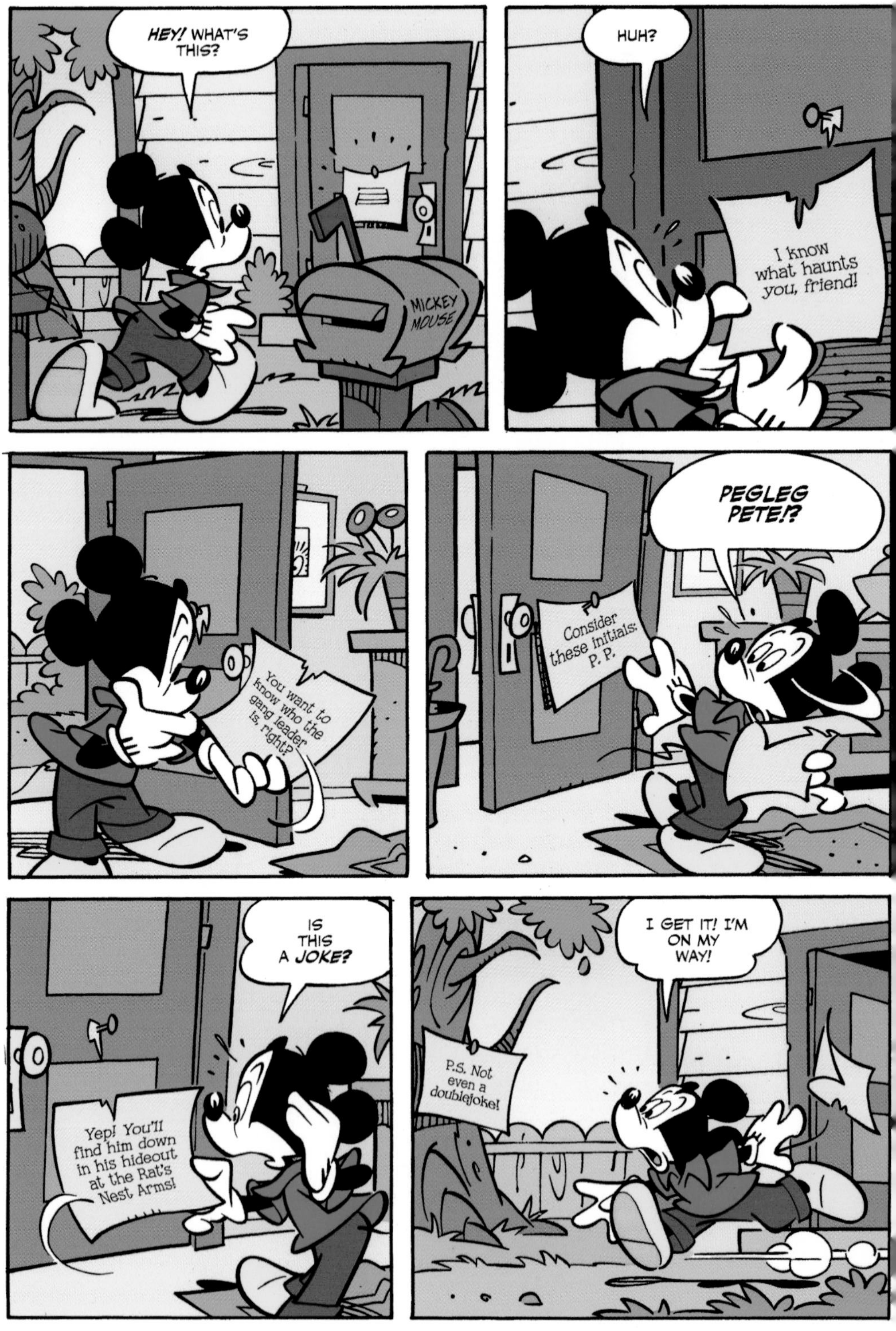
HEY! WHAT'S THIS?
MICKEY MOUSE
HUH?
I know what haunts you, friend!
You want to know who the gang leader is, right?
Consider these initials: P. P.
PEGLEG PETE!?
IS THIS A JOKE?
Yep! You'll find him down in his hideout at the Rat's Nest Arms!
I GET IT! I'M ON MY WAY!
P.S. Not even a doublejoke!

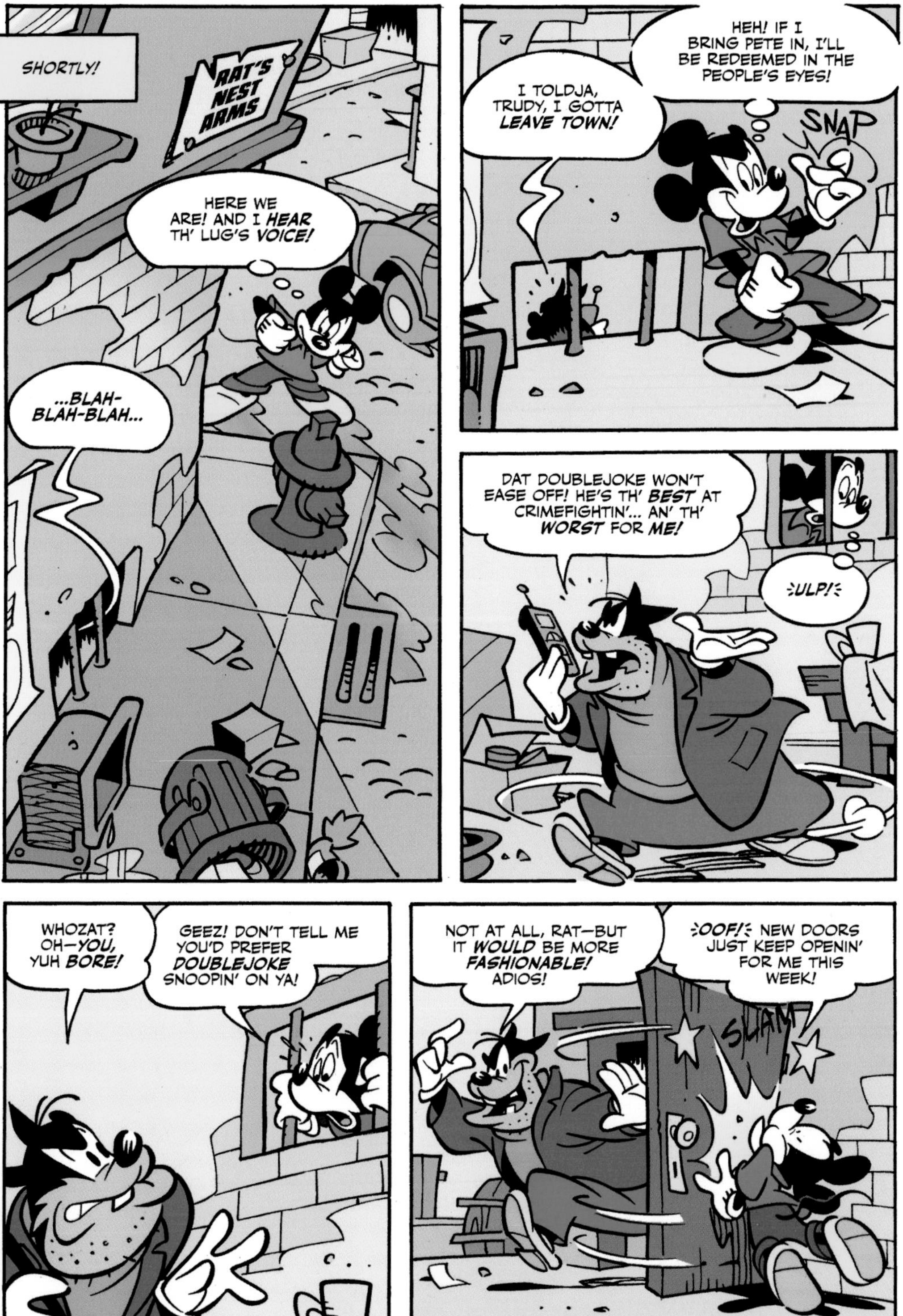
SHORTLY!
RAT'S NEST ARMS
HERE WE ARE! AND I HEAR TH' LUG'S VOICE!
...BLAH-BLAH-BLAH...
I TOLDJA, TRUDY, I GOTTA LEAVE TOWN!
HEH! IF I BRING PETE IN, I'LL BE REDEEMED IN THE PEOPLE'S EYES!
SNAP
DAT DOUBLEJOKE WON'T EASE OFF! HE'S TH' BEST AT CRIMEFIGHTIN'... AN' TH' WORST FOR ME!
ULP!
WHOZAT? OH—YOU, YUH BORE!
GEEZ! DON'T TELL ME YOU'D PREFER DOUBLEJOKE SNOOPIN' ON YA!
NOT AT ALL, RAT—BUT IT WOULD BE MORE FASHIONABLE! ADIOS!
OOF! NEW DOORS JUST KEEP OPENIN' FOR ME THIS WEEK!
SLAM

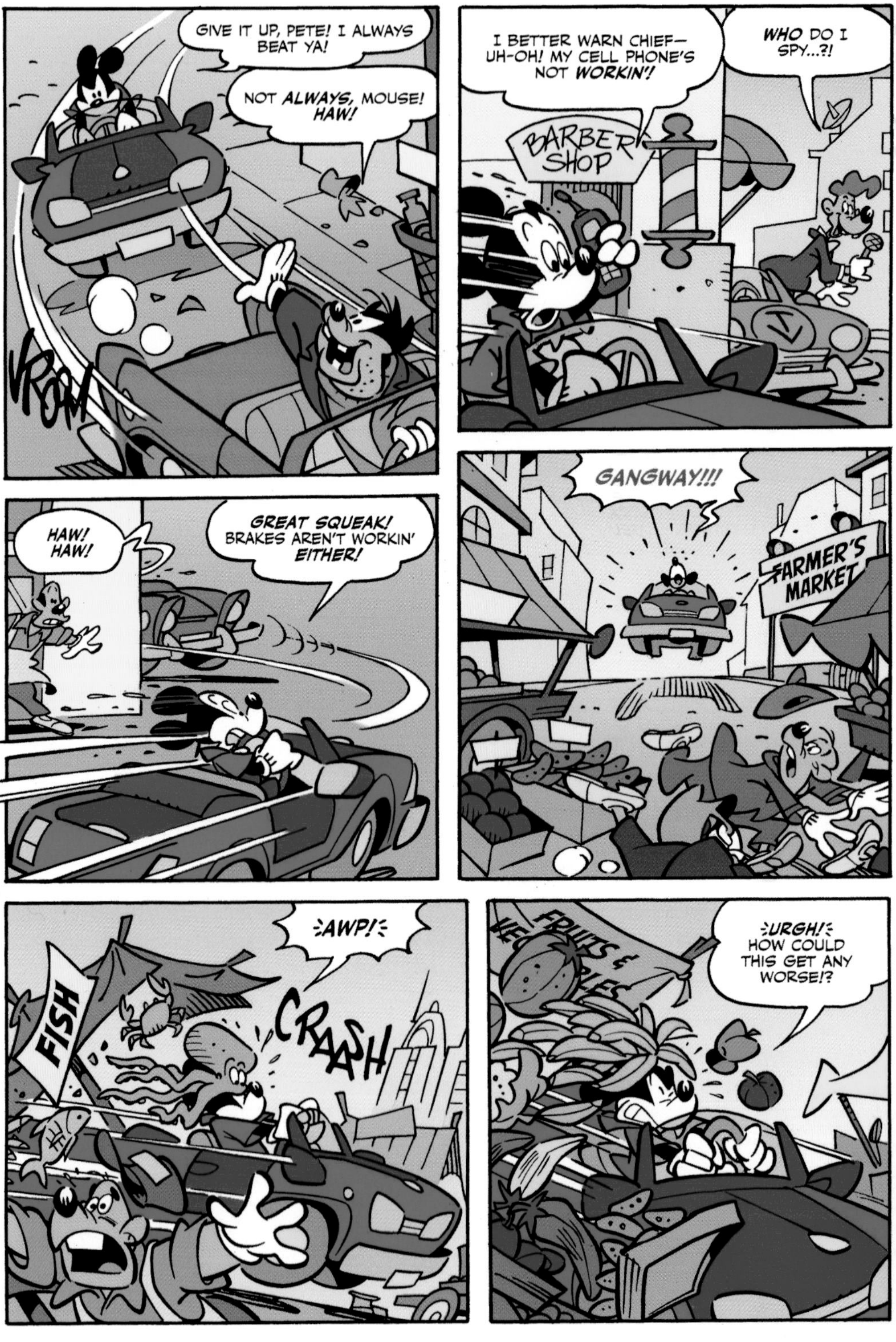
GIVE IT UP, PETE! I ALWAYS BEAT YA!
NOT ALWAYS, MOUSE! HAW!
VROM
I BETTER WARN CHIEF— UH-OH! MY CELL PHONE'S NOT WORKIN'!
WHO DO I SPY...?!
BARBER SHOP
HAW! HAW!
GREAT SQUEAK! BRAKES AREN'T WORKIN' EITHER!
GANGWAY!!!
FARMER'S MARKET
AWP!
FISH
CRAASH
URGH! HOW COULD THIS GET ANY WORSE!?

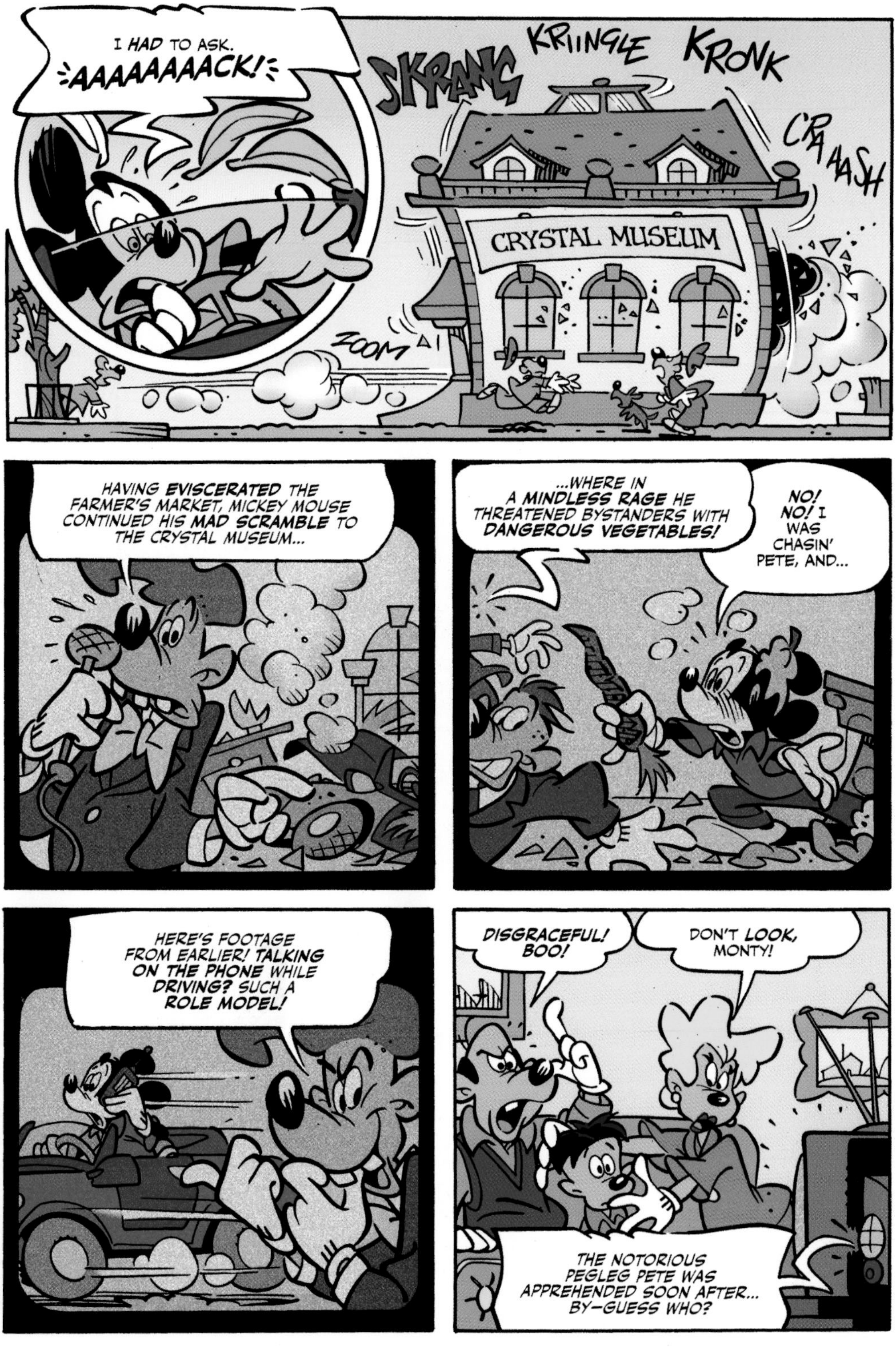

I HAD TO ASK. AAAAAAAACK!
SKRANG
KRIINGLE
KRONK
CRAAASH
CRYSTAL MUSEUM
ZOOM
HAVING EVISCERATED THE FARMER'S MARKET, MICKEY MOUSE CONTINUED HIS MAD SCRAMBLE TO THE CRYSTAL MUSEUM...
...WHERE IN A MINDLESS RAGE HE THREATENED BYSTANDERS WITH DANGEROUS VEGETABLES!
NO! NO! I WAS CHASIN' PETE, AND...
HERE'S FOOTAGE FROM EARLIER! TALKING ON THE PHONE WHILE DRIVING? SUCH A ROLE MODEL!
DISGRACEFUL! BOO!
DON'T LOOK, MONTY!
THE NOTORIOUS PEGLEG PETE WAS APPREHENDED SOON AFTER... BY—GUESS WHO?

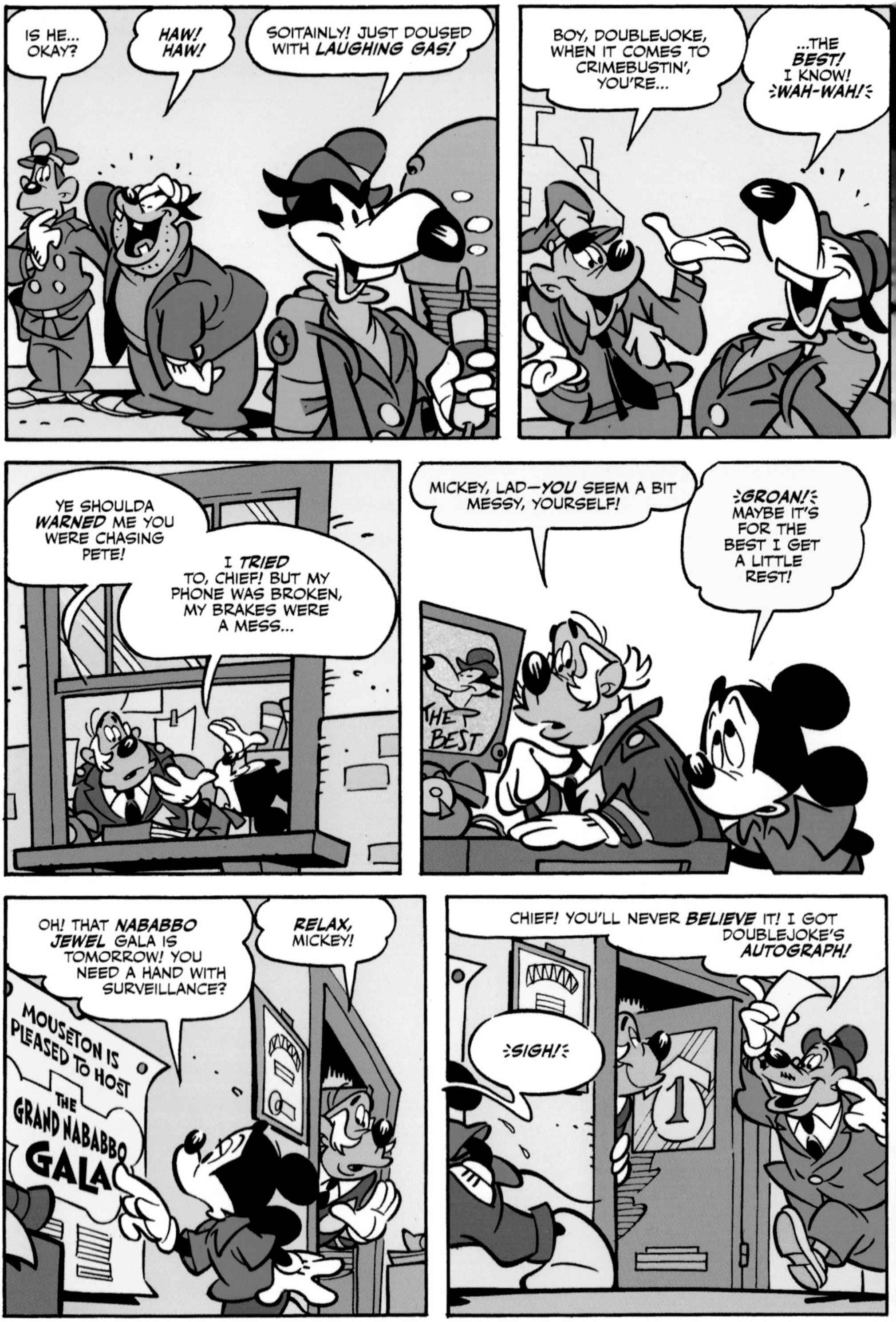
IS HE... OKAY?
HAW! HAW!
SOITAINLY! JUST DOUSED WITH LAUGHING GAS!
BOY, DOUBLEJOKE, WHEN IT COMES TO CRIMEBUSTIN', YOU'RE...
...THE BEST! I KNOW! WAH-WAH!
YE SHOULDA WARNED ME YOU WERE CHASING PETE!
I TRIED TO, CHIEF! BUT MY PHONE WAS BROKEN, MY BRAKES WERE A MESS...
MICKEY, LAD—YOU SEEM A BIT MESSY, YOURSELF!
GROAN! MAYBE IT'S FOR THE BEST I GET A LITTLE REST!
THE BEST
OH! THAT NABABBO JEWEL GALA IS TOMORROW! YOU NEED A HAND WITH SURVEILLANCE?
RELAX, MICKEY!
MOUSETON IS PLEASED TO HOST THE GRAND NABABBO GALA
CHIEF! YOU'LL NEVER BELIEVE IT! I GOT DOUBLEJOKE'S AUTOGRAPH!
SIGH!
1

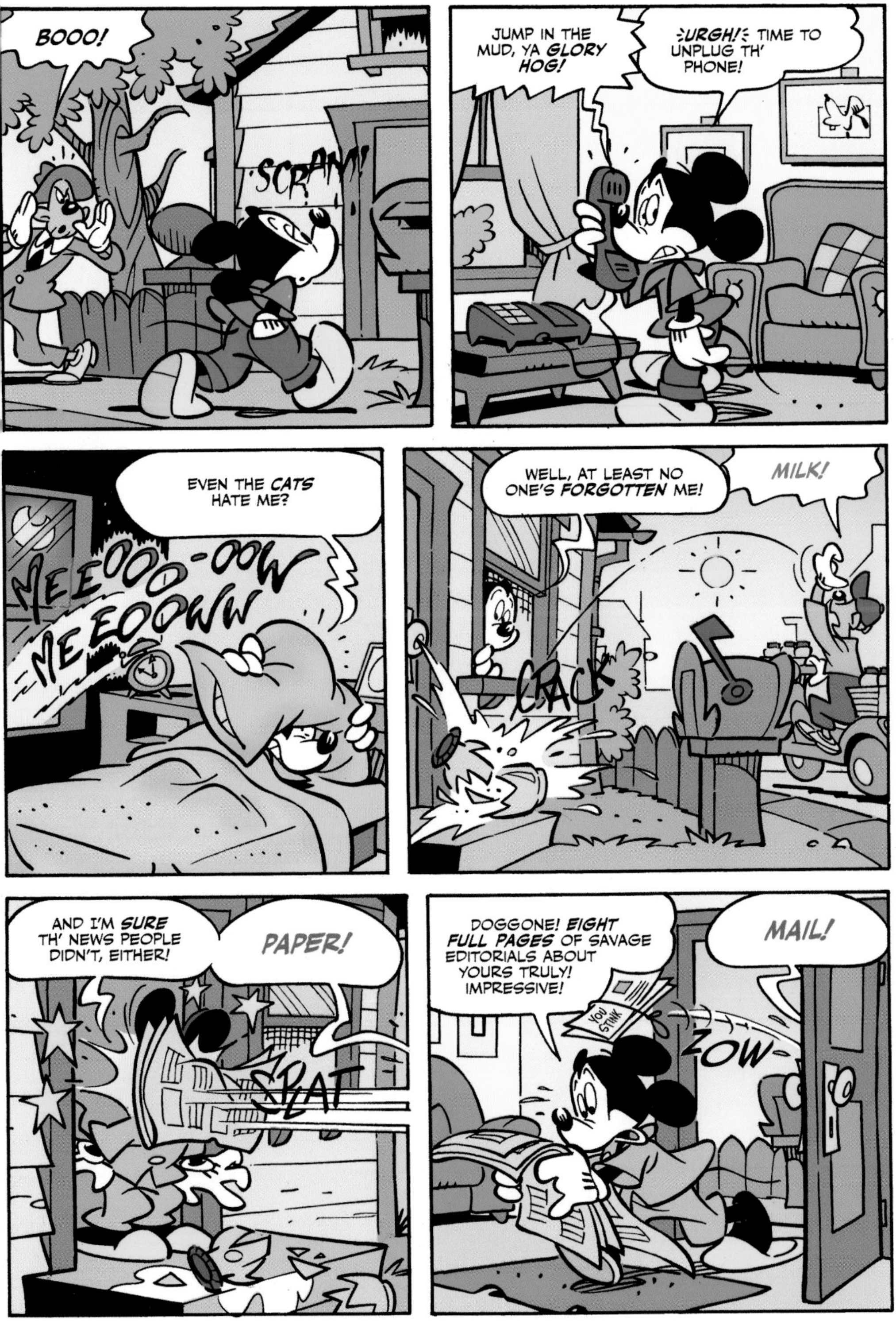
BOOO!
SCRAM!
JUMP IN THE MUD, YA GLORY HOG!
URGH! TIME TO UNPLUG TH' PHONE!
EVEN THE CATS HATE ME?
MEEOOO-OOW
MEEOOWW
WELL, AT LEAST NO ONE'S FORGOTTEN ME!
MILK!
CRACK
AND I'M SURE TH' NEWS PEOPLE DIDN'T, EITHER!
PAPER!
SPLAT
DOGGONE! EIGHT FULL PAGES OF SAVAGE EDITORIALS ABOUT YOURS TRULY! IMPRESSIVE!
MAIL!
YOU STINK
ZOW

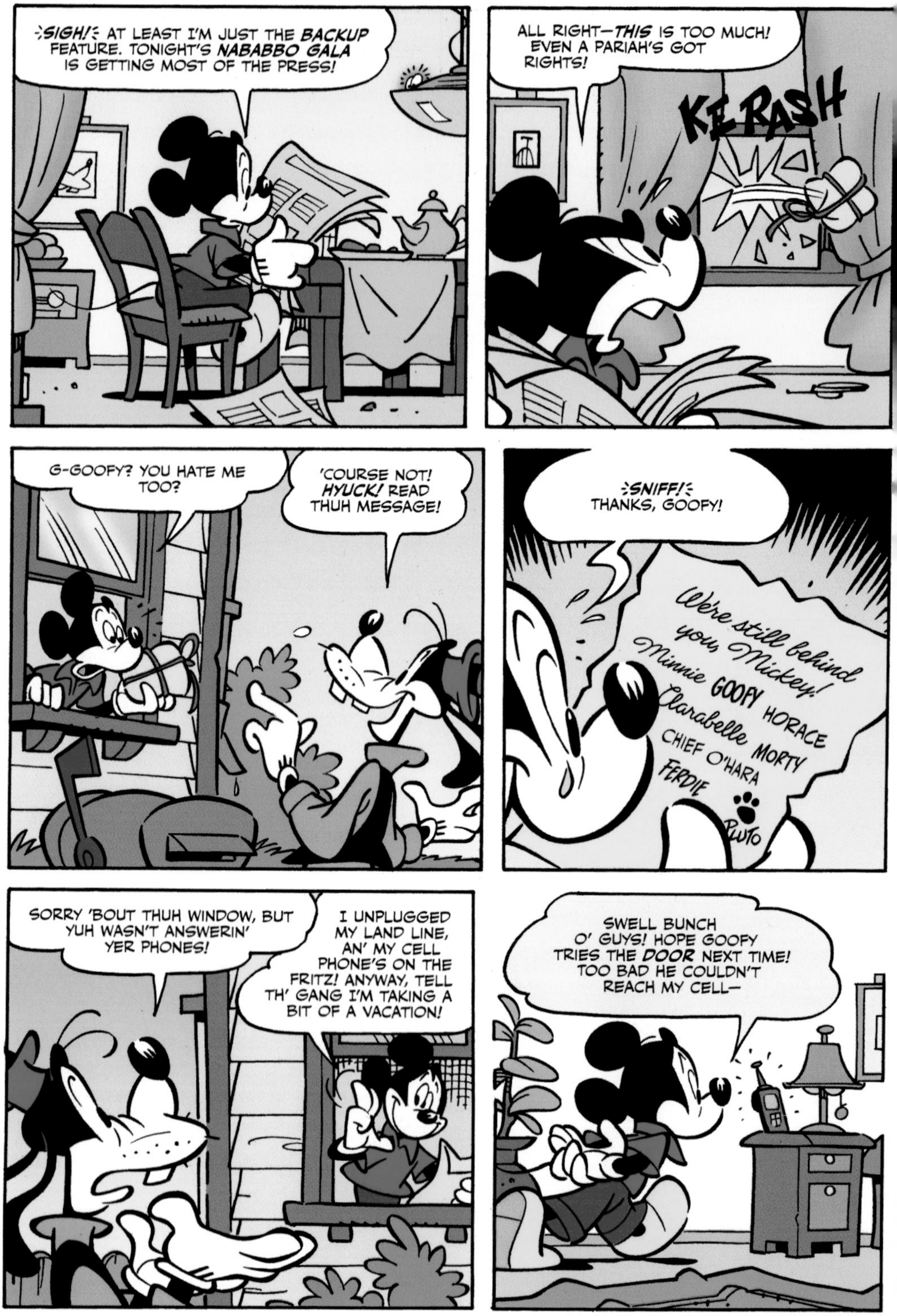

:SIGH!: AT LEAST I'M JUST THE BACKUP FEATURE. TONIGHT'S NABABBO GALA IS GETTING MOST OF THE PRESS!
ALL RIGHT—THIS IS TOO MUCH! EVEN A PARIAH'S GOT RIGHTS!
KERASH
G-GOOFY? YOU HATE ME TOO?
'COURSE NOT! HYUCK! READ THUH MESSAGE!
:SNIFF!: THANKS, GOOFY!
We're still behind you, Mickey!
Minnie GOOFY HORACE
Clarabelle MORTY
CHIEF O'HARA
FERDIE
PLUTO
SORRY 'BOUT THUH WINDOW, BUT YUH WASN'T ANSWERIN' YER PHONES!
I UNPLUGGED MY LAND LINE, AN' MY CELL PHONE'S ON THE FRITZ! ANYWAY, TELL TH' GANG I'M TAKING A BIT OF A VACATION!
SWELL BUNCH O' GUYS! HOPE GOOFY TRIES THE DOOR NEXT TIME! TOO BAD HE COULDN'T REACH MY CELL—

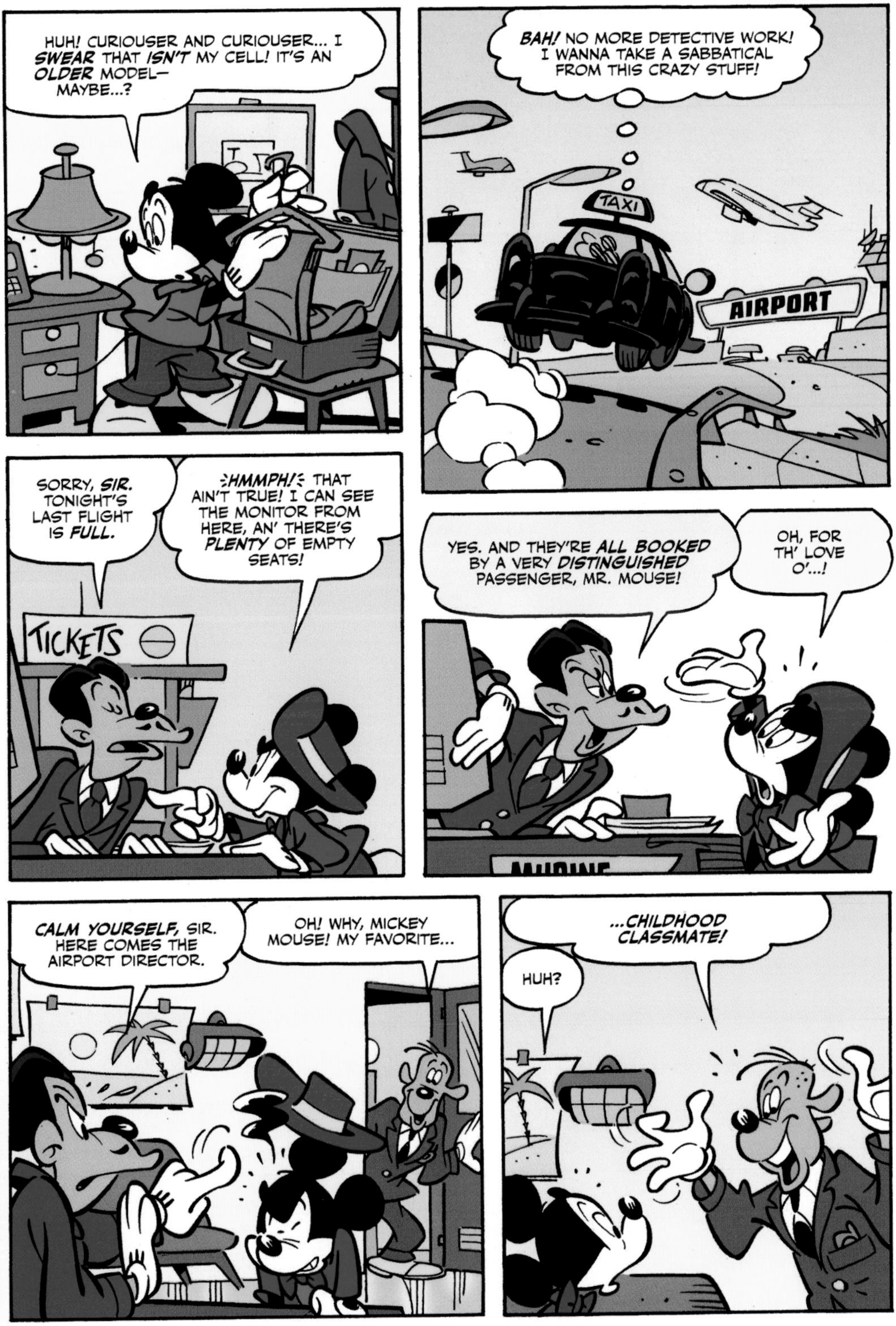
HUH! CURIOUSER AND CURIOUSER... I SWEAR THAT ISN'T MY CELL! IT'S AN OLDER MODEL— MAYBE...?
BAH! NO MORE DETECTIVE WORK! I WANNA TAKE A SABBATICAL FROM THIS CRAZY STUFF!
TAXI
AIRPORT
SORRY, SIR. TONIGHT'S LAST FLIGHT IS FULL.
HMMPH! THAT AIN'T TRUE! I CAN SEE THE MONITOR FROM HERE, AN' THERE'S PLENTY OF EMPTY SEATS!
TICKETS
YES. AND THEY'RE ALL BOOKED BY A VERY DISTINGUISHED PASSENGER, MR. MOUSE!
OH, FOR TH' LOVE O'...!
CALM YOURSELF, SIR. HERE COMES THE AIRPORT DIRECTOR.
OH! WHY, MICKEY MOUSE! MY FAVORITE...
...CHILDHOOD CLASSMATE!
HUH?

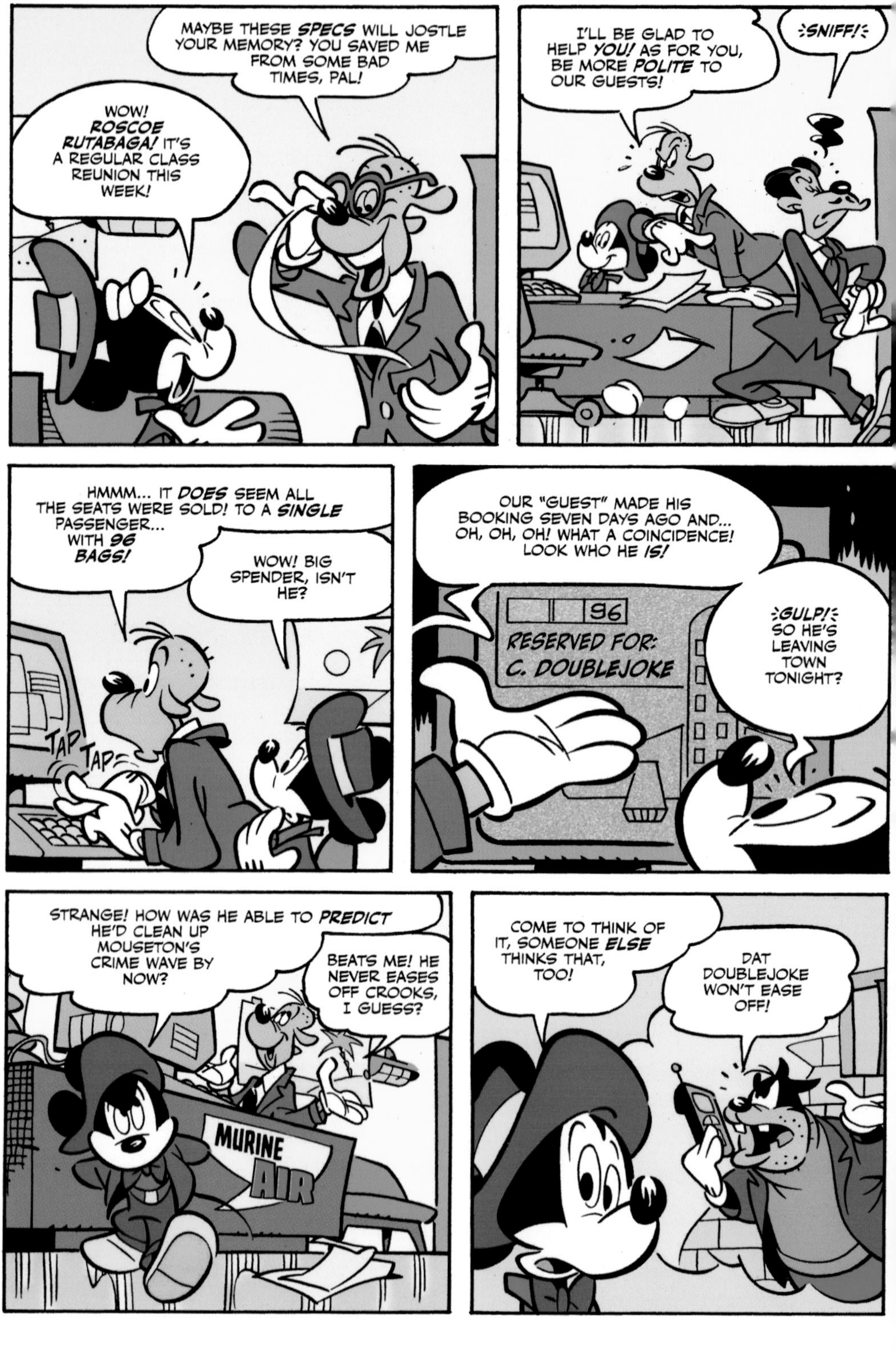
MAYBE THESE SPECS WILL JOSTLE YOUR MEMORY? YOU SAVED ME FROM SOME BAD TIMES, PAL!
WOW! ROSCOE RUTABAGA! IT'S A REGULAR CLASS REUNION THIS WEEK!
I'LL BE GLAD TO HELP YOU! AS FOR YOU, BE MORE POLITE TO OUR GUESTS!
SNIFF!
HMMM... IT DOES SEEM ALL THE SEATS WERE SOLD! TO A SINGLE PASSENGER... WITH 96 BAGS!
WOW! BIG SPENDER, ISN'T HE?
TAP TAP
OUR "GUEST" MADE HIS BOOKING SEVEN DAYS AGO AND... OH, OH, OH! WHAT A COINCIDENCE! LOOK WHO HE IS!
96
RESERVED FOR: C. DOUBLEJOKE
GULP! SO HE'S LEAVING TOWN TONIGHT?
STRANGE! HOW WAS HE ABLE TO PREDICT HE'D CLEAN UP MOUSETON'S CRIME WAVE BY NOW?
BEATS ME! HE NEVER EASES OFF CROOKS, I GUESS?
MURINE AIR
COME TO THINK OF IT, SOMEONE ELSE THINKS THAT, TOO!
DAT DOUBLEJOKE WON'T EASE OFF!

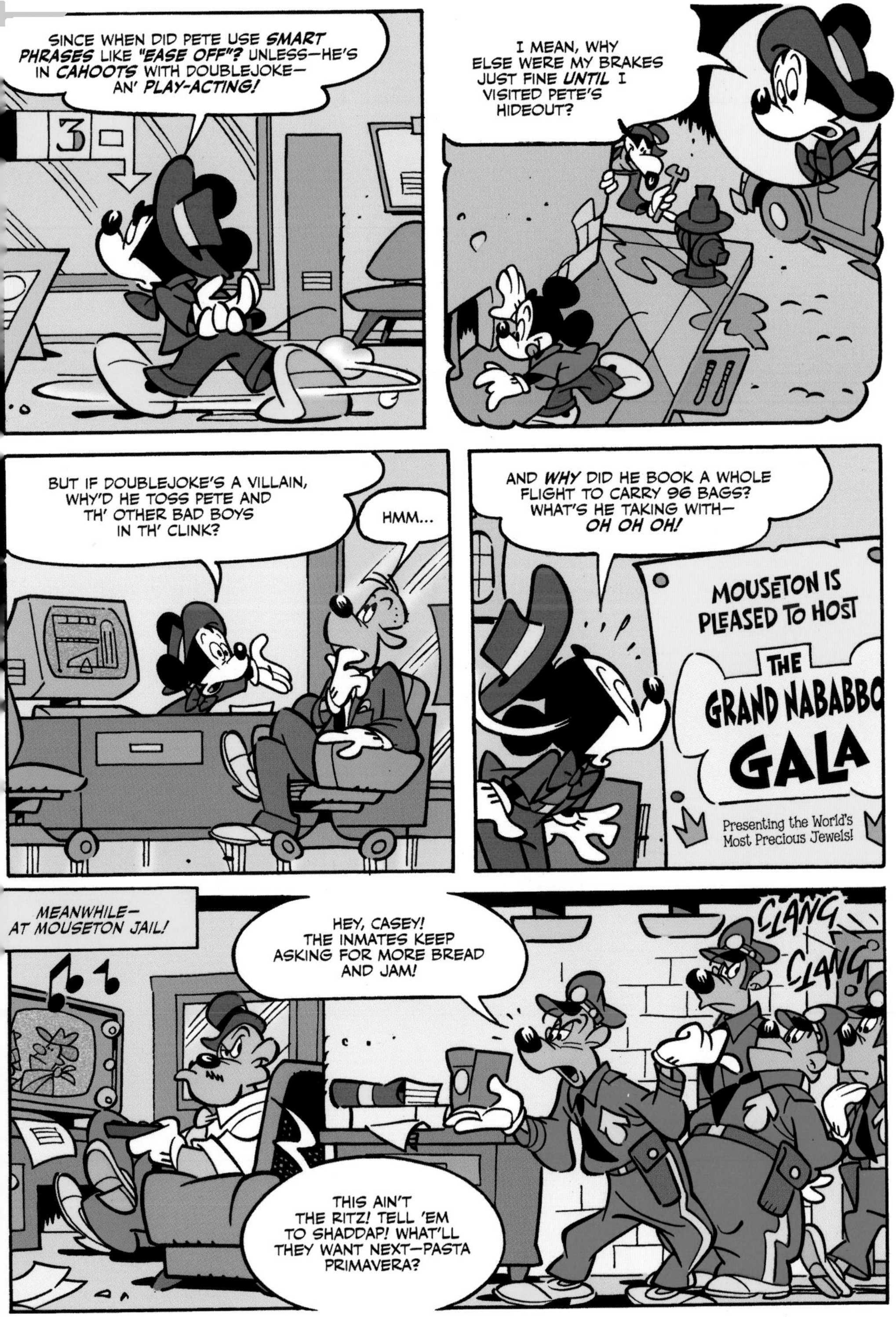
SINCE WHEN DID PETE USE SMART PHRASES LIKE "EASE OFF"? UNLESS—HE'S IN CAHOOTS WITH DOUBLEJOKE— AN' PLAY-ACTING!
I MEAN, WHY ELSE WERE MY BRAKES JUST FINE UNTIL I VISITED PETE'S HIDEOUT?
BUT IF DOUBLEJOKE'S A VILLAIN, WHY'D HE TOSS PETE AND TH' OTHER BAD BOYS IN TH' CLINK?
HMM...
AND WHY DID HE BOOK A WHOLE FLIGHT TO CARRY 96 BAGS? WHAT'S HE TAKING WITH— OH OH OH!
MOUSETON IS PLEASED TO HOST
THE GRAND NABABBO GALA
Presenting the World's Most Precious Jewels!
MEANWHILE— AT MOUSETON JAIL!
HEY, CASEY! THE INMATES KEEP ASKING FOR MORE BREAD AND JAM!
CLANG CLANG
THIS AIN'T THE RITZ! TELL 'EM TO SHADDAP! WHAT'LL THEY WANT NEXT—PASTA PRIMAVERA?

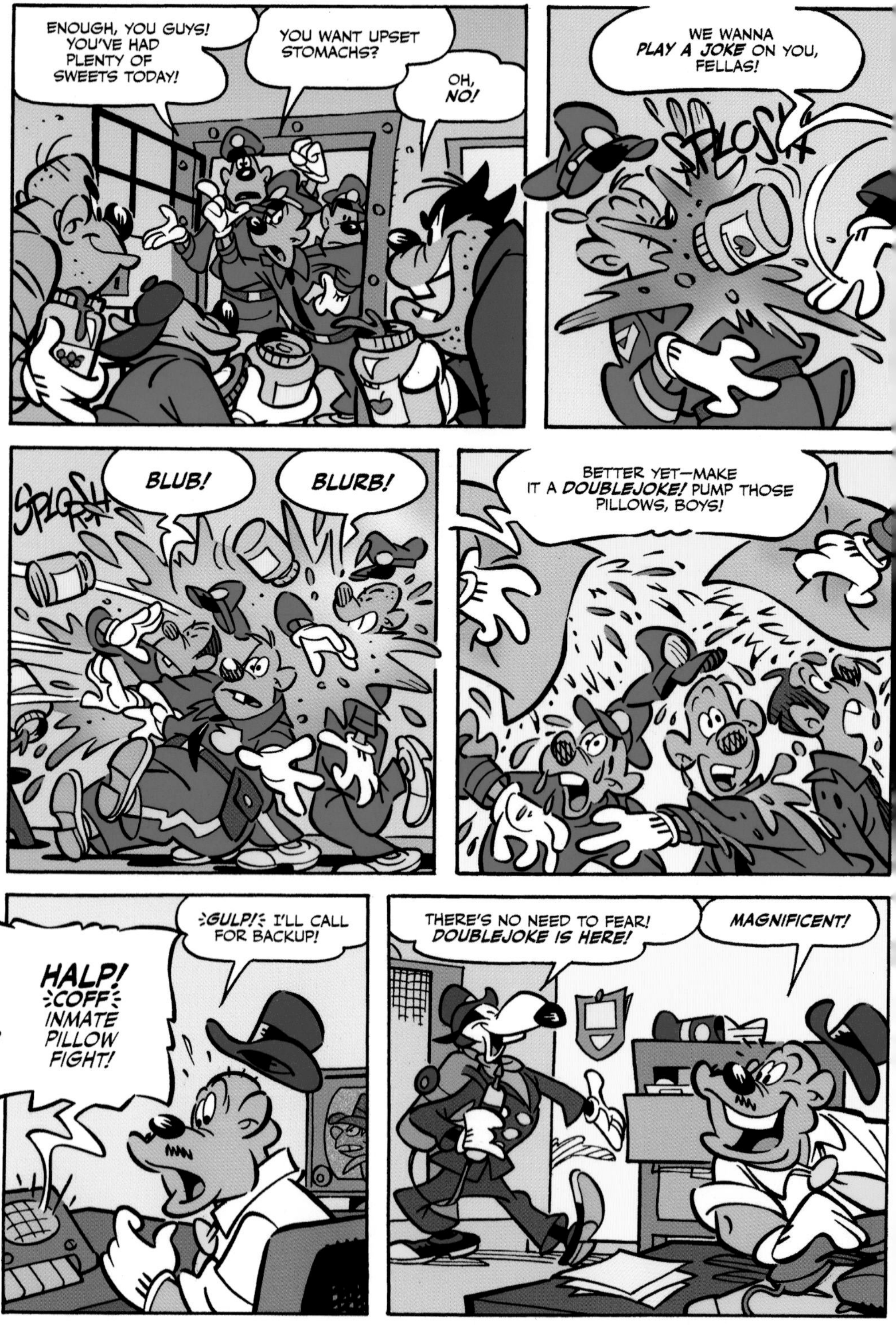
ENOUGH, YOU GUYS! YOU'VE HAD PLENTY OF SWEETS TODAY!
YOU WANT UPSET STOMACHS?
OH, NO!
WE WANNA PLAY A JOKE ON YOU, FELLAS!
SPLOSH
SPLOOSH
BLUB!
BLURB!
BETTER YET—MAKE IT A DOUBLEJOKE! PUMP THOSE PILLOWS, BOYS!
HALP! COFF INMATE PILLOW FIGHT!
GULP! I'LL CALL FOR BACKUP!
THERE'S NO NEED TO FEAR! DOUBLEJOKE IS HERE!
MAGNIFICENT!

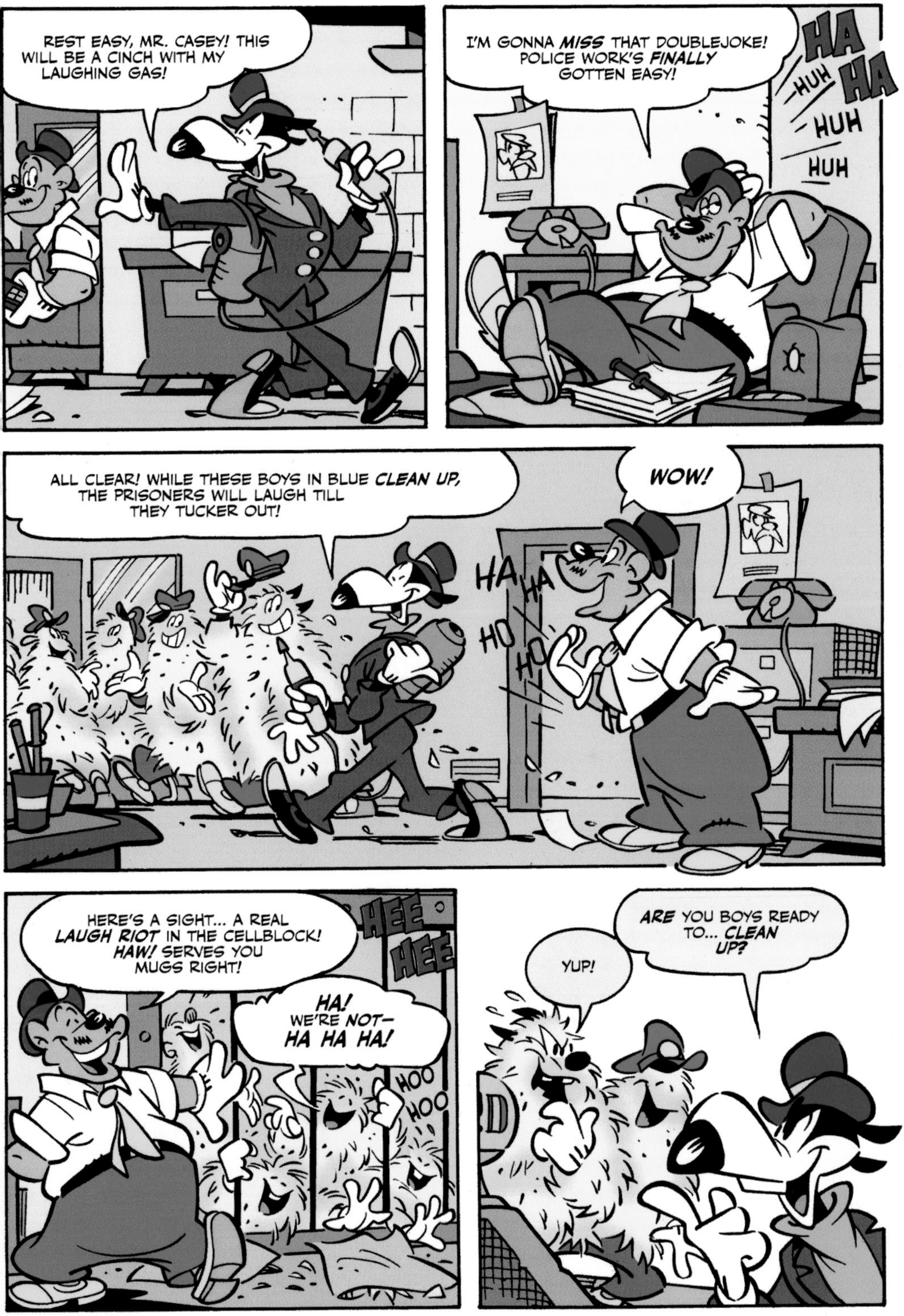
REST EASY, MR. CASEY! THIS WILL BE A CINCH WITH MY LAUGHING GAS!
I'M GONNA *MISS* THAT DOUBLEJOKE! POLICE WORK'S *FINALLY* GOTTEN EASY!
HA HA
HUH HUH HUH
ALL CLEAR! WHILE THESE BOYS IN BLUE *CLEAN UP,* THE PRISONERS WILL LAUGH TILL THEY TUCKER OUT!
WOW!
HA HA
HO HO
HERE'S A SIGHT... A REAL *LAUGH RIOT* IN THE CELLBLOCK! *HAW!* SERVES YOU MUGS RIGHT!
HEE HEE
HA! WE'RE *NOT— HA HA HA!*
HOO HOO
YUP!
ARE YOU BOYS READY TO... *CLEAN UP?*

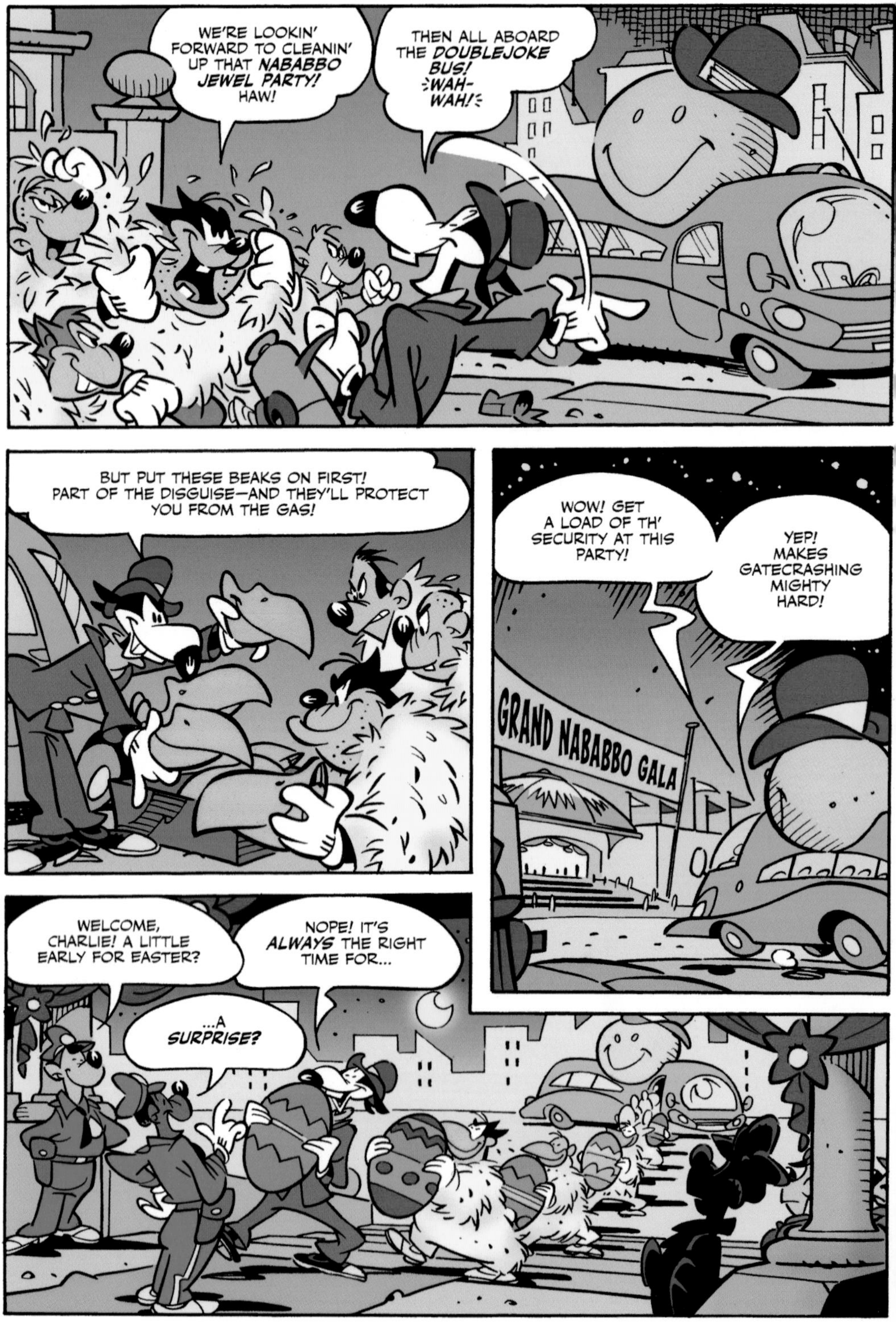
WE'RE LOOKIN' FORWARD TO CLEANIN' UP THAT NABABBO JEWEL PARTY! HAW!
THEN ALL ABOARD THE DOUBLEJOKE BUS! WAH-WAH!
BUT PUT THESE BEAKS ON FIRST! PART OF THE DISGUISE—AND THEY'LL PROTECT YOU FROM THE GAS!
WOW! GET A LOAD OF TH' SECURITY AT THIS PARTY!
YEP! MAKES GATECRASHING MIGHTY HARD!
GRAND NABABBO GALA
WELCOME, CHARLIE! A LITTLE EARLY FOR EASTER?
NOPE! IT'S ALWAYS THE RIGHT TIME FOR...
...A SURPRISE?

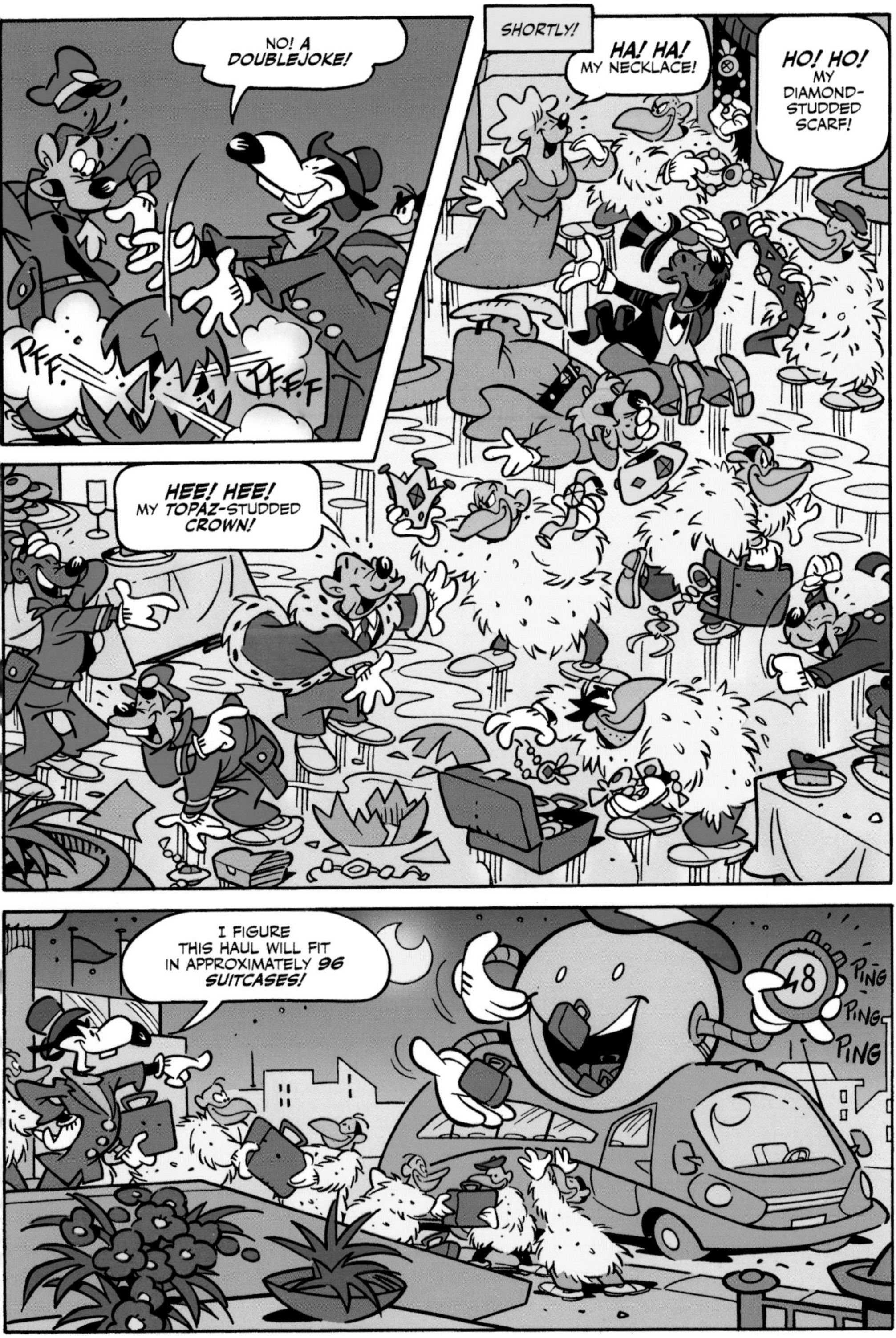
NO! A DOUBLEJOKE!
PFF.
PFF.F
SHORTLY!
HA! HA! MY NECKLACE!
HO! HO! MY DIAMOND-STUDDED SCARF!
HEE! HEE! MY TOPAZ-STUDDED CROWN!
I FIGURE THIS HAUL WILL FIT IN APPROXIMATELY 96 SUITCASES!
48
PING
PING
PING

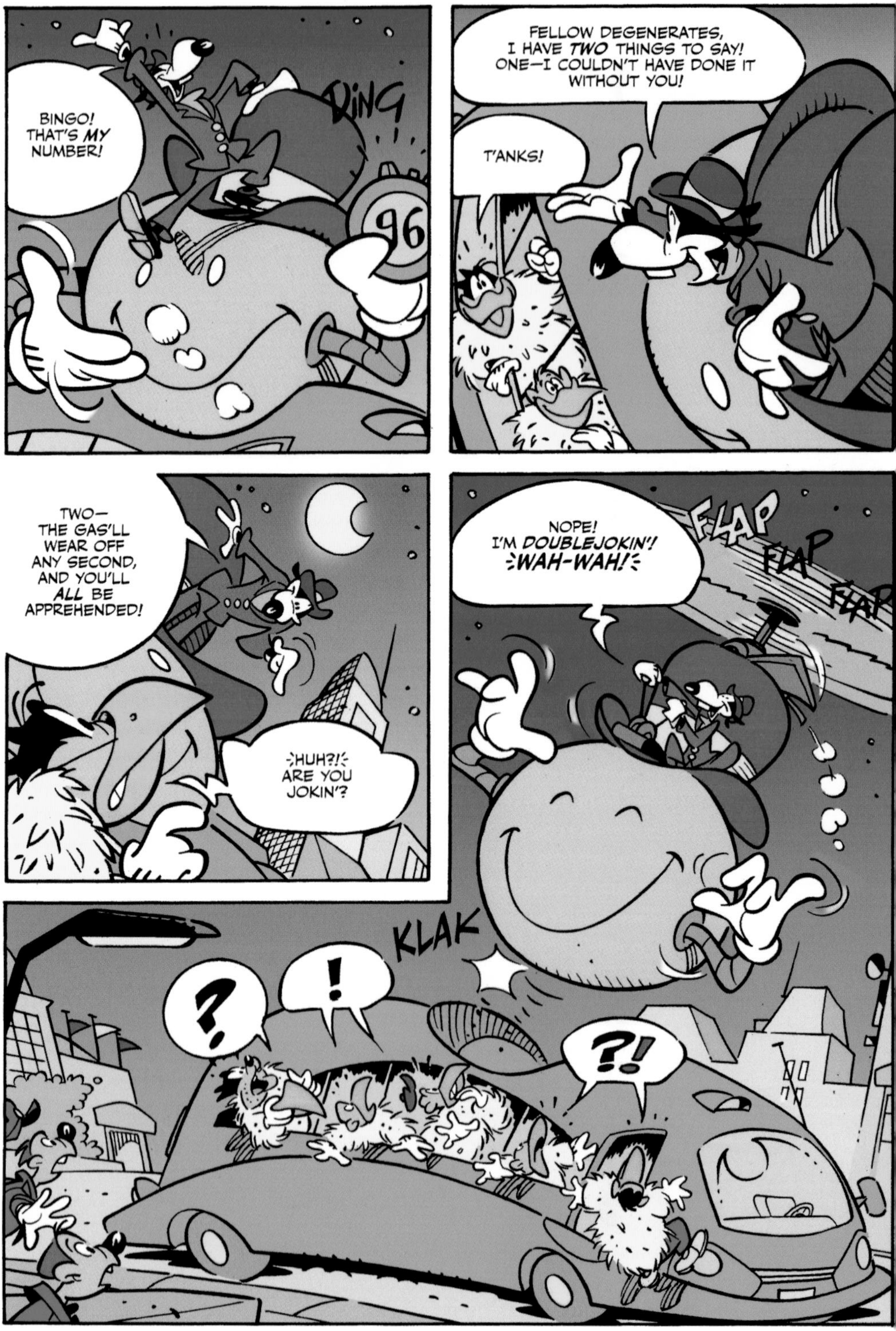
BINGO! THAT'S MY NUMBER!
DING
96
FELLOW DEGENERATES, I HAVE TWO THINGS TO SAY! ONE—I COULDN'T HAVE DONE IT WITHOUT YOU!
T'ANKS!
TWO— THE GAS'LL WEAR OFF ANY SECOND, AND YOU'LL ALL BE APPREHENDED!
HUH?! ARE YOU JOKIN'?
NOPE! I'M DOUBLEJOKIN'! WAH-WAH!
FLAP
FLAP
FLAP
KLAK
?
!
?!

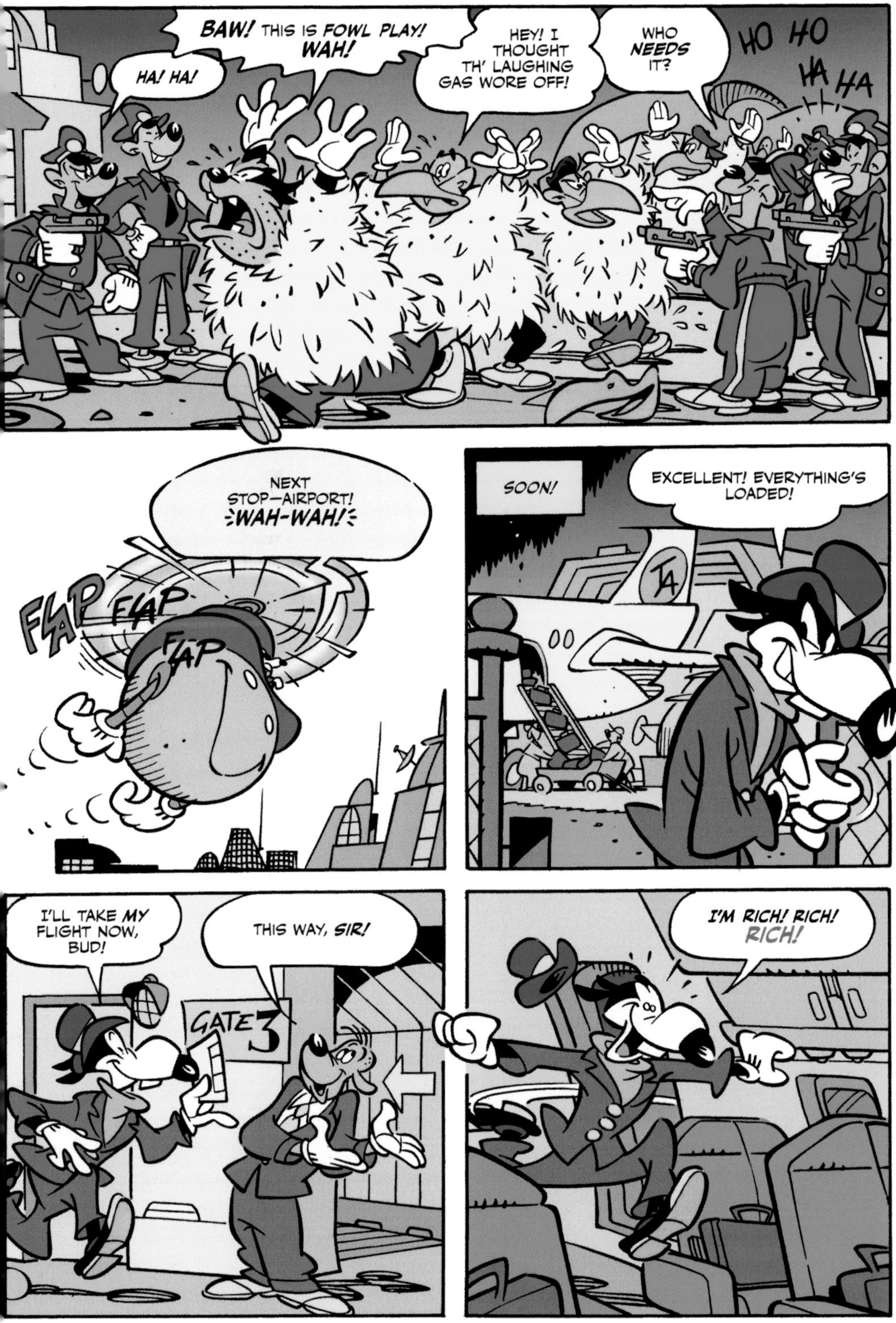

HA! HA!
BAW! THIS IS FOWL PLAY! WAH!
HEY! I THOUGHT TH' LAUGHING GAS WORE OFF!
WHO NEEDS IT?
HO HO HA HA
NEXT STOP—AIRPORT! WAH-WAH!
FLAP FLAP FLAP
SOON!
EXCELLENT! EVERYTHING'S LOADED!
TA
I'LL TAKE MY FLIGHT NOW, BUD!
THIS WAY, SIR!
GATE 3
I'M RICH! RICH! RICH!

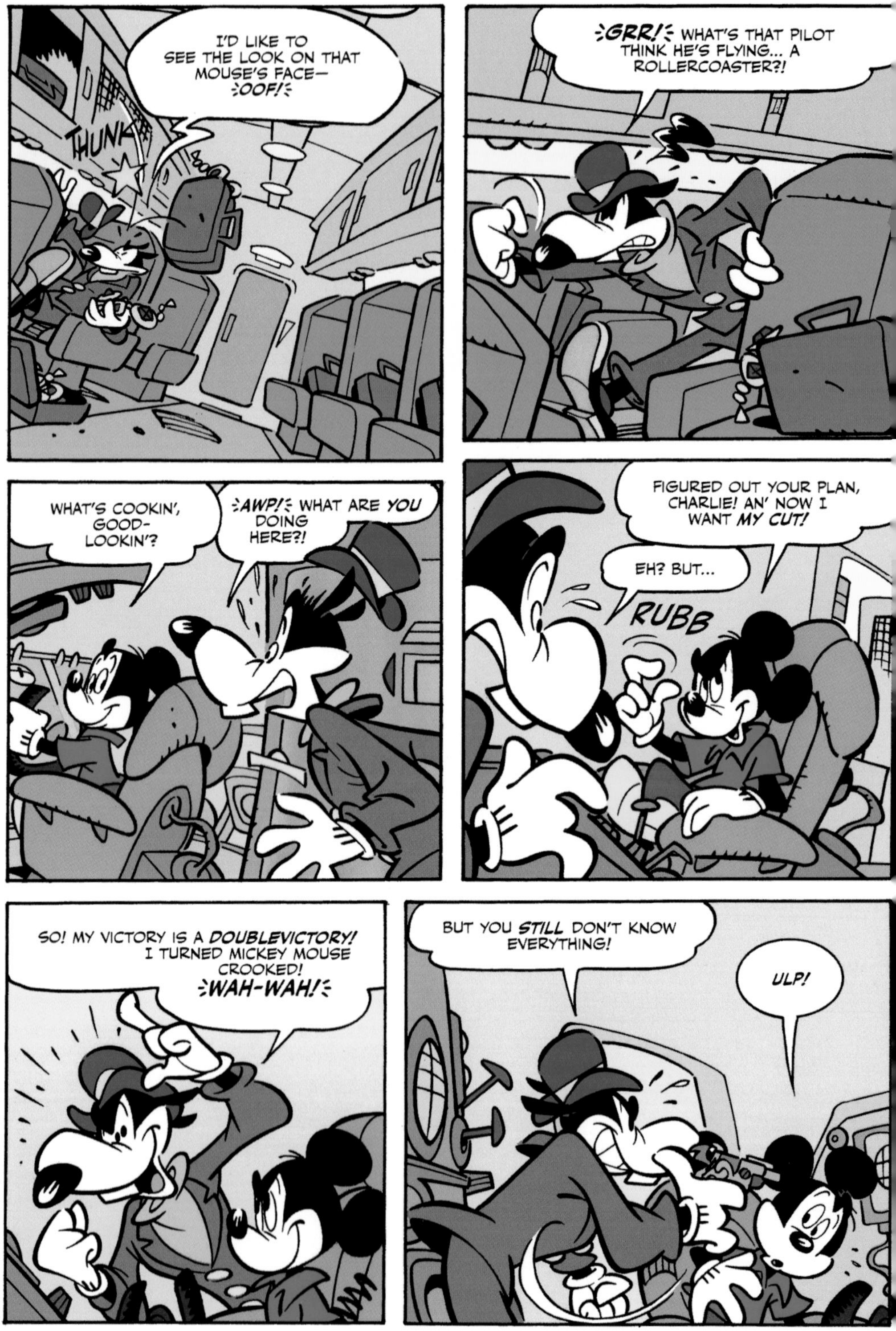
THUNK
I'D LIKE TO SEE THE LOOK ON THAT MOUSE'S FACE— OOF!
GRR! WHAT'S THAT PILOT THINK HE'S FLYING... A ROLLERCOASTER?!
WHAT'S COOKIN', GOOD-LOOKIN'?
AWP! WHAT ARE YOU DOING HERE?!
FIGURED OUT YOUR PLAN, CHARLIE! AN' NOW I WANT MY CUT!
EH? BUT...
RUBB
SO! MY VICTORY IS A DOUBLEVICTORY! I TURNED MICKEY MOUSE CROOKED! WAH-WAH!
BUT YOU STILL DON'T KNOW EVERYTHING!
ULP!

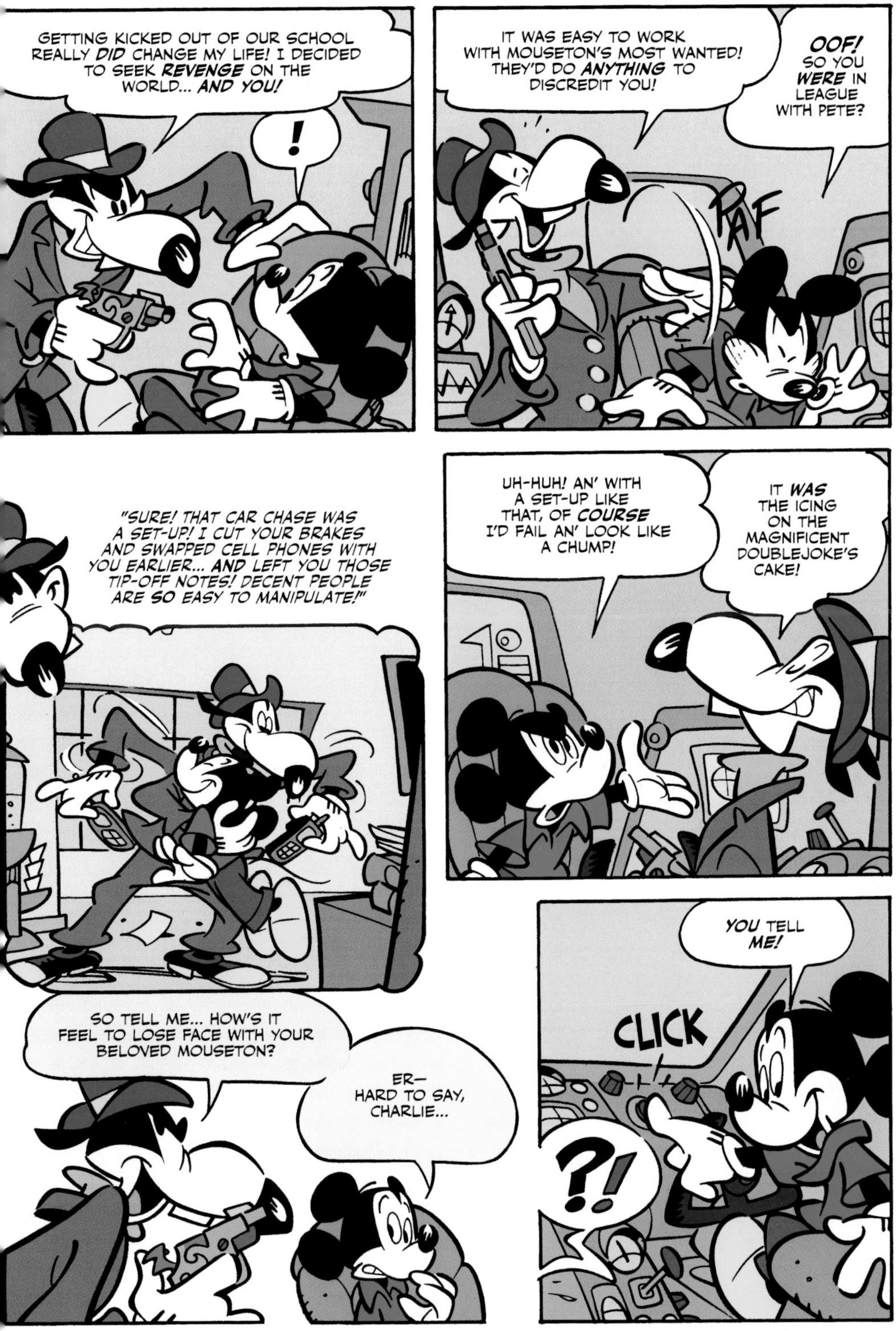
GETTING KICKED OUT OF OUR SCHOOL REALLY DID CHANGE MY LIFE! I DECIDED TO SEEK REVENGE ON THE WORLD... AND YOU!
!
IT WAS EASY TO WORK WITH MOUSETON'S MOST WANTED! THEY'D DO ANYTHING TO DISCREDIT YOU!
OOF! SO YOU WERE IN LEAGUE WITH PETE?
PAF
"SURE! THAT CAR CHASE WAS A SET-UP! I CUT YOUR BRAKES AND SWAPPED CELL PHONES WITH YOU EARLIER... AND LEFT YOU THOSE TIP-OFF NOTES! DECENT PEOPLE ARE SO EASY TO MANIPULATE!"
UH-HUH! AN' WITH A SET-UP LIKE THAT, OF COURSE I'D FAIL AN' LOOK LIKE A CHUMP!
IT WAS THE ICING ON THE MAGNIFICENT DOUBLEJOKE'S CAKE!
SO TELL ME... HOW'S IT FEEL TO LOSE FACE WITH YOUR BELOVED MOUSETON?
ER— HARD TO SAY, CHARLIE...
YOU TELL ME!
CLICK
?!

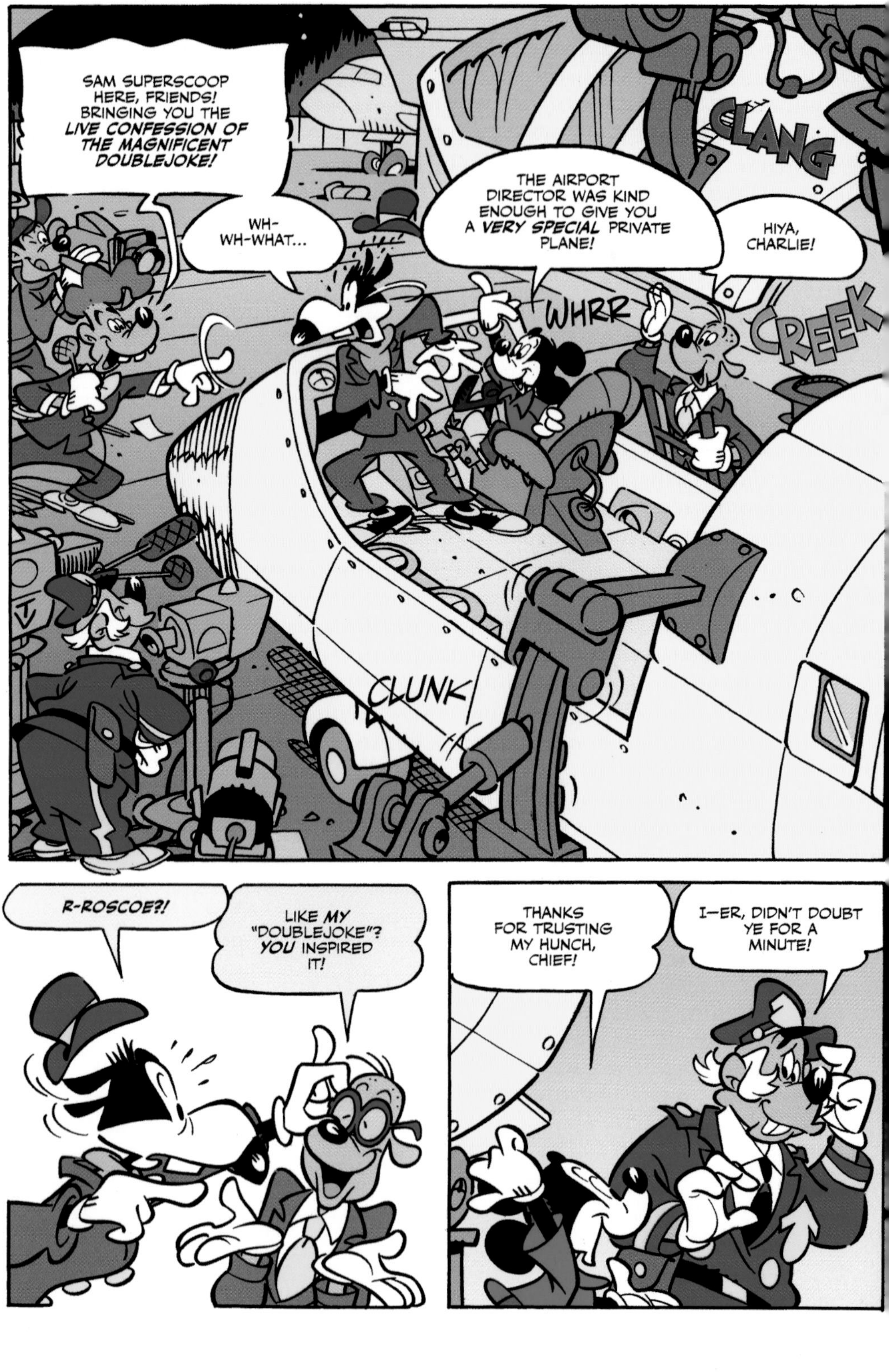
SAM SUPERSCOOP HERE, FRIENDS! BRINGING YOU THE *LIVE CONFESSION OF THE MAGNIFICENT DOUBLEJOKE!*
CLANG
WH- WH-WHAT...
THE AIRPORT DIRECTOR WAS KIND ENOUGH TO GIVE YOU A *VERY SPECIAL* PRIVATE PLANE!
WHRR
HIYA, CHARLIE!
CREEK
CLUNK
R-ROSCOE?!
LIKE *MY* "DOUBLEJOKE"? *YOU* INSPIRED IT!
THANKS FOR TRUSTING MY HUNCH, CHIEF!
I—ER, DIDN'T DOUBT YE FOR A MINUTE!

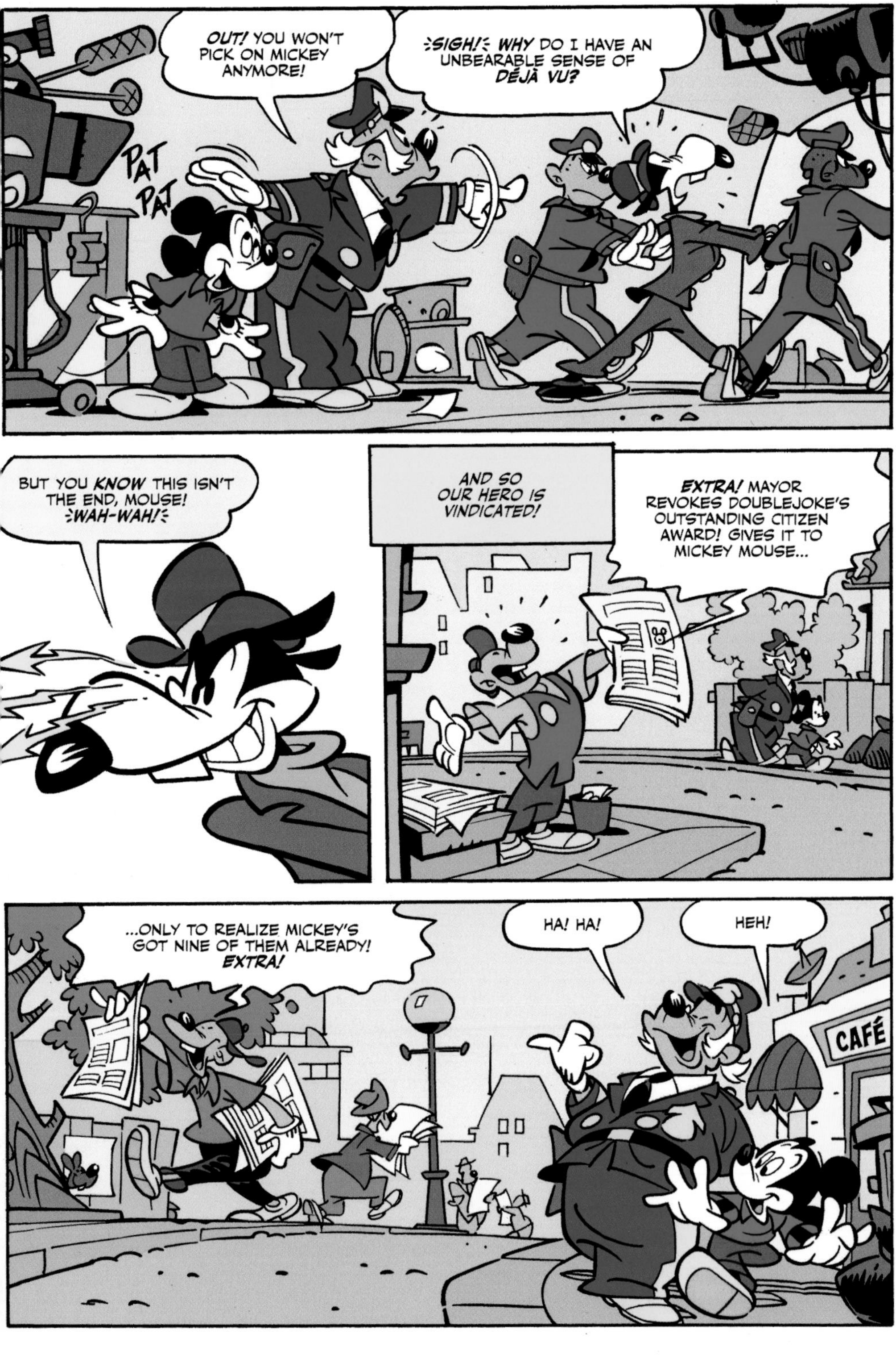
PAT PAT
OUT! YOU WON'T PICK ON MICKEY ANYMORE!
SIGH! WHY DO I HAVE AN UNBEARABLE SENSE OF DÉJÀ VU?
BUT YOU KNOW THIS ISN'T THE END, MOUSE! WAH-WAH!
AND SO OUR HERO IS VINDICATED!
EXTRA! MAYOR REVOKES DOUBLEJOKE'S OUTSTANDING CITIZEN AWARD! GIVES IT TO MICKEY MOUSE...
...ONLY TO REALIZE MICKEY'S GOT NINE OF THEM ALREADY! EXTRA!
HA! HA!
HEH!
CAFÉ

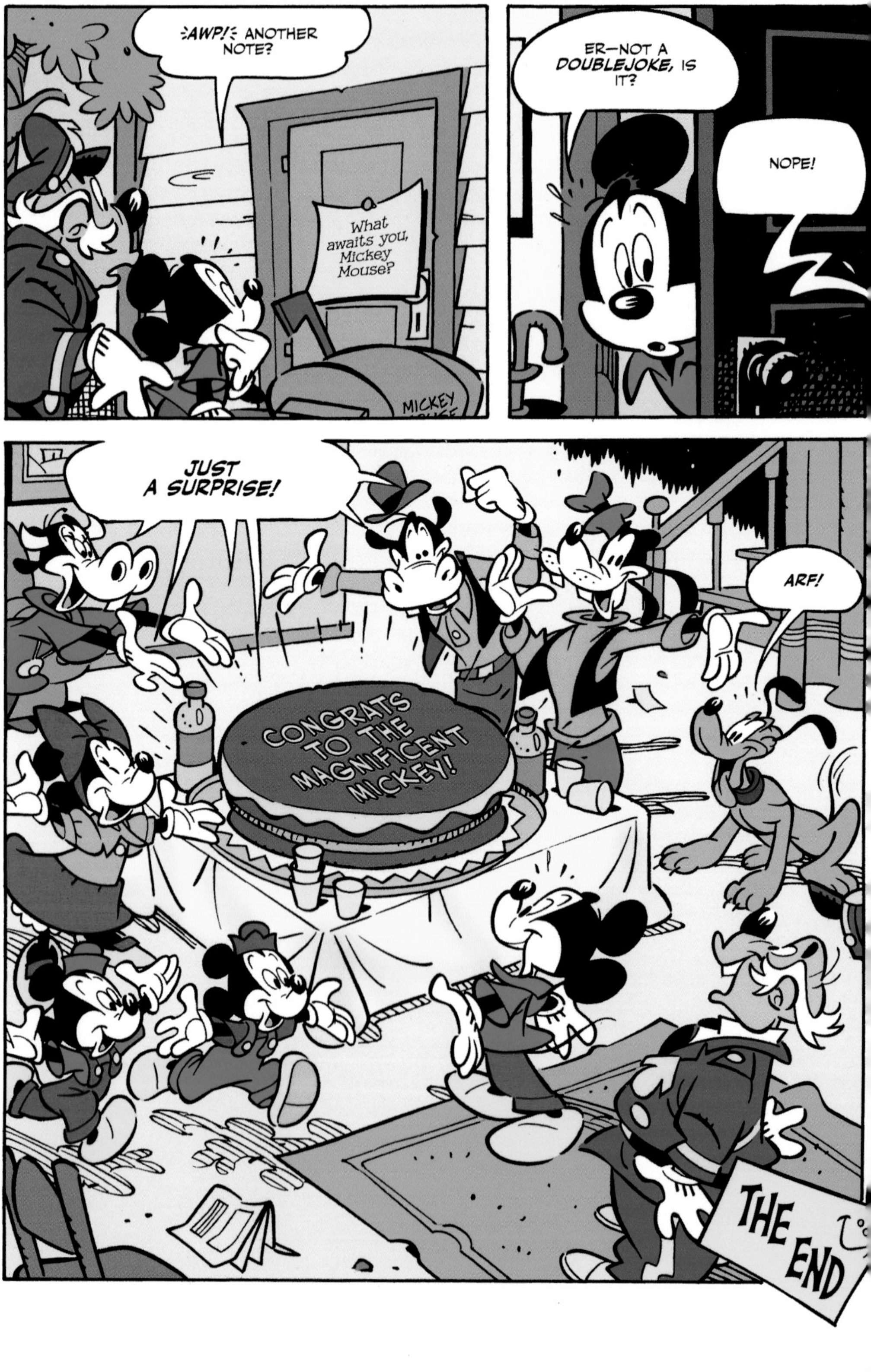
AWP! ANOTHER NOTE?
What awaits you, Mickey Mouse?
MICKEY
ER—NOT A DOUBLEJOKE, IS IT?
NOPE!
JUST A SURPRISE!
ARF!
CONGRATS TO THE MAGNIFICENT MICKEY!
THE END

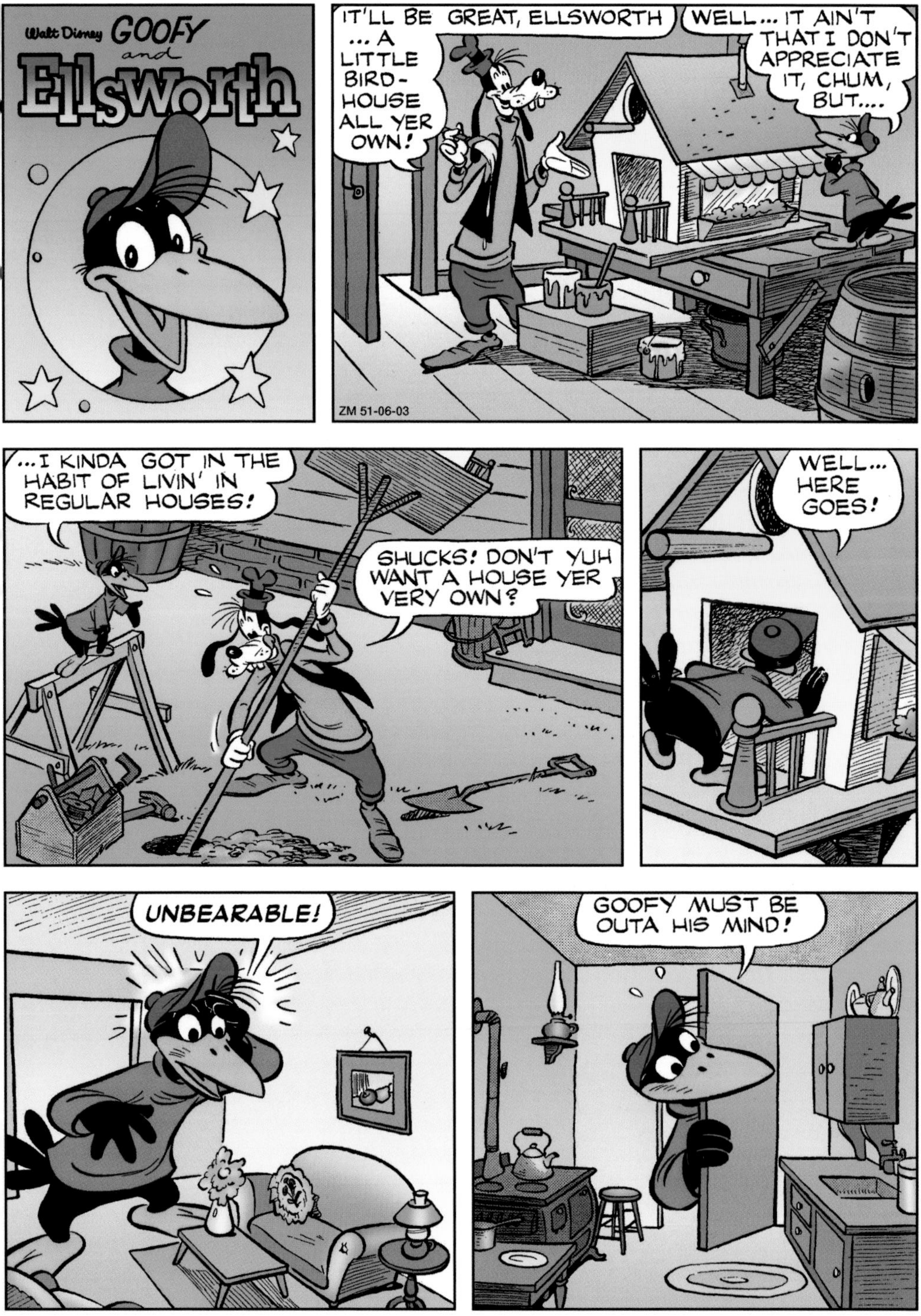
Walt Disney GOOFY and Ellsworth
IT'LL BE GREAT, ELLSWORTH ... A LITTLE BIRD-HOUSE ALL YER OWN!
WELL... IT AIN'T THAT I DON'T APPRECIATE IT, CHUM, BUT....
ZM 51-06-03
...I KINDA GOT IN THE HABIT OF LIVIN' IN REGULAR HOUSES!
SHUCKS! DON'T YUH WANT A HOUSE YER VERY OWN?
WELL... HERE GOES!
UNBEARABLE!
GOOFY MUST BE OUTA HIS MIND!

Originally published in *Mickey Mouse* Sunday comic strip (USA, 1951)

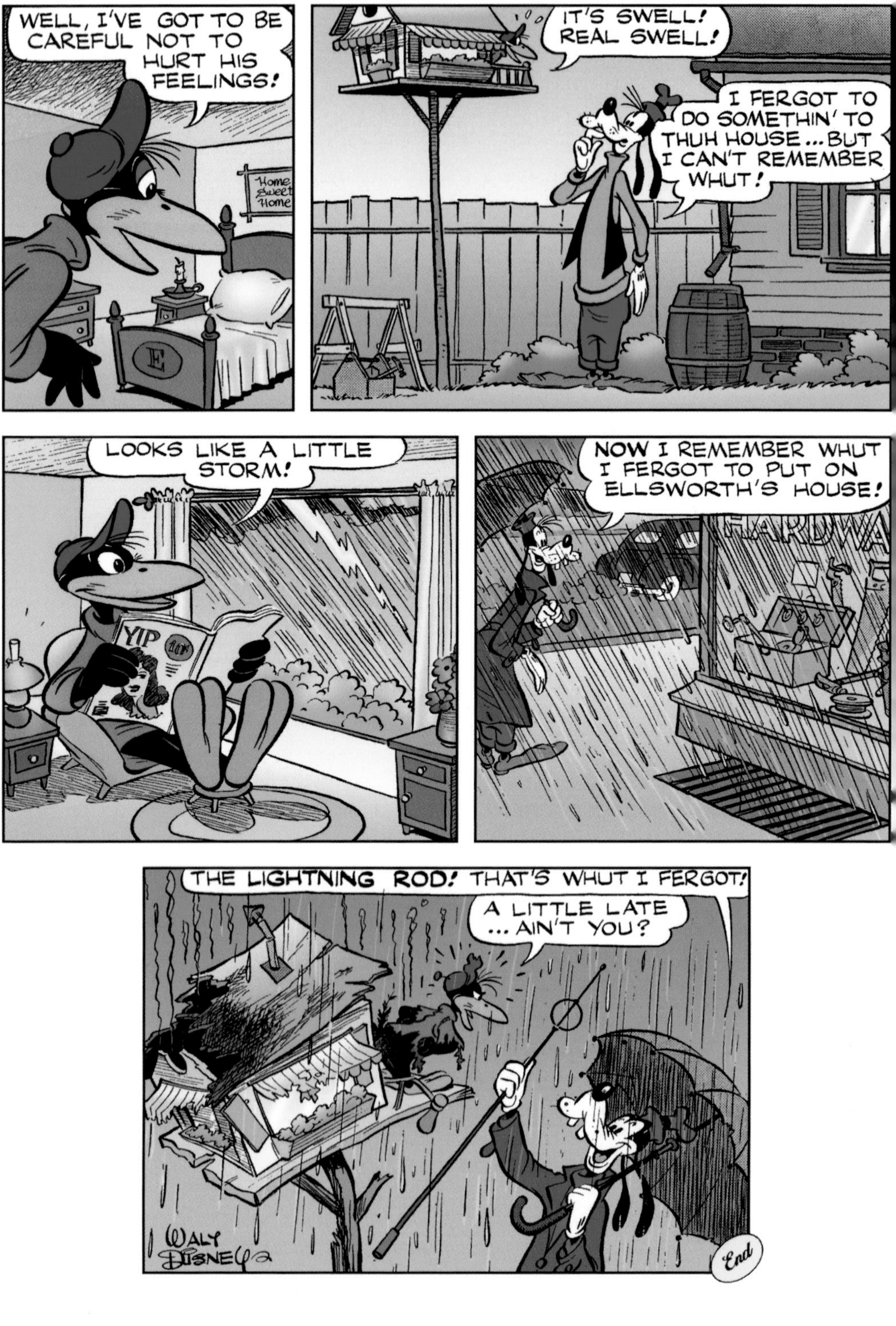
WELL, I'VE GOT TO BE CAREFUL NOT TO HURT HIS FEELINGS!
Home Sweet Home
IT'S SWELL! REAL SWELL!
I FERGOT TO DO SOMETHIN' TO THUH HOUSE...BUT I CAN'T REMEMBER WHUT!
LOOKS LIKE A LITTLE STORM!
YIP 10¢
NOW I REMEMBER WHUT I FERGOT TO PUT ON ELLSWORTH'S HOUSE!
HARDWA
THE LIGHTNING ROD! THAT'S WHUT I FERGOT!
A LITTLE LATE ...AIN'T YOU?
WALT DISNEY
End

Walt Disney's

MICKEY MOUSE in EARLY TO BID

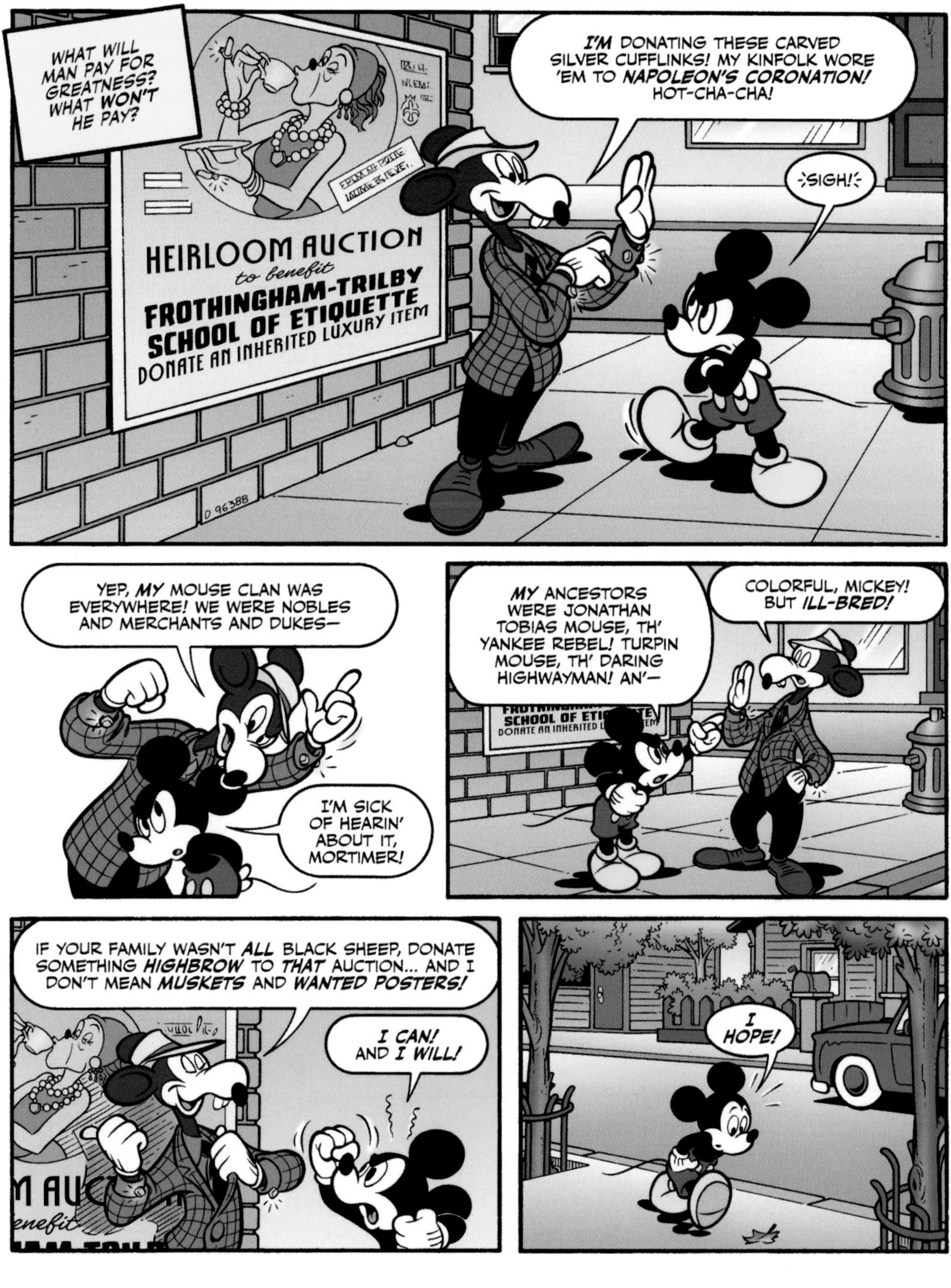
WHAT WILL MAN PAY FOR GREATNESS? WHAT WON'T HE PAY?
HEIRLOOM AUCTION to benefit FROTHINGHAM-TRILBY SCHOOL OF ETIQUETTE DONATE AN INHERITED LUXURY ITEM
I'M DONATING THESE CARVED SILVER CUFFLINKS! MY KINFOLK WORE 'EM TO NAPOLEON'S CORONATION! HOT-CHA-CHA!
SIGH!
YEP, MY MOUSE CLAN WAS EVERYWHERE! WE WERE NOBLES AND MERCHANTS AND DUKES—
I'M SICK OF HEARIN' ABOUT IT, MORTIMER!
MY ANCESTORS WERE JONATHAN TOBIAS MOUSE, TH' YANKEE REBEL! TURPIN MOUSE, TH' DARING HIGHWAYMAN! AN'—
COLORFUL, MICKEY! BUT ILL-BRED!
IF YOUR FAMILY WASN'T ALL BLACK SHEEP, DONATE SOMETHING HIGHBROW TO THAT AUCTION... AND I DON'T MEAN MUSKETS AND WANTED POSTERS!
I CAN! AND I WILL!
I HOPE!

Originally published in *Kalle Anka & C:o* #37/1997 (Sweden, 1997)

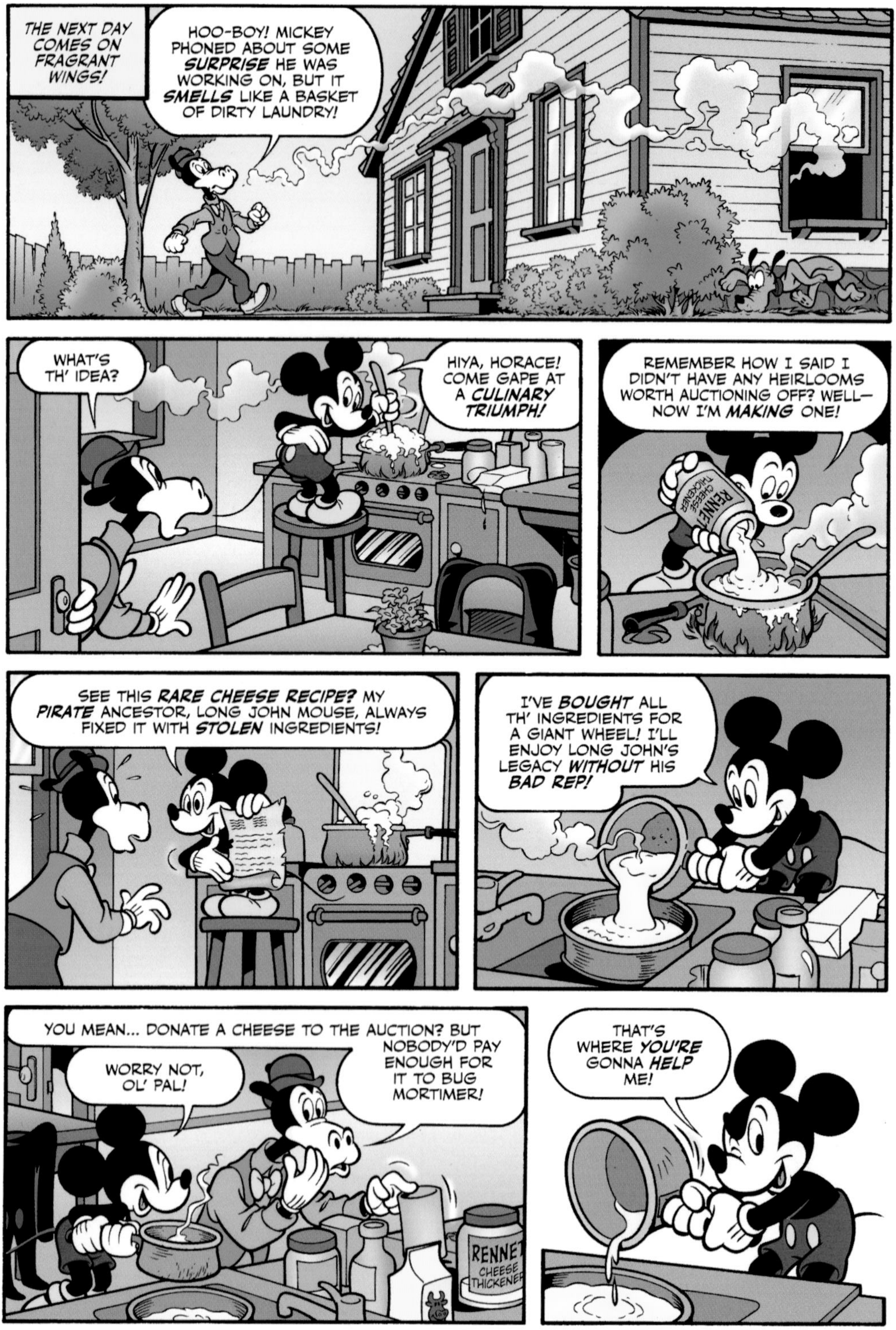

THE NEXT DAY COMES ON FRAGRANT WINGS!
HOO-BOY! MICKEY PHONED ABOUT SOME SURPRISE HE WAS WORKING ON, BUT IT SMELLS LIKE A BASKET OF DIRTY LAUNDRY!
WHAT'S TH' IDEA?
HIYA, HORACE! COME GAPE AT A CULINARY TRIUMPH!
REMEMBER HOW I SAID I DIDN'T HAVE ANY HEIRLOOMS WORTH AUCTIONING OFF? WELL— NOW I'M MAKING ONE!
RENNET CHEESE THICKENER
SEE THIS RARE CHEESE RECIPE? MY PIRATE ANCESTOR, LONG JOHN MOUSE, ALWAYS FIXED IT WITH STOLEN INGREDIENTS!
I'VE BOUGHT ALL TH' INGREDIENTS FOR A GIANT WHEEL! I'LL ENJOY LONG JOHN'S LEGACY WITHOUT HIS BAD REP!
YOU MEAN... DONATE A CHEESE TO THE AUCTION? BUT NOBODY'D PAY ENOUGH FOR IT TO BUG MORTIMER!
WORRY NOT, OL' PAL!
RENNET CHEESE THICKENER
THAT'S WHERE YOU'RE GONNA HELP ME!

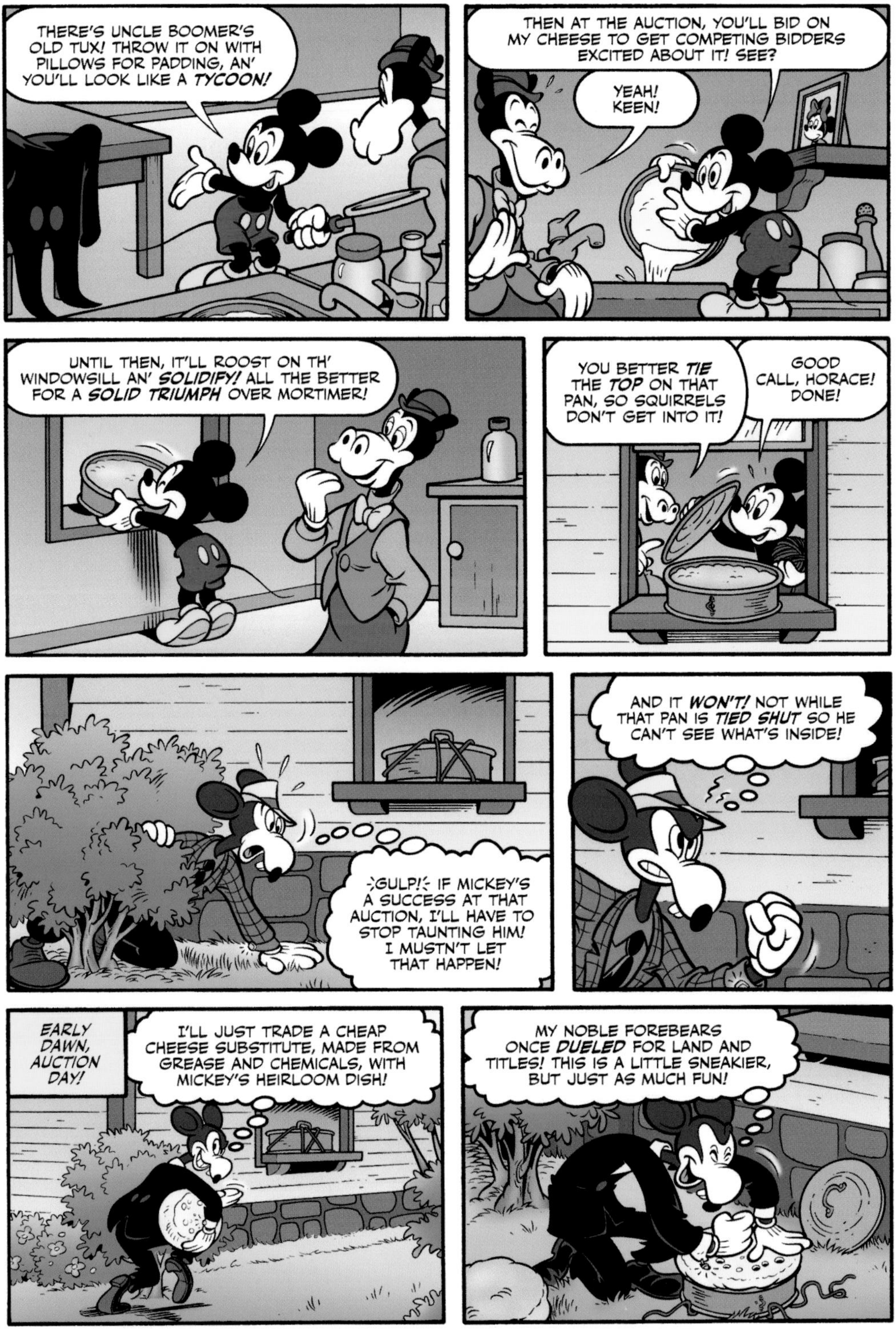
THERE'S UNCLE BOOMER'S OLD TUX! THROW IT ON WITH PILLOWS FOR PADDING, AN' YOU'LL LOOK LIKE A *TYCOON!*
THEN AT THE AUCTION, YOU'LL BID ON MY CHEESE TO GET COMPETING BIDDERS EXCITED ABOUT IT! SEE?
YEAH! KEEN!
UNTIL THEN, IT'LL ROOST ON TH' WINDOWSILL AN' *SOLIDIFY!* ALL THE BETTER FOR A *SOLID TRIUMPH* OVER MORTIMER!
YOU BETTER *TIE* THE *TOP* ON THAT PAN, SO SQUIRRELS DON'T GET INTO IT!
GOOD CALL, HORACE! DONE!
-GULP!- IF MICKEY'S A SUCCESS AT THAT AUCTION, I'LL HAVE TO STOP TAUNTING HIM! I MUSTN'T LET THAT HAPPEN!
AND IT *WON'T!* NOT WHILE THAT PAN IS *TIED SHUT* SO HE CAN'T SEE WHAT'S INSIDE!
EARLY DAWN, AUCTION DAY!
I'LL JUST TRADE A CHEAP CHEESE SUBSTITUTE, MADE FROM GREASE AND CHEMICALS, WITH MICKEY'S HEIRLOOM DISH!
MY NOBLE FOREBEARS ONCE *DUELED* FOR LAND AND TITLES! THIS IS A LITTLE SNEAKIER, BUT JUST AS MUCH FUN!

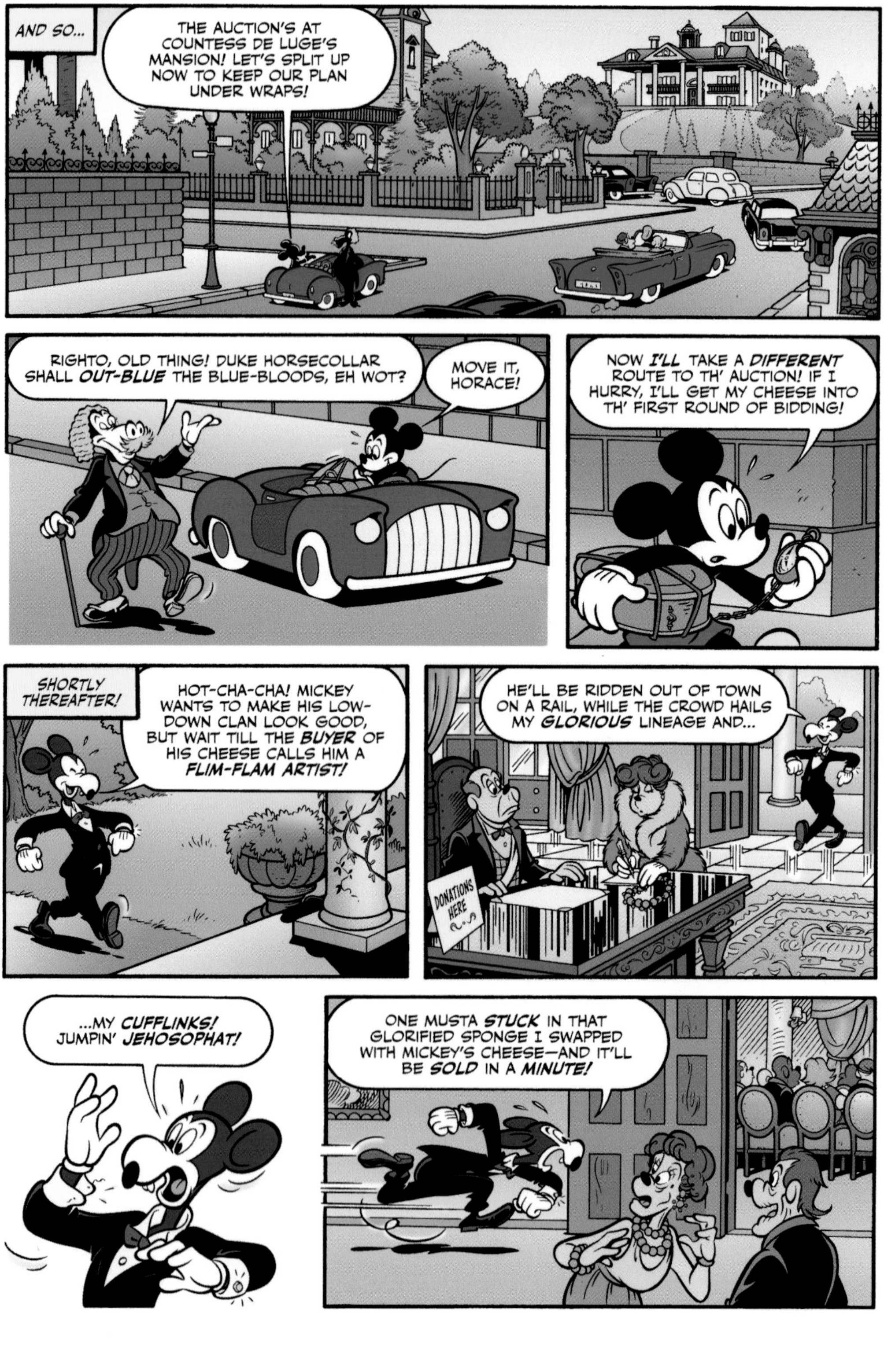
AND SO...
THE AUCTION'S AT COUNTESS DE LUGE'S MANSION! LET'S SPLIT UP NOW TO KEEP OUR PLAN UNDER WRAPS!
RIGHTO, OLD THING! DUKE HORSECOLLAR SHALL OUT-BLUE THE BLUE-BLOODS, EH WOT?
MOVE IT, HORACE!
NOW I'LL TAKE A DIFFERENT ROUTE TO TH' AUCTION! IF I HURRY, I'LL GET MY CHEESE INTO TH' FIRST ROUND OF BIDDING!
SHORTLY THEREAFTER!
HOT-CHA-CHA! MICKEY WANTS TO MAKE HIS LOW-DOWN CLAN LOOK GOOD, BUT WAIT TILL THE BUYER OF HIS CHEESE CALLS HIM A FLIM-FLAM ARTIST!
HE'LL BE RIDDEN OUT OF TOWN ON A RAIL, WHILE THE CROWD HAILS MY GLORIOUS LINEAGE AND...
DONATIONS HERE
...MY CUFFLINKS! JUMPIN' JEHOSOPHAT!
ONE MUSTA STUCK IN THAT GLORIFIED SPONGE I SWAPPED WITH MICKEY'S CHEESE—AND IT'LL BE SOLD IN A MINUTE!

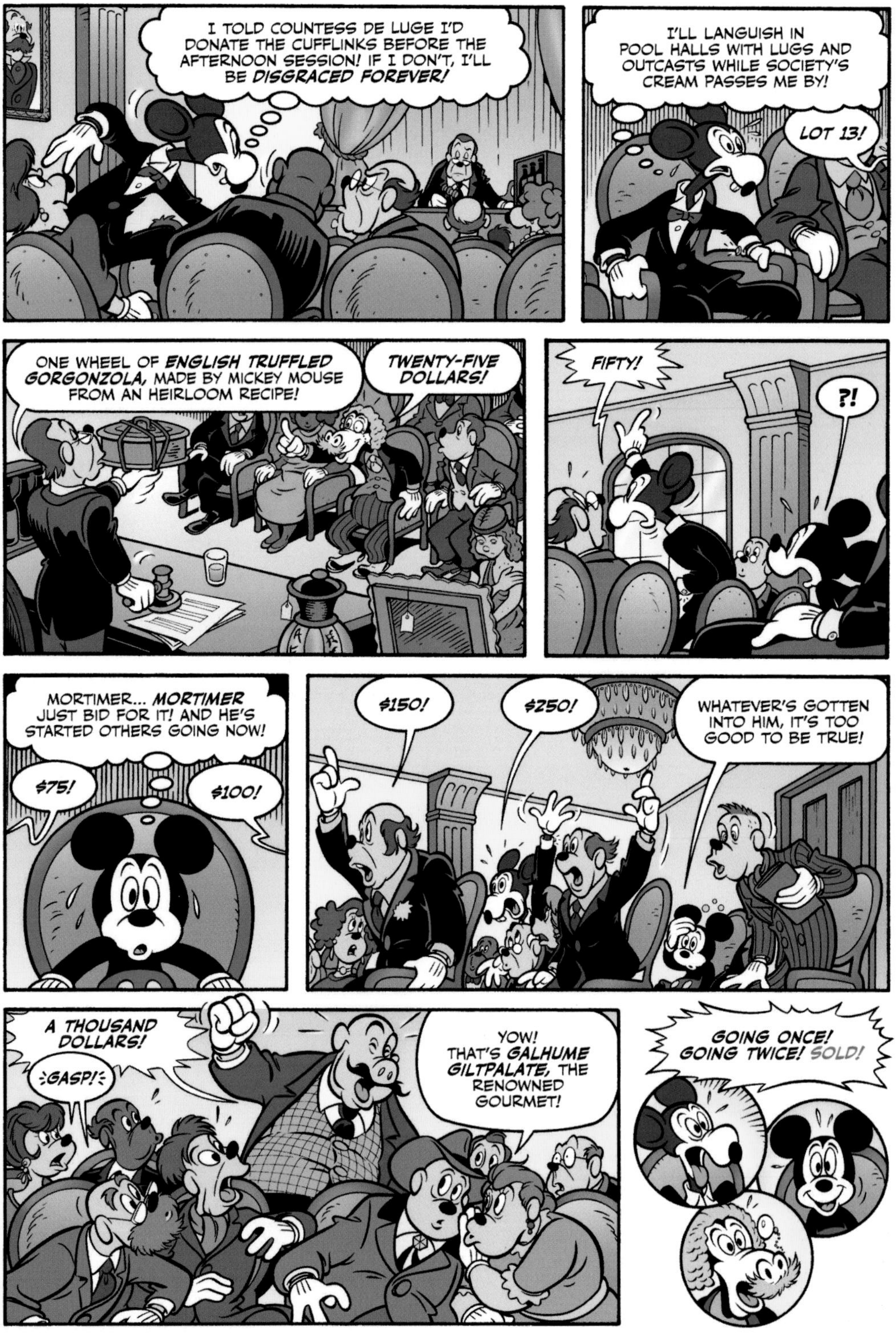
I TOLD COUNTESS DE LUGE I'D DONATE THE CUFFLINKS BEFORE THE AFTERNOON SESSION! IF I DON'T, I'LL BE DISGRACED FOREVER!
I'LL LANGUISH IN POOL HALLS WITH LUGS AND OUTCASTS WHILE SOCIETY'S CREAM PASSES ME BY!
LOT 13!
ONE WHEEL OF ENGLISH TRUFFLED GORGONZOLA, MADE BY MICKEY MOUSE FROM AN HEIRLOOM RECIPE!
TWENTY-FIVE DOLLARS!
FIFTY!
?!
MORTIMER... MORTIMER JUST BID FOR IT! AND HE'S STARTED OTHERS GOING NOW!
$75!
$100!
$150!
$250!
WHATEVER'S GOTTEN INTO HIM, IT'S TOO GOOD TO BE TRUE!
A THOUSAND DOLLARS!
GASP!
YOW! THAT'S GALHUME GILTPALATE, THE RENOWNED GOURMET!
GOING ONCE! GOING TWICE! SOLD!

THAT TAKES TH' CAKE... AN' TH' ICE CREAM, TOO! BY MORTIMER'S DEFINITION, I'M A *HIGHBROW* NOW!

SO HEIRLOOMS MEAN CLASS, EH? THAT MAKES MY *PIRATE* ANCESTOR SOCIETY'S MOST—

ENOUGH, MICKEY! I *GOTTA GET* THAT *CHEESE!*

OH, I GET IT, MORTIMER, OLD TUB! YOU WANT WHATEVER *ANYONE ELSE* WANTS!

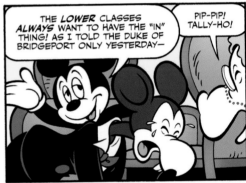

THE *LOWER* CLASSES *ALWAYS* WANT TO HAVE THE "IN" THING! AS I TOLD THE DUKE OF BRIDGEPORT ONLY YESTERDAY—

PIP-PIP! TALLY-HO!

LISTEN, YOU! I DON'T WANT JUST *ANY* CHEESE! I NEED *THAT* ONE! AND AS ITS FORMER OWNER, ONLY *YOU* CAN TALK THAT GUY INTO RETURNING IT!

AFTER WHAT *YOU* SAID ABOUT MY RELATIVES?!

PUH-LEEEZE! I'LL *NEVER* BADMOUTH THEM AGAIN!

FER GOSH SAKES, SIMMER DOWN! I'LL SEE WHAT I CAN DO!

BUT ALAS!

SORRY, MAC! MR. GILTPLATE JUST LEFT FOR THE *EATER'S CIRCLE GOURMETS' CONVENTION*... IN *PICKLEBURG!*

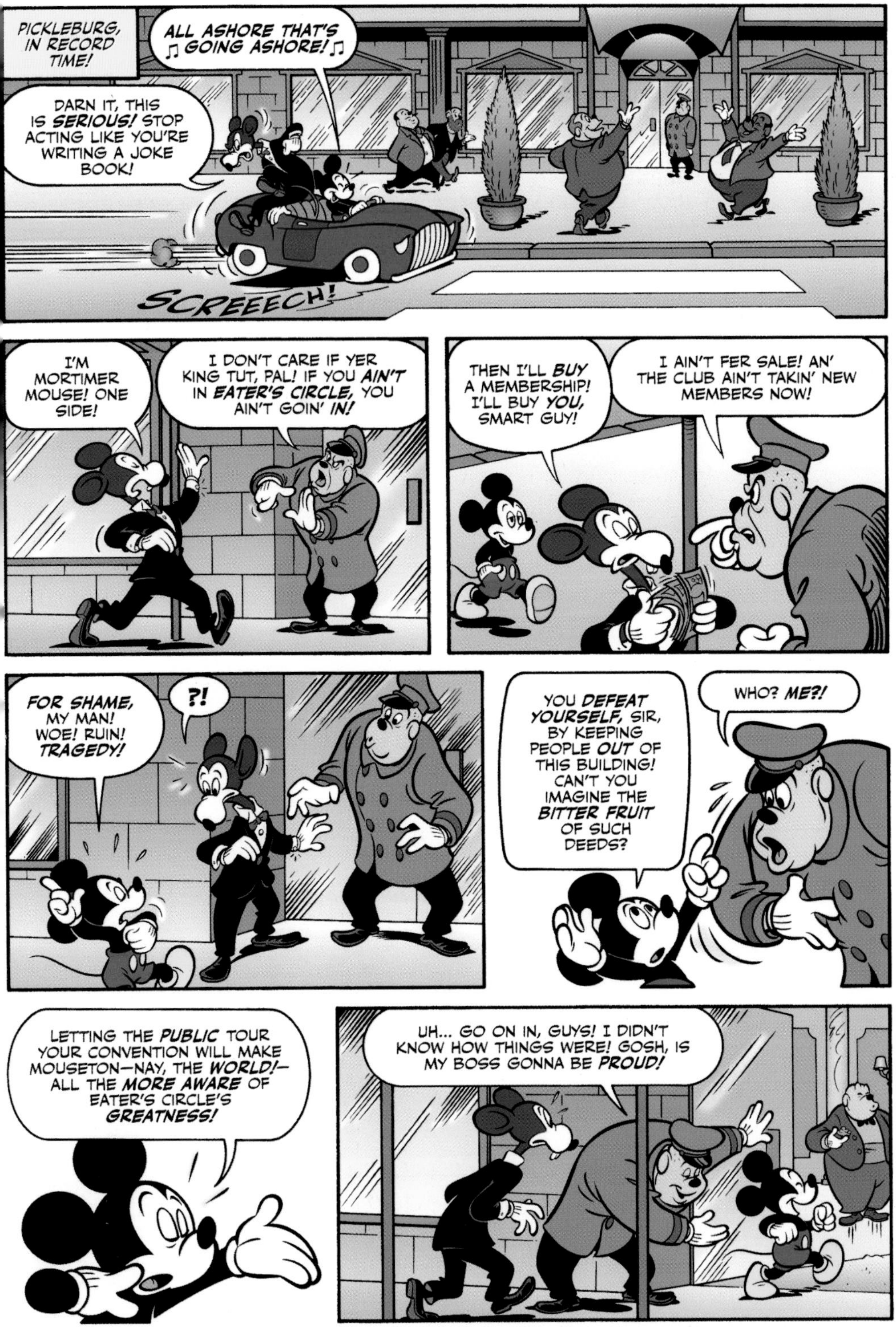
PICKLEBURG, IN RECORD TIME!
ALL ASHORE THAT'S ♫ GOING ASHORE! ♫
DARN IT, THIS IS SERIOUS! STOP ACTING LIKE YOU'RE WRITING A JOKE BOOK!
SCREEECH!
I'M MORTIMER MOUSE! ONE SIDE!
I DON'T CARE IF YER KING TUT, PAL! IF YOU AIN'T IN EATER'S CIRCLE, YOU AIN'T GOIN' IN!
THEN I'LL BUY A MEMBERSHIP! I'LL BUY YOU, SMART GUY!
I AIN'T FER SALE! AN' THE CLUB AIN'T TAKIN' NEW MEMBERS NOW!
FOR SHAME, MY MAN! WOE! RUIN! TRAGEDY!
?!
YOU DEFEAT YOURSELF, SIR, BY KEEPING PEOPLE OUT OF THIS BUILDING! CAN'T YOU IMAGINE THE BITTER FRUIT OF SUCH DEEDS?
WHO? ME?!
LETTING THE PUBLIC TOUR YOUR CONVENTION WILL MAKE MOUSETON—NAY, THE WORLD!—ALL THE MORE AWARE OF EATER'S CIRCLE'S GREATNESS!
UH... GO ON IN, GUYS! I DIDN'T KNOW HOW THINGS WERE! GOSH, IS MY BOSS GONNA BE PROUD!

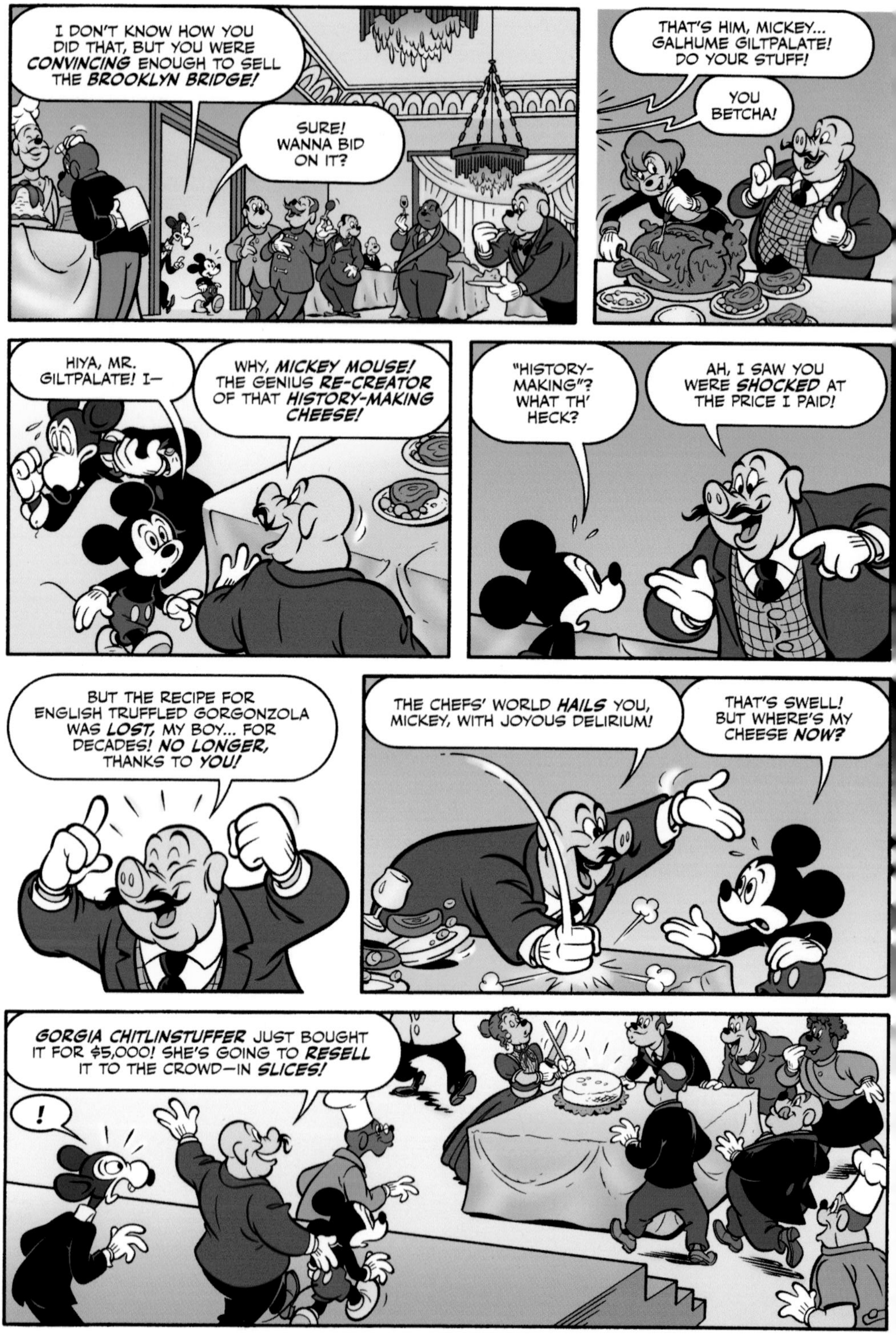
I DON'T KNOW HOW YOU DID THAT, BUT YOU WERE *CONVINCING* ENOUGH TO SELL THE *BROOKLYN BRIDGE!*
SURE! WANNA BID ON IT?
THAT'S HIM, MICKEY... GALHUME GILTPALATE! DO YOUR STUFF!
YOU BETCHA!
HIYA, MR. GILTPALATE! I—
WHY, *MICKEY MOUSE!* THE GENIUS *RE-CREATOR* OF THAT *HISTORY-MAKING CHEESE!*
"HISTORY-MAKING"? WHAT TH' HECK?
AH, I SAW YOU WERE *SHOCKED* AT THE PRICE I PAID!
BUT THE RECIPE FOR ENGLISH TRUFFLED GORGONZOLA WAS *LOST,* MY BOY... FOR DECADES! *NO LONGER,* THANKS TO *YOU!*
THE CHEFS' WORLD *HAILS* YOU, MICKEY, WITH JOYOUS DELIRIUM!
THAT'S SWELL! BUT WHERE'S MY CHEESE *NOW?*
GORGIA CHITLINSTUFFER JUST BOUGHT IT FOR $5,000! SHE'S GOING TO *RESELL* IT TO THE CROWD—IN *SLICES!*
!

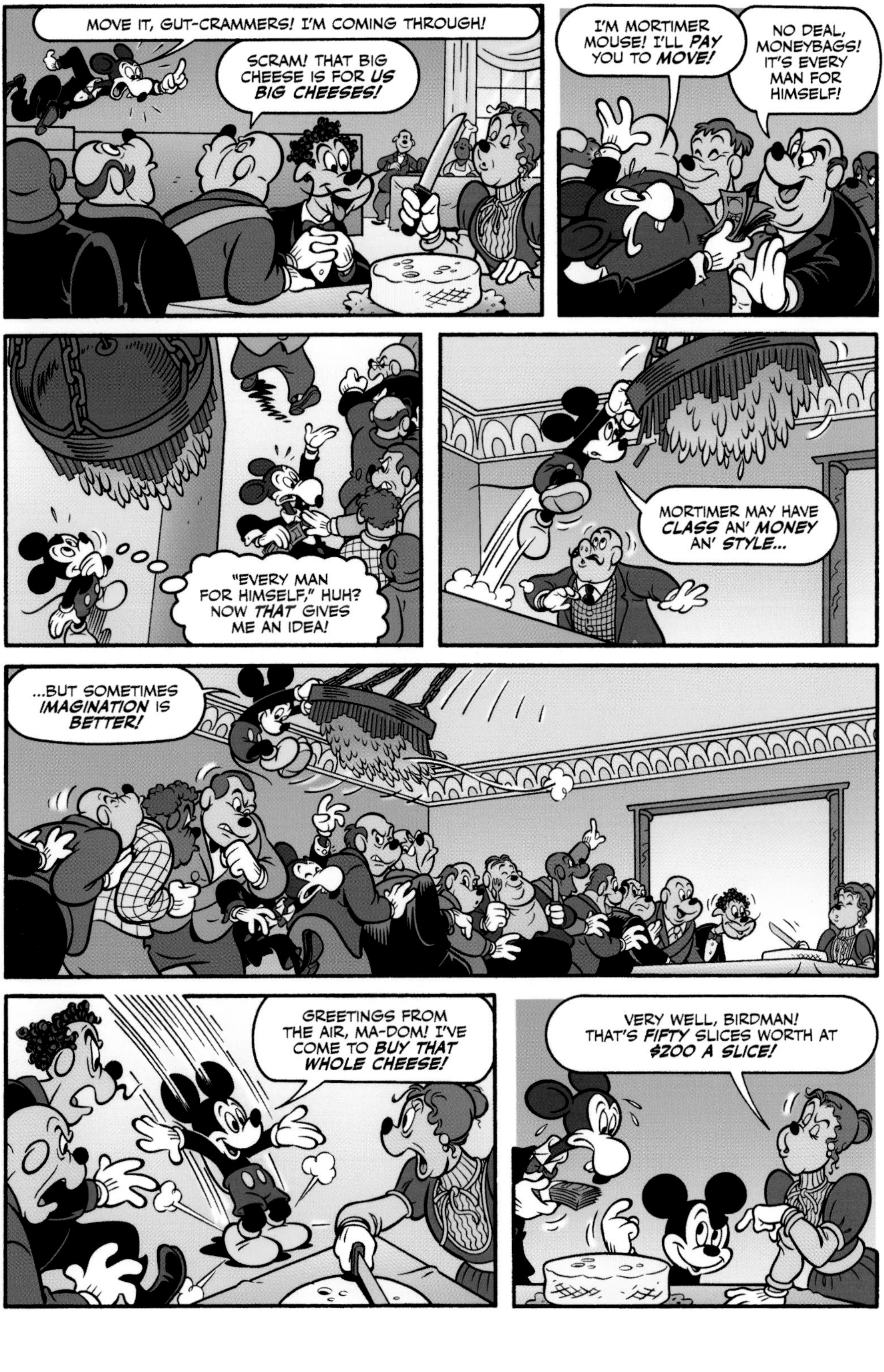
MOVE IT, GUT-CRAMMERS! I'M COMING THROUGH!
SCRAM! THAT BIG CHEESE IS FOR US BIG CHEESES!
I'M MORTIMER MOUSE! I'LL PAY YOU TO MOVE!
NO DEAL, MONEYBAGS! IT'S EVERY MAN FOR HIMSELF!
"EVERY MAN FOR HIMSELF," HUH? NOW THAT GIVES ME AN IDEA!
MORTIMER MAY HAVE CLASS AN' MONEY AN' STYLE...
...BUT SOMETIMES IMAGINATION IS BETTER!
GREETINGS FROM THE AIR, MA-DOM! I'VE COME TO BUY THAT WHOLE CHEESE!
VERY WELL, BIRDMAN! THAT'S FIFTY SLICES WORTH AT $200 A SLICE!

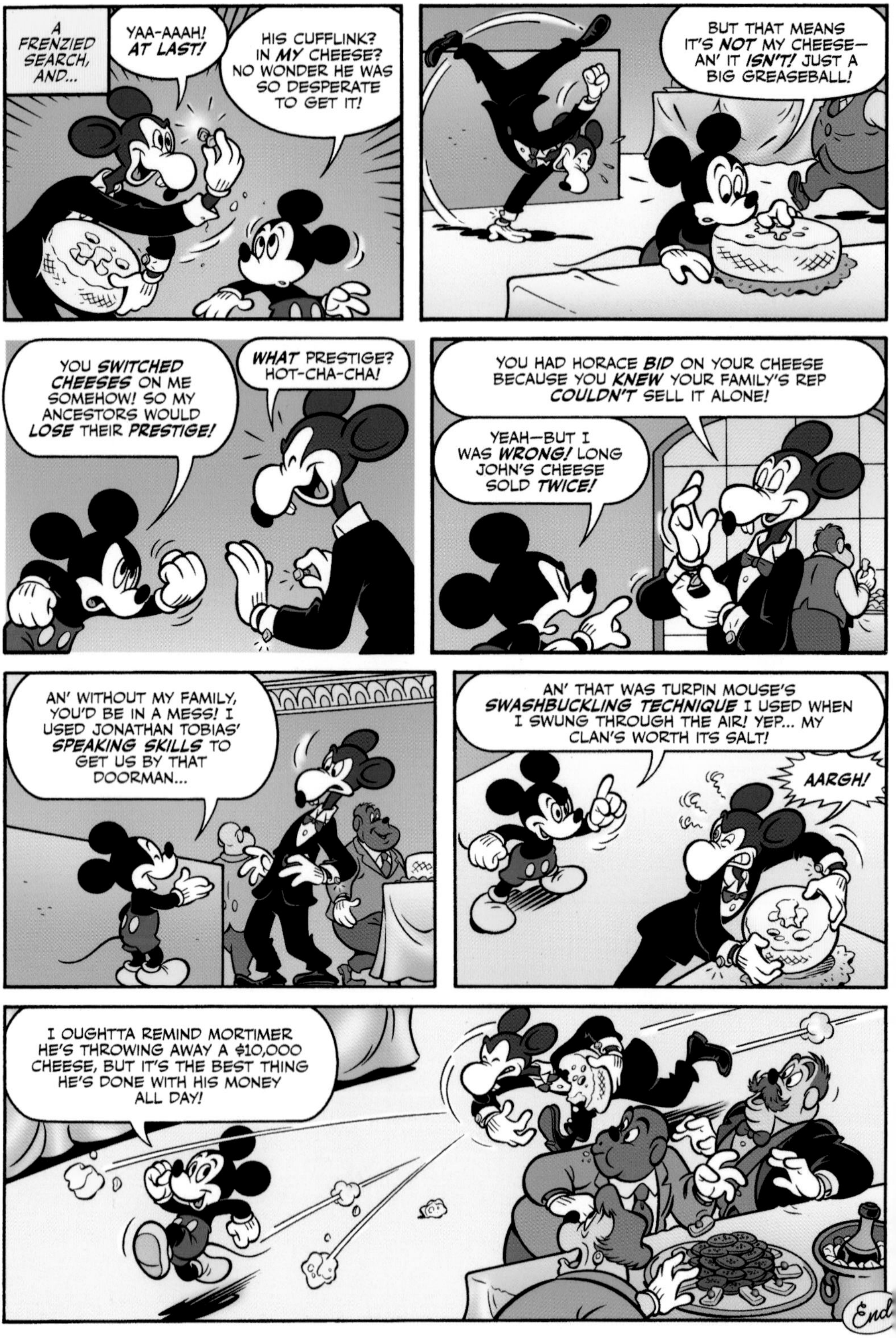
A FRENZIED SEARCH, AND...
YAA-AAAH! AT LAST!
HIS CUFFLINK? IN MY CHEESE? NO WONDER HE WAS SO DESPERATE TO GET IT!
BUT THAT MEANS IT'S NOT MY CHEESE— AN' IT ISN'T! JUST A BIG GREASEBALL!
YOU SWITCHED CHEESES ON ME SOMEHOW! SO MY ANCESTORS WOULD LOSE THEIR PRESTIGE!
WHAT PRESTIGE? HOT-CHA-CHA!
YOU HAD HORACE BID ON YOUR CHEESE BECAUSE YOU KNEW YOUR FAMILY'S REP COULDN'T SELL IT ALONE!
YEAH—BUT I WAS WRONG! LONG JOHN'S CHEESE SOLD TWICE!
AN' WITHOUT MY FAMILY, YOU'D BE IN A MESS! I USED JONATHAN TOBIAS' SPEAKING SKILLS TO GET US BY THAT DOORMAN...
AN' THAT WAS TURPIN MOUSE'S SWASHBUCKLING TECHNIQUE I USED WHEN I SWUNG THROUGH THE AIR! YEP... MY CLAN'S WORTH ITS SALT!
AARGH!
I OUGHTTA REMIND MORTIMER HE'S THROWING AWAY A $10,000 CHEESE, BUT IT'S THE BEST THING HE'S DONE WITH HIS MONEY ALL DAY!
End

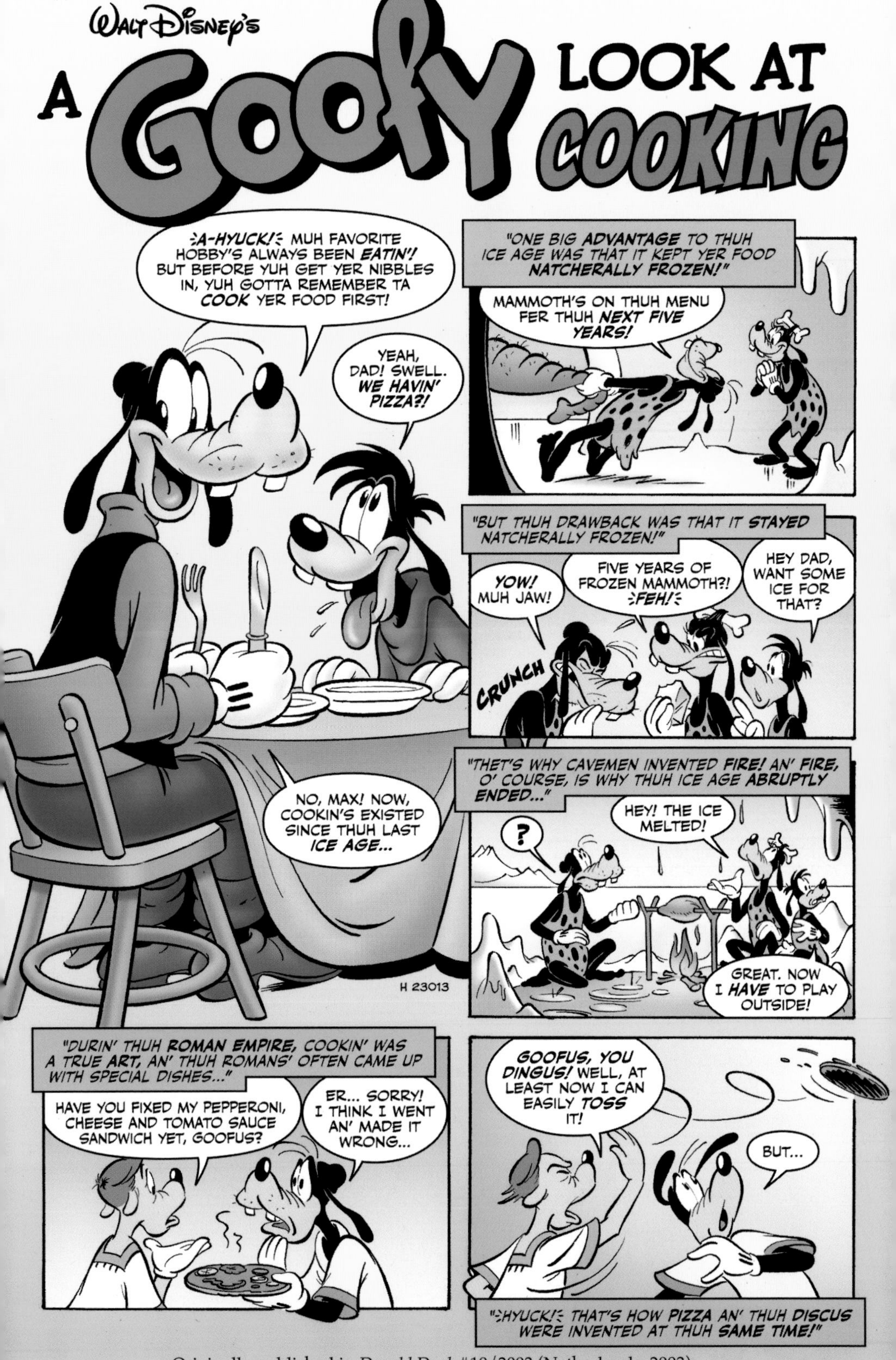
WALT DISNEY'S
A GOOFY LOOK AT COOKING
A-HYUCK! MUH FAVORITE HOBBY'S ALWAYS BEEN EATIN'! BUT BEFORE YUH GET YER NIBBLES IN, YUH GOTTA REMEMBER TA COOK YER FOOD FIRST!
YEAH, DAD! SWELL. WE HAVIN' PIZZA?!
NO, MAX! NOW, COOKIN'S EXISTED SINCE THUH LAST ICE AGE...
H 23013
"ONE BIG ADVANTAGE TO THUH ICE AGE WAS THAT IT KEPT YER FOOD NATCHERALLY FROZEN!"
MAMMOTH'S ON THUH MENU FER THUH NEXT FIVE YEARS!
"BUT THUH DRAWBACK WAS THAT IT STAYED NATCHERALLY FROZEN!"
YOW! MUH JAW!
FIVE YEARS OF FROZEN MAMMOTH?! FEH!
HEY DAD, WANT SOME ICE FOR THAT?
CRUNCH
"THET'S WHY CAVEMEN INVENTED FIRE! AN' FIRE, O' COURSE, IS WHY THUH ICE AGE ABRUPTLY ENDED..."
?
HEY! THE ICE MELTED!
GREAT. NOW I HAVE TO PLAY OUTSIDE!
"DURIN' THUH ROMAN EMPIRE, COOKIN' WAS A TRUE ART, AN' THUH ROMANS' OFTEN CAME UP WITH SPECIAL DISHES..."
HAVE YOU FIXED MY PEPPERONI, CHEESE AND TOMATO SAUCE SANDWICH YET, GOOFUS?
ER... SORRY! I THINK I WENT AN' MADE IT WRONG...
GOOFUS, YOU DINGUS! WELL, AT LEAST NOW I CAN EASILY TOSS IT!
BUT...
"HYUCK! THAT'S HOW PIZZA AN' THUH DISCUS WERE INVENTED AT THUH SAME TIME!"

Originally published in *Donald Duck* #10/2003 (Netherlands, 2003)

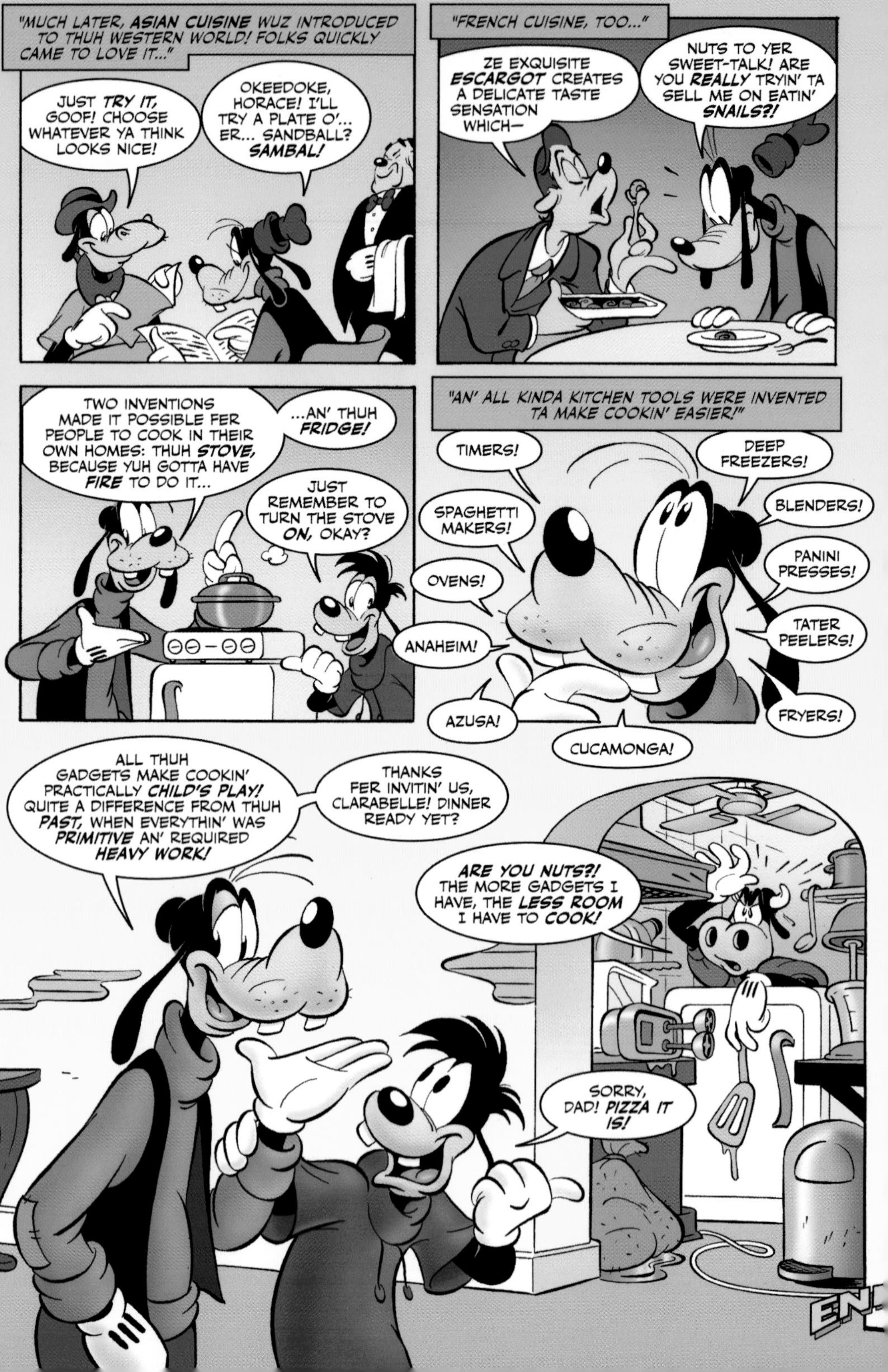
"MUCH LATER, ASIAN CUISINE WUZ INTRODUCED TO THUH WESTERN WORLD! FOLKS QUICKLY CAME TO LOVE IT..."
JUST TRY IT, GOOF! CHOOSE WHATEVER YA THINK LOOKS NICE!
OKEEDOKE, HORACE! I'LL TRY A PLATE O'... ER... SANDBALL? SAMBAL!
"FRENCH CUISINE, TOO..."
ZE EXQUISITE ESCARGOT CREATES A DELICATE TASTE SENSATION WHICH—
NUTS TO YER SWEET-TALK! ARE YOU REALLY TRYIN' TA SELL ME ON EATIN' SNAILS?!
TWO INVENTIONS MADE IT POSSIBLE FER PEOPLE TO COOK IN THEIR OWN HOMES: THUH STOVE, BECAUSE YUH GOTTA HAVE FIRE TO DO IT...
...AN' THUH FRIDGE!
JUST REMEMBER TO TURN THE STOVE ON, OKAY?
"AN' ALL KINDA KITCHEN TOOLS WERE INVENTED TA MAKE COOKIN' EASIER!"
TIMERS!
DEEP FREEZERS!
SPAGHETTI MAKERS!
BLENDERS!
PANINI PRESSES!
OVENS!
TATER PEELERS!
ANAHEIM!
FRYERS!
AZUSA!
CUCAMONGA!
ALL THUH GADGETS MAKE COOKIN' PRACTICALLY CHILD'S PLAY! QUITE A DIFFERENCE FROM THUH PAST, WHEN EVERYTHIN' WAS PRIMITIVE AN' REQUIRED HEAVY WORK!
THANKS FER INVITIN' US, CLARABELLE! DINNER READY YET?
ARE YOU NUTS?! THE MORE GADGETS I HAVE, THE LESS ROOM I HAVE TO COOK!
SORRY, DAD! PIZZA IT IS!

Walt Disney's

Mickey Mouse in The Mouse Collector

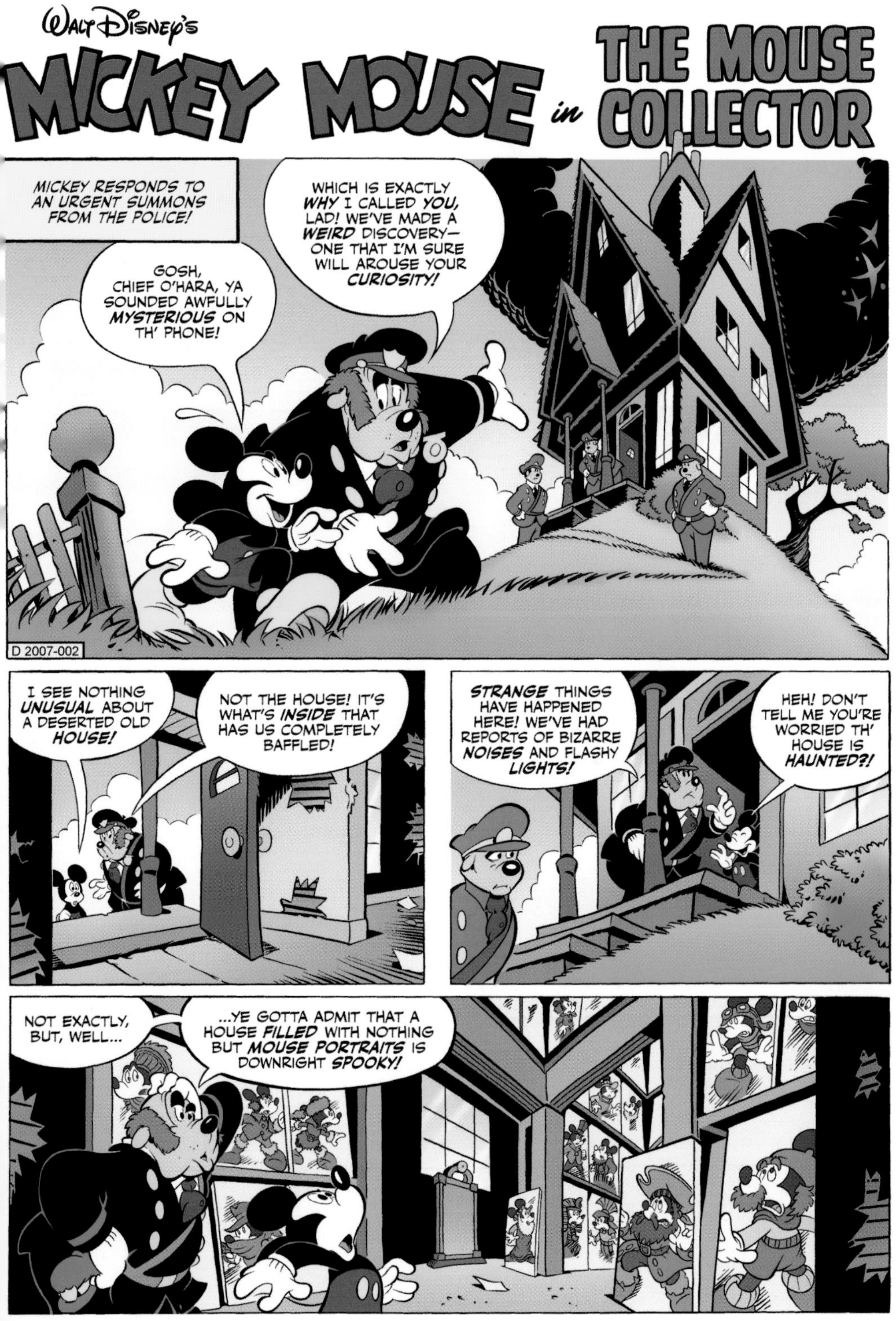

MICKEY RESPONDS TO AN URGENT SUMMONS FROM THE POLICE!
GOSH, CHIEF O'HARA, YA SOUNDED AWFULLY MYSTERIOUS ON TH' PHONE!
WHICH IS EXACTLY WHY I CALLED YOU, LAD! WE'VE MADE A WEIRD DISCOVERY— ONE THAT I'M SURE WILL AROUSE YOUR CURIOSITY!
D 2007-002
I SEE NOTHING UNUSUAL ABOUT A DESERTED OLD HOUSE!
NOT THE HOUSE! IT'S WHAT'S INSIDE THAT HAS US COMPLETELY BAFFLED!
STRANGE THINGS HAVE HAPPENED HERE! WE'VE HAD REPORTS OF BIZARRE NOISES AND FLASHY LIGHTS!
HEH! DON'T TELL ME YOU'RE WORRIED TH' HOUSE IS HAUNTED?!
NOT EXACTLY, BUT, WELL...
...YE GOTTA ADMIT THAT A HOUSE FILLED WITH NOTHING BUT MOUSE PORTRAITS IS DOWNRIGHT SPOOKY!

Originally published in *Le Journal de Mickey* #2998 (France, 2009)

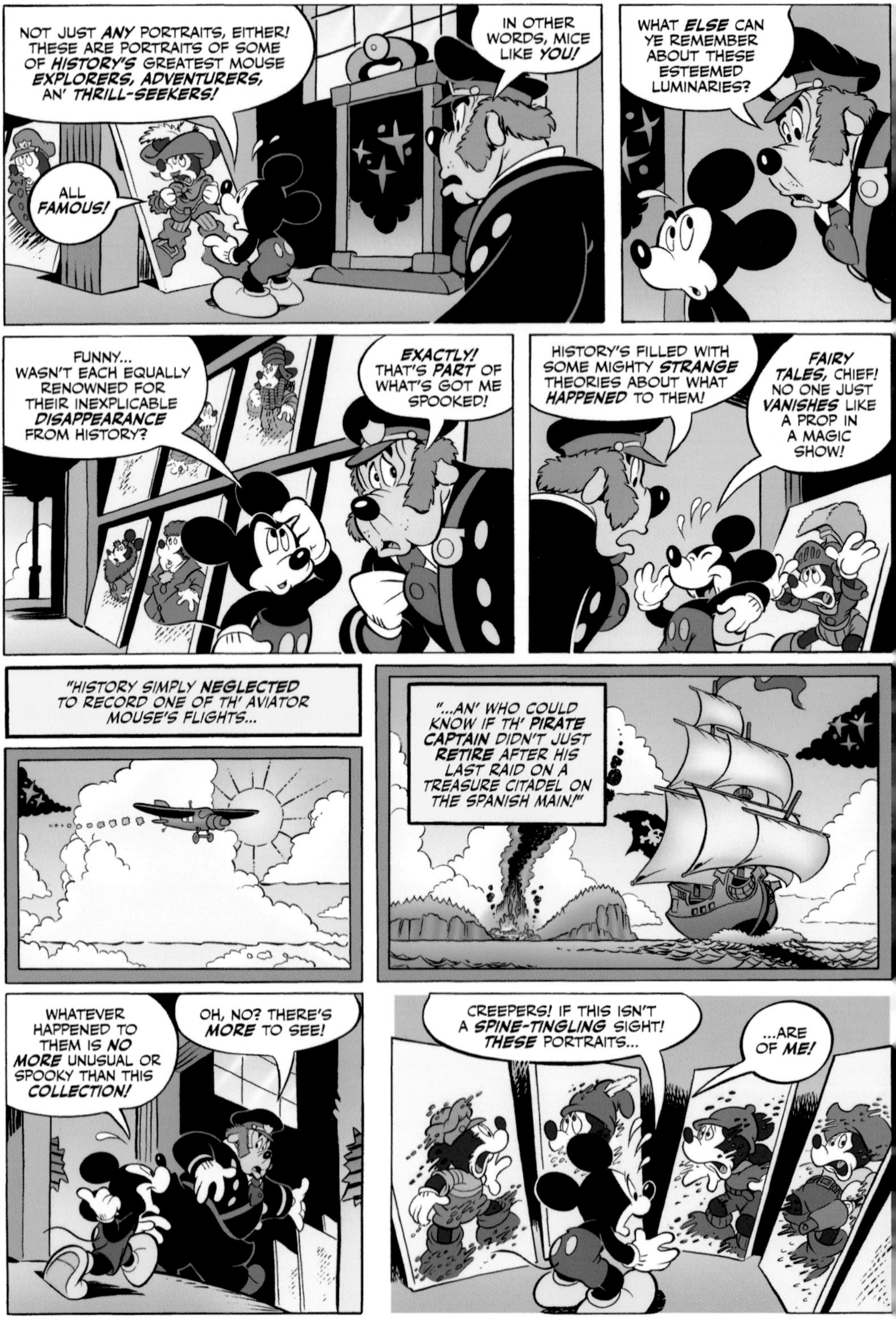
NOT JUST ANY PORTRAITS, EITHER! THESE ARE PORTRAITS OF SOME OF HISTORY'S GREATEST MOUSE EXPLORERS, ADVENTURERS, AN' THRILL-SEEKERS!
ALL FAMOUS!
IN OTHER WORDS, MICE LIKE YOU!
WHAT ELSE CAN YE REMEMBER ABOUT THESE ESTEEMED LUMINARIES?
FUNNY... WASN'T EACH EQUALLY RENOWNED FOR THEIR INEXPLICABLE DISAPPEARANCE FROM HISTORY?
EXACTLY! THAT'S PART OF WHAT'S GOT ME SPOOKED!
HISTORY'S FILLED WITH SOME MIGHTY STRANGE THEORIES ABOUT WHAT HAPPENED TO THEM!
FAIRY TALES, CHIEF! NO ONE JUST VANISHES LIKE A PROP IN A MAGIC SHOW!
"HISTORY SIMPLY NEGLECTED TO RECORD ONE OF TH' AVIATOR MOUSE'S FLIGHTS...
"...AN' WHO COULD KNOW IF TH' PIRATE CAPTAIN DIDN'T JUST RETIRE AFTER HIS LAST RAID ON A TREASURE CITADEL ON THE SPANISH MAIN!"
WHATEVER HAPPENED TO THEM IS NO MORE UNUSUAL OR SPOOKY THAN THIS COLLECTION!
OH, NO? THERE'S MORE TO SEE!
CREEPERS! IF THIS ISN'T A SPINE-TINGLING SIGHT! THESE PORTRAITS...
...ARE OF ME!

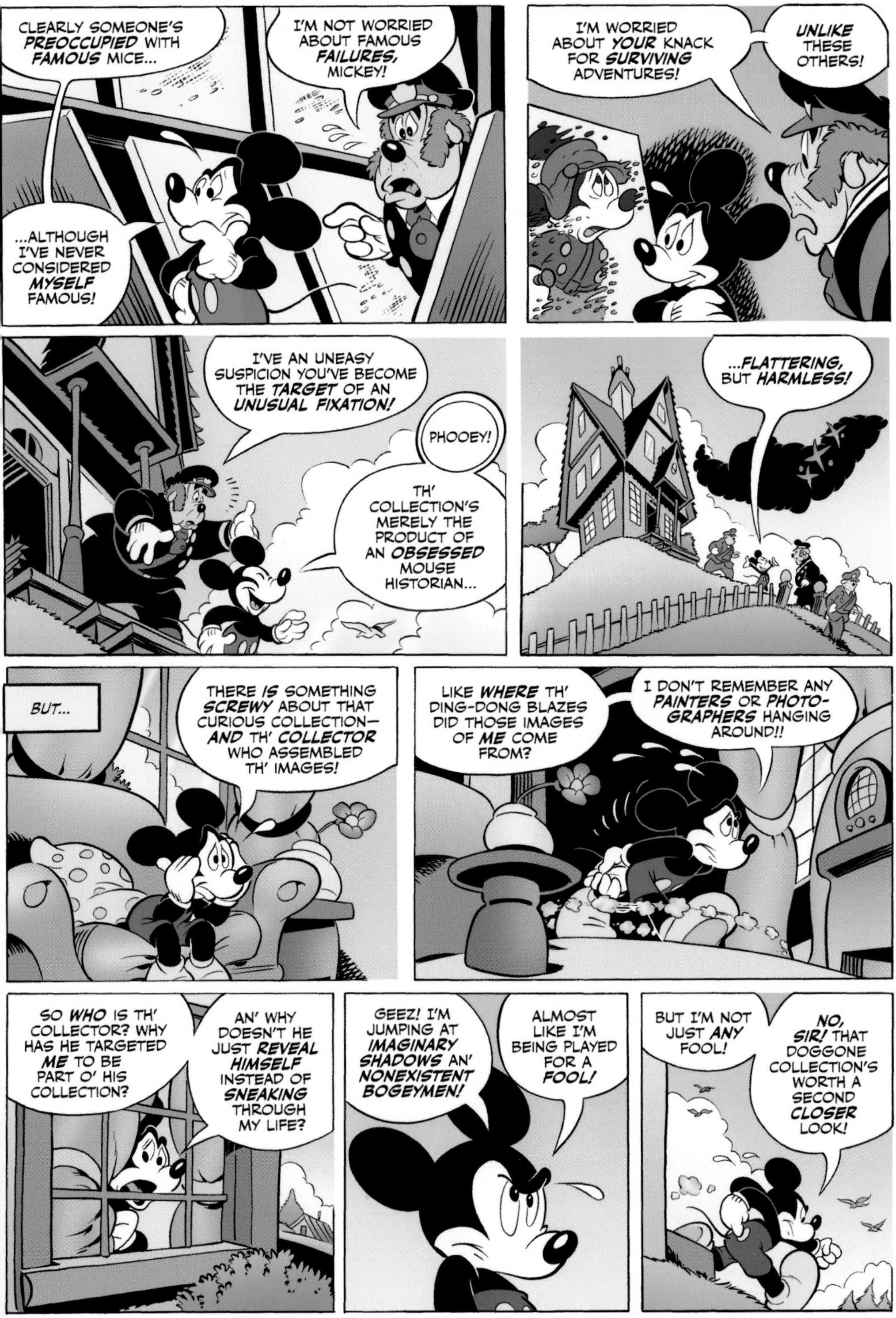
CLEARLY SOMEONE'S PREOCCUPIED WITH FAMOUS MICE...
...ALTHOUGH I'VE NEVER CONSIDERED MYSELF FAMOUS!
I'M NOT WORRIED ABOUT FAMOUS FAILURES, MICKEY!
I'M WORRIED ABOUT YOUR KNACK FOR SURVIVING ADVENTURES!
UNLIKE THESE OTHERS!
I'VE AN UNEASY SUSPICION YOU'VE BECOME THE TARGET OF AN UNUSUAL FIXATION!
PHOOEY!
TH' COLLECTION'S MERELY THE PRODUCT OF AN OBSESSED MOUSE HISTORIAN...
...FLATTERING, BUT HARMLESS!
BUT...
THERE IS SOMETHING SCREWY ABOUT THAT CURIOUS COLLECTION— AND TH' COLLECTOR WHO ASSEMBLED TH' IMAGES!
LIKE WHERE TH' DING-DONG BLAZES DID THOSE IMAGES OF ME COME FROM?
I DON'T REMEMBER ANY PAINTERS OR PHOTOGRAPHERS HANGING AROUND!!
SO WHO IS TH' COLLECTOR? WHY HAS HE TARGETED ME TO BE PART O' HIS COLLECTION?
AN' WHY DOESN'T HE JUST REVEAL HIMSELF INSTEAD OF SNEAKING THROUGH MY LIFE?
GEEZ! I'M JUMPING AT IMAGINARY SHADOWS AN' NONEXISTENT BOGEYMEN!
ALMOST LIKE I'M BEING PLAYED FOR A FOOL!
BUT I'M NOT JUST ANY FOOL!
NO, SIR! THAT DOGGONE COLLECTION'S WORTH A SECOND CLOSER LOOK!

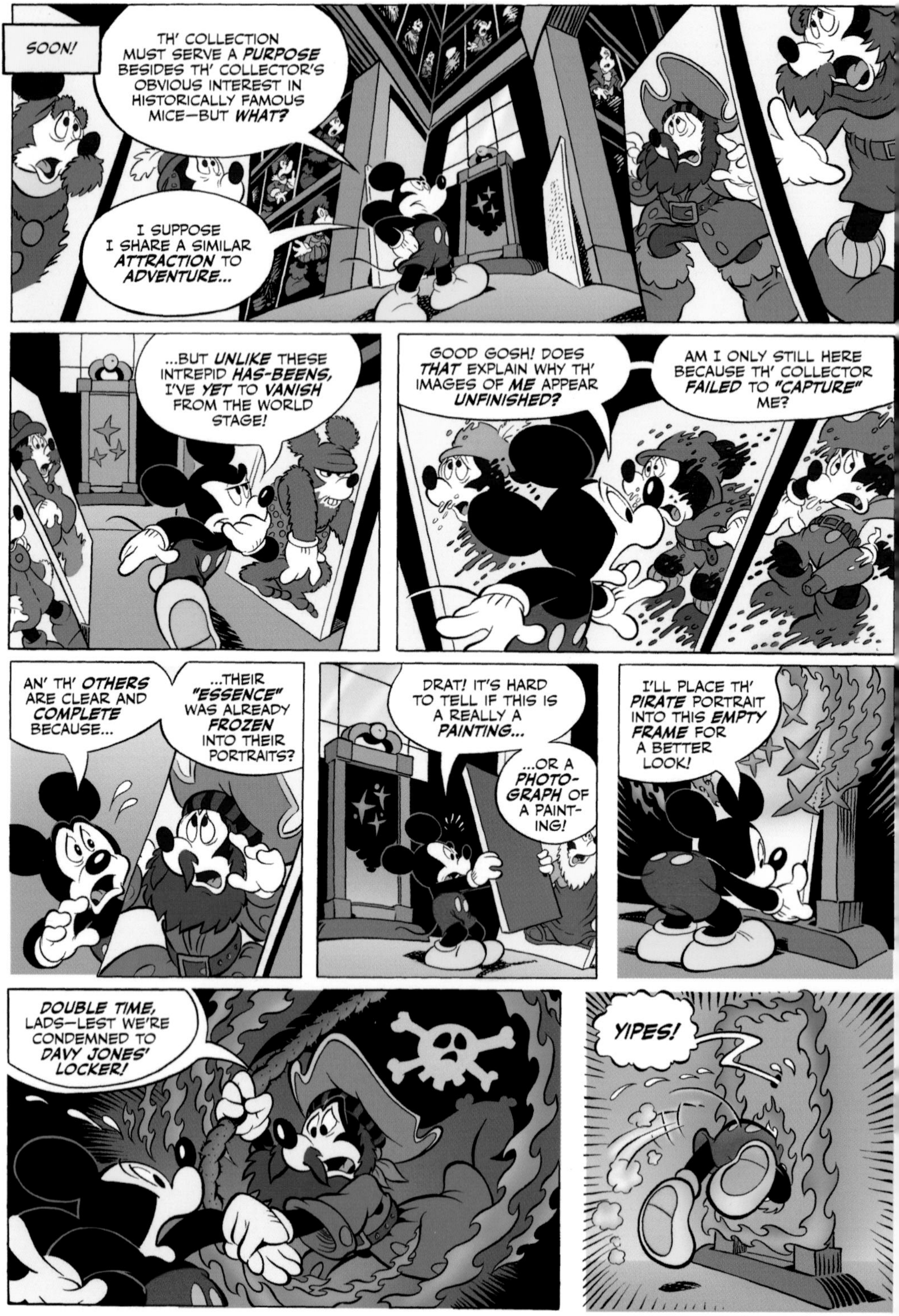
SOON!
TH' COLLECTION MUST SERVE A PURPOSE BESIDES TH' COLLECTOR'S OBVIOUS INTEREST IN HISTORICALLY FAMOUS MICE—BUT WHAT?
I SUPPOSE I SHARE A SIMILAR ATTRACTION TO ADVENTURE...
...BUT UNLIKE THESE INTREPID HAS-BEENS, I'VE YET TO VANISH FROM THE WORLD STAGE!
GOOD GOSH! DOES THAT EXPLAIN WHY TH' IMAGES OF ME APPEAR UNFINISHED?
AM I ONLY STILL HERE BECAUSE TH' COLLECTOR FAILED TO "CAPTURE" ME?
AN' TH' OTHERS ARE CLEAR AND COMPLETE BECAUSE...
...THEIR "ESSENCE" WAS ALREADY FROZEN INTO THEIR PORTRAITS?
DRAT! IT'S HARD TO TELL IF THIS IS A REALLY A PAINTING...
...OR A PHOTO-GRAPH OF A PAINT-ING!
I'LL PLACE TH' PIRATE PORTRAIT INTO THIS EMPTY FRAME FOR A BETTER LOOK!
DOUBLE TIME, LADS—LEST WE'RE CONDEMNED TO DAVY JONES' LOCKER!
YIPES!

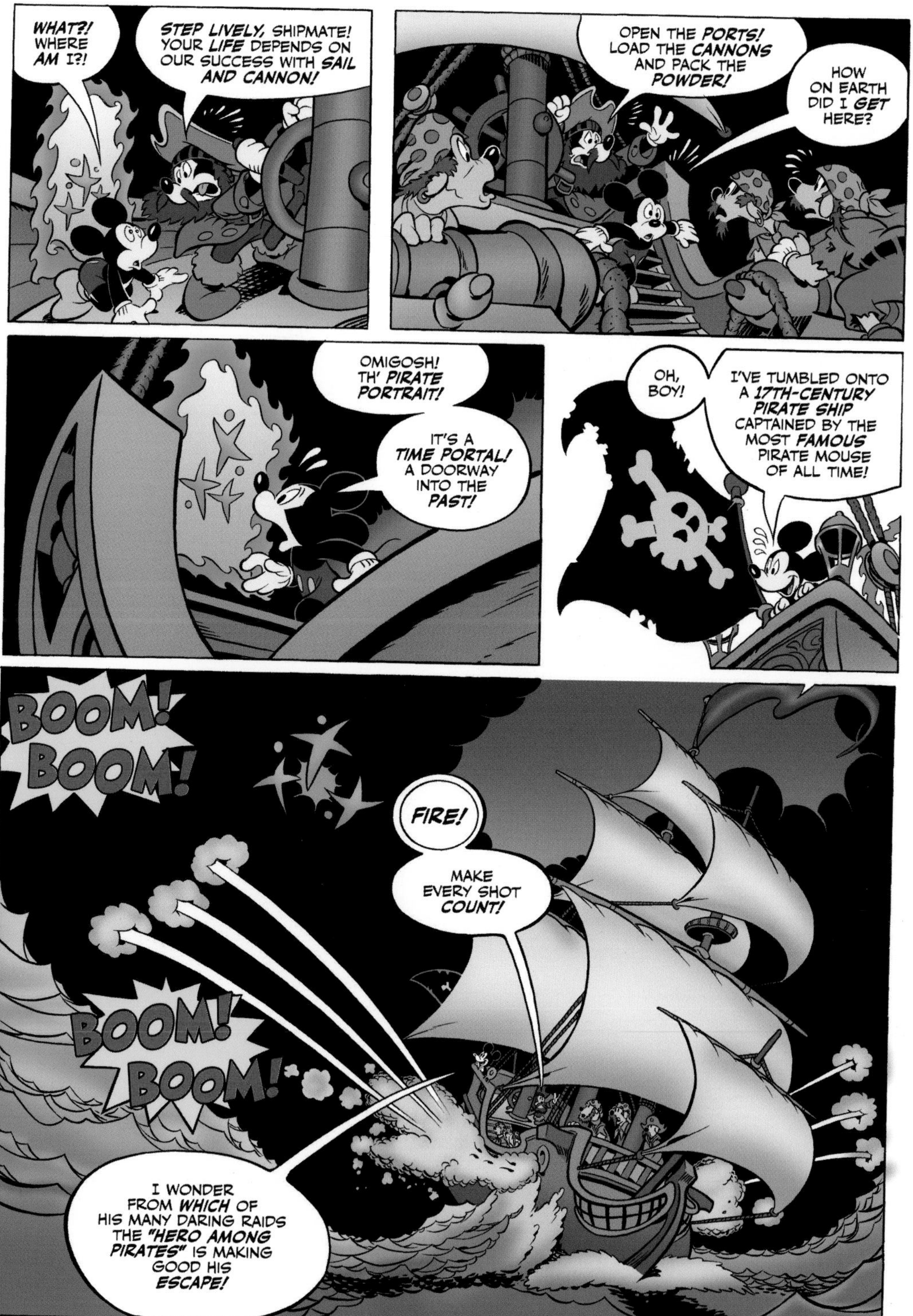
WHAT?! WHERE AM I?!
STEP LIVELY, SHIPMATE! YOUR LIFE DEPENDS ON OUR SUCCESS WITH SAIL AND CANNON!
OPEN THE PORTS! LOAD THE CANNONS AND PACK THE POWDER!
HOW ON EARTH DID I GET HERE?
OMIGOSH! TH' PIRATE PORTRAIT!
IT'S A TIME PORTAL! A DOORWAY INTO THE PAST!
OH, BOY!
I'VE TUMBLED ONTO A 17TH-CENTURY PIRATE SHIP CAPTAINED BY THE MOST FAMOUS PIRATE MOUSE OF ALL TIME!
BOOM! BOOM!
FIRE!
MAKE EVERY SHOT COUNT!
BOOM! BOOM!
I WONDER FROM WHICH OF HIS MANY DARING RAIDS THE "HERO AMONG PIRATES" IS MAKING GOOD HIS ESCAPE!

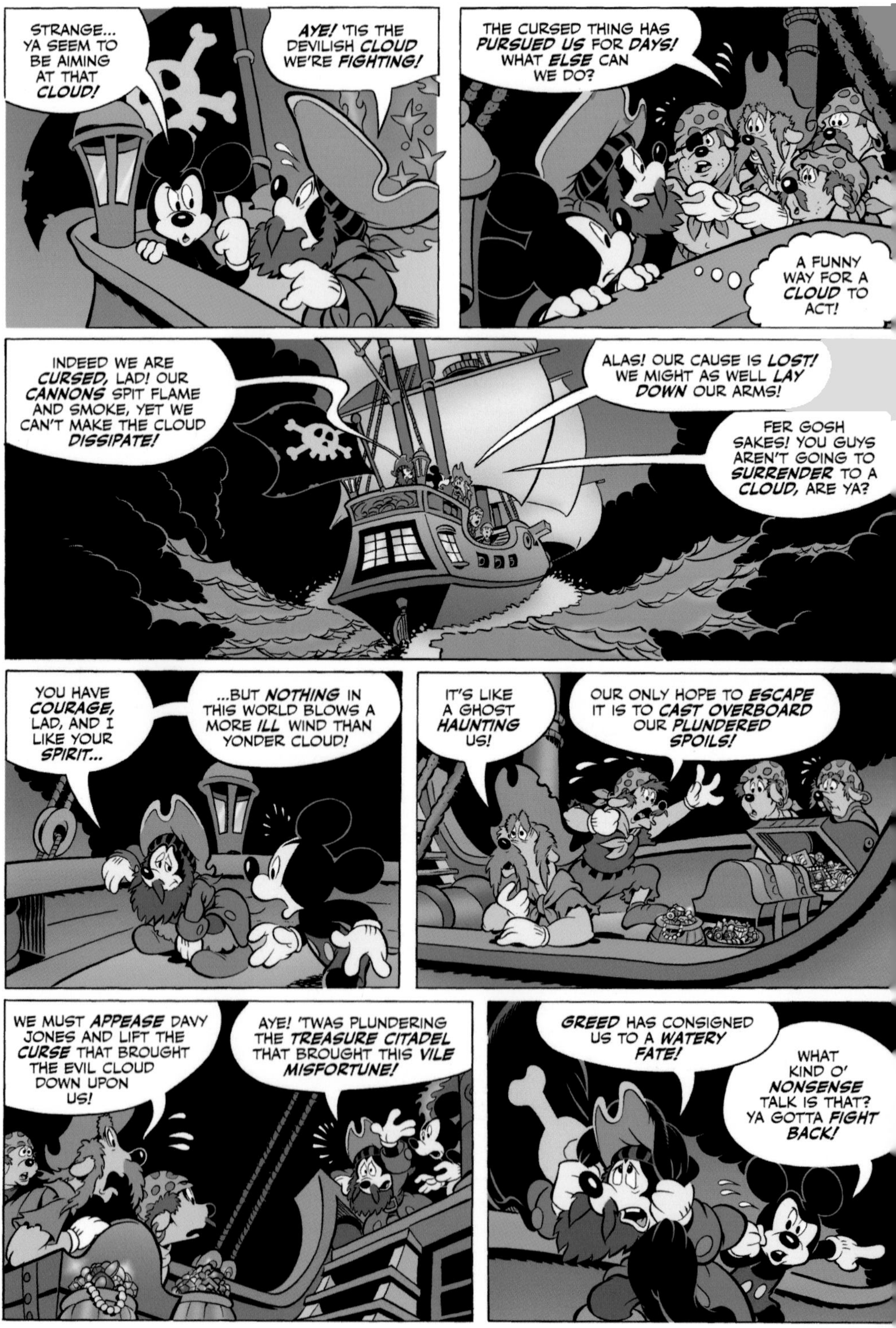
STRANGE... YA SEEM TO BE AIMING AT THAT CLOUD!
AYE! 'TIS THE DEVILISH CLOUD WE'RE FIGHTING!
THE CURSED THING HAS PURSUED US FOR DAYS! WHAT ELSE CAN WE DO?
A FUNNY WAY FOR A CLOUD TO ACT!
INDEED WE ARE CURSED, LAD! OUR CANNONS SPIT FLAME AND SMOKE, YET WE CAN'T MAKE THE CLOUD DISSIPATE!
ALAS! OUR CAUSE IS LOST! WE MIGHT AS WELL LAY DOWN OUR ARMS!
FER GOSH SAKES! YOU GUYS AREN'T GOING TO SURRENDER TO A CLOUD, ARE YA?
YOU HAVE COURAGE, LAD, AND I LIKE YOUR SPIRIT...
...BUT NOTHING IN THIS WORLD BLOWS A MORE ILL WIND THAN YONDER CLOUD!
IT'S LIKE A GHOST HAUNTING US!
OUR ONLY HOPE TO ESCAPE IT IS TO CAST OVERBOARD OUR PLUNDERED SPOILS!
WE MUST APPEASE DAVY JONES AND LIFT THE CURSE THAT BROUGHT THE EVIL CLOUD DOWN UPON US!
AYE! 'TWAS PLUNDERING THE TREASURE CITADEL THAT BROUGHT THIS VILE MISFORTUNE!
GREED HAS CONSIGNED US TO A WATERY FATE!
WHAT KIND O' NONSENSE TALK IS THAT? YA GOTTA FIGHT BACK!

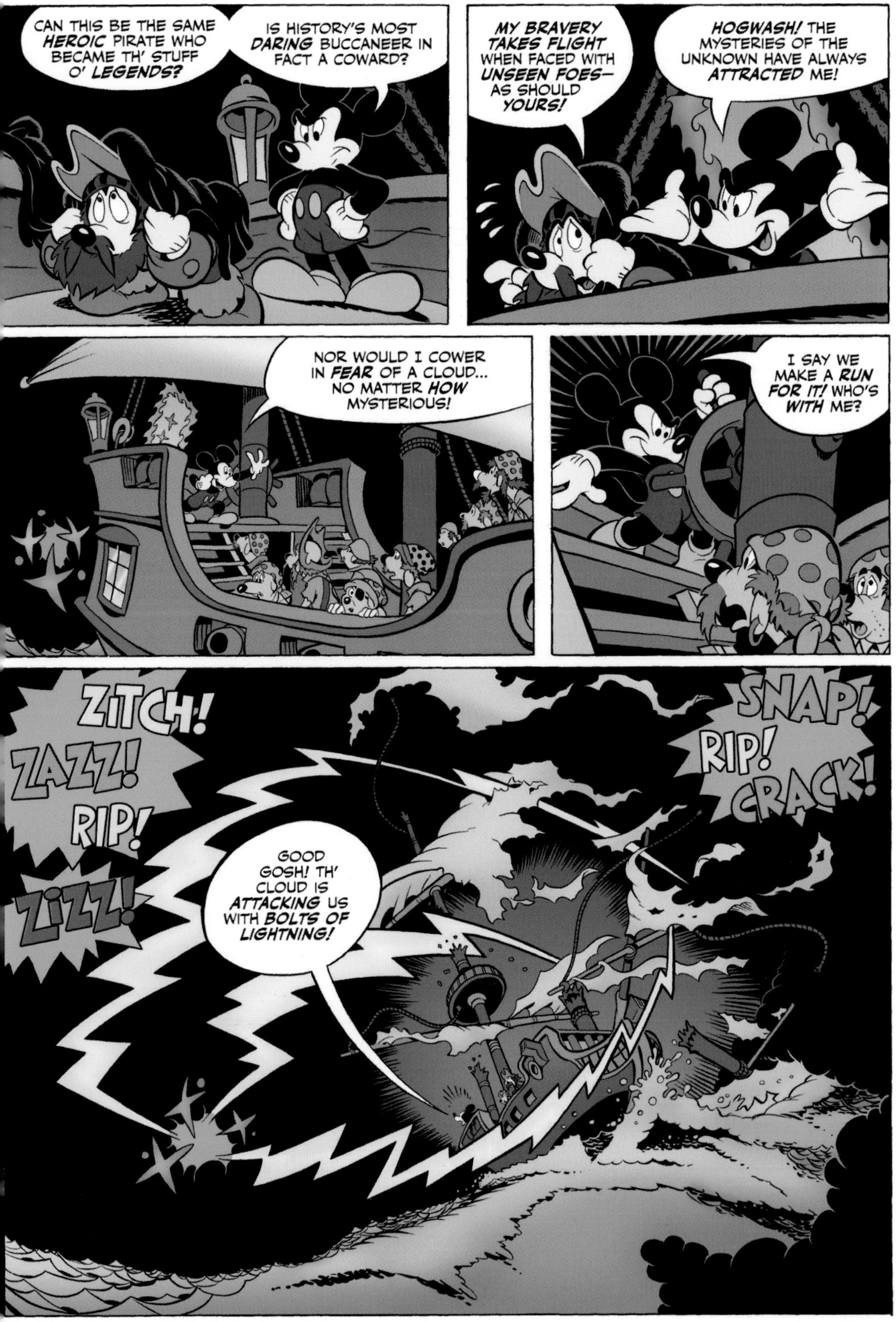

CAN THIS BE THE SAME HEROIC PIRATE WHO BECAME TH' STUFF O' LEGENDS?
IS HISTORY'S MOST DARING BUCCANEER IN FACT A COWARD?
MY BRAVERY TAKES FLIGHT WHEN FACED WITH UNSEEN FOES— AS SHOULD YOURS!
HOGWASH! THE MYSTERIES OF THE UNKNOWN HAVE ALWAYS ATTRACTED ME!
NOR WOULD I COWER IN FEAR OF A CLOUD... NO MATTER HOW MYSTERIOUS!
I SAY WE MAKE A RUN FOR IT! WHO'S WITH ME?
ZITCH!
ZAZZ!
RIP!
ZIZZ!
SNAP!
RIP!
CRACK!
GOOD GOSH! TH' CLOUD IS ATTACKING US WITH BOLTS OF LIGHTNING!

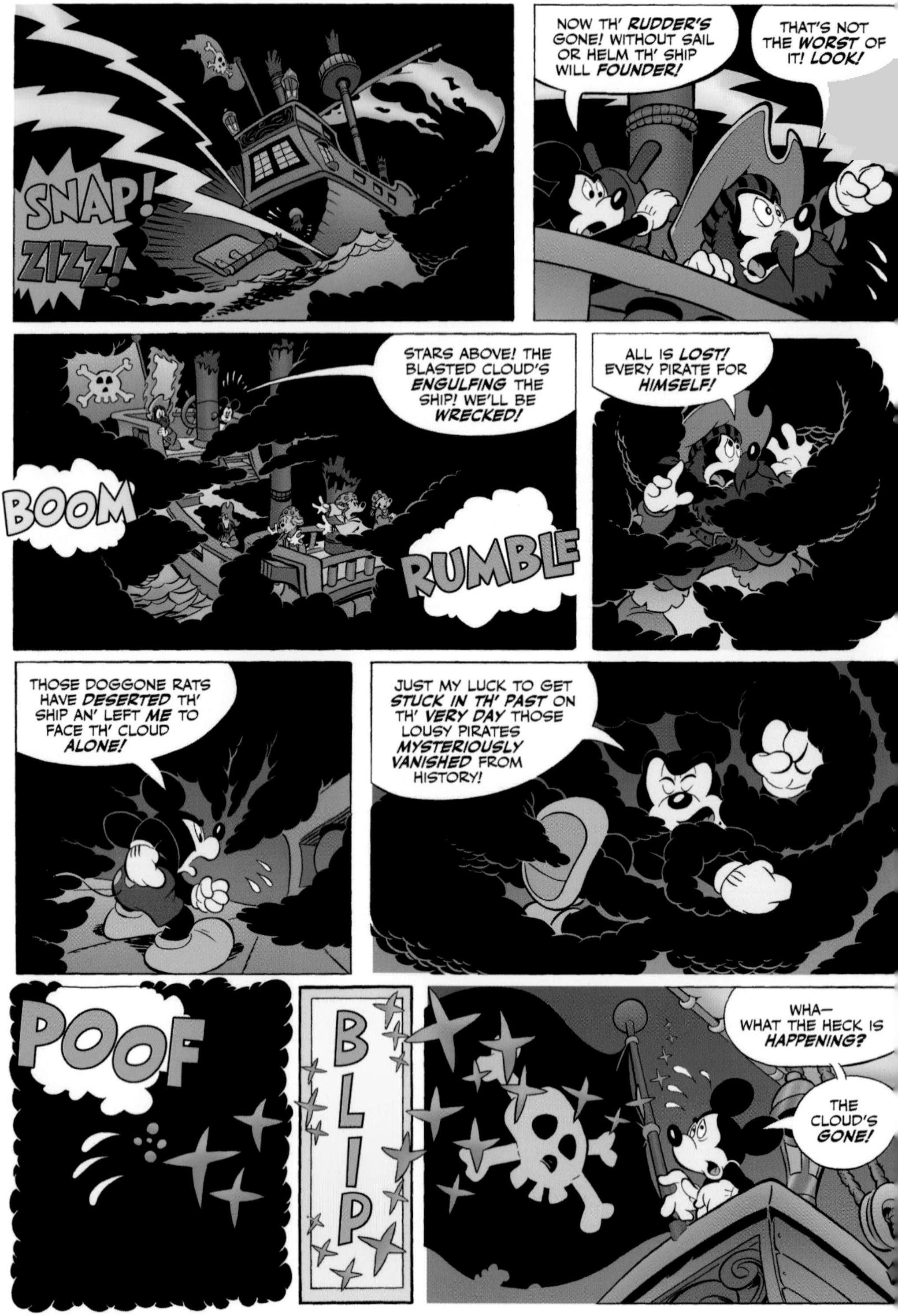
SNAP!
ZIZZ!
NOW TH' RUDDER'S GONE! WITHOUT SAIL OR HELM TH' SHIP WILL FOUNDER!
THAT'S NOT THE WORST OF IT! LOOK!
BOOM
STARS ABOVE! THE BLASTED CLOUD'S ENGULFING THE SHIP! WE'LL BE WRECKED!
RUMBLE
ALL IS LOST! EVERY PIRATE FOR HIMSELF!
THOSE DOGGONE RATS HAVE DESERTED TH' SHIP AN' LEFT ME TO FACE TH' CLOUD ALONE!
JUST MY LUCK TO GET STUCK IN TH' PAST ON TH' VERY DAY THOSE LOUSY PIRATES MYSTERIOUSLY VANISHED FROM HISTORY!
POOF
BLIP
WHA— WHAT THE HECK IS HAPPENING?
THE CLOUD'S GONE!

STEP *LIVELY*, SHIPMATE! YOUR *LIFE* DEPENDS ON OUR SUCCESS WITH *SAIL AND CANNON!*

?

OPEN THE *PORTS!*

HEY!

THIS WHERE I *CAME IN!* DID SOMEONE PRESS THE *REWIND BUTTON?!*

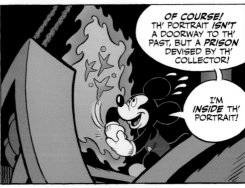

OF COURSE! TH' PORTRAIT *ISN'T* A DOORWAY TO TH' PAST, BUT A *PRISON* DEVISED BY TH' COLLECTOR!

I'M *INSIDE* TH' PORTRAIT!

THE FAMOUS PIRATE MOUSE *DIDN'T* JUST *VANISH* INTO OBSCURITY— HE WAS *STOLEN* FROM HISTORY!

TH' COLLECTOR USED THE *BLACK CLOUD* TO *COLLECT* HIS SHIP AN' CREW *CENTURIES AGO!*

BOOM! BOOM!

THE CLOUD MUST BE A *TOOL* TO *INSTILL FEAR*— TO MAKE TH' SUBJECT *RIPE* TO *COLLECT!*

BUT *I'M* NOT THE ONE WHO'S TRAPPED!

I CAN *EXIT* ANY TIME!

AND NOW I KNOW TH' *PURPOSE* OF TH' COLLECTION!

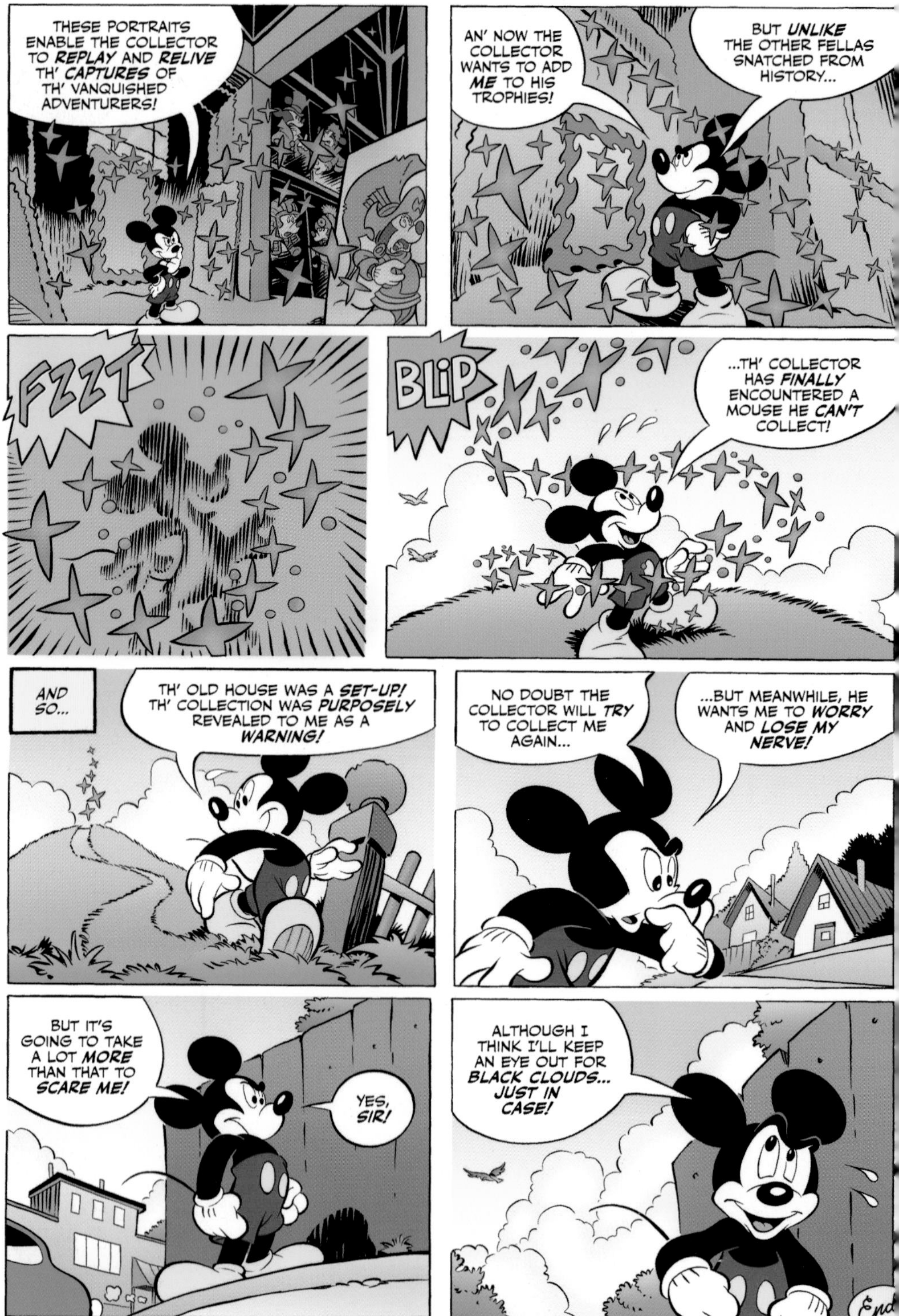
THESE PORTRAITS ENABLE THE COLLECTOR TO REPLAY AND RELIVE TH' CAPTURES OF TH' VANQUISHED ADVENTURERS!
AN' NOW THE COLLECTOR WANTS TO ADD ME TO HIS TROPHIES!
BUT UNLIKE THE OTHER FELLAS SNATCHED FROM HISTORY...
FZZT
BLIP
...TH' COLLECTOR HAS FINALLY ENCOUNTERED A MOUSE HE CAN'T COLLECT!
AND SO...
TH' OLD HOUSE WAS A SET-UP! TH' COLLECTION WAS PURPOSELY REVEALED TO ME AS A WARNING!
NO DOUBT THE COLLECTOR WILL TRY TO COLLECT ME AGAIN...
...BUT MEANWHILE, HE WANTS ME TO WORRY AND LOSE MY NERVE!
BUT IT'S GOING TO TAKE A LOT MORE THAN THAT TO SCARE ME!
YES, SIR!
ALTHOUGH I THINK I'LL KEEP AN EYE OUT FOR BLACK CLOUDS... JUST IN CASE!
End

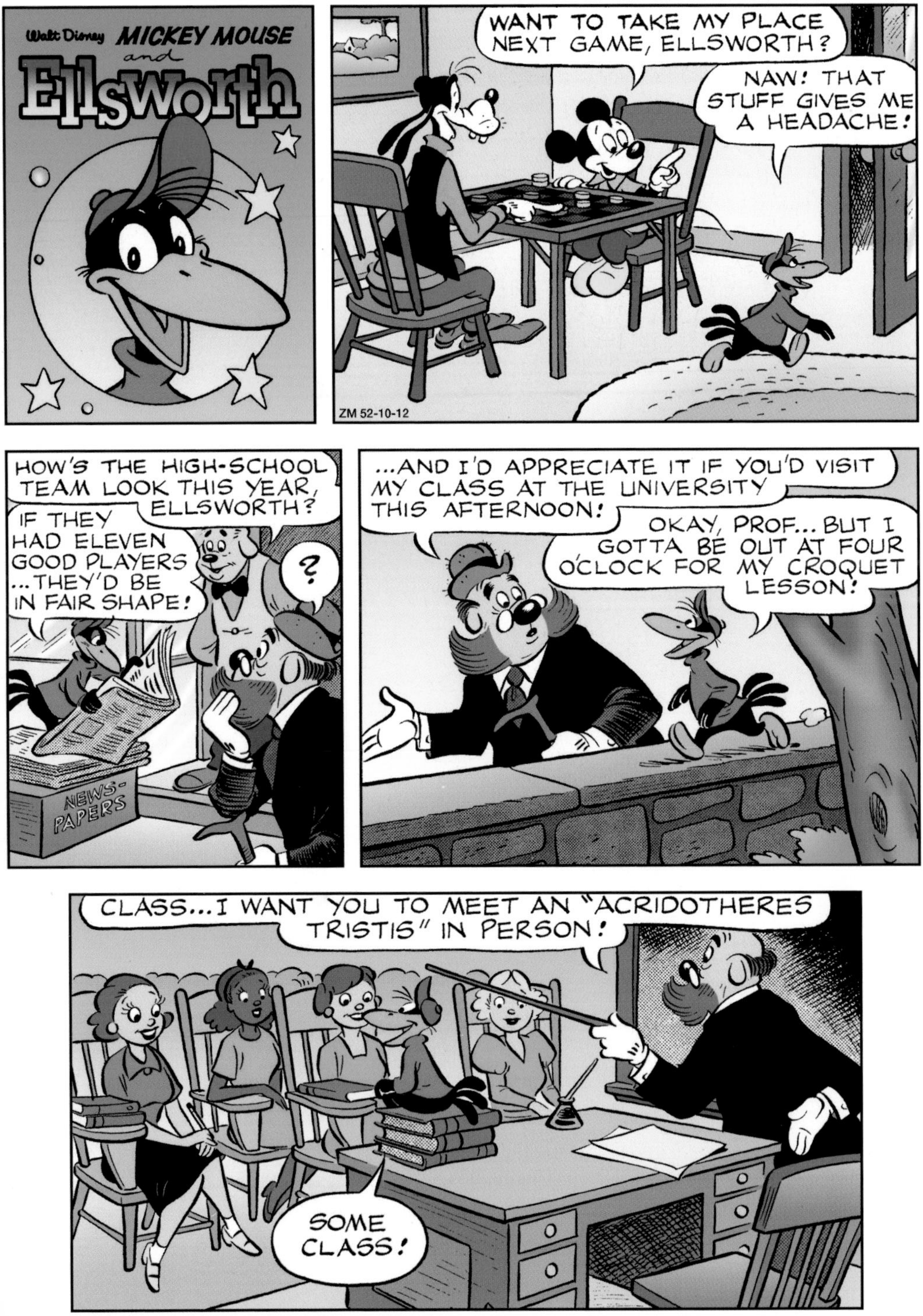
Walt Disney MICKEY MOUSE and Ellsworth
WANT TO TAKE MY PLACE NEXT GAME, ELLSWORTH?
NAW! THAT STUFF GIVES ME A HEADACHE!
ZM 52-10-12
HOW'S THE HIGH-SCHOOL TEAM LOOK THIS YEAR, ELLSWORTH?
IF THEY HAD ELEVEN GOOD PLAYERS ...THEY'D BE IN FAIR SHAPE!
?
NEWS-PAPERS
...AND I'D APPRECIATE IT IF YOU'D VISIT MY CLASS AT THE UNIVERSITY THIS AFTERNOON!
OKAY, PROF... BUT I GOTTA BE OUT AT FOUR O'CLOCK FOR MY CROQUET LESSON!
CLASS...I WANT YOU TO MEET AN "ACRIDOTHERES TRISTIS" IN PERSON!
SOME CLASS!

Originally published in *Mickey Mouse* Sunday comic strip (USA, 1952)

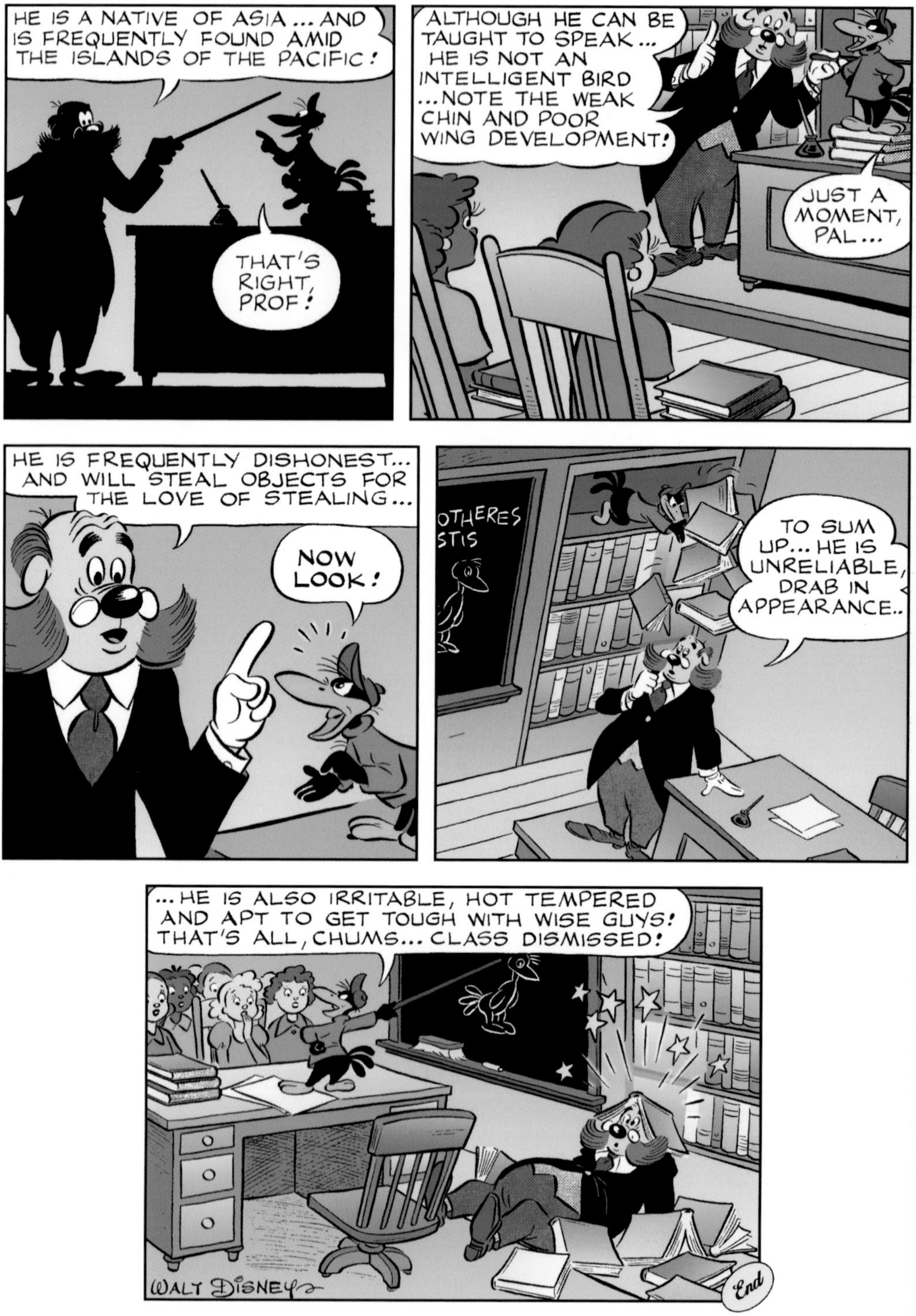
HE IS A NATIVE OF ASIA... AND IS FREQUENTLY FOUND AMID THE ISLANDS OF THE PACIFIC!
THAT'S RIGHT, PROF!
ALTHOUGH HE CAN BE TAUGHT TO SPEAK... HE IS NOT AN INTELLIGENT BIRD ...NOTE THE WEAK CHIN AND POOR WING DEVELOPMENT!
JUST A MOMENT, PAL...
HE IS FREQUENTLY DISHONEST... AND WILL STEAL OBJECTS FOR THE LOVE OF STEALING...
NOW LOOK!
TO SUM UP... HE IS UNRELIABLE, DRAB IN APPEARANCE..
...HE IS ALSO IRRITABLE, HOT TEMPERED AND APT TO GET TOUGH WITH WISE GUYS! THAT'S ALL, CHUMS... CLASS DISMISSED!
WALT DISNEY
End

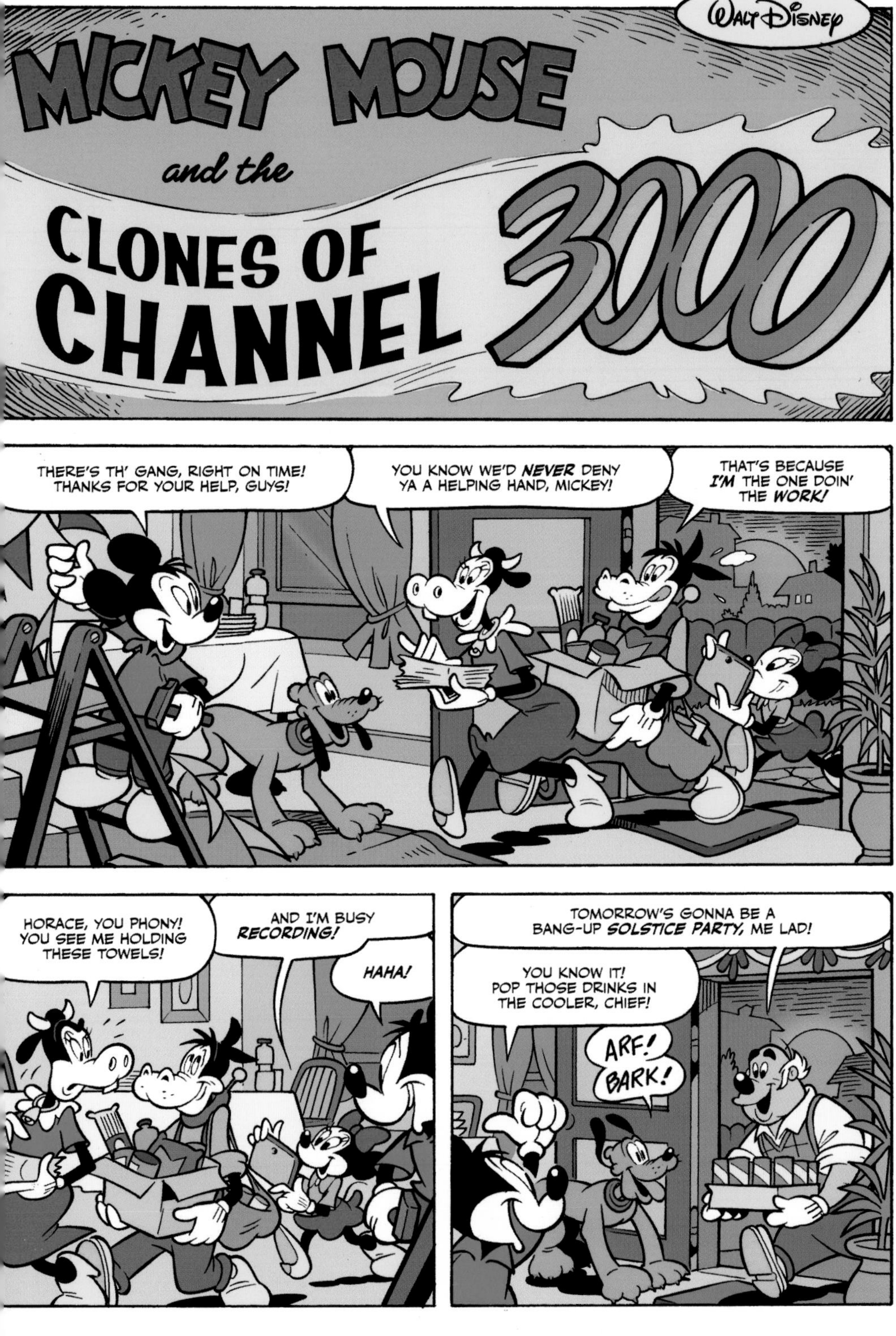
Walt Disney
MICKEY MOUSE
and the
CLONES OF CHANNEL 3000
THERE'S TH' GANG, RIGHT ON TIME! THANKS FOR YOUR HELP, GUYS!
YOU KNOW WE'D NEVER DENY YA A HELPING HAND, MICKEY!
THAT'S BECAUSE I'M THE ONE DOIN' THE WORK!
HORACE, YOU PHONY! YOU SEE ME HOLDING THESE TOWELS!
AND I'M BUSY RECORDING!
HAHA!
TOMORROW'S GONNA BE A BANG-UP SOLSTICE PARTY, ME LAD!
YOU KNOW IT! POP THOSE DRINKS IN THE COOLER, CHIEF!
ARF! BARK!

Originally published in *Topolino* #3000 (Italy, 2013)

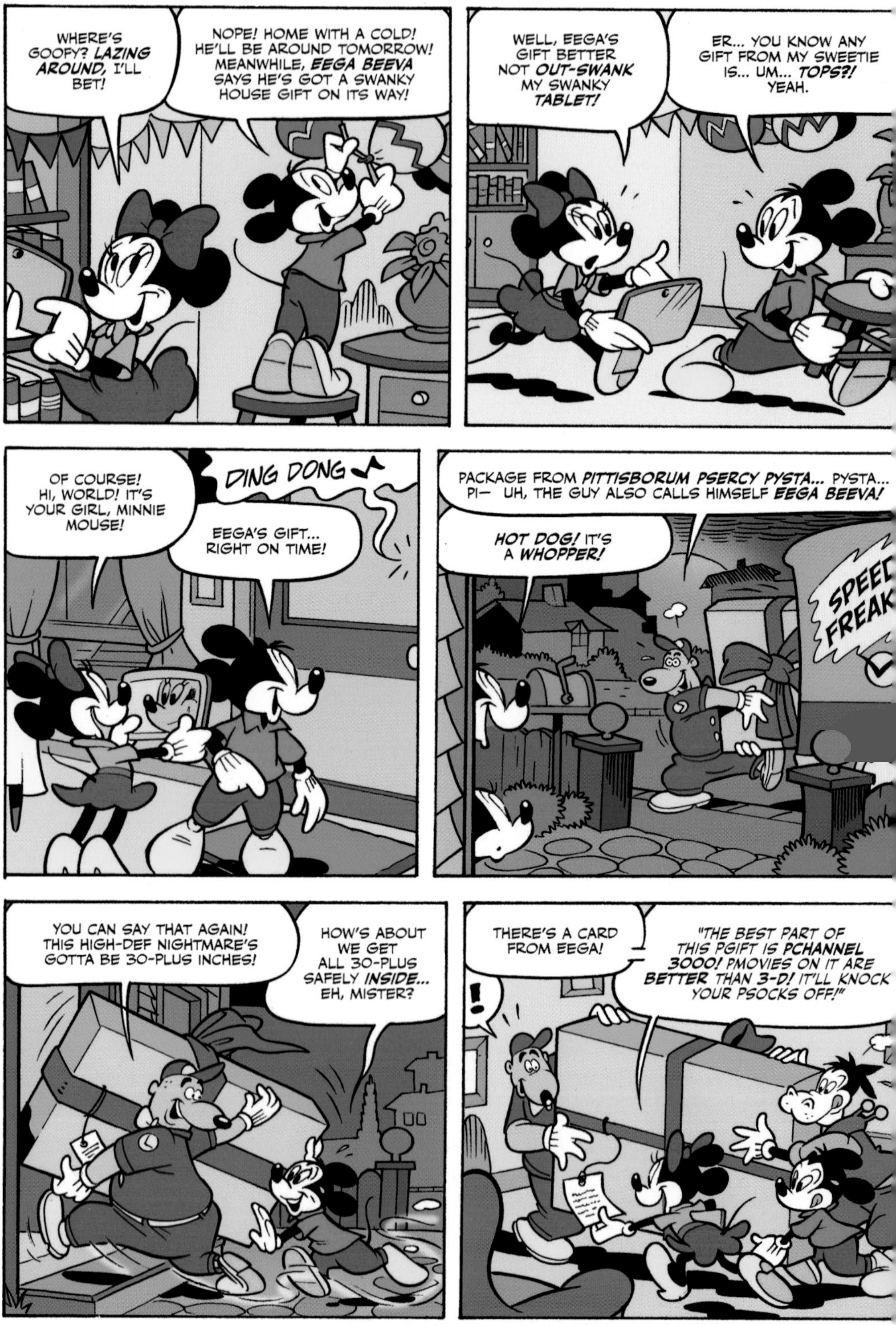

WHERE'S GOOFY? LAZING AROUND, I'LL BET!
NOPE! HOME WITH A COLD! HE'LL BE AROUND TOMORROW! MEANWHILE, EEGA BEEVA SAYS HE'S GOT A SWANKY HOUSE GIFT ON ITS WAY!
WELL, EEGA'S GIFT BETTER NOT OUT-SWANK MY SWANKY TABLET!
ER... YOU KNOW ANY GIFT FROM MY SWEETIE IS... UM... TOPS?! YEAH.
OF COURSE! HI, WORLD! IT'S YOUR GIRL, MINNIE MOUSE!
DING DONG
EEGA'S GIFT... RIGHT ON TIME!
PACKAGE FROM PITTISBORUM PSERCY PYSTA... PYSTA... PI— UH, THE GUY ALSO CALLS HIMSELF EEGA BEEVA!
HOT DOG! IT'S A WHOPPER!
SPEED FREAK
YOU CAN SAY THAT AGAIN! THIS HIGH-DEF NIGHTMARE'S GOTTA BE 30-PLUS INCHES!
HOW'S ABOUT WE GET ALL 30-PLUS SAFELY INSIDE... EH, MISTER?
THERE'S A CARD FROM EEGA!
"THE BEST PART OF THIS PGIFT IS PCHANNEL 3000! PMOVIES ON IT ARE BETTER THAN 3-D! IT'LL KNOCK YOUR PSOCKS OFF!"
!

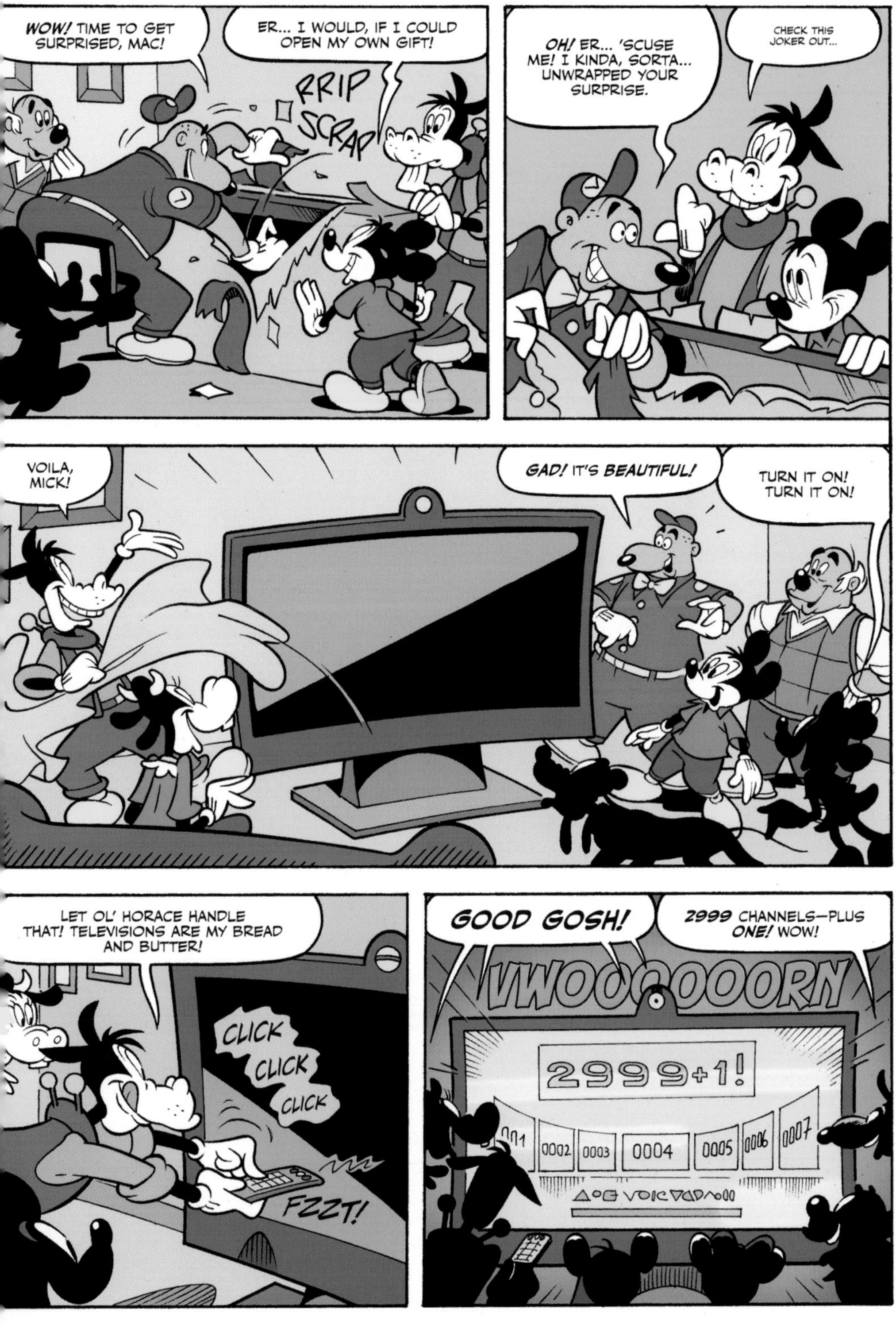
WOW! TIME TO GET SURPRISED, MAC!
ER... I WOULD, IF I COULD OPEN MY OWN GIFT!
RRIP
SCRAP
OH! ER... 'SCUSE ME! I KINDA, SORTA... UNWRAPPED YOUR SURPRISE.
CHECK THIS JOKER OUT...
VOILA, MICK!
GAD! IT'S BEAUTIFUL!
TURN IT ON! TURN IT ON!
LET OL' HORACE HANDLE THAT! TELEVISIONS ARE MY BREAD AND BUTTER!
CLICK
CLICK
CLICK
FZZT!
GOOD GOSH!
2999 CHANNELS—PLUS ONE! WOW!
VWOOOOOOORN
2999+1!
0002
0003
0004
0005
0006
0007

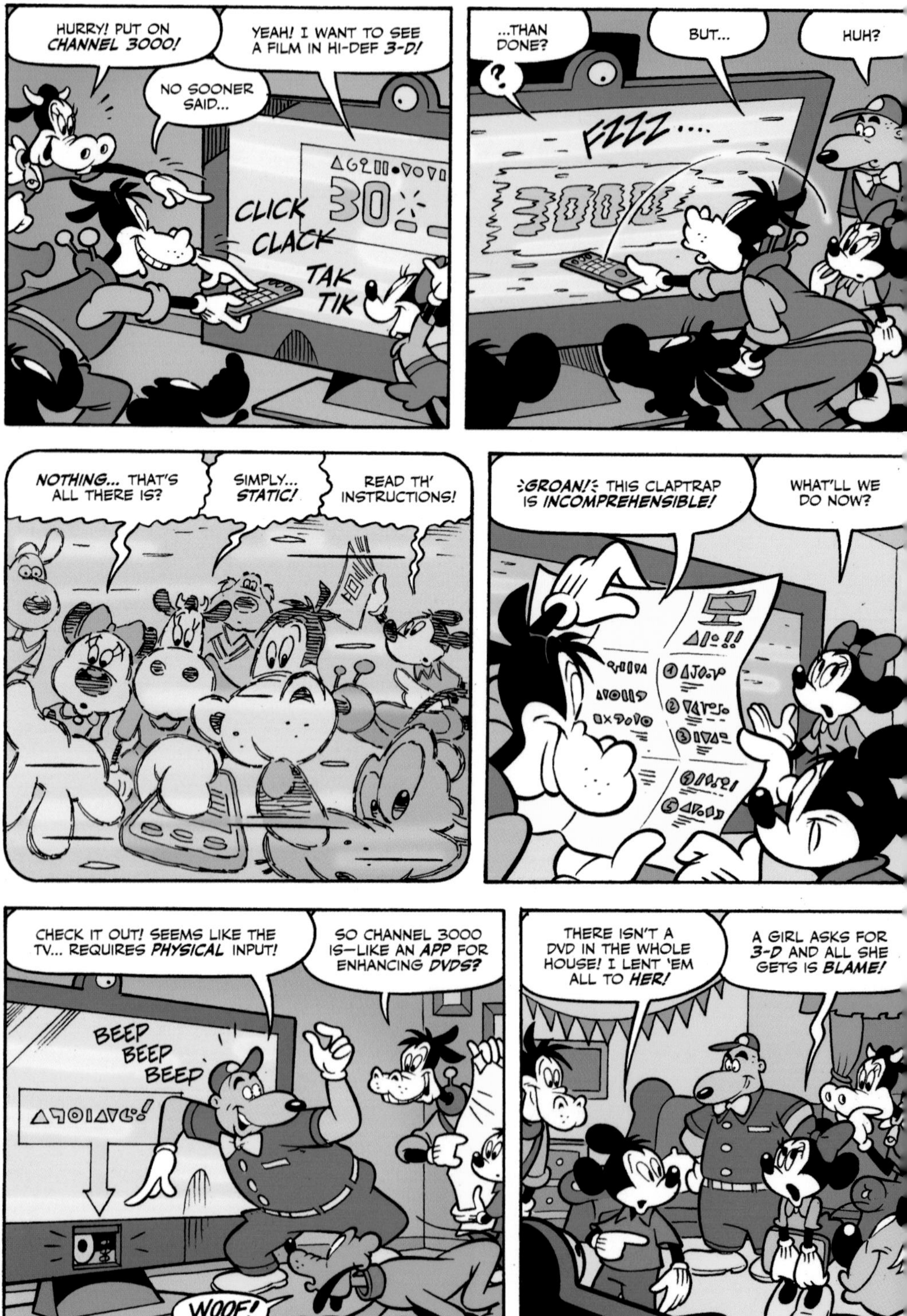
HURRY! PUT ON CHANNEL 3000!
YEAH! I WANT TO SEE A FILM IN HI-DEF 3-D!
NO SOONER SAID...
CLICK
CLACK
TAK
TIK
...THAN DONE?
BUT...
HUH?
FZZZ....
NOTHING... THAT'S ALL THERE IS?
SIMPLY... STATIC!
READ TH' INSTRUCTIONS!
GROAN! THIS CLAPTRAP IS INCOMPREHENSIBLE!
WHAT'LL WE DO NOW?
CHECK IT OUT! SEEMS LIKE THE TV... REQUIRES PHYSICAL INPUT!
SO CHANNEL 3000 IS—LIKE AN APP FOR ENHANCING DVDS?
BEEP
BEEP
BEEP
WOOF!
THERE ISN'T A DVD IN THE WHOLE HOUSE! I LENT 'EM ALL TO HER!
A GIRL ASKS FOR 3-D AND ALL SHE GETS IS BLAME!

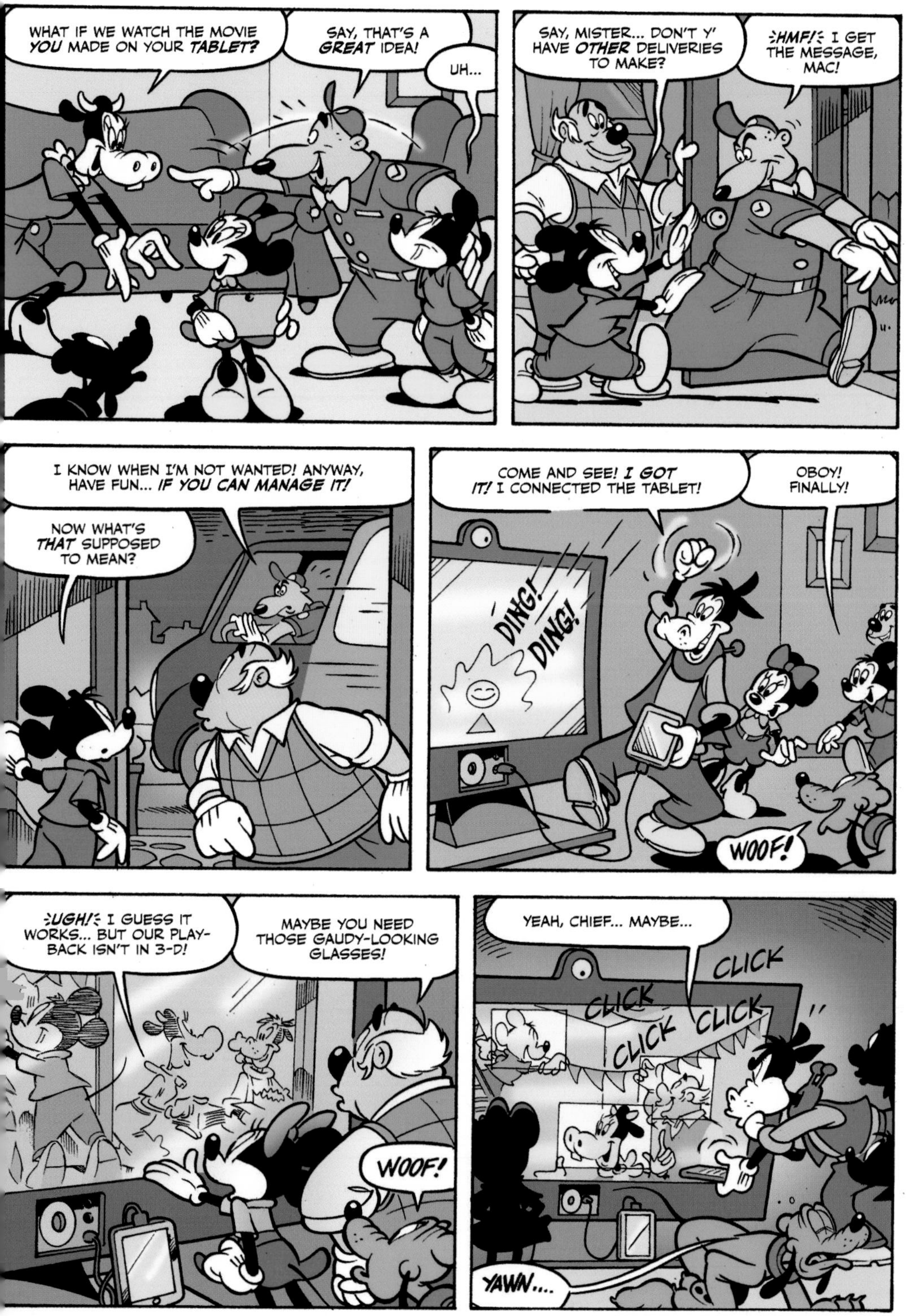
WHAT IF WE WATCH THE MOVIE YOU MADE ON YOUR TABLET?
SAY, THAT'S A GREAT IDEA!
UH...
SAY, MISTER... DON'T Y' HAVE OTHER DELIVERIES TO MAKE?
HMF! I GET THE MESSAGE, MAC!
I KNOW WHEN I'M NOT WANTED! ANYWAY, HAVE FUN... IF YOU CAN MANAGE IT!
NOW WHAT'S THAT SUPPOSED TO MEAN?
COME AND SEE! I GOT IT! I CONNECTED THE TABLET!
OBOY! FINALLY!
DING! DING!
WOOF!
UGH! I GUESS IT WORKS... BUT OUR PLAY-BACK ISN'T IN 3-D!
MAYBE YOU NEED THOSE GAUDY-LOOKING GLASSES!
WOOF!
YEAH, CHIEF... MAYBE...
CLICK
CLICK
CLICK
CLICK
YAWN....

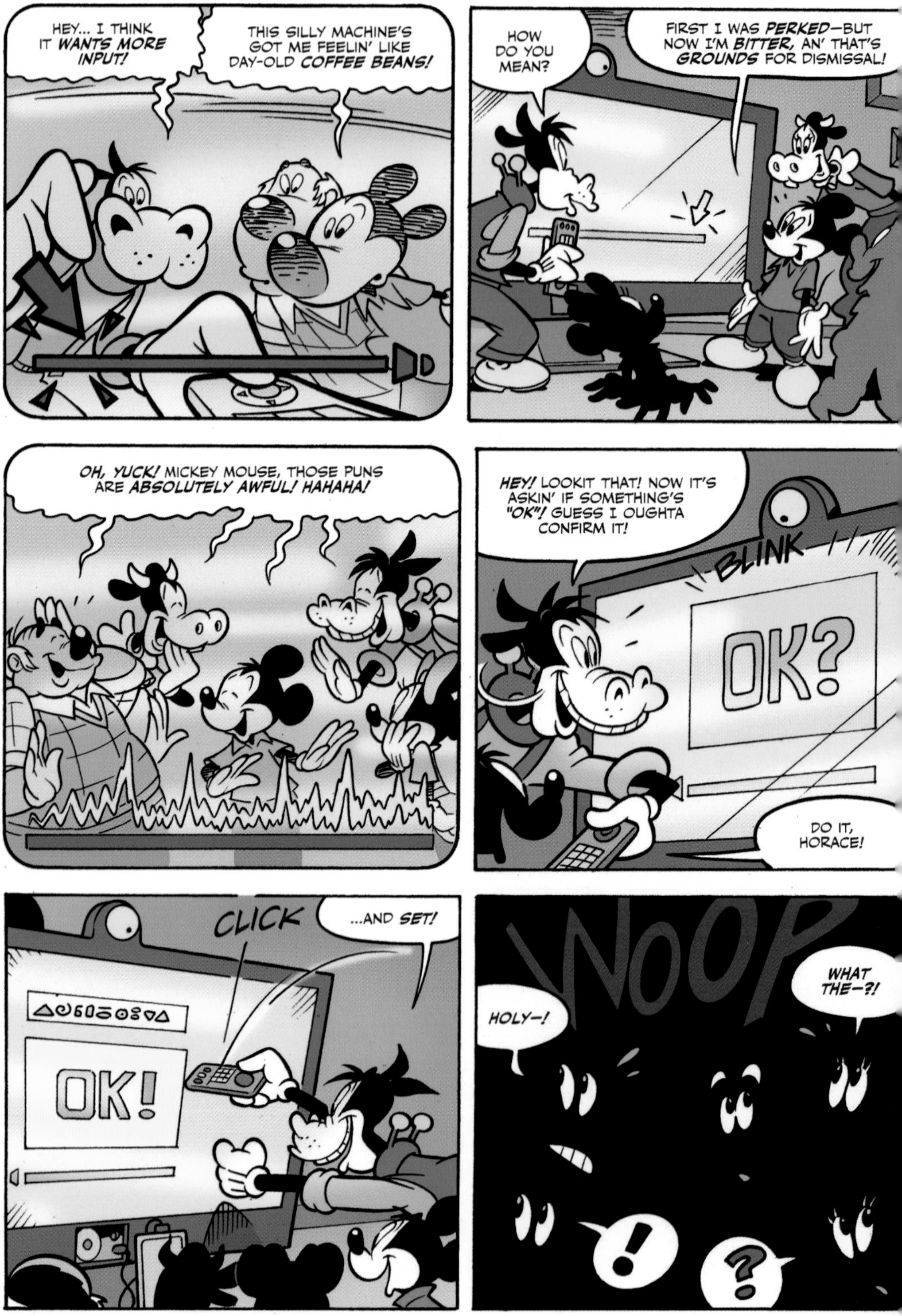
HEY... I THINK IT WANTS MORE INPUT!
THIS SILLY MACHINE'S GOT ME FEELIN' LIKE DAY-OLD COFFEE BEANS!
HOW DO YOU MEAN?
FIRST I WAS PERKED—BUT NOW I'M BITTER, AN' THAT'S GROUNDS FOR DISMISSAL!
OH, YUCK! MICKEY MOUSE, THOSE PUNS ARE ABSOLUTELY AWFUL! HAHAHA!
HEY! LOOKIT THAT! NOW IT'S ASKIN' IF SOMETHING'S "OK"! GUESS I OUGHTA CONFIRM IT!
BLINK
OK?
DO IT, HORACE!
CLICK
...AND SET!
OK!
WOOP
HOLY—!
WHAT THE—?!
!
?

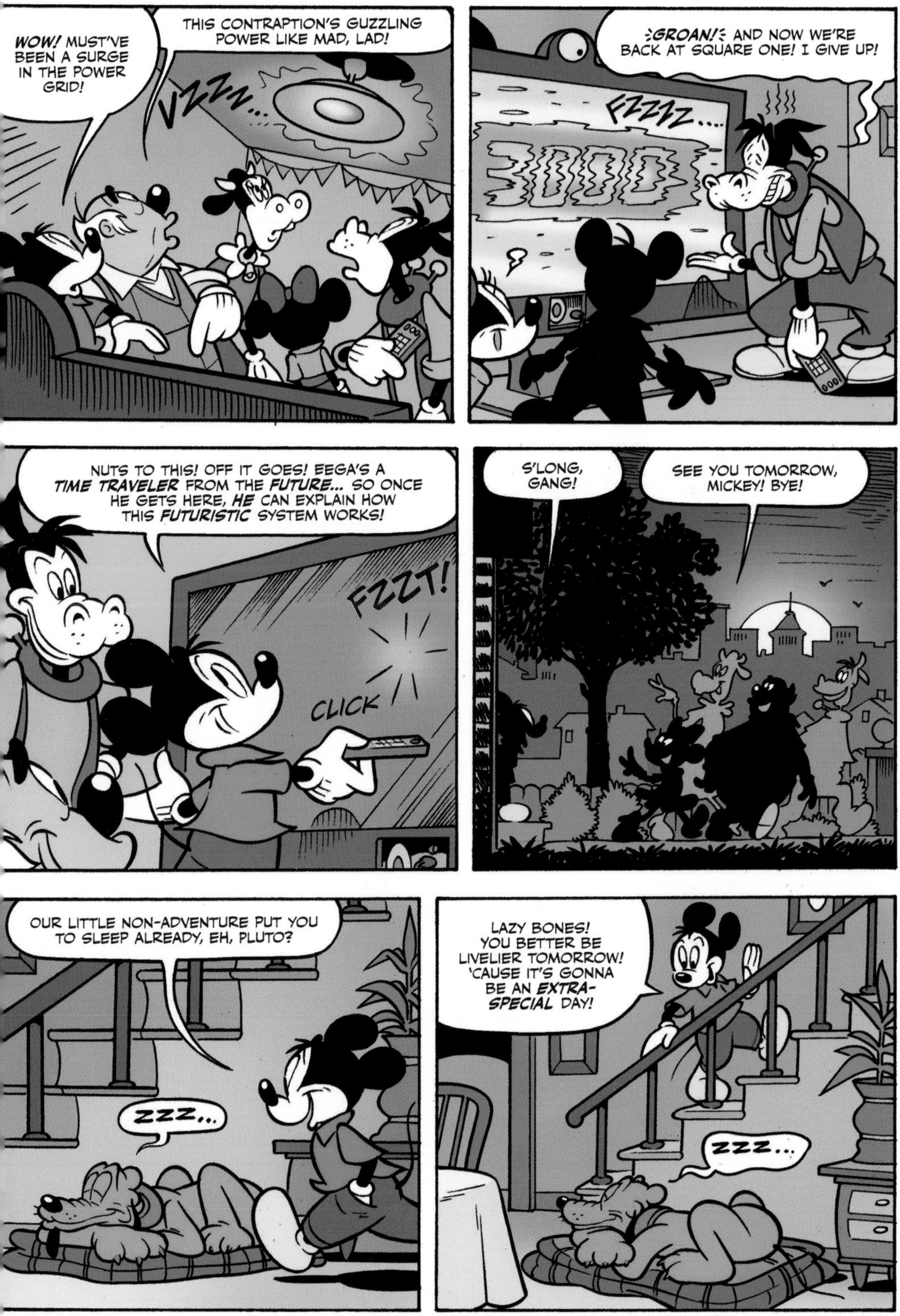
WOW! MUST'VE BEEN A SURGE IN THE POWER GRID!
THIS CONTRAPTION'S GUZZLING POWER LIKE MAD, LAD!
VZZZZ...
:GROAN!: AND NOW WE'RE BACK AT SQUARE ONE! I GIVE UP!
FZZZZ....
3000
NUTS TO THIS! OFF IT GOES! EEGA'S A TIME TRAVELER FROM THE FUTURE... SO ONCE HE GETS HERE, HE CAN EXPLAIN HOW THIS FUTURISTIC SYSTEM WORKS!
FZZT!
CLICK
S'LONG, GANG!
SEE YOU TOMORROW, MICKEY! BYE!
OUR LITTLE NON-ADVENTURE PUT YOU TO SLEEP ALREADY, EH, PLUTO?
ZZZ...
LAZY BONES! YOU BETTER BE LIVELIER TOMORROW! 'CAUSE IT'S GONNA BE AN EXTRA-SPECIAL DAY!
ZZZ...

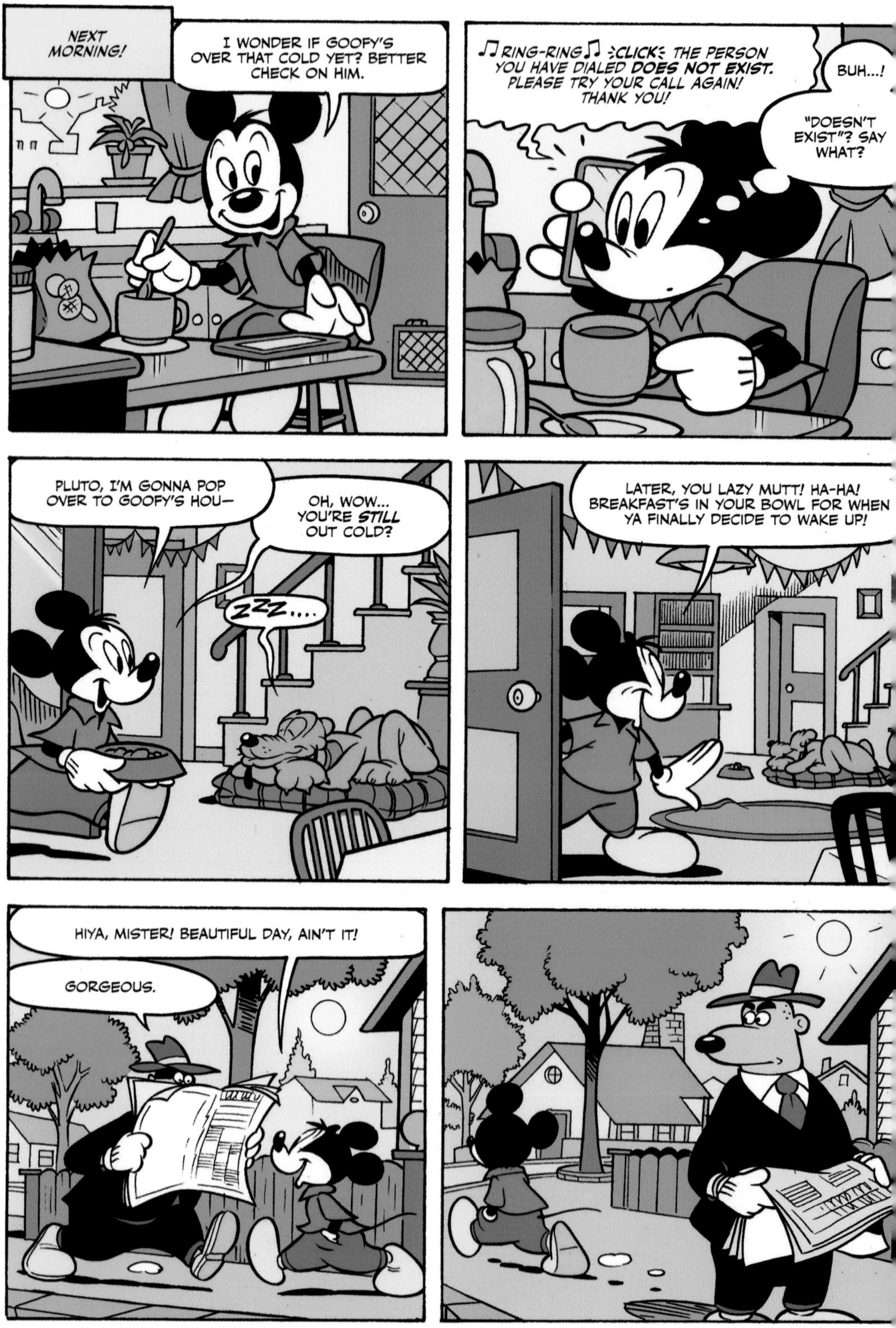
NEXT MORNING!
I WONDER IF GOOFY'S OVER THAT COLD YET? BETTER CHECK ON HIM.
♫RING-RING♫ :CLICK: THE PERSON YOU HAVE DIALED DOES NOT EXIST. PLEASE TRY YOUR CALL AGAIN! THANK YOU!
BUH...!
"DOESN'T EXIST"? SAY WHAT?
PLUTO, I'M GONNA POP OVER TO GOOFY'S HOU—
OH, WOW... YOU'RE STILL OUT COLD?
ZZZ....
LATER, YOU LAZY MUTT! HA-HA! BREAKFAST'S IN YOUR BOWL FOR WHEN YA FINALLY DECIDE TO WAKE UP!
HIYA, MISTER! BEAUTIFUL DAY, AIN'T IT!
GORGEOUS.

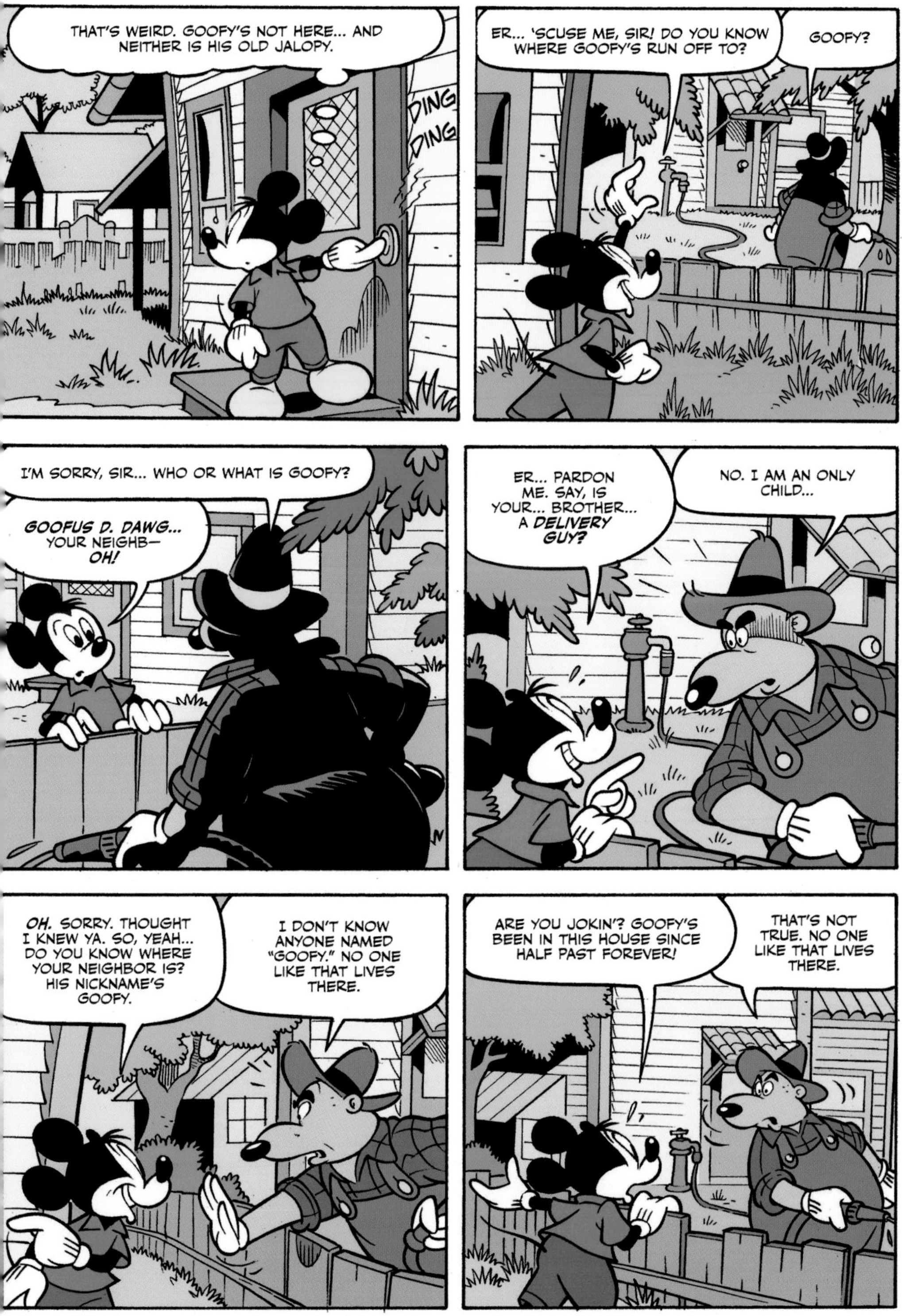
THAT'S WEIRD. GOOFY'S NOT HERE... AND NEITHER IS HIS OLD JALOPY.
DING
DING
ER... 'SCUSE ME, SIR! DO YOU KNOW WHERE GOOFY'S RUN OFF TO?
GOOFY?
I'M SORRY, SIR... WHO OR WHAT IS GOOFY?
GOOFUS D. DAWG... YOUR NEIGHB— OH!
ER... PARDON ME. SAY, IS YOUR... BROTHER... A DELIVERY GUY?
NO. I AM AN ONLY CHILD...
OH. SORRY. THOUGHT I KNEW YA. SO, YEAH... DO YOU KNOW WHERE YOUR NEIGHBOR IS? HIS NICKNAME'S GOOFY.
I DON'T KNOW ANYONE NAMED "GOOFY." NO ONE LIKE THAT LIVES THERE.
ARE YOU JOKIN'? GOOFY'S BEEN IN THIS HOUSE SINCE HALF PAST FOREVER!
THAT'S NOT TRUE. NO ONE LIKE THAT LIVES THERE.

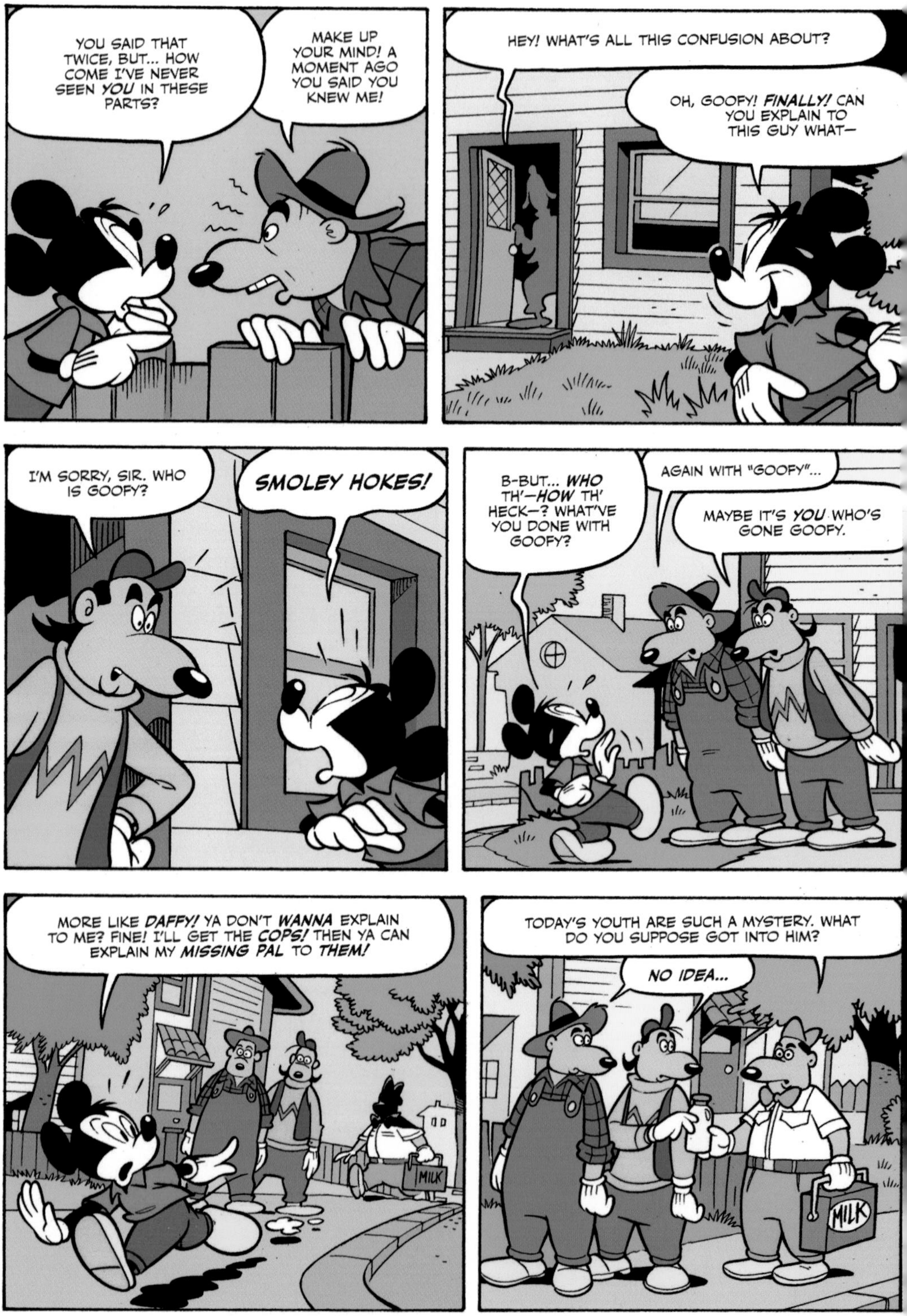
YOU SAID THAT TWICE, BUT... HOW COME I'VE NEVER SEEN *YOU* IN THESE PARTS?
MAKE UP YOUR MIND! A MOMENT AGO YOU SAID YOU KNEW ME!
HEY! WHAT'S ALL THIS CONFUSION ABOUT?
OH, GOOFY! *FINALLY!* CAN YOU EXPLAIN TO THIS GUY WHAT—
I'M SORRY, SIR. WHO IS GOOFY?
SMOLEY HOKES!
B-BUT... *WHO* TH'—*HOW* TH' HECK—? WHAT'VE YOU DONE WITH GOOFY?
AGAIN WITH "GOOFY"...
MAYBE IT'S *YOU* WHO'S GONE GOOFY.
MORE LIKE *DAFFY!* YA DON'T *WANNA* EXPLAIN TO ME? FINE! I'LL GET THE *COPS!* THEN YA CAN EXPLAIN MY *MISSING PAL* TO *THEM!*
MILK
TODAY'S YOUTH ARE SUCH A MYSTERY. WHAT DO YOU SUPPOSE GOT INTO HIM?
NO IDEA...
MILK

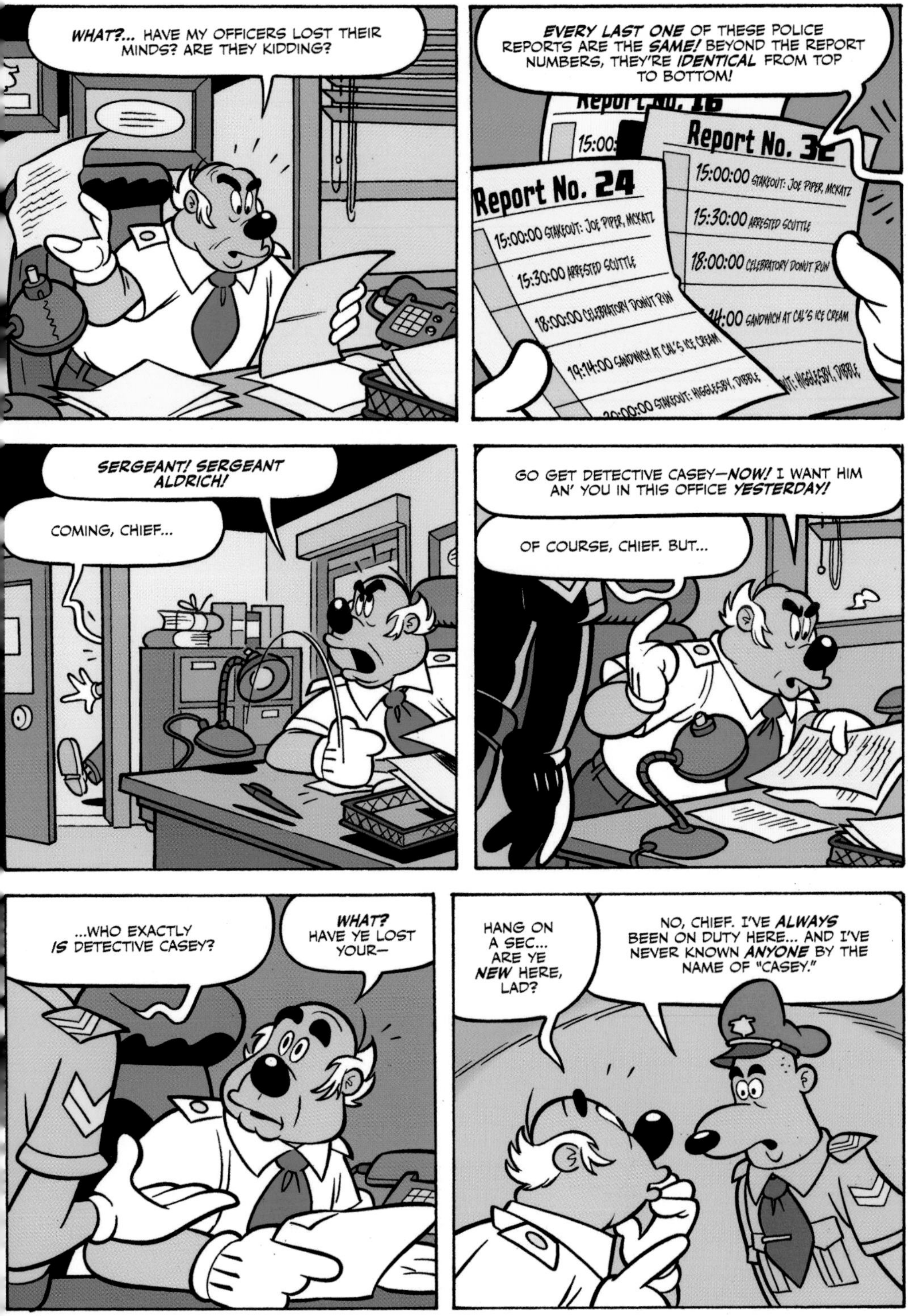
WHAT?... HAVE MY OFFICERS LOST THEIR MINDS? ARE THEY KIDDING?
EVERY LAST ONE OF THESE POLICE REPORTS ARE THE SAME! BEYOND THE REPORT NUMBERS, THEY'RE IDENTICAL FROM TOP TO BOTTOM!
Report No. 24
15:00:00 STAKEOUT: JOE PIPER, MCKATZ
15:30:00 ARRESTED SCUTTLE
18:00:00 CELEBRATORY DONUT RUN
19:14:00 SANDWICH AT CAL'S ICE CREAM
Report No. 32
15:00:00 STAKEOUT: JOE PIPER, MCKATZ
15:30:00 ARRESTED SCUTTLE
18:00:00 CELEBRATORY DONUT RUN
SERGEANT! SERGEANT ALDRICH!
COMING, CHIEF...
GO GET DETECTIVE CASEY—NOW! I WANT HIM AN' YOU IN THIS OFFICE YESTERDAY!
OF COURSE, CHIEF. BUT...
...WHO EXACTLY IS DETECTIVE CASEY?
WHAT? HAVE YE LOST YOUR—
HANG ON A SEC... ARE YE NEW HERE, LAD?
NO, CHIEF. I'VE ALWAYS BEEN ON DUTY HERE... AND I'VE NEVER KNOWN ANYONE BY THE NAME OF "CASEY."

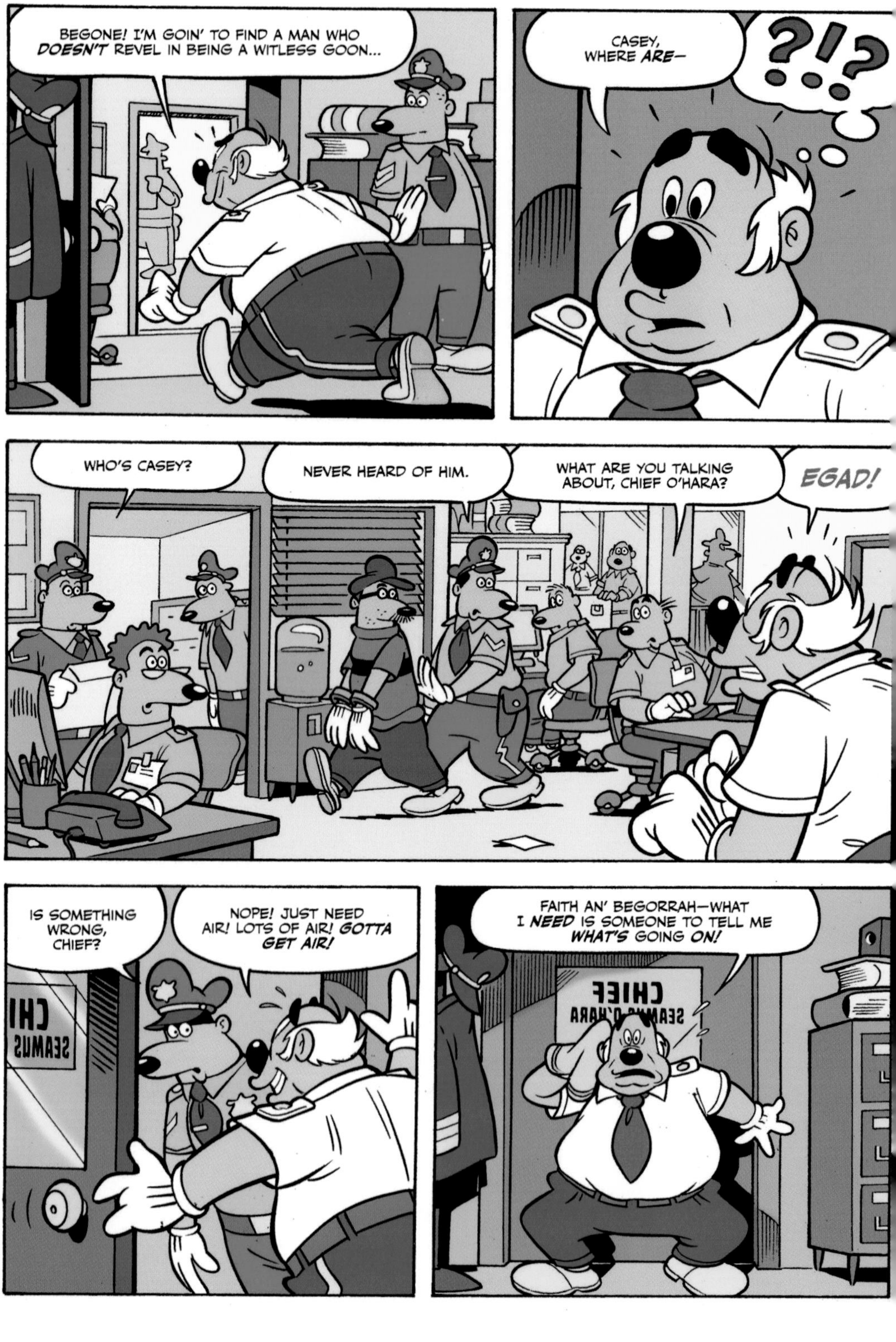
BEGONE! I'M GOIN' TO FIND A MAN WHO DOESN'T REVEL IN BEING A WITLESS GOON...
CASEY, WHERE ARE—
?!?
WHO'S CASEY?
NEVER HEARD OF HIM.
WHAT ARE YOU TALKING ABOUT, CHIEF O'HARA?
EGAD!
IS SOMETHING WRONG, CHIEF?
NOPE! JUST NEED AIR! LOTS OF AIR! GOTTA GET AIR!
FAITH AN' BEGORRAH—WHAT I NEED IS SOMEONE TO TELL ME WHAT'S GOING ON!

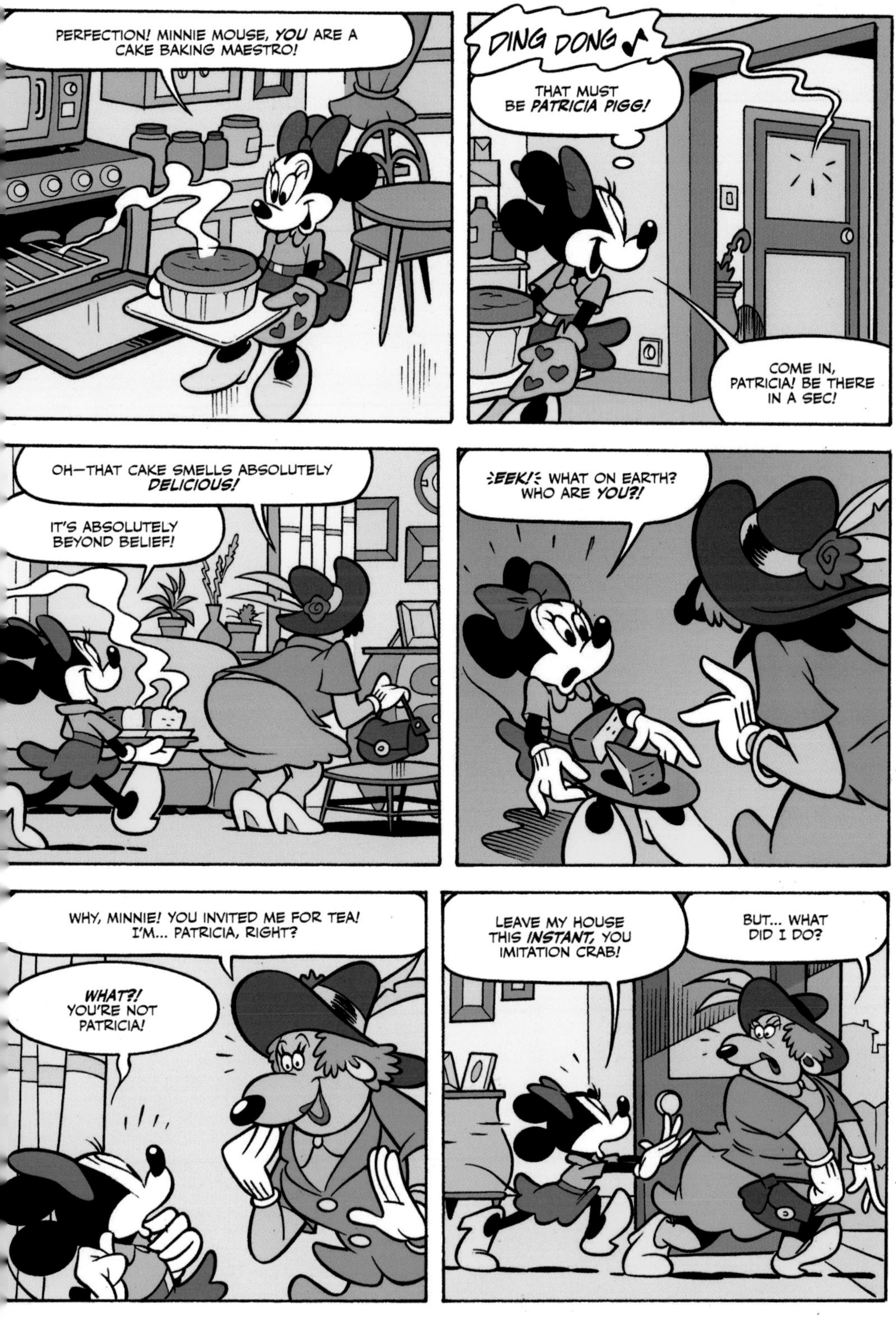
PERFECTION! MINNIE MOUSE, *YOU* ARE A CAKE BAKING MAESTRO!
DING DONG
THAT MUST BE *PATRICIA PIGG!*
COME IN, PATRICIA! BE THERE IN A SEC!
OH—THAT CAKE SMELLS ABSOLUTELY *DELICIOUS!*
IT'S ABSOLUTELY BEYOND BELIEF!
EEK! WHAT ON EARTH? WHO ARE *YOU?!*
WHY, MINNIE! YOU INVITED ME FOR TEA! I'M... PATRICIA, RIGHT?
WHAT?! YOU'RE NOT PATRICIA!
LEAVE MY HOUSE THIS *INSTANT,* YOU IMITATION CRAB!
BUT... WHAT DID I DO?

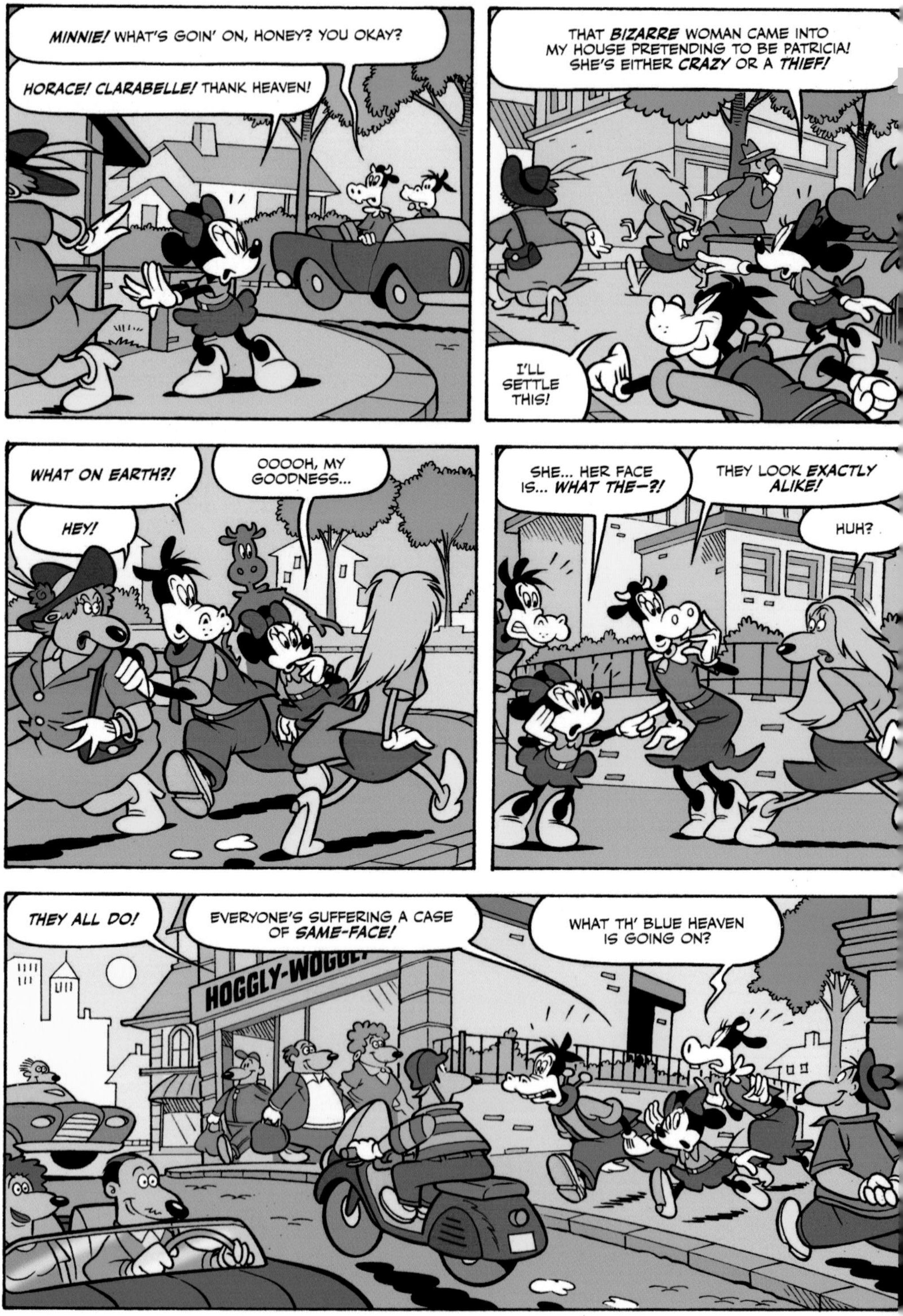
MINNIE! WHAT'S GOIN' ON, HONEY? YOU OKAY?
HORACE! CLARABELLE! THANK HEAVEN!
THAT BIZARRE WOMAN CAME INTO MY HOUSE PRETENDING TO BE PATRICIA! SHE'S EITHER CRAZY OR A THIEF!
I'LL SETTLE THIS!
WHAT ON EARTH?!
HEY!
OOOOH, MY GOODNESS...
SHE... HER FACE IS... WHAT THE—?!
THEY LOOK EXACTLY ALIKE!
HUH?
THEY ALL DO!
EVERYONE'S SUFFERING A CASE OF SAME-FACE!
WHAT TH' BLUE HEAVEN IS GOING ON?
HOGGLY-WOGGLY

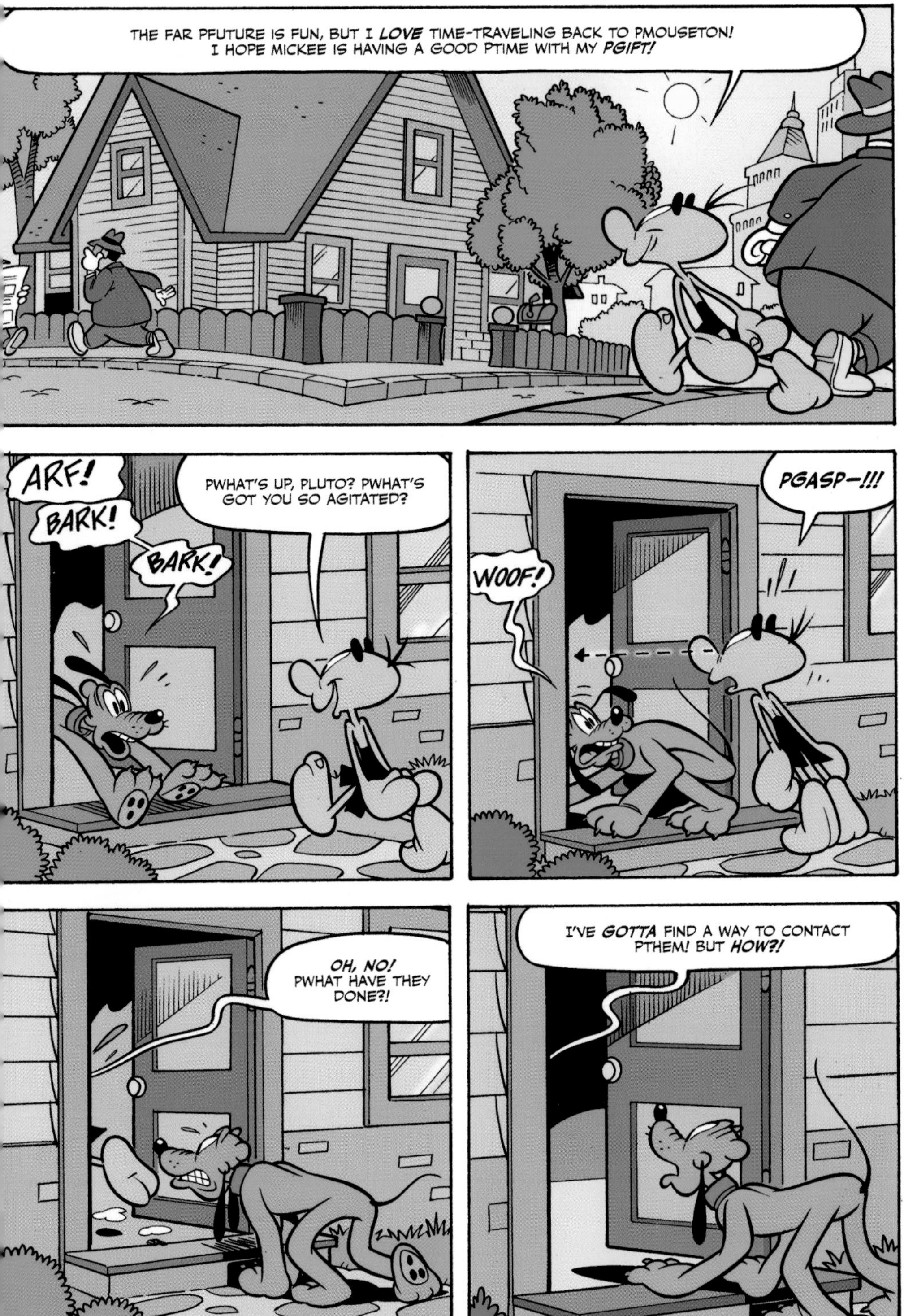
THE FAR PFUTURE IS FUN, BUT I LOVE TIME-TRAVELING BACK TO PMOUSETON! I HOPE MICKEE IS HAVING A GOOD PTIME WITH MY PGIFT!
ARF!
BARK!
BARK!
PWHAT'S UP, PLUTO? PWHAT'S GOT YOU SO AGITATED?
PGASP-!!!
WOOF!
OH, NO! PWHAT HAVE THEY DONE?!
I'VE GOTTA FIND A WAY TO CONTACT PTHEM! BUT HOW?!

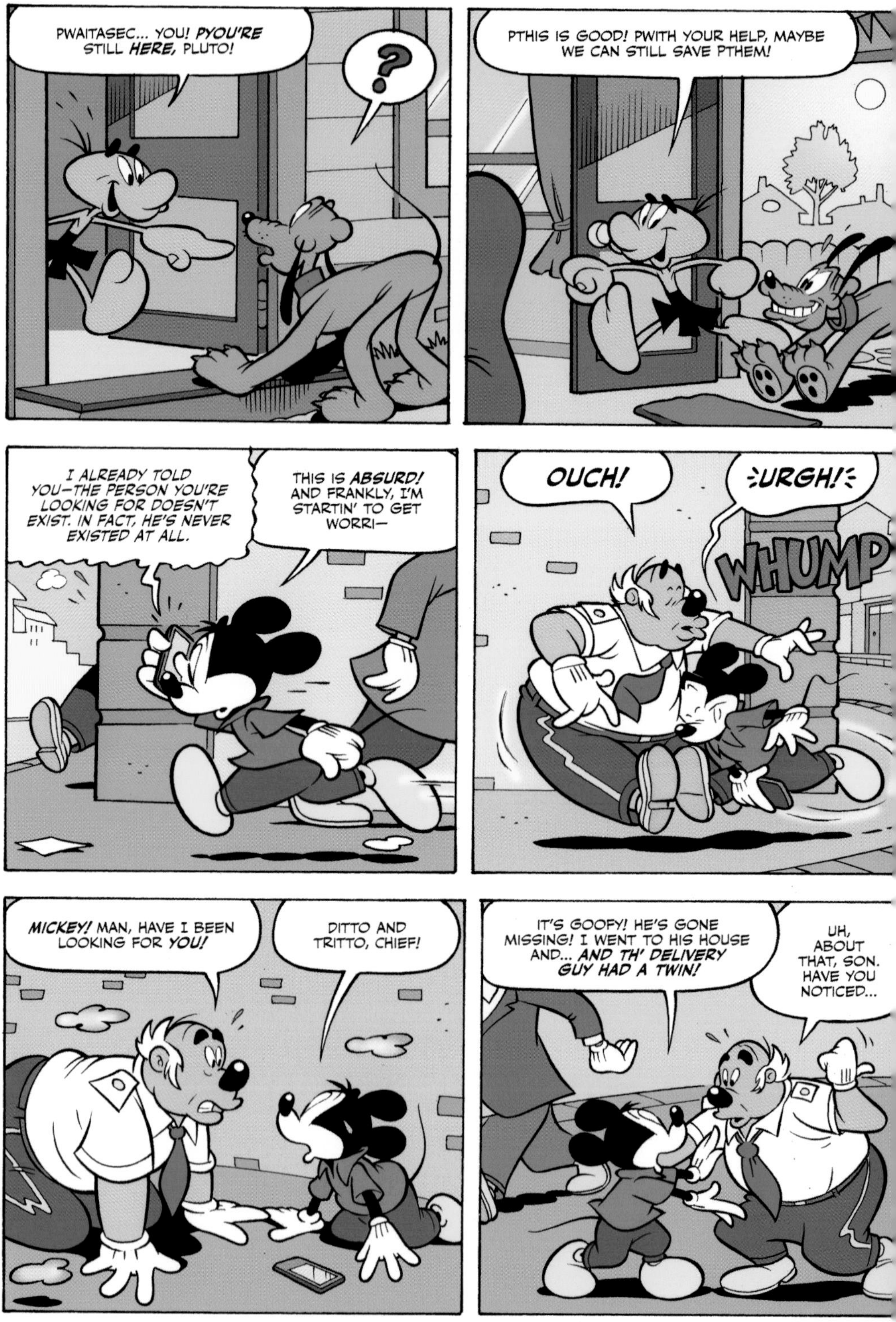
PWAITASEC... YOU! PYOU'RE STILL HERE, PLUTO!
?
PTHIS IS GOOD! PWITH YOUR HELP, MAYBE WE CAN STILL SAVE PTHEM!
I ALREADY TOLD YOU—THE PERSON YOU'RE LOOKING FOR DOESN'T EXIST. IN FACT, HE'S NEVER EXISTED AT ALL.
THIS IS ABSURD! AND FRANKLY, I'M STARTIN' TO GET WORRI—
OUCH!
URGH!
WHUMP
MICKEY! MAN, HAVE I BEEN LOOKING FOR YOU!
DITTO AND TRITTO, CHIEF!
IT'S GOOFY! HE'S GONE MISSING! I WENT TO HIS HOUSE AND... AND TH' DELIVERY GUY HAD A TWIN!
UH, ABOUT THAT, SON. HAVE YOU NOTICED...

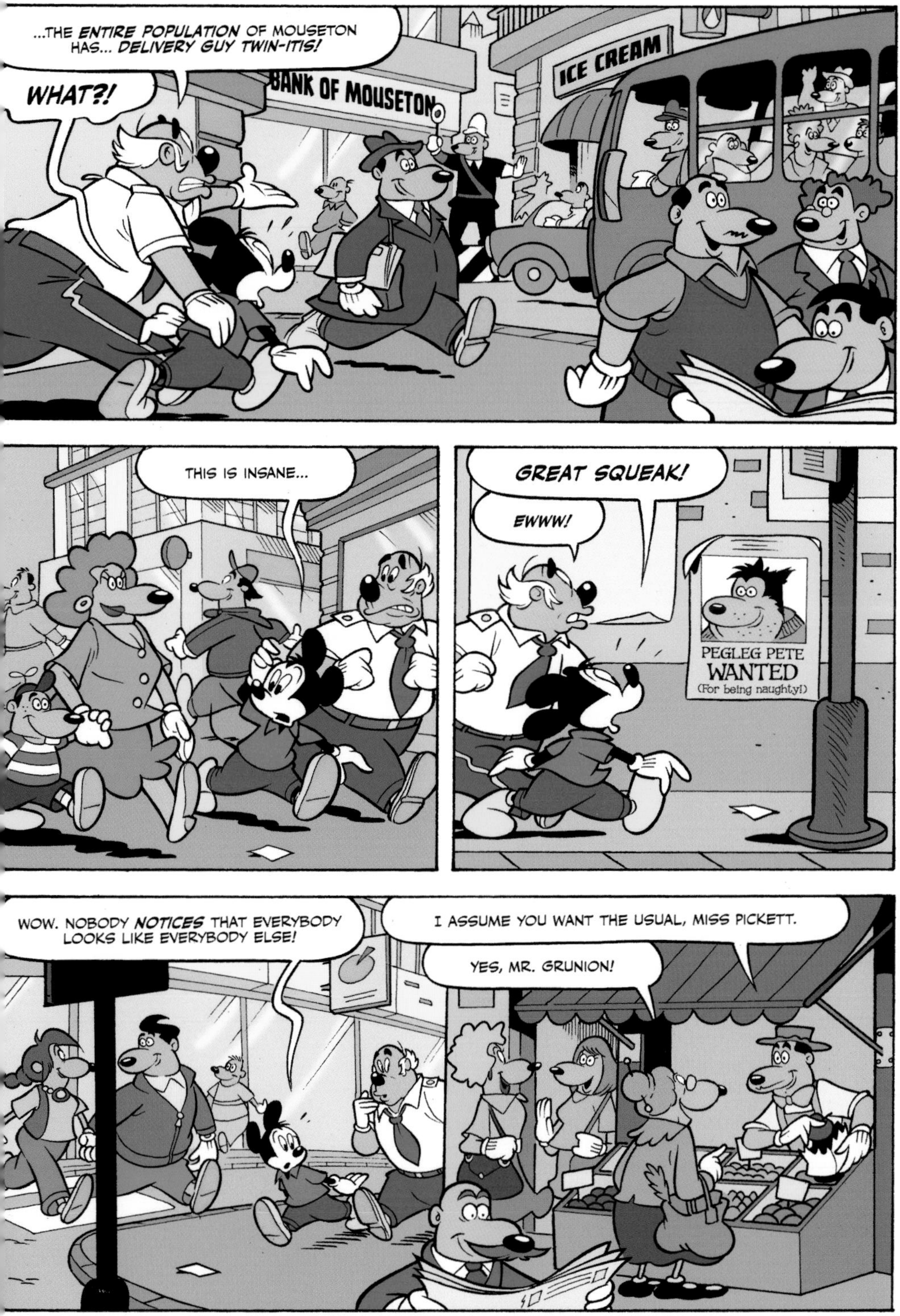
...THE ENTIRE POPULATION OF MOUSETON HAS... DELIVERY GUY TWIN-ITIS!
WHAT?!
BANK OF MOUSETON
ICE CREAM
THIS IS INSANE...
GREAT SQUEAK!
EWWW!
PEGLEG PETE
WANTED
(For being naughty!)
WOW. NOBODY NOTICES THAT EVERYBODY LOOKS LIKE EVERYBODY ELSE!
I ASSUME YOU WANT THE USUAL, MISS PICKETT.
YES, MR. GRUNION!

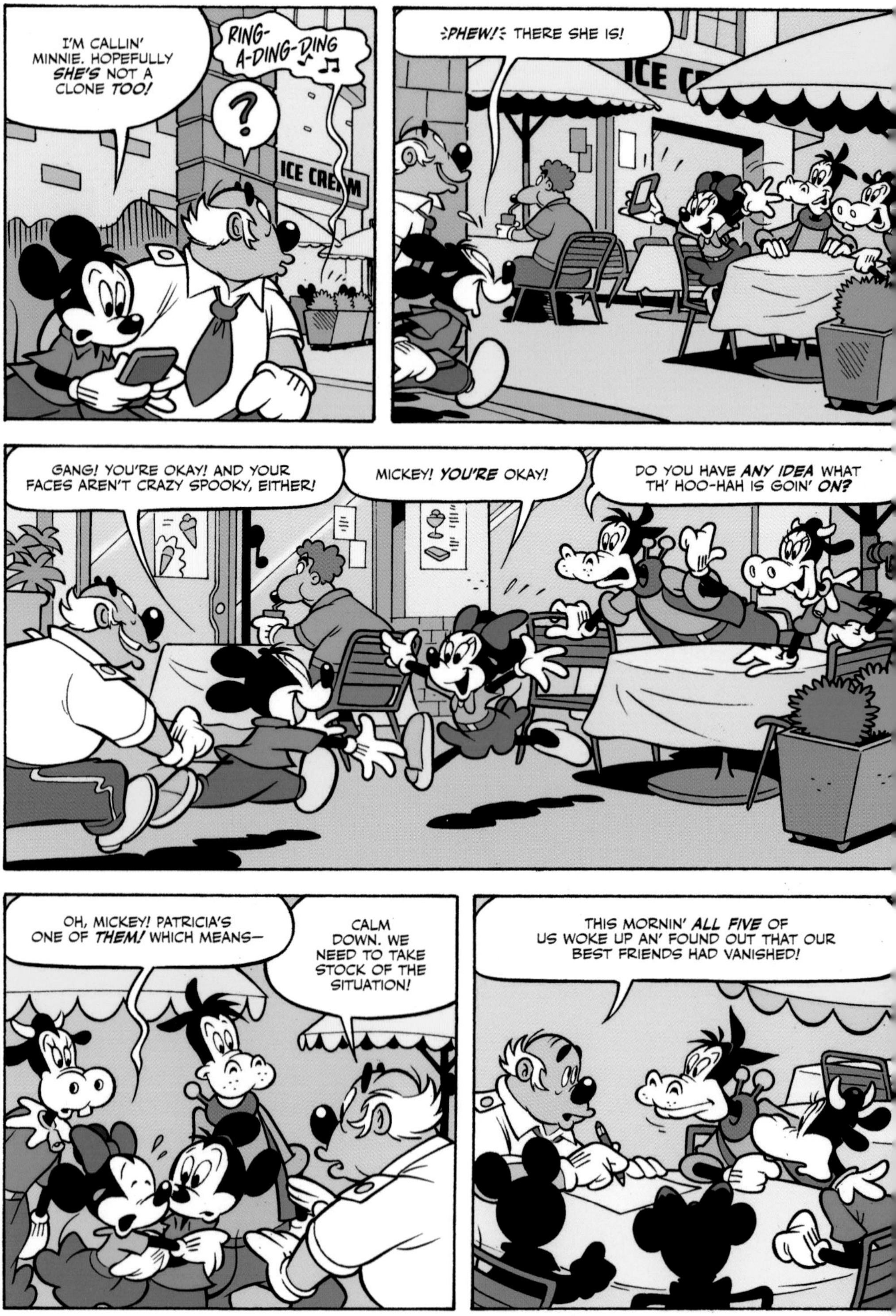
I'M CALLIN' MINNIE. HOPEFULLY SHE'S NOT A CLONE TOO!
RING-A-DING-DING
?
PHEW! THERE SHE IS!
ICE CREAM
GANG! YOU'RE OKAY! AND YOUR FACES AREN'T CRAZY SPOOKY, EITHER!
MICKEY! YOU'RE OKAY!
DO YOU HAVE ANY IDEA WHAT TH' HOO-HAH IS GOIN' ON?
OH, MICKEY! PATRICIA'S ONE OF THEM! WHICH MEANS—
CALM DOWN. WE NEED TO TAKE STOCK OF THE SITUATION!
THIS MORNIN' ALL FIVE OF US WOKE UP AN' FOUND OUT THAT OUR BEST FRIENDS HAD VANISHED!

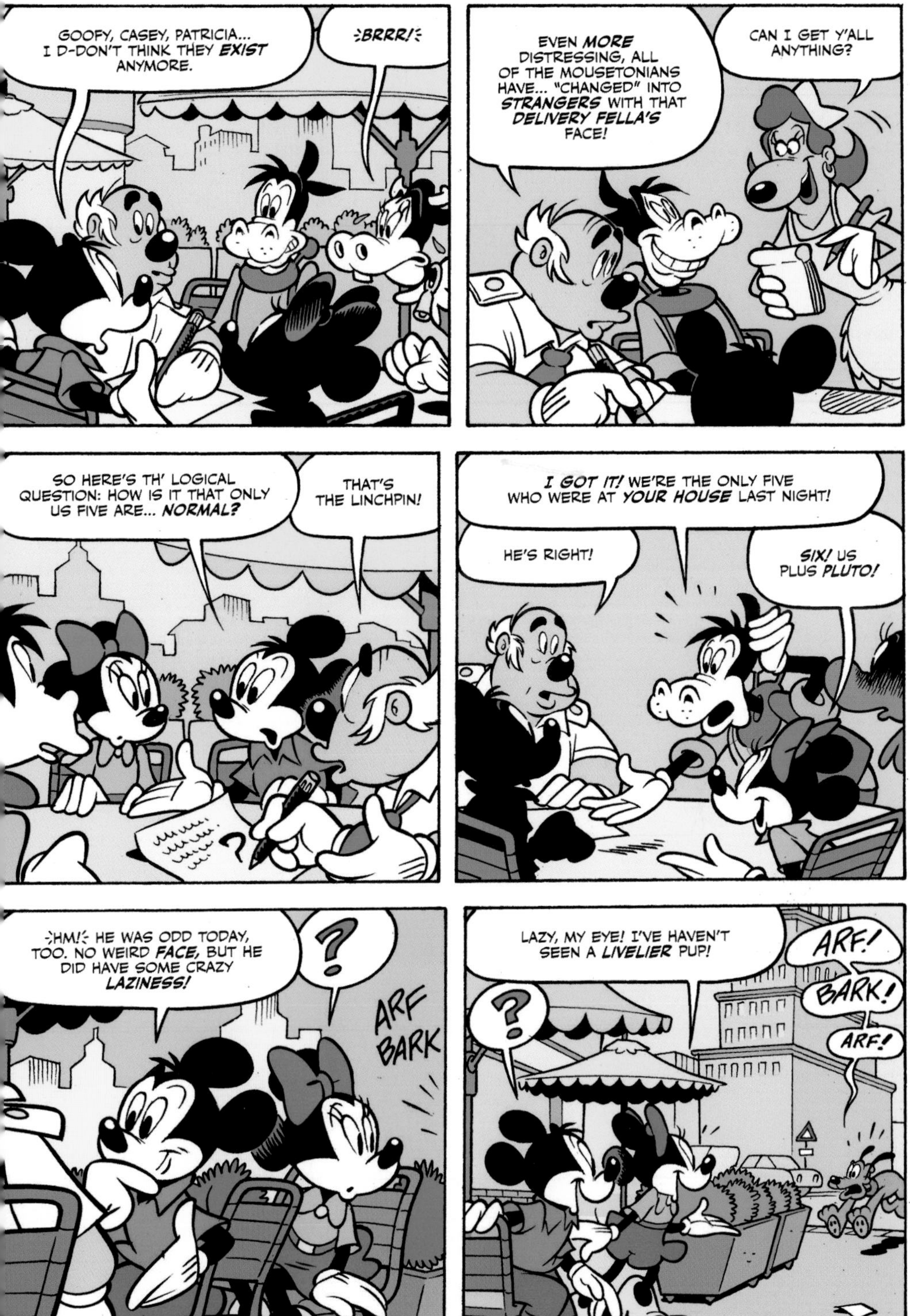
GOOFY, CASEY, PATRICIA... I D-DON'T THINK THEY EXIST ANYMORE.
BRRR!
EVEN MORE DISTRESSING, ALL OF THE MOUSETONIANS HAVE... "CHANGED" INTO STRANGERS WITH THAT DELIVERY FELLA'S FACE!
CAN I GET Y'ALL ANYTHING?
SO HERE'S TH' LOGICAL QUESTION: HOW IS IT THAT ONLY US FIVE ARE... NORMAL?
THAT'S THE LINCHPIN!
I GOT IT! WE'RE THE ONLY FIVE WHO WERE AT YOUR HOUSE LAST NIGHT!
HE'S RIGHT!
SIX! US PLUS PLUTO!
HM! HE WAS ODD TODAY, TOO. NO WEIRD FACE, BUT HE DID HAVE SOME CRAZY LAZINESS!
?
ARF
BARK
LAZY, MY EYE! I'VE HAVEN'T SEEN A LIVELIER PUP!
?
ARF!
BARK!
ARF!

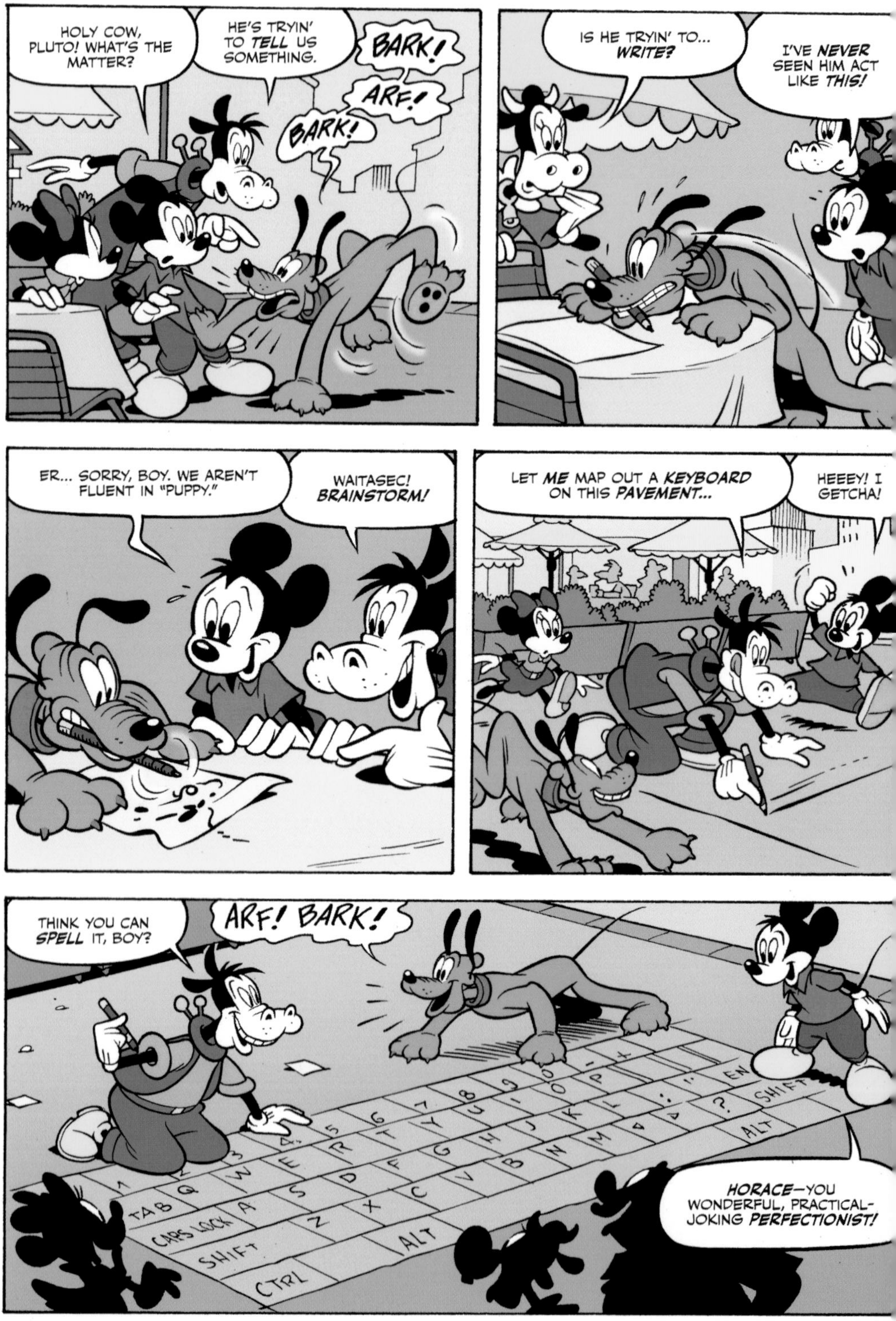
HOLY COW, PLUTO! WHAT'S THE MATTER?
HE'S TRYIN' TO TELL US SOMETHING.
BARK!
ARF!
BARK!
IS HE TRYIN' TO... WRITE?
I'VE NEVER SEEN HIM ACT LIKE THIS!
ER... SORRY, BOY. WE AREN'T FLUENT IN "PUPPY."
WAITASEC! BRAINSTORM!
LET ME MAP OUT A KEYBOARD ON THIS PAVEMENT...
HEEEY! I GETCHA!
THINK YOU CAN SPELL IT, BOY?
ARF! BARK!
HORACE—YOU WONDERFUL, PRACTICAL-JOKING PERFECTIONIST!

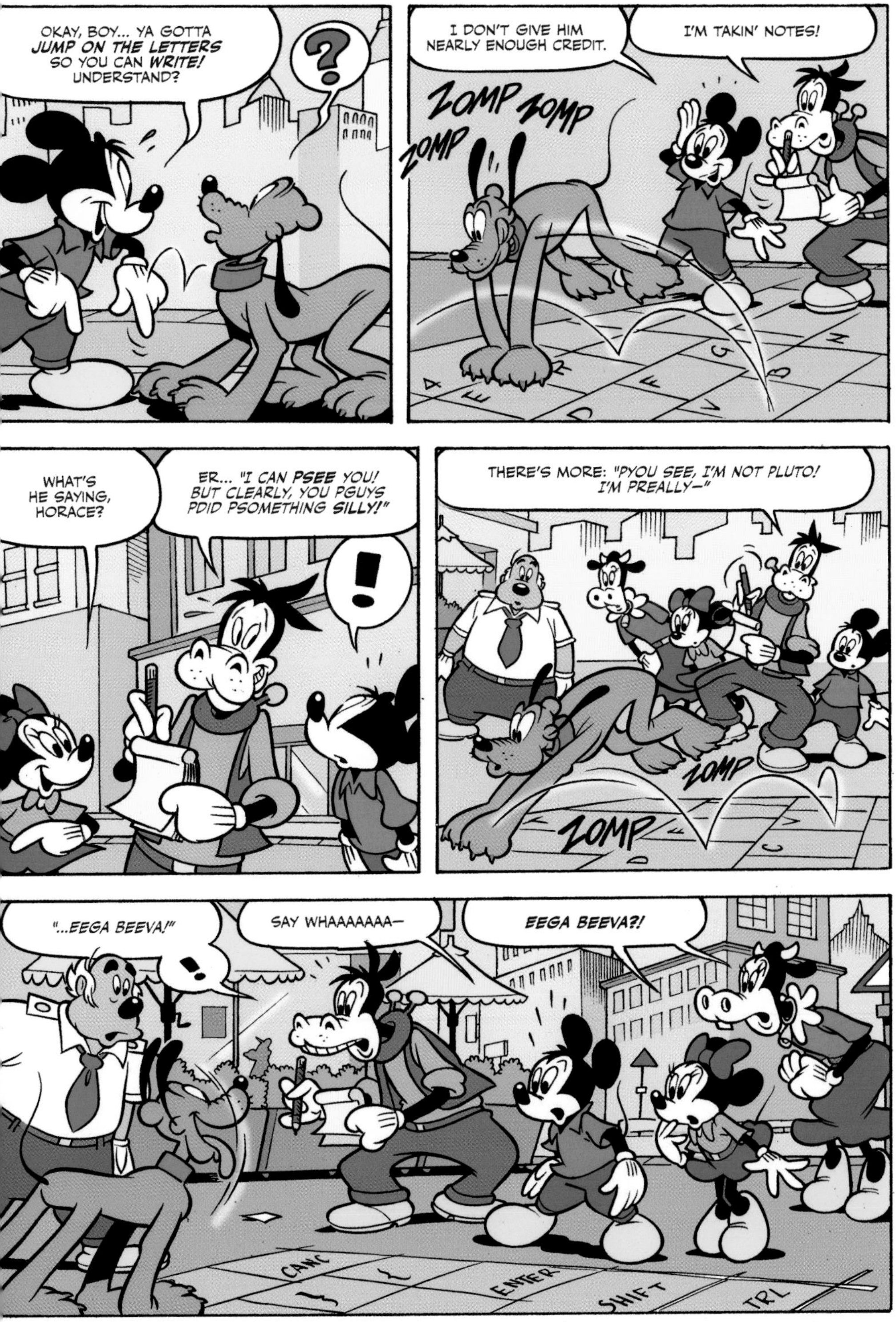

OKAY, BOY... YA GOTTA JUMP ON THE LETTERS SO YOU CAN WRITE! UNDERSTAND?
?
I DON'T GIVE HIM NEARLY ENOUGH CREDIT.
I'M TAKIN' NOTES!
ZOMP ZOMP
ZOMP
WHAT'S HE SAYING, HORACE?
ER... "I CAN PSEE YOU! BUT CLEARLY, YOU PGUYS PDID PSOMETHING SILLY!"
!
THERE'S MORE: "PYOU SEE, I'M NOT PLUTO! I'M PREALLY—"
ZOMP
ZOMP
"...EEGA BEEVA!"
!
SAY WHAAAAAAA—
EEGA BEEVA?!
CANC
ENTER
SHIFT
TRL

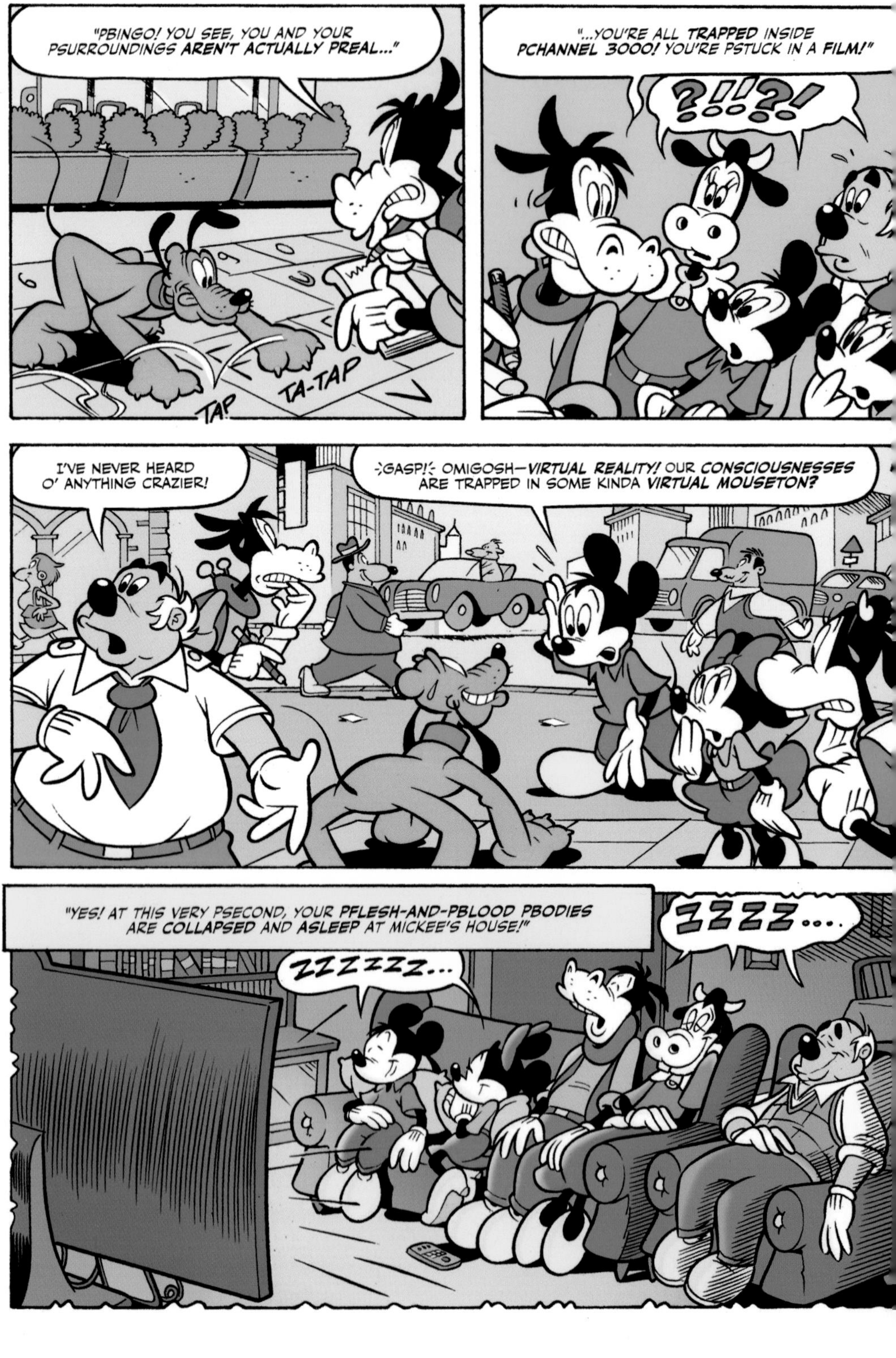
"PBINGO! YOU SEE, YOU AND YOUR PSURROUNDINGS AREN'T ACTUALLY PREAL..."
TA-TAP
TAP
"...YOU'RE ALL TRAPPED INSIDE PCHANNEL 3000! YOU'RE PSTUCK IN A FILM!"
?!!?!
I'VE NEVER HEARD O' ANYTHING CRAZIER!
GASP! OMIGOSH—VIRTUAL REALITY! OUR CONSCIOUSNESSES ARE TRAPPED IN SOME KINDA VIRTUAL MOUSETON?
"YES! AT THIS VERY PSECOND, YOUR PFLESH-AND-PBLOOD PBODIES ARE COLLAPSED AND ASLEEP AT MICKEE'S HOUSE!"
ZZZZ....
ZZZZZZ...

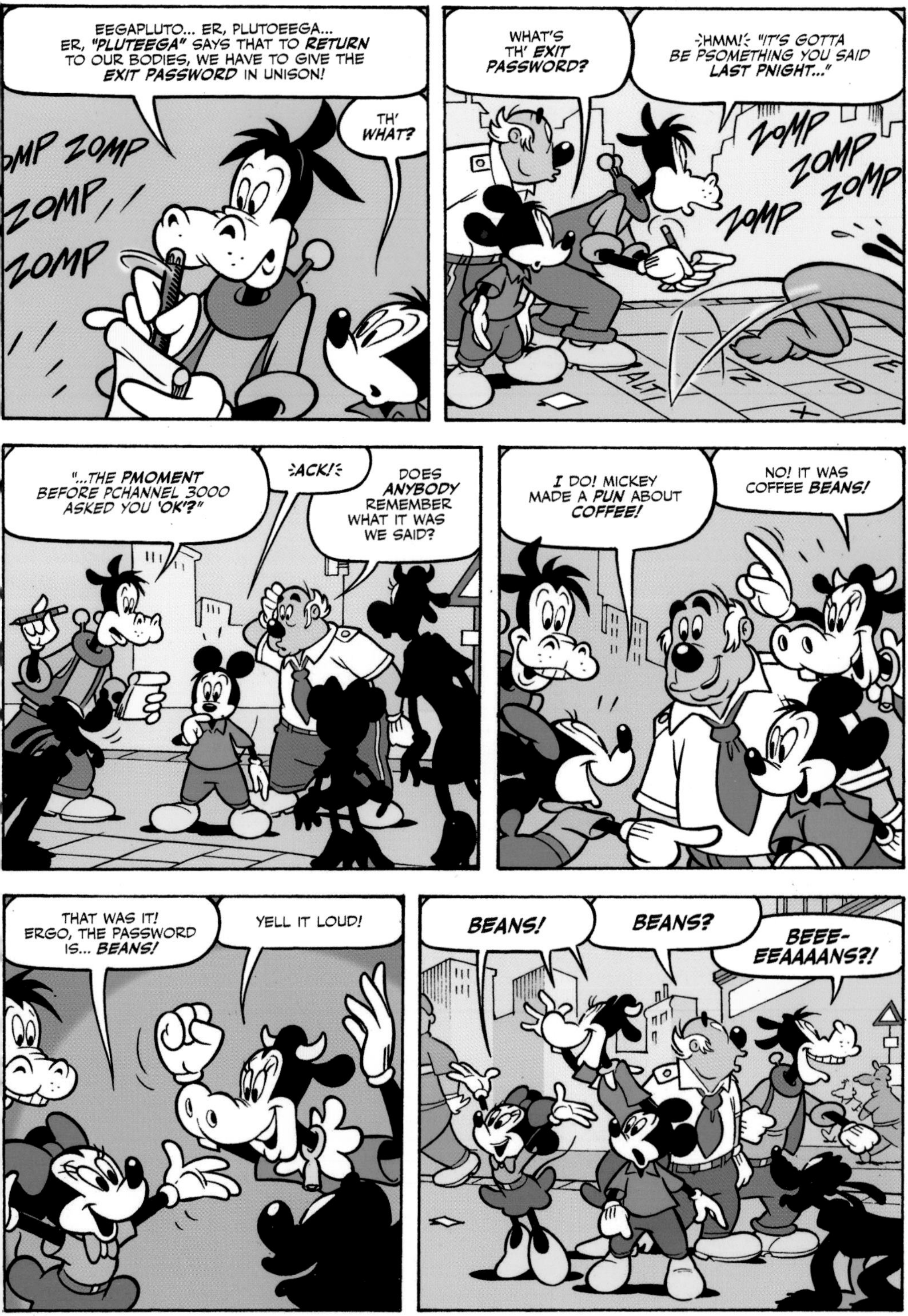
EEGAPLUTO... ER, PLUTOEEGA... ER, "PLUTEEGA" SAYS THAT TO RETURN TO OUR BODIES, WE HAVE TO GIVE THE EXIT PASSWORD IN UNISON!
ZOMP ZOMP
ZOMP
ZOMP
TH' WHAT?
WHAT'S TH' EXIT PASSWORD?
-HMM!- "IT'S GOTTA BE PSOMETHING YOU SAID LAST PNIGHT..."
ZOMP ZOMP ZOMP ZOMP
ALT
"...THE PMOMENT BEFORE PCHANNEL 3000 ASKED YOU 'OK'?"
-ACK!-
DOES ANYBODY REMEMBER WHAT IT WAS WE SAID?
I DO! MICKEY MADE A PUN ABOUT COFFEE!
NO! IT WAS COFFEE BEANS!
THAT WAS IT! ERGO, THE PASSWORD IS... BEANS!
YELL IT LOUD!
BEANS!
BEANS?
BEEE-EEAAAANS?!

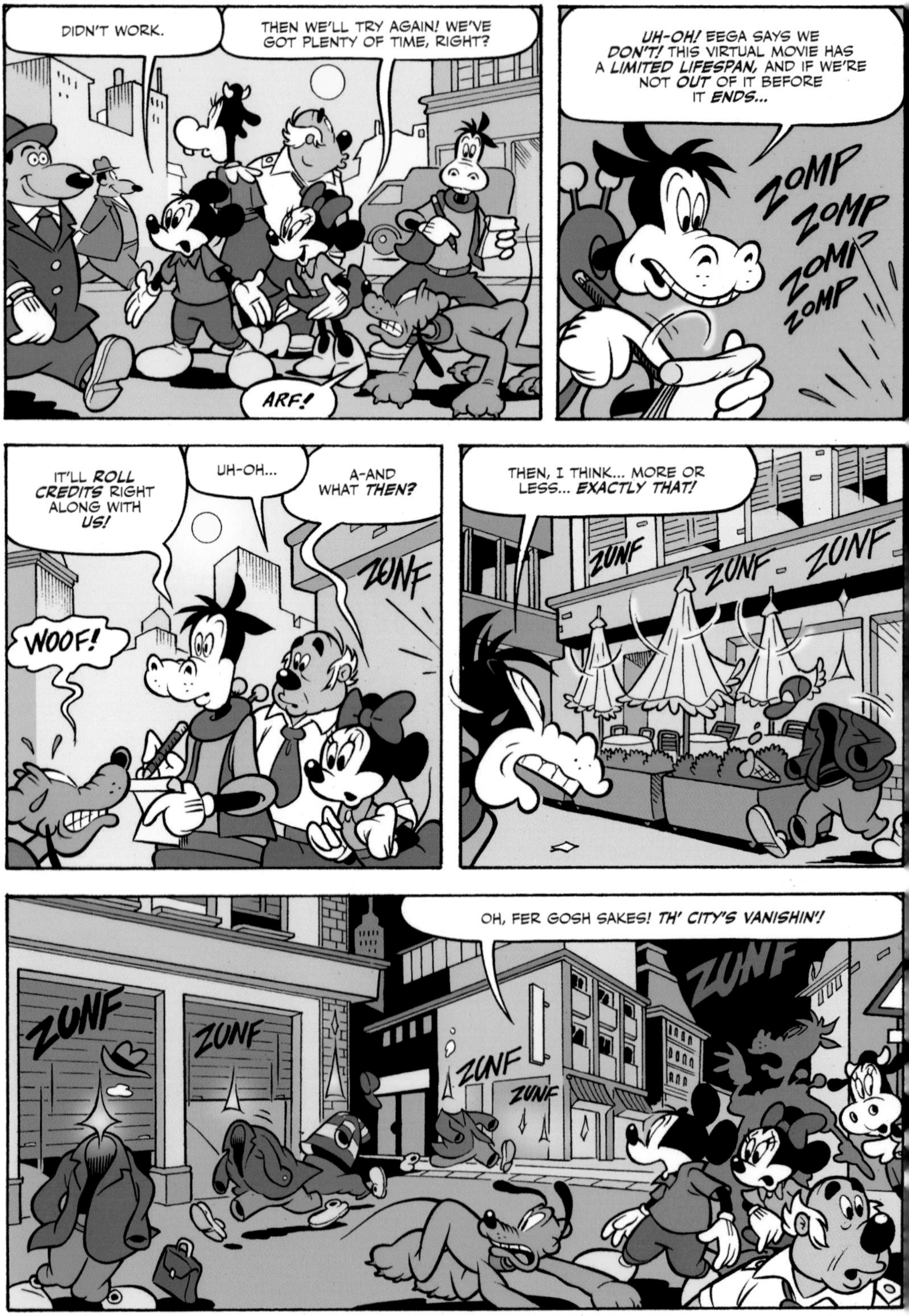
DIDN'T WORK.
THEN WE'LL TRY AGAIN! WE'VE GOT PLENTY OF TIME, RIGHT?
ARF!
UH-OH! EEGA SAYS WE DON'T! THIS VIRTUAL MOVIE HAS A LIMITED LIFESPAN, AND IF WE'RE NOT OUT OF IT BEFORE IT ENDS...
ZOMP
ZOMP
ZOMP
ZOMP
IT'LL ROLL CREDITS RIGHT ALONG WITH US!
UH-OH...
A-AND WHAT THEN?
WOOF!
ZUNF
THEN, I THINK... MORE OR LESS... EXACTLY THAT!
ZUNF
ZUNF
ZUNF
OH, FER GOSH SAKES! TH' CITY'S VANISHIN'!
ZUNF
ZUNF
ZUNF
ZUNF
ZUNF

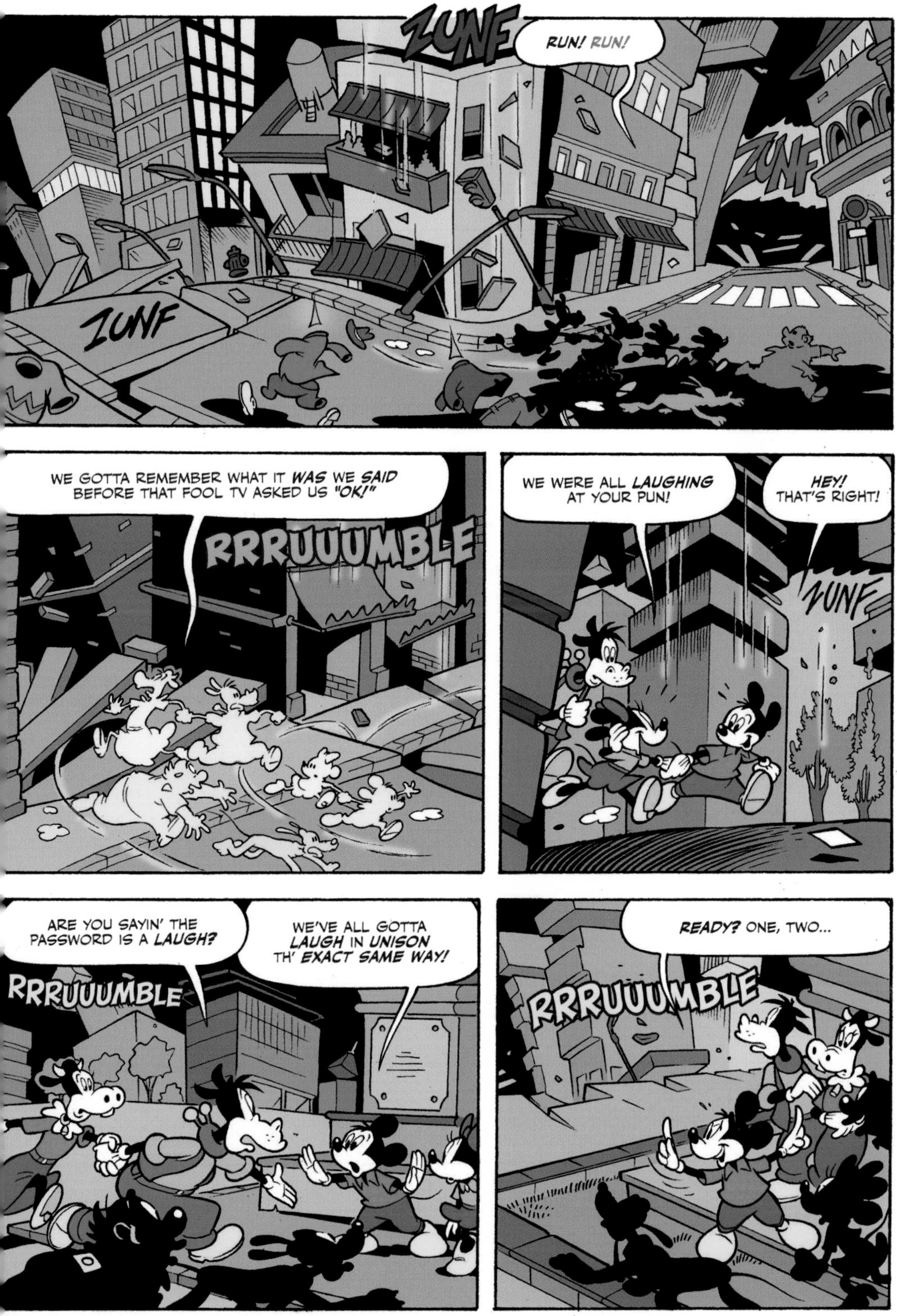
ZUNF
RUN! RUN!
ZUNF
ZUNF
WE GOTTA REMEMBER WHAT IT WAS WE SAID BEFORE THAT FOOL TV ASKED US "OK!"
RRRUUUMBLE
WE WERE ALL LAUGHING AT YOUR PUN!
HEY! THAT'S RIGHT!
ZUNF
ARE YOU SAYIN' THE PASSWORD IS A LAUGH?
WE'VE ALL GOTTA LAUGH IN UNISON TH' EXACT SAME WAY!
RRRUUUMBLE
READY? ONE, TWO...
RRRUUUMBLE

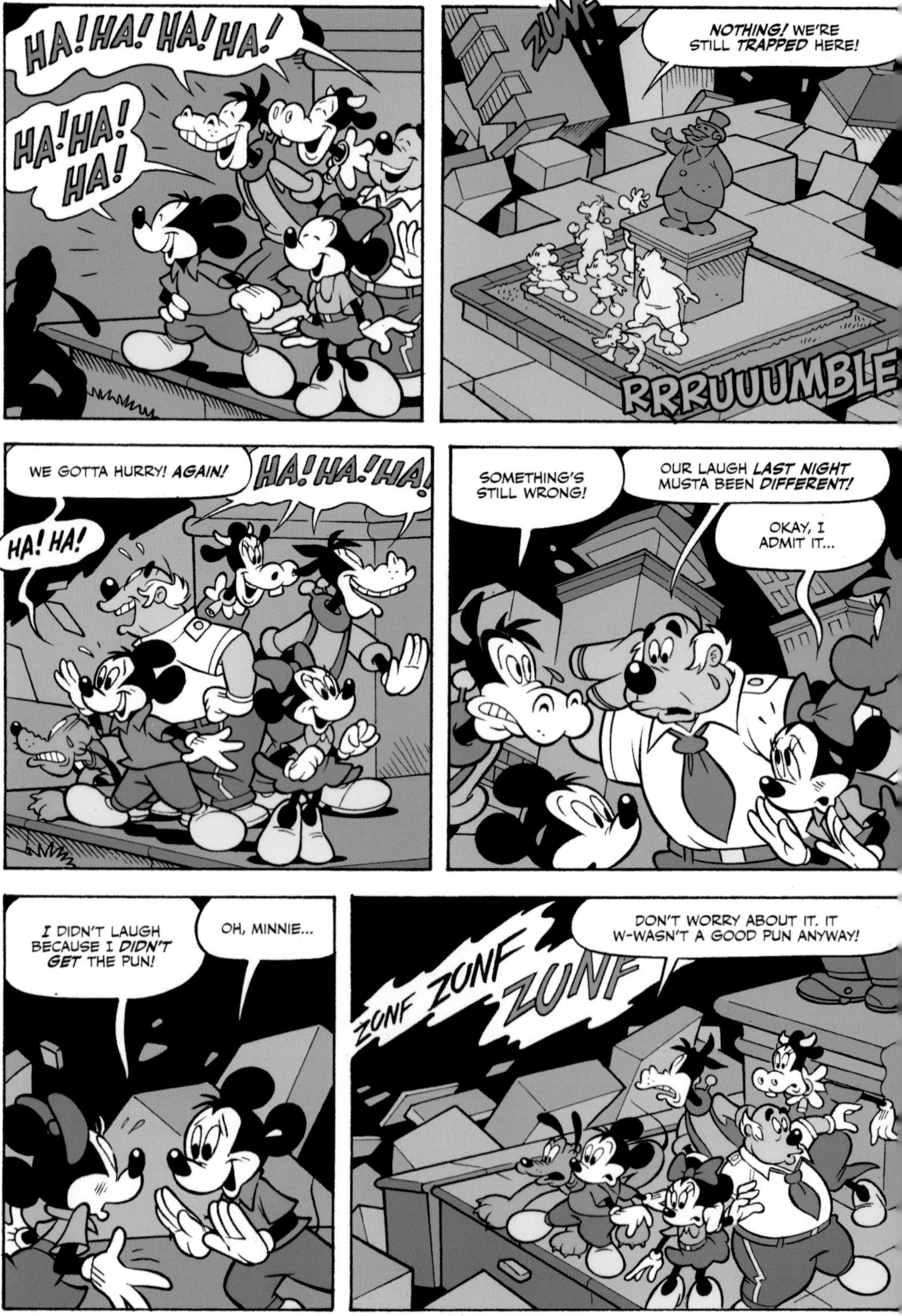
HA! HA! HA! HA!
HA! HA! HA!
ZUNF
NOTHING! WE'RE STILL TRAPPED HERE!
RRRUUUMBLE
WE GOTTA HURRY! AGAIN!
HA! HA! HA!
HA! HA!
SOMETHING'S STILL WRONG!
OUR LAUGH LAST NIGHT MUSTA BEEN DIFFERENT!
OKAY, I ADMIT IT...
I DIDN'T LAUGH BECAUSE I DIDN'T GET THE PUN!
OH, MINNIE...
ZONF ZONF ZUNF
DON'T WORRY ABOUT IT. IT W-WASN'T A GOOD PUN ANYWAY!

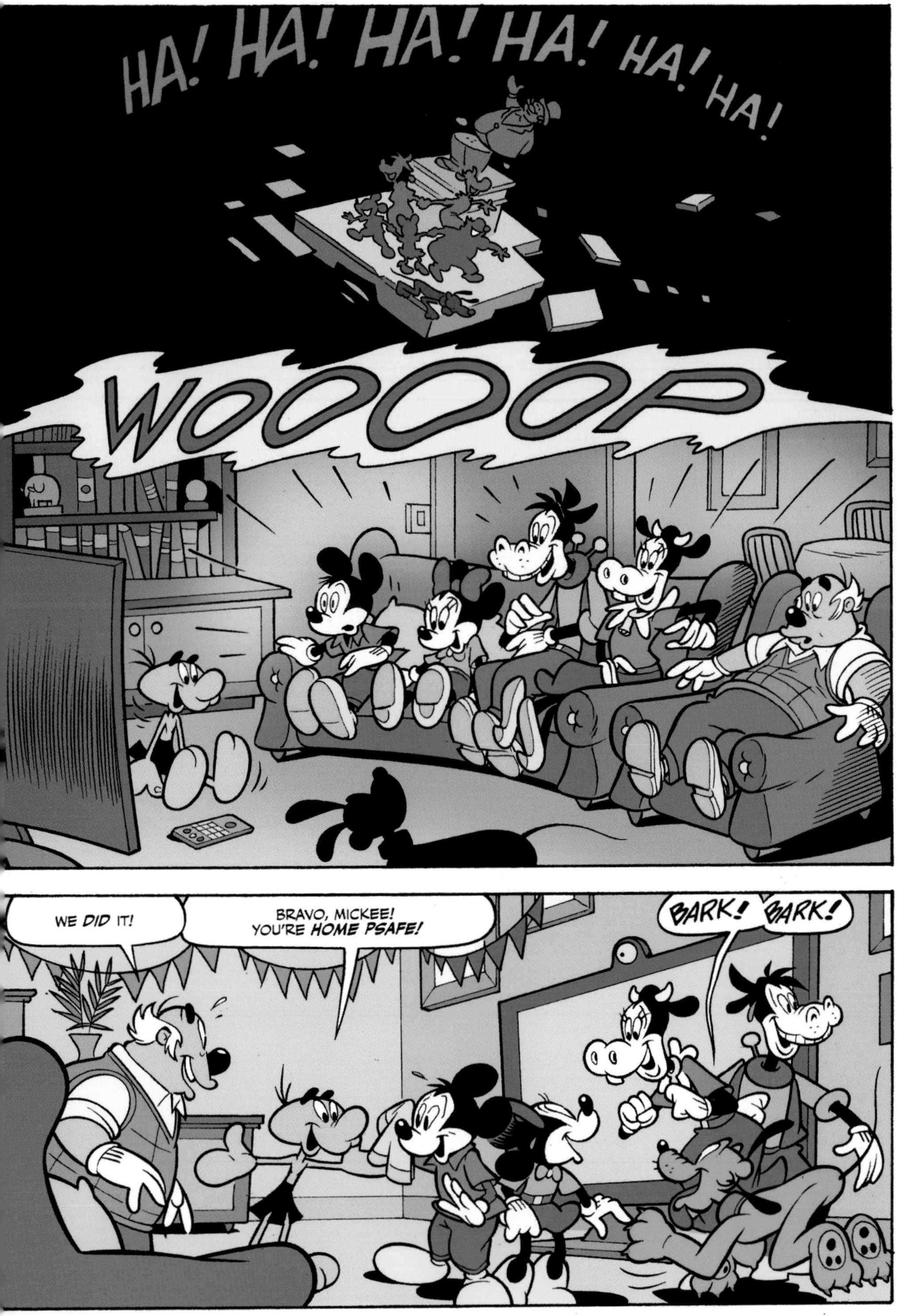
HA! HA! HA! HA! HA! HA!
WOOOOP
WE DID IT!
BRAVO, MICKEE! YOU'RE HOME PSAFE!
BARK! BARK!

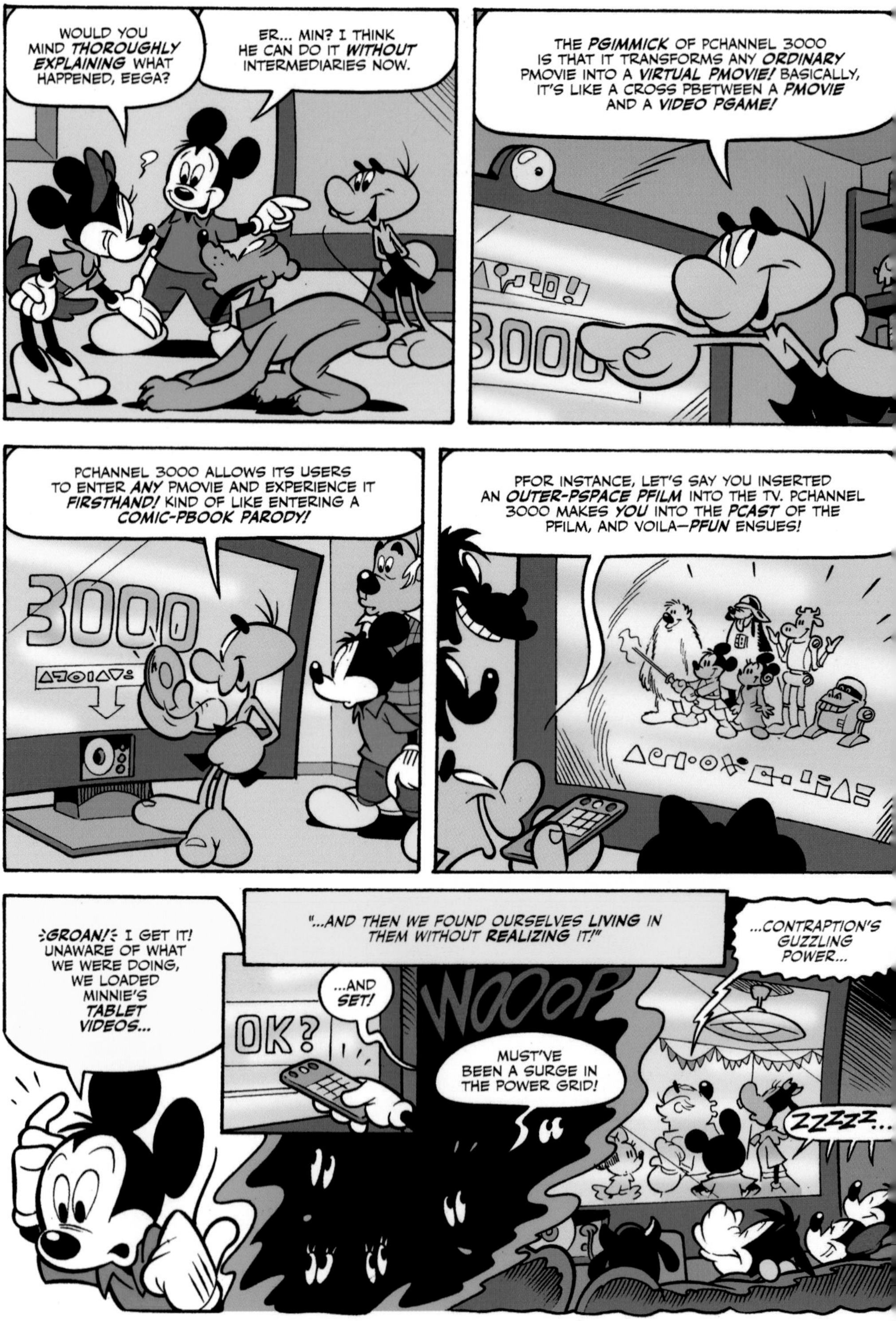

WOULD YOU MIND THOROUGHLY EXPLAINING WHAT HAPPENED, EEGA?
ER... MIN? I THINK HE CAN DO IT WITHOUT INTERMEDIARIES NOW.
THE PGIMMICK OF PCHANNEL 3000 IS THAT IT TRANSFORMS ANY ORDINARY PMOVIE INTO A VIRTUAL PMOVIE! BASICALLY, IT'S LIKE A CROSS PBETWEEN A PMOVIE AND A VIDEO PGAME!
3000
PCHANNEL 3000 ALLOWS ITS USERS TO ENTER ANY PMOVIE AND EXPERIENCE IT FIRSTHAND! KIND OF LIKE ENTERING A COMIC-PBOOK PARODY!
3000
PFOR INSTANCE, LET'S SAY YOU INSERTED AN OUTER-PSPACE PFILM INTO THE TV. PCHANNEL 3000 MAKES YOU INTO THE PCAST OF THE PFILM, AND VOILA—PFUN ENSUES!
GROAN! I GET IT! UNAWARE OF WHAT WE WERE DOING, WE LOADED MINNIE'S TABLET VIDEOS...
"...AND THEN WE FOUND OURSELVES LIVING IN THEM WITHOUT REALIZING IT!"
OK?
...AND SET!
WOOOP
MUST'VE BEEN A SURGE IN THE POWER GRID!
...CONTRAPTION'S GUZZLING POWER...
ZZZZZ...

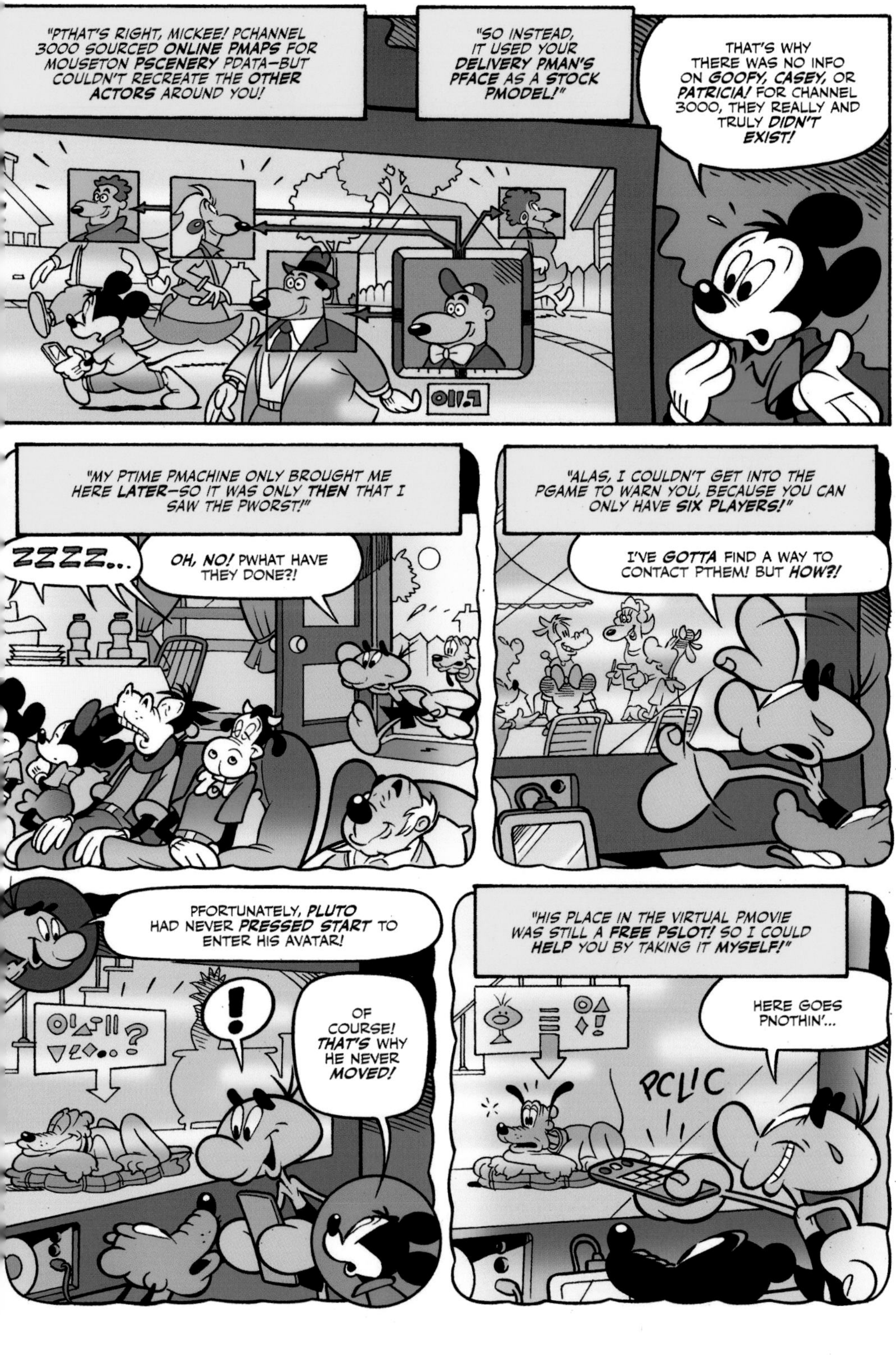
"PTHAT'S RIGHT, MICKEE! PCHANNEL 3000 SOURCED ONLINE PMAPS FOR MOUSETON PSCENERY PDATA—BUT COULDN'T RECREATE THE OTHER ACTORS AROUND YOU!
"SO INSTEAD, IT USED YOUR DELIVERY PMAN'S PFACE AS A STOCK PMODEL!"
THAT'S WHY THERE WAS NO INFO ON GOOFY, CASEY, OR PATRICIA! FOR CHANNEL 3000, THEY REALLY AND TRULY DIDN'T EXIST!
"MY PTIME PMACHINE ONLY BROUGHT ME HERE LATER—SO IT WAS ONLY THEN THAT I SAW THE PWORST!"
ZZZZ...
OH, NO! PWHAT HAVE THEY DONE?!
"ALAS, I COULDN'T GET INTO THE PGAME TO WARN YOU, BECAUSE YOU CAN ONLY HAVE SIX PLAYERS!"
I'VE GOTTA FIND A WAY TO CONTACT PTHEM! BUT HOW?!
PFORTUNATELY, PLUTO HAD NEVER PRESSED START TO ENTER HIS AVATAR!
!
OF COURSE! THAT'S WHY HE NEVER MOVED!
"HIS PLACE IN THE VIRTUAL PMOVIE WAS STILL A FREE PSLOT! SO I COULD HELP YOU BY TAKING IT MYSELF!"
HERE GOES PNOTHIN'...
PCLIC

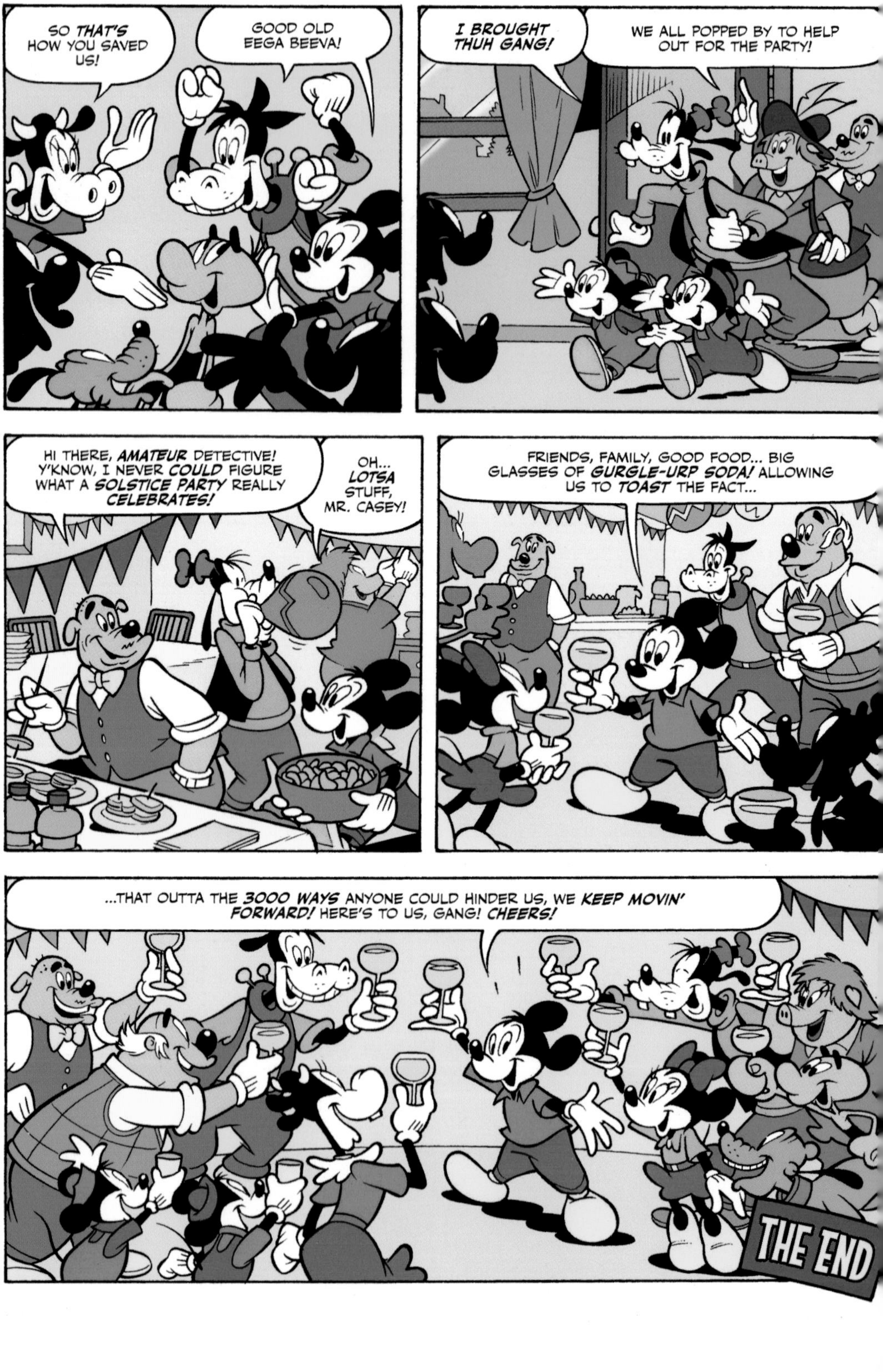
SO THAT'S HOW YOU SAVED US!
GOOD OLD EEGA BEEVA!
I BROUGHT THUH GANG!
WE ALL POPPED BY TO HELP OUT FOR THE PARTY!
HI THERE, AMATEUR DETECTIVE! Y'KNOW, I NEVER COULD FIGURE WHAT A SOLSTICE PARTY REALLY CELEBRATES!
OH... LOTSA STUFF, MR. CASEY!
FRIENDS, FAMILY, GOOD FOOD... BIG GLASSES OF GURGLE-URP SODA! ALLOWING US TO TOAST THE FACT...
...THAT OUTTA THE 3000 WAYS ANYONE COULD HINDER US, WE KEEP MOVIN' FORWARD! HERE'S TO US, GANG! CHEERS!
THE END

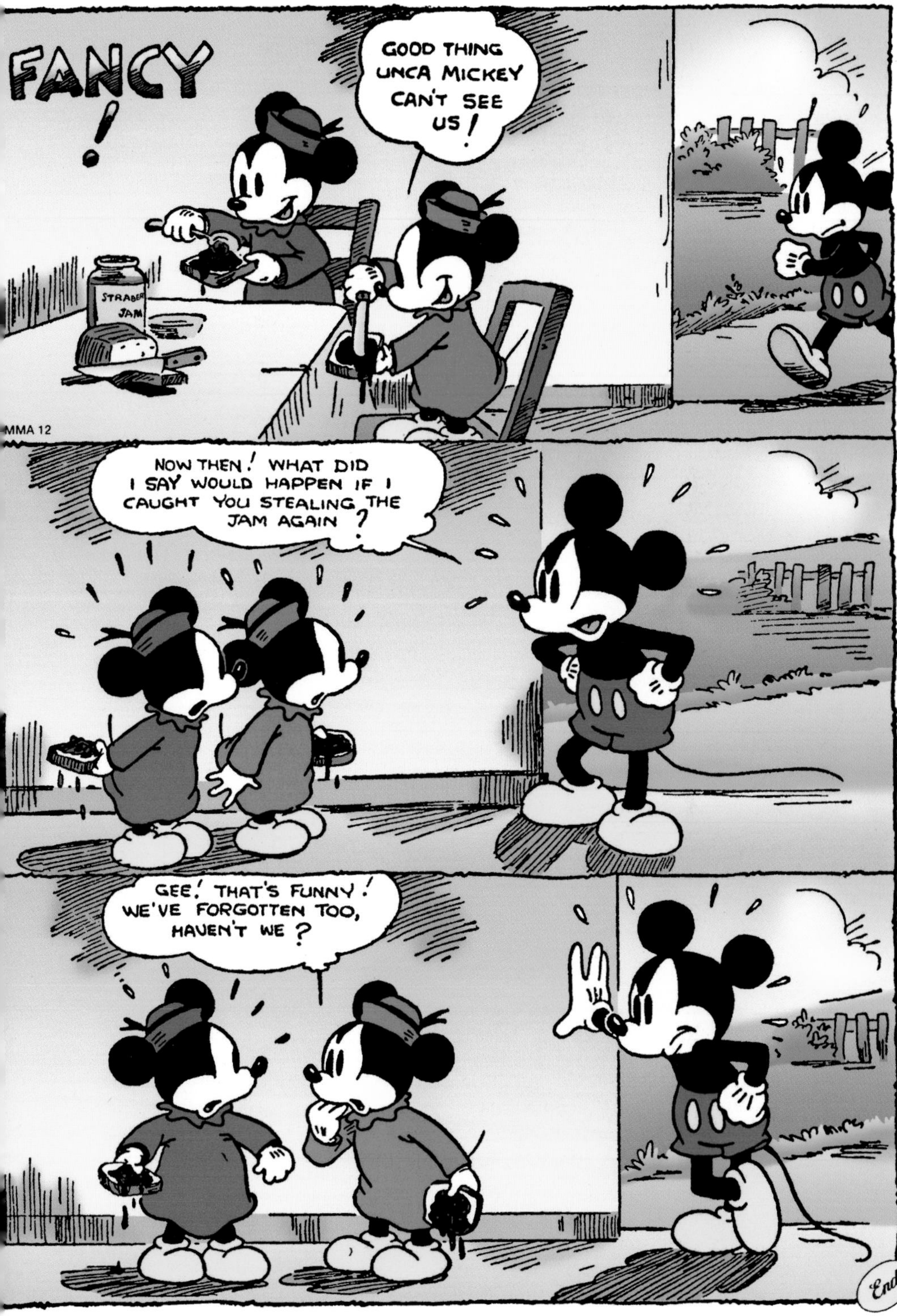
FANCY!
GOOD THING UNCA MICKEY CAN'T SEE US!
STRABERY JAM
MMA 12
NOW THEN! WHAT DID I SAY WOULD HAPPEN IF I CAUGHT YOU STEALING THE JAM AGAIN?
GEE! THAT'S FUNNY! WE'VE FORGOTTEN TOO, HAVEN'T WE?
End

Originally published in *Mickey Mouse Annual* #12 (United Kingdom, 1941)

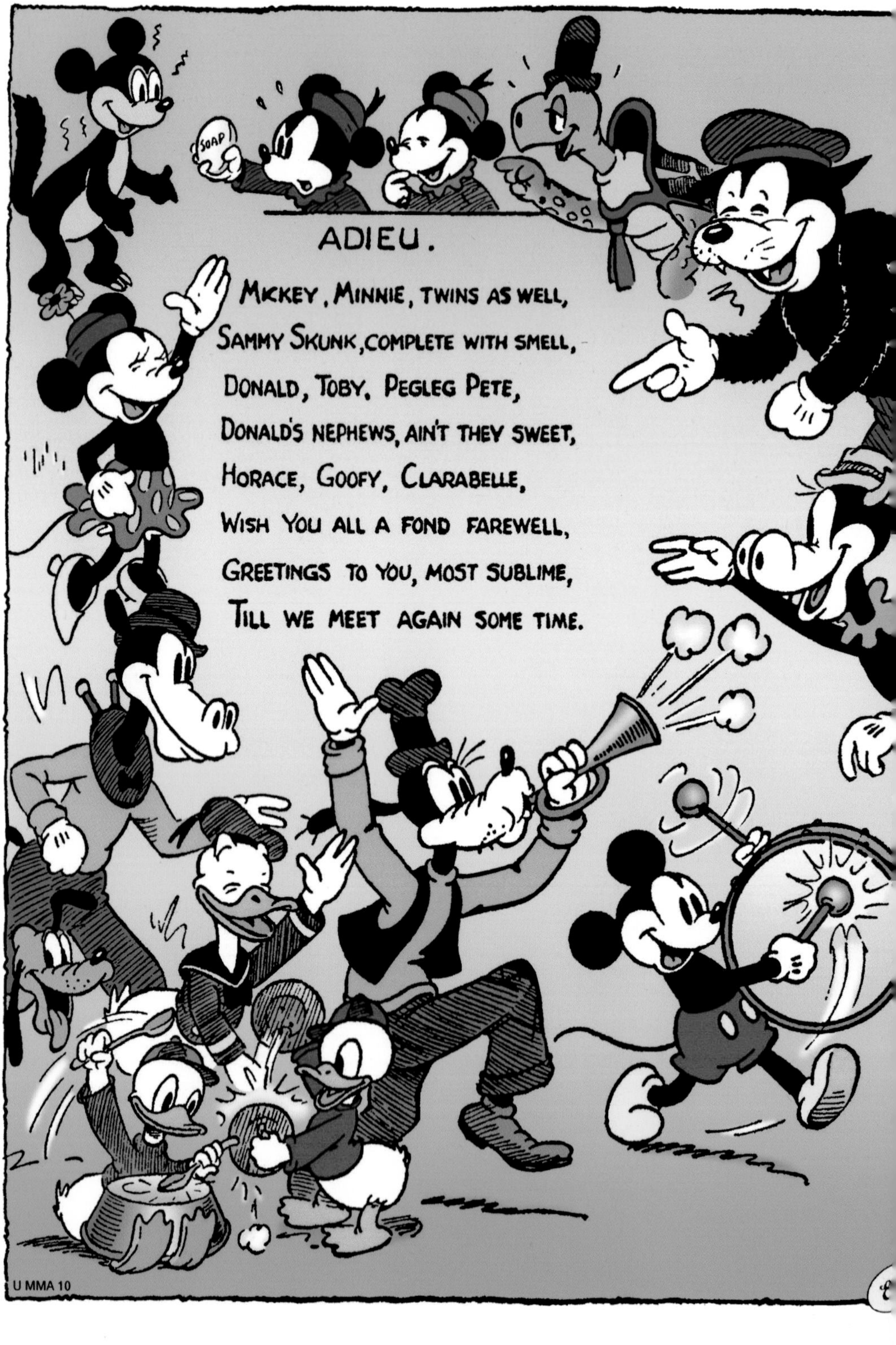
SOAP
ADIEU.
MICKEY, MINNIE, TWINS AS WELL,
SAMMY SKUNK, COMPLETE WITH SMELL,
DONALD, TOBY, PEGLEG PETE,
DONALD'S NEPHEWS, AIN'T THEY SWEET,
HORACE, GOOFY, CLARABELLE,
WISH YOU ALL A FOND FAREWELL,
GREETINGS TO YOU, MOST SUBLIME,
TILL WE MEET AGAIN SOME TIME.
U MMA 10

Originally published in *Mickey Mouse Annual* #10 (United Kingdom, 1939)

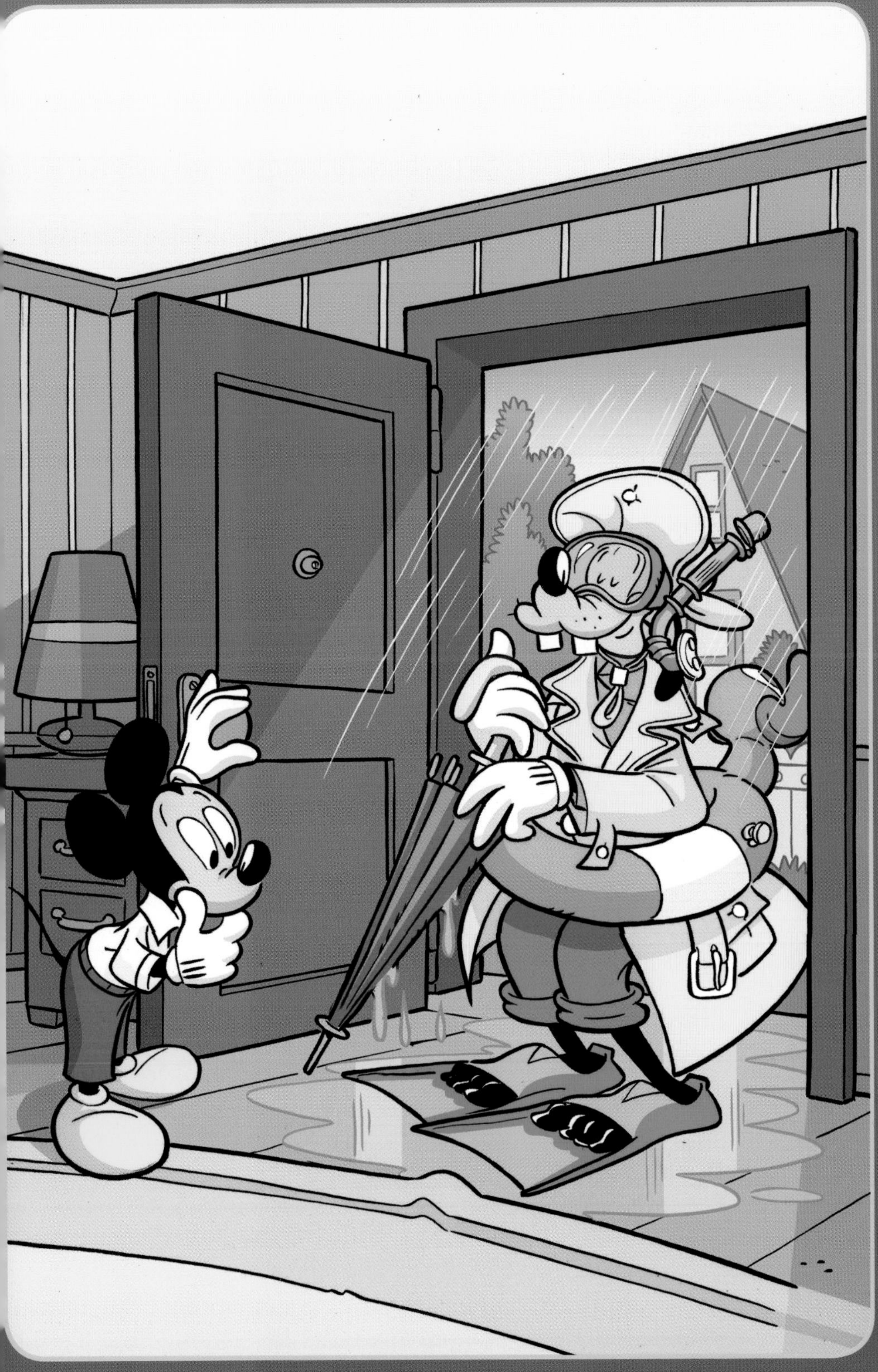

Art by Marco Mazzarello, Colors by Ronda Pattison

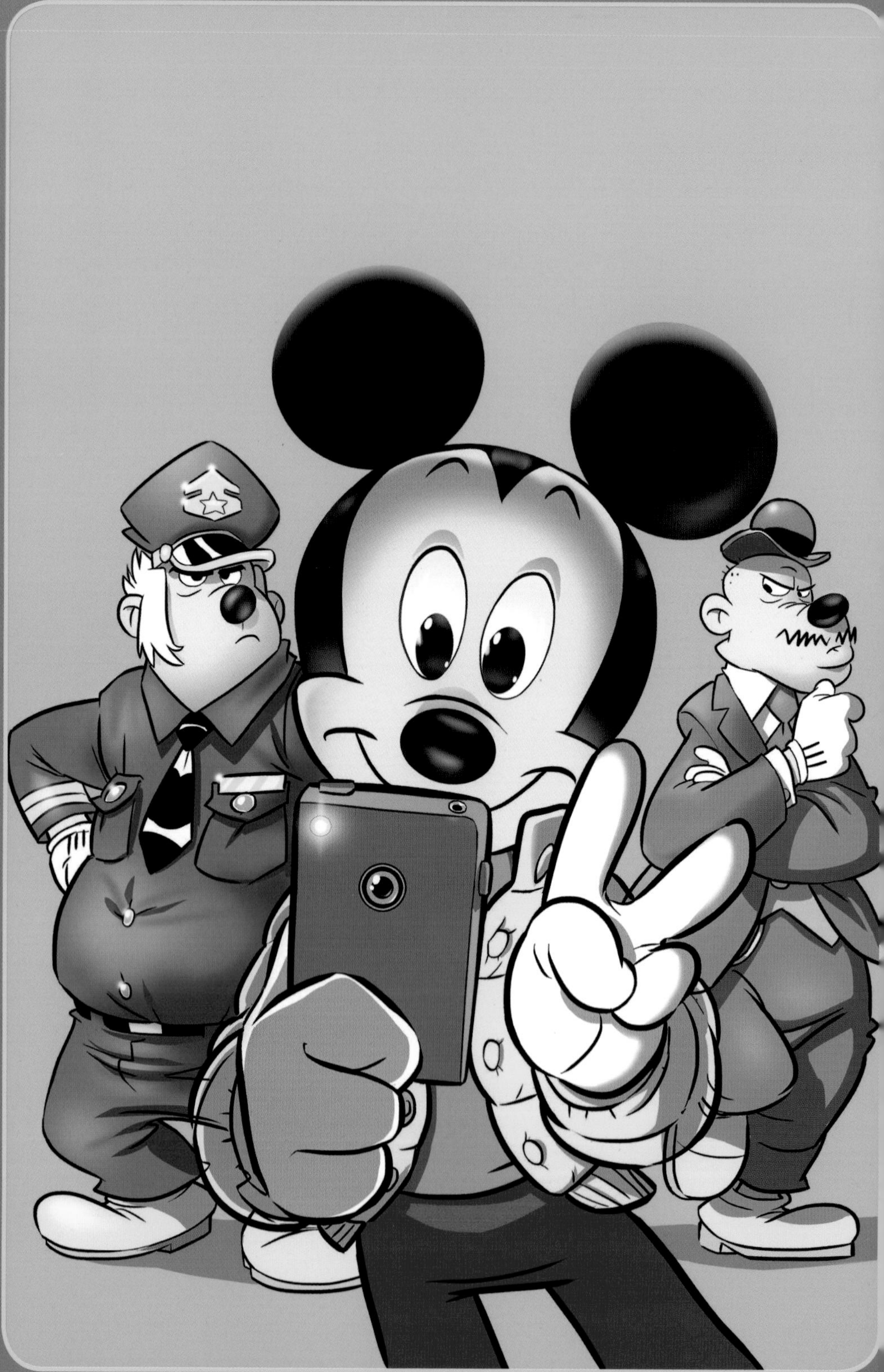

Art by Claudio Sciarrone

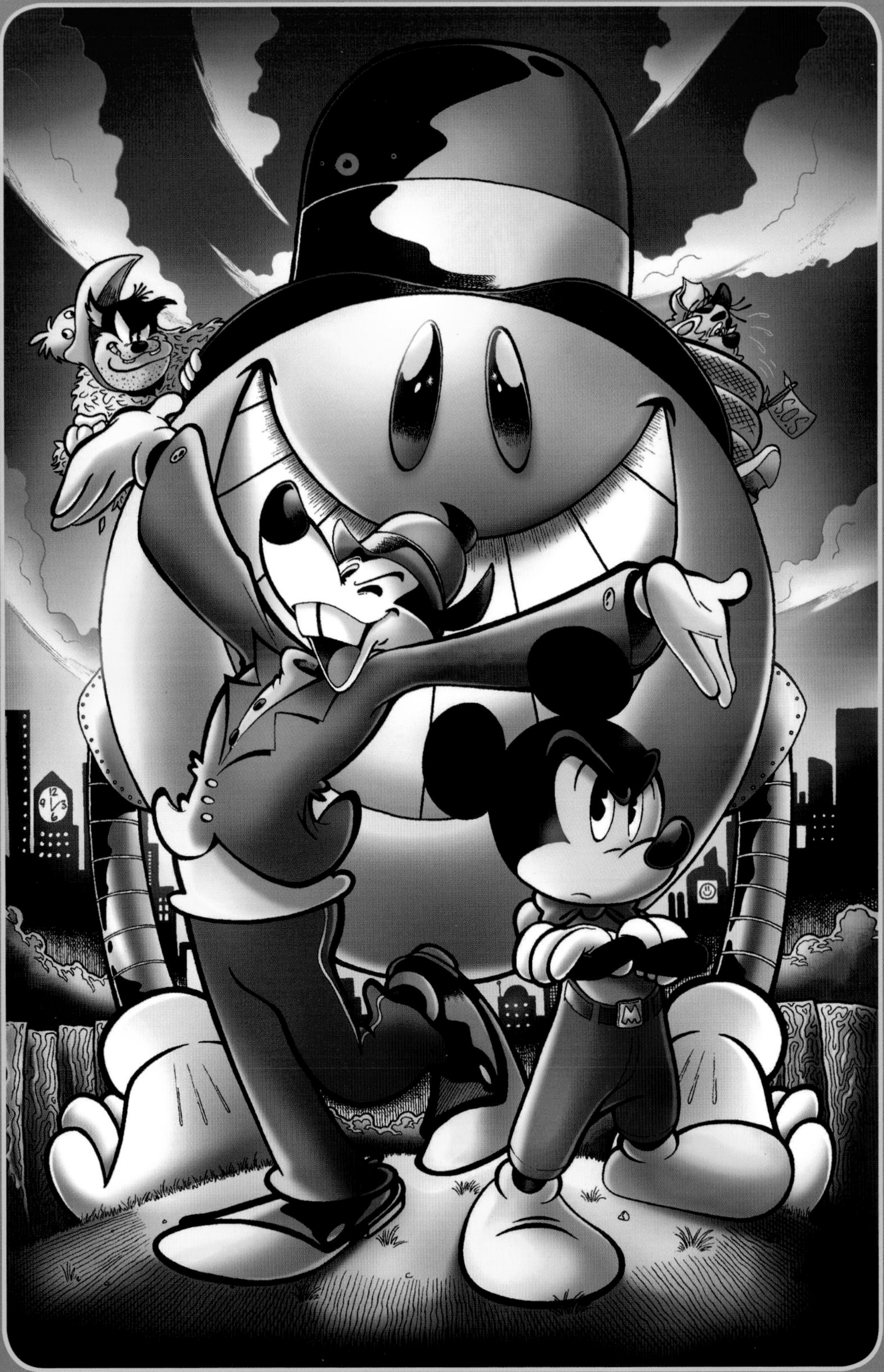
S.O.S

Art by Jonathan H. Gray, Colors by Marco Colletti

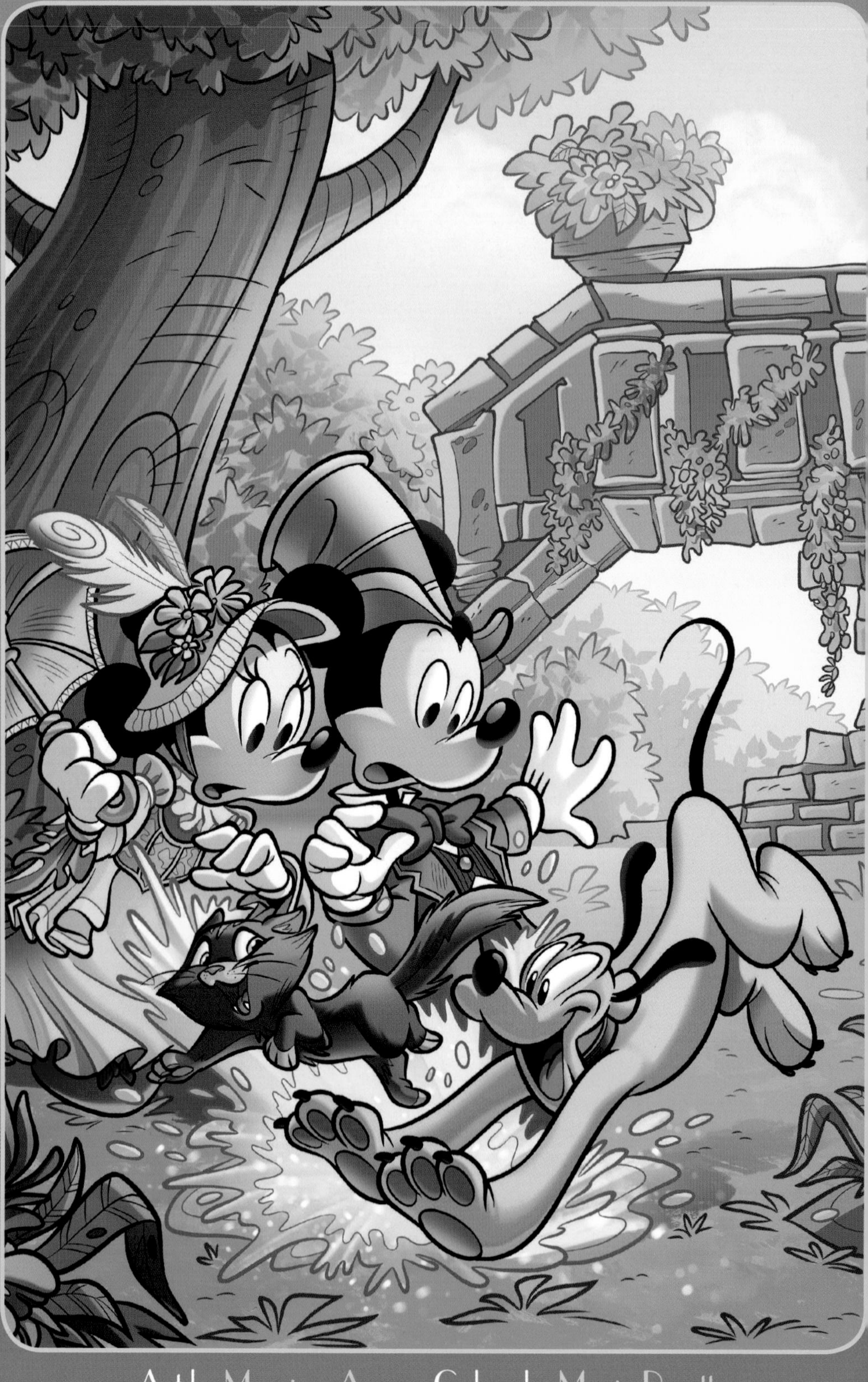

Art by Massimo Asaro, Colors by Mario Perotta

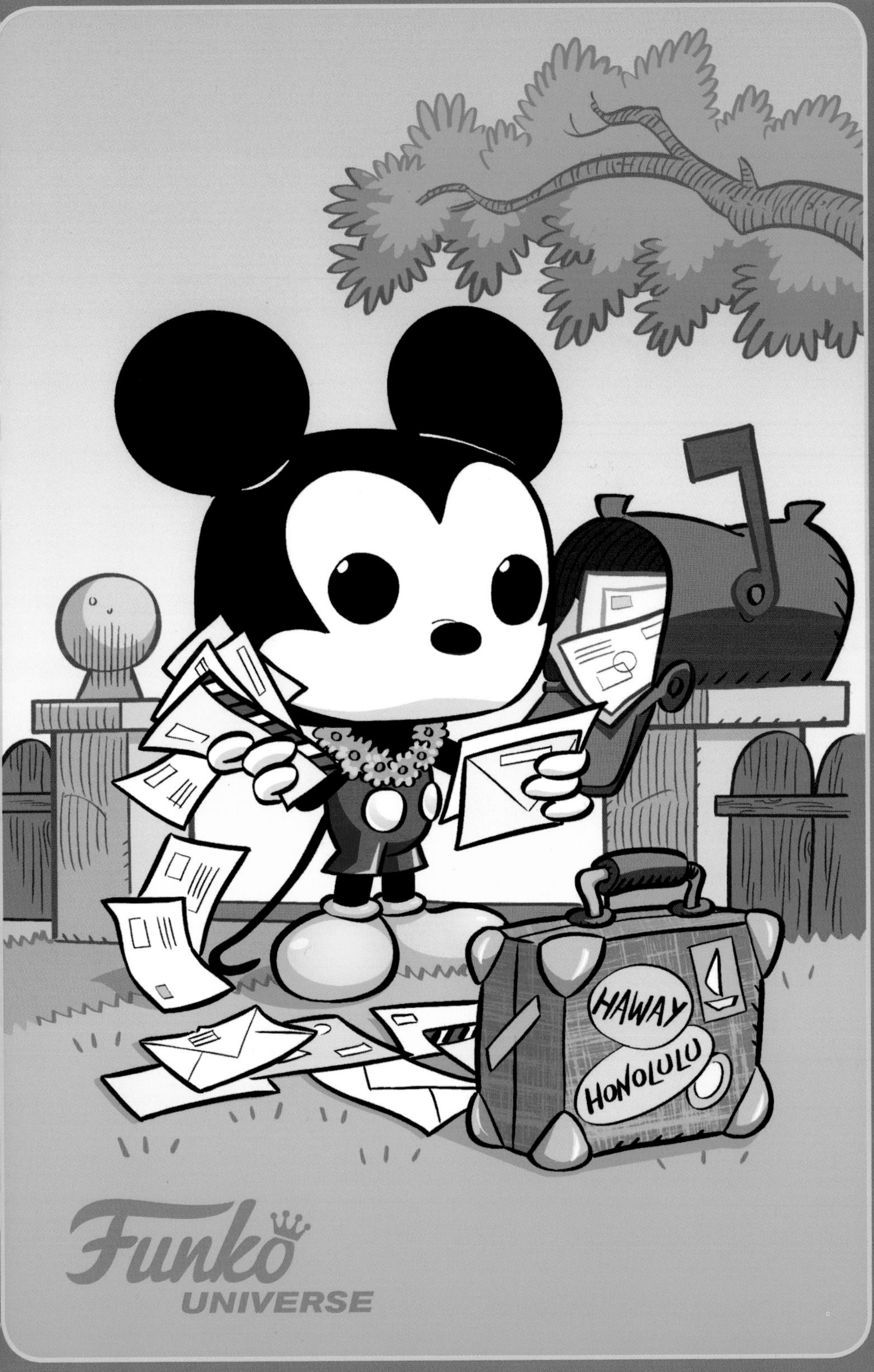
HAWAY
HONOLULU
Funko
UNIVERSE

Art by Marco Gervasio, Colors by Ronda Pattison

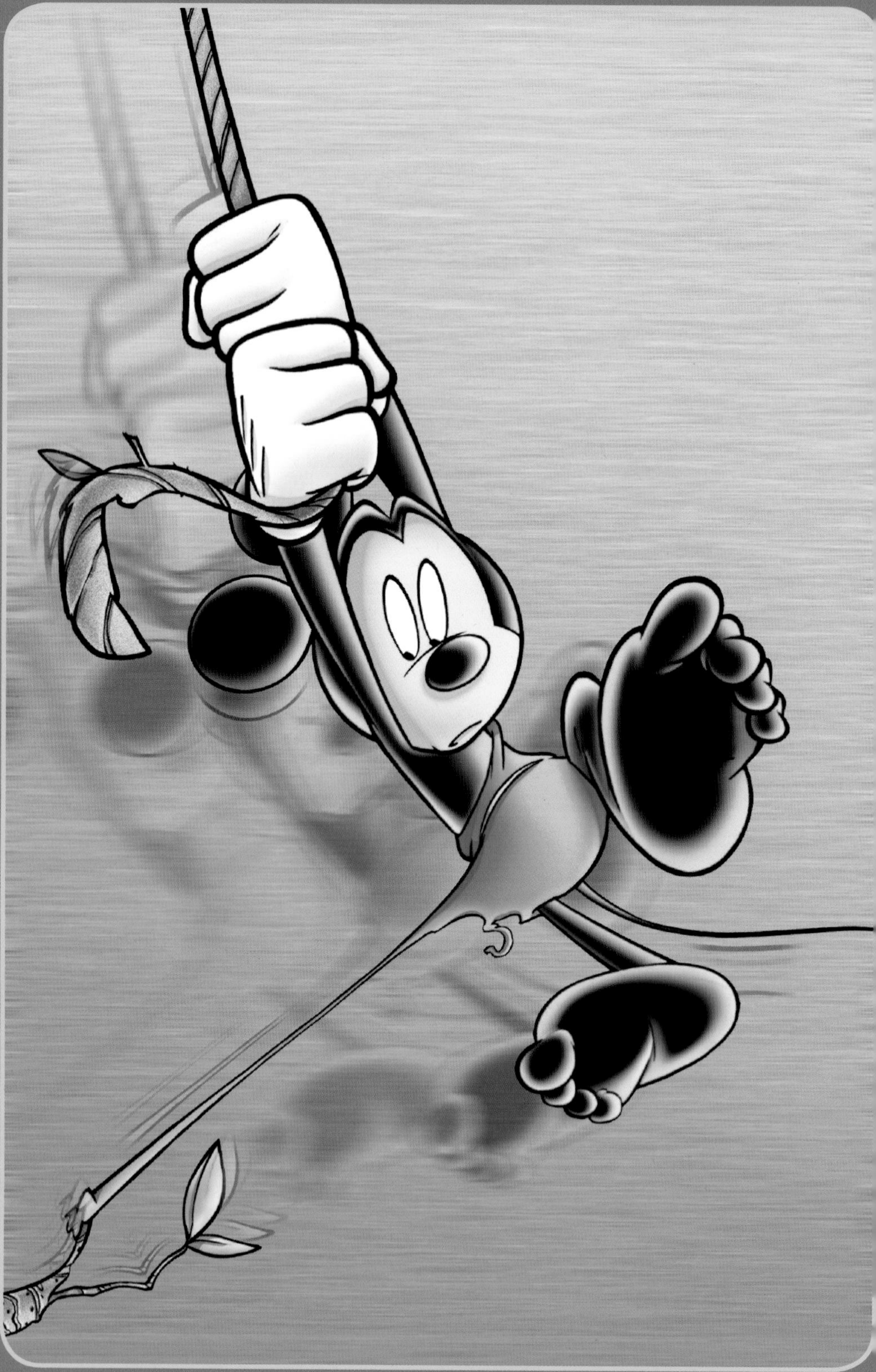

Art by Marco Ghiglione, Colors by Disney Italia and Ronda Pattison

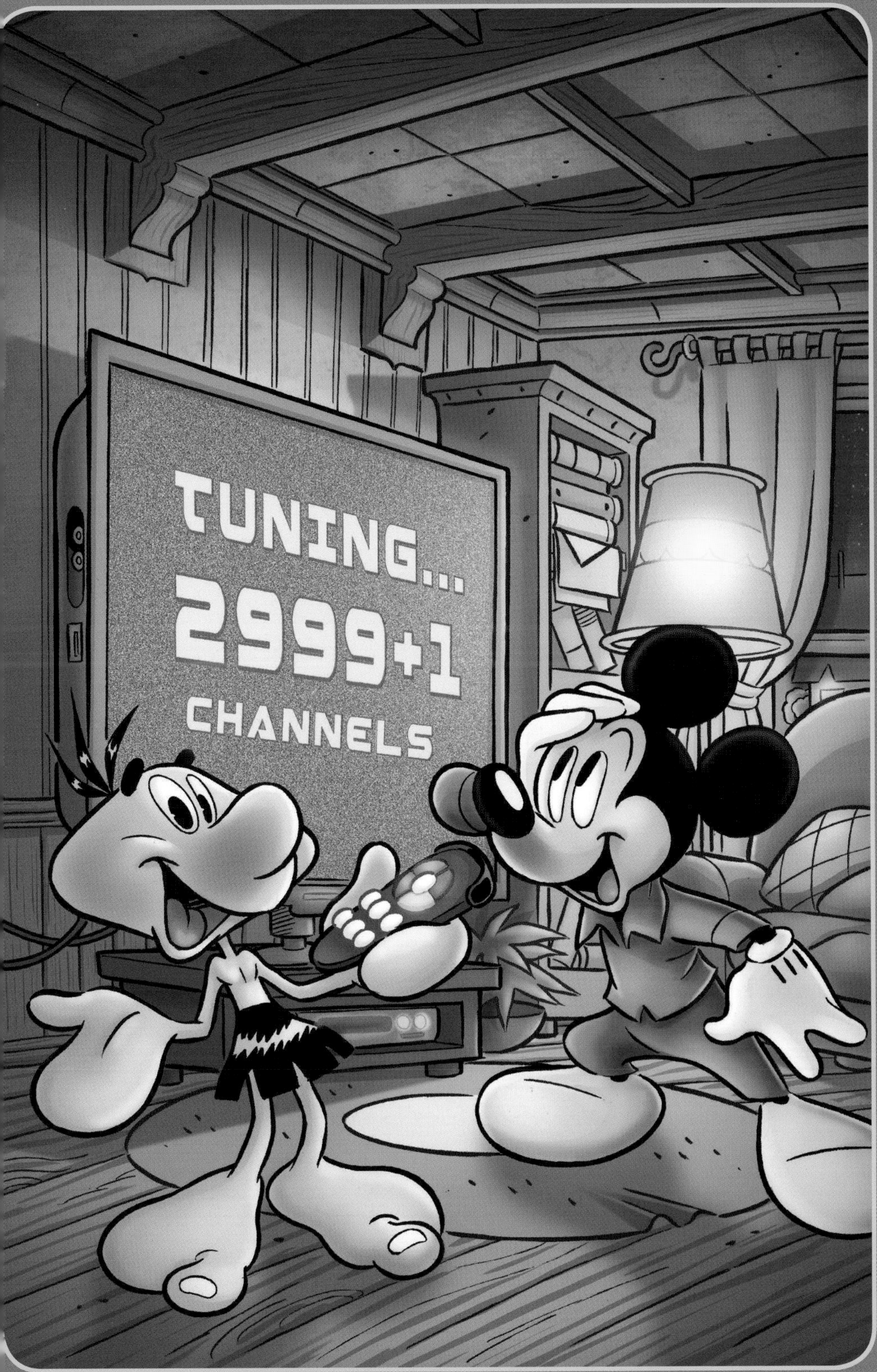
TUNING...
2999+1
CHANNELS
Art by Andrea Freccero, Colors by Fabio Lo Monaco

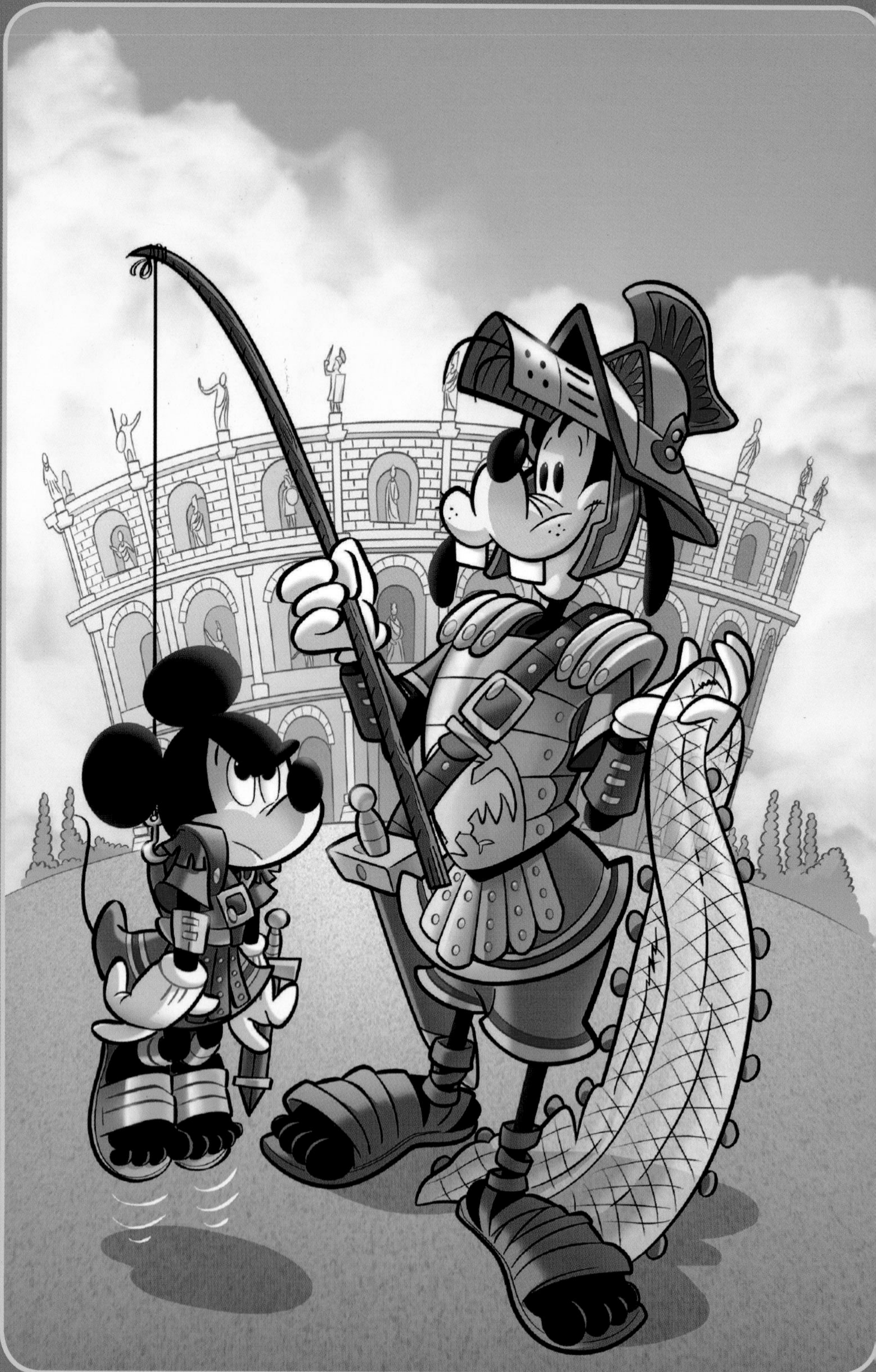

Art by Marco Gervasio, Colors by Mario Perotta

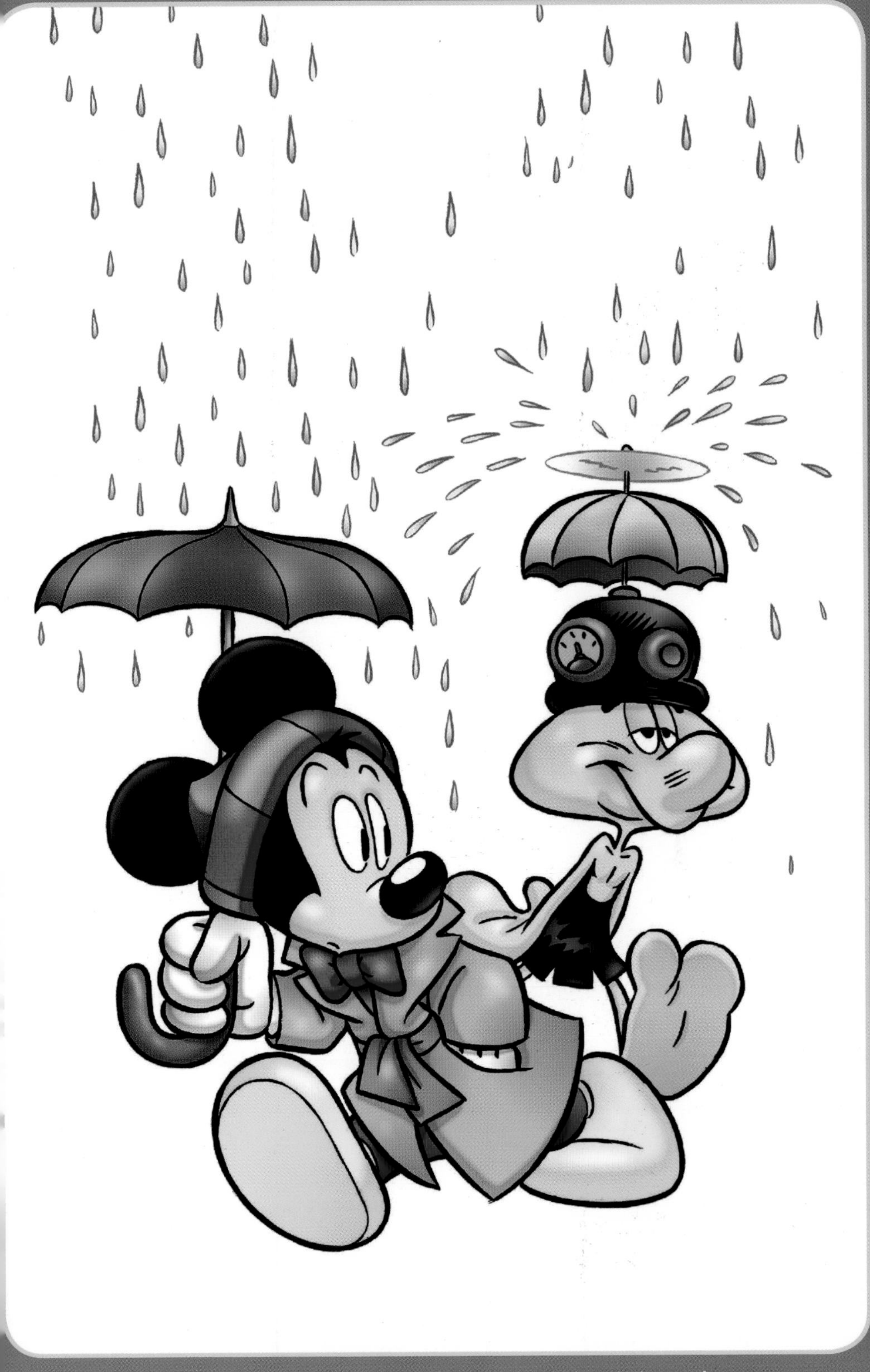

Art by Andrea Freccero, Colors by Max Monteduro